STARS
of
CHAOS

SHA PO LANG

4

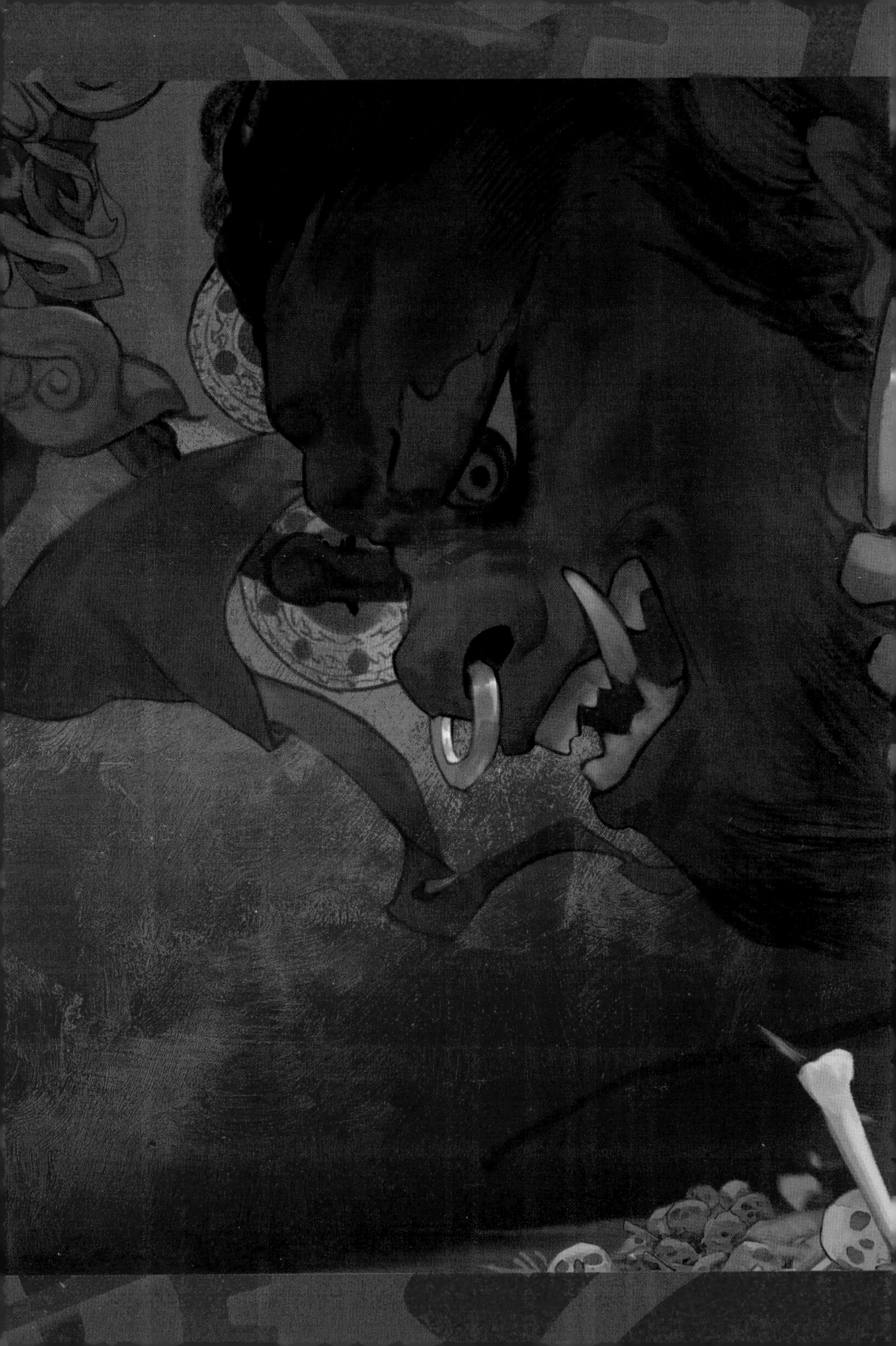

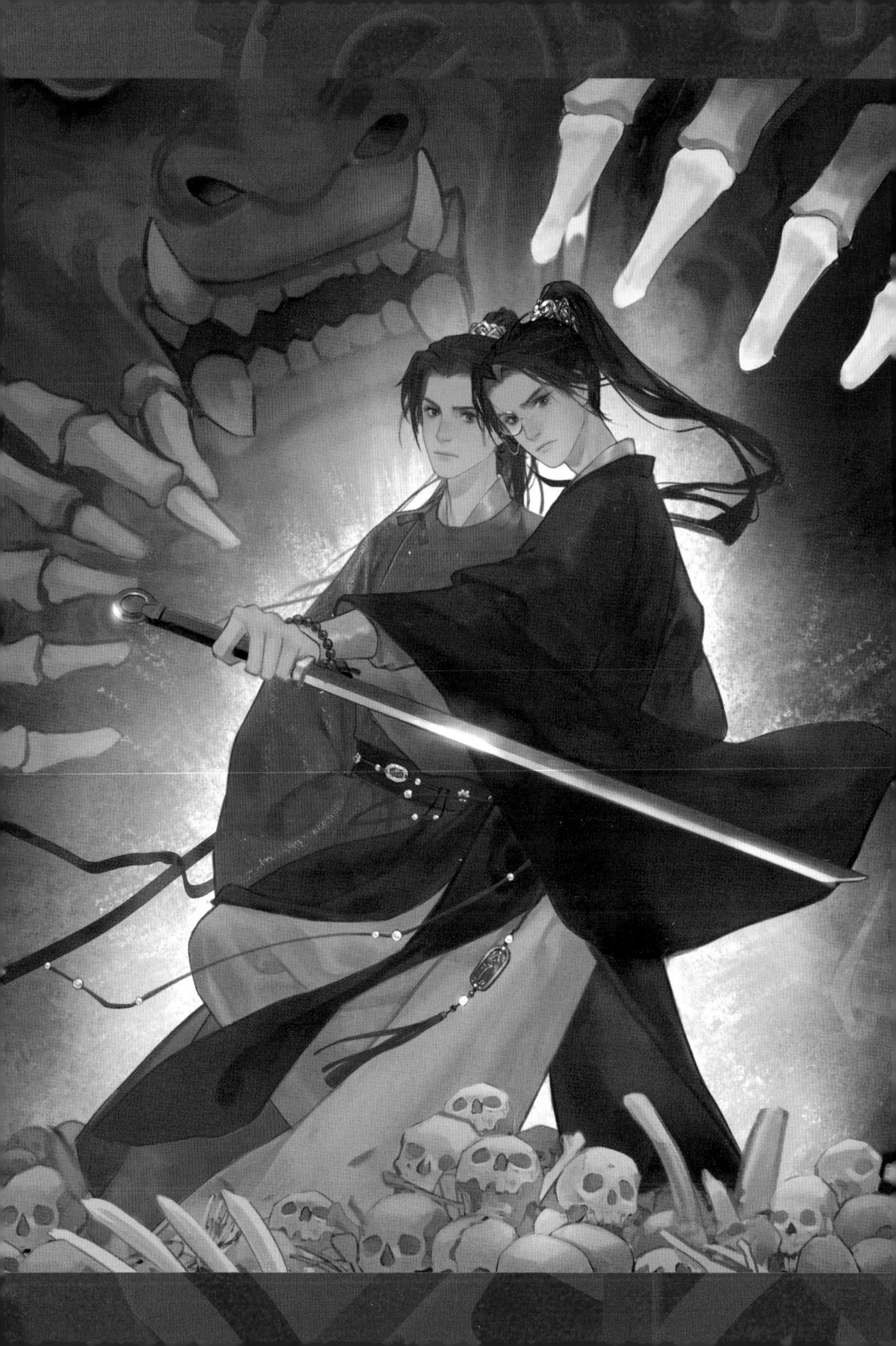

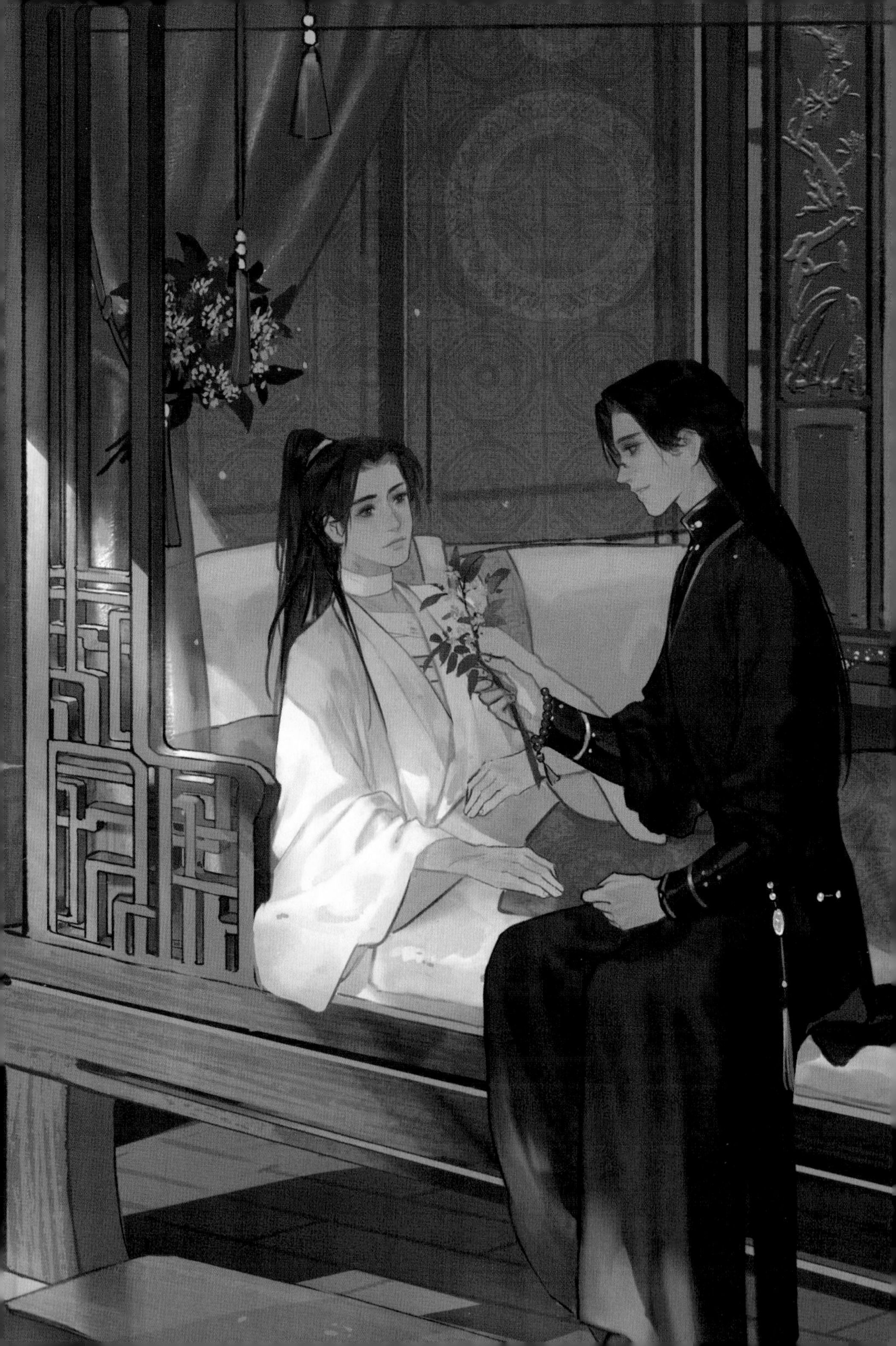

STARS
of
CHAOS
SHA PO LANG

4

WRITTEN BY

priest

ILLUSTRATED BY

罐一一

TRANSLATED BY

Lily & Louise

Seven Seas

Seven Seas Entertainment

STARS OF CHAOS:
SHA PO LANG VOL. 4

Published originally under the title of 《杀破狼》 (Sha Po Lang)
Author © priest
English edition rights under license granted by 北京晋江原创网络科技有限公司
(Beijing Jinjiang Original Network Technology Co., Ltd.)
English edition copyright © 2024 Seven Seas Entertainment, Inc.
Arranged through JS Agency Co., Ltd
All rights reserved

Cover and Interior Illustrations by 罐一一 (eleven small jars)

No portion of this book may be reproduced or transmitted in any form without written
permission from the copyright holders. This is a work of fiction. Names, characters, places,
and incidents are the products of the author's imagination or are used fictitiously.
Any resemblance to actual events, locales, or persons, living or dead, is entirely coincidental.
Any information or opinions expressed by the creators of this book belong to those individual
creators and do not necessarily reflect the views of Seven Seas Entertainment or its employees.

Seven Seas press and purchase enquiries can be sent
to Marketing Manager Lauren Hill at press@gomanga.com.
Information regarding the distribution and purchase of digital editions
is available from Digital Manager CK Russell at digital@gomanga.com.

Seven Seas and the Seven Seas logo are trademarks of
Seven Seas Entertainment. All rights reserved.

Follow Seven Seas Entertainment online at
sevenseasentertainment.com.

TRANSLATION: Lily, Louise
COVER DESIGN: M. A. Lewife
INTERIOR DESIGN: Clay Gardner
INTERIOR LAYOUT: Karis Page
PROOFREADER: Kate Kishi, Hnä
COPY EDITOR: Jehanne Bell
EDITOR: Kelly Quinn Chiu
PREPRESS TECHNICIAN: Melanie Ujimori, Jules Valera
MANAGING EDITOR: Alyssa Scavetta
EDITOR-IN-CHIEF: Julie Davis
PUBLISHER: Lianne Sentar
VICE PRESIDENT: Adam Arnold
PRESIDENT: Jason DeAngelis

ISBN: 978-1-63858-942-6
Printed in Canada
First Printing: September 2024
10 9 8 7 6 5 4 3 2 1

TABLE OF CONTENTS

ARC 12: TREASON

ARC 13: GOVERNMENT REFORMS

ARC 14: DIVERGENT PATHS

APPENDIXES

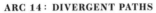

The Mandate of Heaven
comes to light

ARC 12

TREASON

91

THE YELLOW ROBES

YANG RONGGUI was a strikingly handsome man of towering stature. In his youth, he had been known far and wide as a noble young master of outstanding talent. Now slightly past his prime, he had cultivated a short mustache that endowed him with an aura of steady maturity. His conduct toward others was beyond reproach, and his manner of speech was genuine and profound. He was nothing at all like the hideous character of Xu Ling's imagination.

But at this moment, the real Xu Ling had yet to meet him, for the honored imperial envoys Yang Ronggui now hosted were a pair of imposters.

After seeing Prince Yan's entourage off with all due respect, Yang Ronggui stroked a hand over his mustache. He was a deeply shrewd man who seldom revealed his true thoughts, but Zheng Kun, the prefectural magistrate of Yangzhou, had long served at his side. Though it was impossible to tell from his expression, Zheng Kun sensed that Yang Ronggui was in a rather good mood. Thus, he stepped closer and remarked, "It seems Governor Yang has much in common with His Highness Prince Yan."

Prince Yan appeared to understand the deep and hidden currents of officialdom. He had no real intention of getting to the bottom of this case. Rather, he was only using it as a pretext to raise a fuss and consolidate his own strength.

Yang Ronggui smiled. "His Highness Prince Yan is a remarkable young man. With a little more polish, he's sure to accomplish great things. As for Assistant Minister Xu, he is an uncommon exemplar of a pure official, perfectly upright in conduct. I had hoped the Marquis of Anding would join us tonight since I'd heard they'd traveled together, but it seems it wasn't meant to be. The marquis was in a hurry to attend to military affairs and merely passed Yangzhou Prefecture's front gates on his way to the Jiangbei Garrison. What a pity I missed meeting Great Liang's God of War in person."

Zheng Kun was a clever man and unparalleled bootlicker who had served with Yang Ronggui for years. He immediately surmised what Governor Yang was driving at: Prince Yan was an inexperienced youngster. Though he possessed great ambition, he had revealed his intentions with only a few words and would be easy to handle. As for that Xu Ling with him, he was a blockhead who had addled his brain by reading too many books; there was no need to waste any effort on him. Most remarkable of all, whether out of a desire to avoid suspicion by mixing military affairs with politics or due to Prince Yan's own deliberate machinations, the ever-irksome Marquis of Anding had taken himself out of the picture. Thus, they could cast aside their misgivings and put everything they had into the imminent battle.

Yang Ronggui met Zheng Kun's eyes and smiled. "With these common miscreants spreading their wicked slander all the way to the capital, it's perfectly reasonable that His Highness has to come look into things," he said. "Instruct your subordinates to prepare themselves. We who walk the straight and narrow path have nothing to fear from his investigation."

"Yes, Your Excellency." Zhang Kun smiled. "Rest assured that all will be put in order."

Only after dismissing the ebullient Zheng Kun did the satisfaction on Yang Ronggui's face subside. Malice flooded his eyes. He had known dealing with Prince Yan would be no simple task, but he never expected such a monumental challenge. If not for Assistant Minister Lü's prior warning, he might really have been duped. Prince Yan was a cunning character who manipulated the imperial court with ease—his abilities went without saying. How could he possibly be a mere inexperienced youngster?

The great plan Yang Ronggui and his allies had devised in the shadows was a tightly kept secret of which not even Zheng Kun was aware. If Prince Yan had taken swift action, sweeping in like a bolt of lightning out of the blue and judging things as they stood, it would have been easier to deal with. But the young prince was focusing his energies and taking his time instead... There was a good chance things were about to go awry.

This matter would have to be resolved as quickly as possible.

While Yang Ronggui and company led the "imperial envoys" to tour the sparsely populated refugee camps on the city's outskirts, Chang Geng and Xu Ling were conducting their own undercover investigation into the refugees' fate. Watching the noble Prince Yan stroll the streets filled with commoners, Commissioner Xu was perplexed. His Highness took to the city like a fish to water, striking up conversations with small-time merchants and people of all walks of life, adapting gracefully to his circumstances. With the fake Prince Yan acting as a decoy, hardly anyone took notice of them. Xu Ling, trailing in Prince Yan's wake, made several friends who would happily have him over for a meal in only a matter of days.

Their investigation gradually took shape.

"You say there used to be a bunch of refugee camps outside the city, but you don't know where they've all gone...? Your High— Proprietor, be careful!" Xu Ling was chatting with an innkeeper while staring at Prince Yan with his heart in his throat. They were currently in a small tavern in the Yangzhou outskirts owned by a retired armed escort surnamed Sun. He had a fierce visage and an aggressive personality, and would readily remove patrons by force if they crossed him. Thanks to his fine wine-making skills, however, no few members of the jianghu patronized his tavern. Only in this way had his business shakily survived till now.

Innkeeper Sun and Prince Yan seemed to get on like a house on fire. By now, the tavern had already closed for the day. Buoyed by the excitement of their new acquaintance, Prince Yan had carved a horizontal plaque for his friend on the spot and was presently standing on a bench to personally hang it over the doorway. The bench was missing a leg and swayed precariously even when untouched—how could it possibly support a person standing on it?

The innkeeper laughed boisterously. "Your proprietor's martial skills are excellent. There's no need for a fair-faced pencil-pusher like yourself to worry about him—but why are you asking about the refugees? With those foreign dogs occupying Jiangnan, there're no shortage of displaced souls out there. Even if they cover the ground with their dead bodies, who's going to keep track?"

Xu Ling hurried to respond. "I hear there are over a hundred thousand refugees in Jiangbei. Our boss sent us to scout the canal banks in hopes of employing some of them in his factories. But we've traveled all this way and hardly seen anyone—how are we supposed to find workers?"

Innkeeper Sun had by now drunk nearly a catty of yellow wine.

His face was deeply flushed, and his gaze seemed to drift. He glanced muzzily at Xu Ling and bared his yellowed teeth in a grin. "What is this, some kind of interrogation?"

Xu Ling froze.

Chang Geng took the hammer and nimbly tapped an iron nail into the lintel of the little tavern's doorway before leaping down from his perch, the three-legged bench remaining still as stone throughout. Watching the flustered Commissioner Xu, he shook his head with a smile—Xu Ling had dedicated his entire childhood to studying, his ears plugged to anything beyond his own window. After entering the imperial court as a government official, he spent all his time mucking about in the capital. When had he ever had the opportunity to interact with hardened travelers who risked their lives roaming the jianghu?

Innkeeper Sun glanced at Chang Geng and slurred, "A white dragon disguised as a fish—you're no simple proprietor."

Xu Ling, terrified, promptly broke into a cold sweat, but Chang Geng was unfazed. Accepting the wine jug offered by Innkeeper Sun, he knocked back half its contents. "White dragons or black dragons—I don't know what you mean by this. But those who make a habit of taking the crooked path at night will inevitably encounter a demon. And I am that demon."

Innkeeper Sun studied Chang Geng, something profound in his gaze. Then he smiled. "So. How exactly did the esteemed imperial envoy find me?"

Chang Geng's identity had been exposed, yet his expression was placid. "It was simple, really. I just noticed this little tavern seems to be doing a bit too well in terms of business. Every day, you receive no more than two or three tables' worth of customers, yet you seem to go through an endless stream of food and drink—can you even finish it all?"

Innkeeper Sun eyed him. All signs of drunkenness had vanished from his face, and his gaze now sharpened into a malevolent glint. Xu Ling's eyes were keen; he spotted the vicious dagger winking beneath the man's outer robe.

Xu Ling shot to his feet. "Your Highness!"

The handful of people who had been busy napping, doing the accounts, and waiting on customers in the tavern rose as one, their eyes flashing. Every one of them bore a weapon at their waist, all clearly adept martial artists. The pair of Black Iron Battalion guards escorting the prince stepped out to block the door as Xu Ling's hand instinctively tightened around the sword he carried for self-defense.

Chang Geng set the wine jar lightly on the table. "On our way here, I kept wondering where so many refugees could possibly be hidden. The worst-case scenario would doubtless be that Yang Ronggui is so unhinged he swept them all up and buried them alive in the name of suppressing the plague—"

"Your Highness knows your underlings well," Innkeeper Sun said with a terrifying smile. "As expected of the leader of those government dogs."

"The leader of those government dogs is my elder brother, not me," Chang Geng said blandly. "But no matter how unhinged Yang Ronggui may be, he is not so capable as all that. If he really did massacre the refugees, rebellion would have broken out, and the nearby Jiangbei Garrison would be alerted."

Innkeeper Sun shot him a cold look. "Yang Ronggui claimed refugee settlements had already been built near the mountains. He intended to send the refugees to cultivate virgin land and help them put down roots. Every refugee was registered and given a numbered tablet, which granted them entry into a different mountain settlement. The policies for dividing land and rent collection were all made clear. He also allowed small groups of refugees to appoint their own leaders. Those who refused to go could do as they pleased, but if they left the limits of Yangzhou City, they would no longer receive alms. The sick were quarantined and treated in a separate side courtyard; all the doctors in Yangzhou City were present to tend them."

Any members of the jianghu with even the slightest connection to the government or the criminal underworld would have long found a place for themselves even if they had to flee their homes. Those who were reduced to refugee status were those without such connections—truly impoverished common folk. Over the course of their lives, the greatest wish of these people was to find a place to settle down and live a good life. As long as they were alive, as long as each day was a bit better than the last and they had something to look forward to, they would never cause any trouble.

If Yang Ronggui had made grand promises of better accommodations, people would have become suspicious. But Yang Ronggui had been clear that he would task the refugees with developing unworked farmland. He had even dutifully explained his policies upfront in concrete terms. Perhaps the rent was slightly higher than what local landlords had charged in the past, but the precarity of the refugees' circumstances was sufficient to keep them in line and following Yang Ronggui's orders.

Xu Ling was utterly confused. He'd originally expected Yang Ronggui to be a useless, sinecure-holding glutton who had shirked his duties by concealing an epidemic in his district. This account, however, painted him as someone quite capable. If these policies had been adopted as these people claimed, how could Jiangbei possibly have become so overrun with refugees?

"Sending the refugees to clear land for agriculture isn't a terrible solution," said Xu Ling. "But if Governor Yang has been doing such a fine job resettling the refugees, why would he falsify reports of the plague?"

"The esteemed imperial envoy subsists on the imperial coffers and lives an innocent and unaffected life, free of worry. Where, one wonders, does all that money come from?" Innkeeper Sun mused, dangerously sarcastic.

Xu Ling gaped at him for a long moment before grasping his point. "You mean to tell me that Yang Ronggui pocketed the money the imperial court allocated for the resettlement of refugees?!"

Xu Ling regretted his words the instant they escaped his mouth; they were too obviously naïve. As expected, Prince Yan and Innkeeper Sun burst into laughter. Xu Ling's face burned, and he hastily added, "I just didn't think Yang Ronggui would have the audacity. Our enemies lie across the river, and the Jiangbei Garrison is right next door. How does he have the gall to..."

"The Jiangbei Garrison cannot mobilize at will," Chang Geng said, his voice low. "The foreigners watch this bank with covetous eyes. Should the enemy troops make their move, the consequences don't bear thinking about. If Yang Ronggui covers his tracks well, Zhong-lao and his people might not have the means to monitor the situation."

Innkeeper Sun scoffed. Clearly, this explanation didn't satisfy him.

"Yang Ronggui only needs to take control of the northbound relay stations and he can hide the truth from the masses." Chang Geng turned to Innkeeper Sun. "Sun-xiong is so familiar with the situation—you've surely done your part in gathering up the refugees as well. Let me guess: there are many fishermen in the Liangjiang region. There is also the Shahai Gang that operates on both land

and sea. I wonder to which group my dear friend Innkeeper Sun belongs?"

It took Xu Ling a moment to catch on. He felt that this "Shahai Gang" sounded vaguely familiar. Innkeeper Sun turned his head and smiled, revealing a terrifying knife scar that stretched from his ear to his lower jaw. Only then did Xu Ling remember—the Shahai Gang's sphere of influence extended from the Jiangnan region all the way south to Fujian Province. It was a huge bandit gang.

This Innkeeper Sun was no armed escort; he was an outlaw. This inn was no Apricot Blossom Village either, but a hive of criminal activity!

Xu Ling tensed. He stepped forward, using his frail scholar's body without even the strength to truss a chicken to shield Prince Yan. "You...you are..."

Chang Geng cupped his hands politely. "Those who make a living doing lowly work value loyalty far more than scholarly intellectuals with their noses stuck in books. The true-hearted may be found among the outlaws of the greenwood. Please forgive my disrespect."

Innkeeper Sun glanced at the Black Iron Battalion guards standing behind him. "Prince Yan needn't be so polite." His tone was hostile. "You came here to ferret out how much Yang Ronggui has embezzled, the fate of the refugees under his watch, and whether there really is an epidemic. I'll give it to you straight: the first day those sick refugees were taken to the side courtyards to be 'treated,' they were each fed a bowl of herbal medicine. That night, a huge fire broke out in the settlement and in the end, not a single person made it out of those courtyards. Their bodies were burned to ash, leaving no evidence behind. As for the others, they were either sent off to those 'mountain settlements' and locked away in groups, or they followed us brothers and joined the gang."

Chang Geng's expression was unchanged. "It seems even if we didn't come, it would be only a matter of time before rebellion broke out."

"It's a typical case of oppressive government policies forcing the common people to revolt." Innkeeper Sun smiled grimly. "That said, though they never caught wind of Yang Ronggui massacring refugees, I have no doubt that the Jiangbei Garrison would move out at once if the refugees actually rebel. Even if they're incapable of taking down corrupt officials or foreign adversaries, they're more than enough to handle some insignificant commonfolk. There are so many different roads to walk in life, yet all lead to dead ends."

Xu Ling had seen with his own eyes the discipline of the Jiangbei Garrison, as well as the state of the battlefield on the twin banks of the Yangtze River. He was about to refute Innkeeper Sun's words when Chang Geng raised a hand to stop him.

"If all roads lead to dead ends," Chang Geng said calmly, "why would Sun-xiong be guarding the tree stump and waiting here for us rabbits?"

Innkeeper Sun's eyes flashed like lightning. "I've been waiting *respectfully* for you here because I want to see whether the imperial court's envoy will do his job. If your esteemed self is no more than a sinecure-holding loafer who colludes with snakes and rats, then even if we must face the Northern Camp's cannon fire, we will risk our lives and fight! The question now is whether you have the guts to treat with us—but I can't open the door for a wolf to enter our stronghold. If you and that pretty boy with you wish to get to the bottom of this, leave all your henchmen—these here in plain sight and those in the shadows—behind and follow me."

Xu Ling's protest was immediate. "Your Highness, you mustn't!"

Chang Geng smiled. "That's more than I could have asked for. Lead the way."

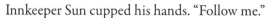

Innkeeper Sun cupped his hands. "Follow me."

He was first to stride out the door. But he had taken only a few steps when he turned and caught sight of the horizontal plaque Prince Yan had inscribed for this criminal stronghold disguised as a little tavern. The old bandit's expression finally wavered. Four words were starkly carved on that narrow strip of wood: MAY JUSTICE REIGN ETERNAL.

If someone were, at that very moment, to see the "Prince Yan" standing in the Governor of Liangjiang's estate, they would surely be flabbergasted.

This Prince Yan was incredibly charming when in the presence of others. Yet the instant he closed the door to his room, he promptly transformed into a preening, featherbrained idiot. He was, of course, none other than the master of disguise, Cao Chunhua.

Governor Yang had taken great pains to welcome them with hospitality. The room was elegantly appointed and sumptuously outfitted with a number of delicate golden devices that burned violet gold. A large western mirror the height of an adult man stood against one wall, in which every minute detail of one's features was reflected clearly. "Prince Yan," who had only just been standing tall and straight as a pine tree outside, sashayed his way in with a twist of his hips, as if he wouldn't be satisfied till he'd twisted his legs into a knot. Prancing over to the mirror, he tilted his face this way and that, spending nearly an incense stick's time making eyes at his own image. No matter how long he cupped his own cheeks and ogled himself, it wasn't enough.

Beside him, "Xu Ling" kept his eyes lowered like a wooden mannequin. Perhaps he'd grown numb to such antics; he refused to involve himself in this idiocy.

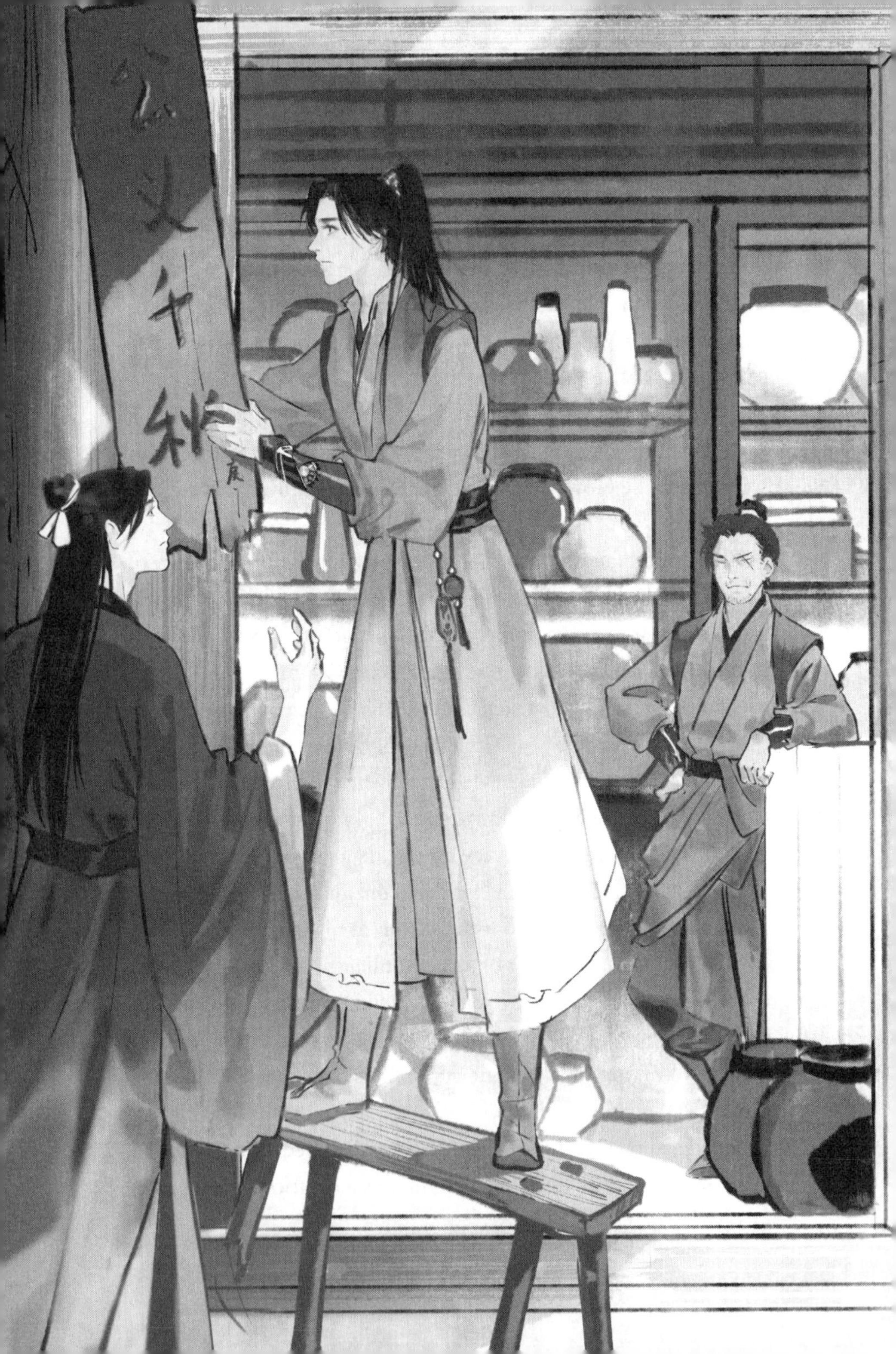

Prince Yan—or rather, Cao Chunhua—clicked his tongue. "Never mind the rest of his body, just my dage's face alone is beyond compare," he sighed in heartfelt appreciation. "No matter how much I touch it, I can't get enough."

Xu Ling sneered. "Go touch the real thing if you've got the balls."

"This face of mine is plenty real," Prince Yan raised his chin in satisfaction. "Real enough to pass for the original at least—ay, speaking of which, why wouldn't he let me perfect the ruse? If the marquis is here, I could've made a mask of his face. Why bother with this nonsense about him heading directly to Jiangbei to avoid arousing suspicion or some such thing?"

"It's for your own good," Xu Ling said. "Saves you from accidentally desecrating Marshal Gu's face with those clodhopping paws of yours and getting chopped in half by the Black Iron Battalion."

Rolling his eyes, Prince Yan turned back to continue admiring the masterpiece that was his face with single-minded devotion.

A member of his personal guard ran in with a report. "Your Highness, Commissioner Xu, Governor Yang urgently seeks a meeting. He is waiting for you outside."

Prince Yan and Xu Ling exchanged a glance.

"We've played our parts, and both the host and guests have thoroughly enjoyed themselves," Prince Yan murmured. "Logically speaking, our next step would be to go all in and start accepting their bribes, right? There are probably whole chests of treasure and countless beauties waiting for us out there. They can have the female beauties, but let's keep the male beauties, shall we? Our boss ordered us to collect material evidence, but what about witness testimonies?"

Xu Ling glanced back, an ache developing in his stomach as he took in Prince Yan's handsome face and the way he practically salivated through the words *male beauties*. But before he could spit out

a sarcastic retort, he was interrupted by the sound of urgent footsteps. Even as the guards standing outside shouted for them to stop,
the intruders charged straight in. The raucous clamor of clashing
arms soon followed.

Xu Ling's face fell. "Did we slip up somehow?" he muttered
quietly. "Or was it..."

He was still speaking when the imposter Prince Yan's depraved
expression faded entirely, his countenance taking on the stern lines
of the genuine article. He swept forward and flung open the door,
standing with his hands clasped behind his back beneath his broad
sleeves. He glared down at the group of armored swordsmen that
had barged into the courtyard, Yang Ronggui at their head.

"Governor Yang, what is the meaning of this?" Prince Yan demanded, affecting an imperious tone. Behind him, Xu Ling surrep-
titiously put a hand to his waist, prepared to fight their way out if
their identities had been exposed.

But to everyone's surprise, Yang Ronggui, who had arrived radi-
ating killing intent, stepped forward and fell to his knees. "Your
Highness," he cried out, voice booming, "this lower official is inept.
The local bandit gangs have risen in rebellion and sealed off the
postal routes from Yangzhou to the Jiangbei Garrison. This lower
official had no choice but to gather the guard of all the nearby cities
here and ask them to lay down their lives to protect Your Highness
from harm! There is no time to lose; please make preparations to
leave at once, your Highness."

"Prince Yan" glanced back at "Xu Ling." Xu Ling subtly shook
his head; he hadn't grasped Yang Ronggui's game. Prince Yan was
forced to improvise. "I understand. Governor Yang, please rise..."

Yang Ronggui continued in a ringing voice, "This lower official
seeks to raise another matter. The current emperor is muddleheaded

and incompetent, and the dynasty is in decline. Our nation has been plagued with a bevy of troubles both at home and abroad, with foreigners eyeing us greedily from without and violent mobs revolting within. Our troops lack a strong leader. Thus, I am willing to risk the condemnation of all to follow in the footsteps of my forebears and support Your Highness's ascension to the imperial throne!"

As he finished, the ranks of armed guards behind him parted to allow four men carrying an article of clothing between them to step forward. The fake Prince Yan's eyes nearly popped out of his skull as he stared in astonishment—it was a near-perfect replica of the yellow imperial dragon robe!

"I have spared no effort in performing my duties for the sake of Great Liang," Yang Ronggui continued. "During this time of national crisis, I dared not hoard my private possessions and offered up all I had to save the state. I have handed over what few family assets I possess, even my own wife's dowry, to the imperial court in exchange for war beacon tickets. Yet still, our inept ruler questions my loyalty. I have suffered an injustice greater than any known to history. Should a wise ruler appear, I am willing to lay my life on the line to support his rise!"

This speech resounded like a fervent plea. But in reality, it contained three layers of threat and accusation:

First: *While it's true I took bribes and bent the law, I was forced to do so because of your war beacon tickets. I may be guilty, but you, Prince Yan, drove me to it.*

Second: *It matters not whether gangs of bandits truly rise in revolt. If I say they are in revolt, then they are in revolt.*

Third: *To don the yellow robes or to die as a casualty of a refugee insurrection—the choice is yours, Your Highness.*

When they had first arrived in Yangzhou, the real Prince Yan had instructed them to stall for as much time as possible with this villainous Yang bastard. He never warned them they might encounter such a farce. For a moment, the pair of imposter envoys were both confounded.

Finally, Xu Ling sucked in a deep breath and barked out, "Open rebellion—Governor Yang, have you lost your mind? The Marquis of Anding is a stone's throw away in the Jiangbei Garrison. Do you think Great Liang's countless elite troops are all dead?"

Yang Ronggui smiled. "Commissioner Xu exaggerates," he said, his voice heavy with meaning. "How would a government official dare harbor thoughts of rebellion? His Majesty has been murdered by Dongying assassins and the nation stands on the verge of catastrophe. The crown prince is young; we have no choice but to propose this inferior plan and ask His Highness to ascend the throne."

92

RUNNING ABOUT

NEITHER GU YUN NOR ZHONG CHAN—nor even the entirety of Great Liang's military—had much confidence in their ability to win naval battles. They had no choice but to pour all their energy into the problem. With the assistance of Ge Chen, the expert sent from the Lingshu Institute, they dismantled the Far Western dragon warship in its entirety and analyzed it from top to bottom. They needed to know everything there was to know about the Far Western navy's combat maneuvers and the flexibility of their tactics during battle—speed, defense, firepower, and violet gold carrying capacity all factored in.

When the two armies inevitably clashed, they would have tens of thousands of sea dragon warships, large and small, under their command. It couldn't be compared to Gu Yun's madcap flight across the Yangtze River with only twenty-some martial experts at his disposal; anything could happen. What sorts of conditions might they encounter, and how should they meet them? In the heat of battle, many decisions that seemed to be made on the spur of the moment were in fact based on a foundation laid by the commander in chief's extensive experience and preparation.

Furthermore, they had to consider how Great Liang's navy ought to develop in the future, the structure of its leadership, the types of battleships to commission from the Lingshu Institute, training methods for the sailors, allocation of violet gold, and so on and so forth.

Gu Yun's position was even more complicated. He was acting as commander in chief over military operations on all four borders, so the front here at Jiangnan was far from his only concern. He spent his daylight hours patrolling and familiarizing himself with the battlefront that was the Liangjiang region. After returning with the setting sun, he would spend his nights speaking at length with either old General Zhong or Yao Zhen. Since Chang Geng had left with Xu Ling, Gu Yun had essentially been working around the clock, so busy he barely had time for a sip of water.

Today, he was once again consulting with Yao Zhen. When Gu Yun rose to leave, he suddenly felt one of his feet go numb. He swayed in place, his heart pounding as he struggled for breath. Yao Zhen hastily caught him by the arm. "Marshal, what's wrong?"

"It's nothing, I'm just famished." Gu Yun flashed a smile, then continued, self-mocking, "To be honest with you, I could eat a donkey burger the size of a horse cart right now."

Yao Zheng frowned slightly. Gu Yun couldn't see his own complexion at this moment, but people often said young folk were "full of hot blood." A person's essence, breath, and spirit showed on their face, and whether one was really full of vim and vigor could be determined at a glance from the color of their lips and cheeks.

"Why don't you come stay at my place tonight?" Yao Zhen asked. "My wife has few hobbies, but she's very fond of cooking. I'll have her prepare some plain congee and side dishes. I can't offer any exotic delicacies, but at the very least you can enjoy a hot, home-cooked meal that suits your taste."

In the past, Gu Yun would have instantly invited himself over after hearing these words. But recently, he seemed to have developed a strange new condition. The more tired he was, the more difficult it was for him to keep food down. All he wanted to do was to lie down and sleep. He said politely, "Many thanks, but perhaps another time. It's already so late; it wouldn't do for me to impose on the madam like that."

Yao Zhen couldn't insist without crossing the bounds of propriety. He accompanied Gu Yun back to the commander's tent. But he still felt ill at ease, so he added before leaving, "So long as the green hills remain, one needn't worry about firewood. Please take care of yourself, Marshal."

"We have enough to get through the winter at least, so you can rest assured." Gu Yun waved a hand, then lifted his head, stretching his stiff neck. Catching sight of the starry galaxies strewn across the black satin of the sky, he sighed. "I remember back in the day, despite brimming with talent, Chongze-xiong lacked ambition. You didn't even want to take credit for the great achievement of quelling Prince Wei's rebellion. You preferred to guard your own patch of earth and live a peaceful life with your family—yet now look at you, pressed into leading the war effort. Truly, fate makes fools of us all."

Yao Zhen smiled bitterly. "The imperial court is rife with partisanship as it is. I am but a powerless scholar—why should I add to the mess? What good is all that plotting and scheming? Rather than buzzing around the rich like a fly and trying to shamelessly crawl up the ladder, it's much better to settle far from the machinations of the capital and idle the days away. Here, I have my family. We needn't worry about food and drink, and everyone honors their word—how is that not a blessing?"

The truth was, Yao Chongze was too smart; he knew very well how to seek advantage while avoiding harm. As early as Prince Wei's rebellion, he had recognized that beneath Great Liang's façade of prosperity lay a fading empire entering its final days. He had no desire to toil his life away for this wretched imperial court. His greatest ambition was to hold this mid-level official position and laze around awaiting death.

Unfortunately, no eggs remain intact when the nest overturns. He could no longer shirk his responsibilities by playing the fool.

Refusing to relent, Gu Yun asked, "Then what will you do after the war is over?"

In response, Yao Zhen launched into an impassioned speech. "If the time comes that the nation is once again at peace, then I'll put all this behind me. If, after everything, the imperial court is still so noxiously corrupt, why should I bother wading into the muck? Marshal Gu holds the Black Iron Tiger Tally—but are you really happier now than you were in your youth, when you returned in triumph from the south and feasted with the rest of us loafers in the company of dancing girls?"

Gu Yun had nothing to say.

Yao Zhen smiled in recollection. "This lower official remembers to this day a time when Marshal Gu was deep in his cups. You were balanced with one foot on a narrow banister, swaying to and fro with an ornamental saber borrowed from a sword dancer. You etched characters into falling flower petals with such skill that even the queen of flowers[1] blushed. You know, that incident remains a much-told tale…"

Gu Yun was so embarrassed his tongue nearly tied itself into a knot. "I was too young back then. Please don't mention such—such absurd incidents again."

Yao Zhen laughed, utterly oblivious, and cast his eyes southward. "The day we recover Jiangnan, I'll play host and we can get drunk

---

1 Nickname for the most famous courtesan in a brothel.

on maiden red wine and play with dancing girls in the warm spring breeze. When the time comes, please do me the honor of joining me."

How would I dare play with anyone else? Gu Yun thought. *I've got one at home who's more than enough.*

But such craven words weren't fit to be spoken before an old friend, so Gu Yun only offered a mysterious smile.

Their late-night reminiscence on youthful indiscretions had reached this awkward standstill when Ge Chen burst in with a sheet of billow paper in his hand and alarm written all over his face. "My lord, bad news—Yang Ronggui has launched a revolt!"

The letter was from the fake Prince Yan. Fearing his wooden bird would be intercepted by their enemies, he hadn't dared mention the ruse involving the double Prince Yans, nor did he indicate that the letter was meant for the Jiangbei Garrison. In his plea for help, he wrote that for the time being, they were feigning cooperation with the insurgents, that he'd no idea what Yang Ronggui planned to do with them next, and so on and so forth.

Gu Yun and Yao Zhen were both stunned. Certainly Gu Yun had considered the possibility that, failing to bribe the imperial envoy, Yang Ronggui might resort to desperate measures. But after leading the Black Iron Battalion for so many years, Gu Yun tended to look down his nose at these local garrisons. In his mind, twenty personal guards were sufficient to flatten Yangzhou Prefecture—not to mention, Chang Geng wasn't the type to be so easily cowed. Gu Yun grabbed the billow paper from Ge Chen only to find that the script scrawled across it didn't belong to Chang Geng at all. The message had been hastily penned, and its contents grew more concerning with every word read, ending with the final, most alarming line of all: *His Majesty has suffered an assassination attempt, his current status is unknown.*

Possibilities raced through Gu Yun's mind as he worked himself up into a cold sweat. Detaining Prince Yan in the south while assassinating the emperor in the capital... Now that he thought about it, such a plot wasn't impossible so long as one had the guts to do the deed! If not for the Linyuan Pavilion's wooden birds, given Yangzhou City's current lockdown, this news would have been completely blocked. Yang Ronggui and his collaborators could have secretly escorted Prince Yan north all the way to the capital with the Jiangbei Garrison none the wiser.

If Li Feng was really dead and the throne vacant, it would change everything.

"Marshal?" Yao Zhen ventured, petrified.

"Send word to old General Zhong and ask him to lend me a few armored hawks; I'll return them later—hurry!" With this, Gu Yun completely forgot about his dizzy exhaustion from a moment ago. "Xiao-Ge, you stay put. Figure out some way to contact the capital and find out what's going on. I'm taking some men and heading to Yangzhou."

At this moment, the imposter Prince Yan and Xu Ling had finished packing their bags and been "invited" aboard the metaphorical pirate ship. They departed Yangzhou with the rebel army and marched north, on their way to force an abdication. The rebels kept a low profile the entire journey. The fact that barely a whisper had leaked of something as major as a plague in Jiangbei was sufficient to demonstrate the control Yang Ronggui and his traitorous faction exerted over the relay posts along the canal banks.

Evening found the entourage resting at one such relay post. Prince Yan and Xu Ling were forced to share a room, an insult to their stations. Their personal guards had long since been dispatched. Instead, they were surrounded by layer upon layer of Yang Ronggui's people. They wouldn't have been able to fly out even if they sprouted wings.

Only in the latter half of the night did Prince Yan finally peek out through the crack in the window. Seeing that their guards had relaxed slightly, he rubbed his face and said to Xu Ling in a low voice, "Had I known how difficult this mission would be, I would've stayed put in the barbarian grasslands. His Highness owes me big time—who knows whether Ge Pangxiao's received our wooden bird. Even the young master's gotten embroiled in this mess. Your dad would be worried sick if he knew."

Xu Ling was about to respond when his expression suddenly turned grim. The men guarding the rear entrance had inexplicably and silently collapsed. In the next moment, a dark shadow darted into the courtyard, so fast it seemed to fly. Everything Xu Ling carried that could be used for self-defense had long been confiscated. He grabbed a porcelain cup from the table and flung it at the intruder with surprising force. With a tilt of the head, the intruder narrowly dodged the projectile before sweeping the porcelain cup into his sleeves. He stole soundlessly through the back window, his movements astonishingly nimble. Despite the flurry of activity, the wind chime hanging over the window didn't so much as stir.

The man jumped down and yanked off his mask. "It's me," he signed.

It was Gu Yun.

"Xu Ling" had never met Gu Yun before and started in surprise, but "Prince Yan" gasped sharply, his face lighting up. Gu Yun had already felt something was a bit off—the force with which Xu Ling had thrown the cup was too strong. But he didn't have the time to consider this just now. He peered outside and frowned. "How did you end up like this?" he signed rapidly. "What happened to your guards?"

Gu Yun's hands were still moving when Prince Yan threw himself at him like a fledgling bird diving back into the forest, his gait so charmingly coquettish as to elicit gasps of amazement. Few knew that Gu Yun had a dog's nose capable of sniffing out any fishy individual who came within a meter of him. Not only did the Prince Yan before him lack the ever-present scent of pacifying fragrance, he smelled faintly of rouge and powder. Gu Yun took a swift step back and grabbed this imposter by the throat. "Who are you?"

"Prince Yan" hadn't expected to be exposed the moment they met. Utterly thwarted, he flailed and mouthed, *Uncle Shiliu, it's me.*

The only people who called Gu Yun "Uncle Shiliu" were Ge Chen and Cao Chunhua, who had followed Chang Geng from Yanhui Town to the capital all those years ago. The two of them had gradually stopped addressing him by this moniker once they came of age.

Gu Yun's grip went slack. "Xiao-Cao?" he asked, shocked.

While Gu Yun was secretly making contact with his double, elsewhere, the real Prince Yan had vanished into thin air. On the third day of the seventh month, a confidential letter from Yangzhou passed through the nine gates of the Imperial City and landed in the hands of Lü Chang in the capital.

When he read the missive, Lü Chang couldn't help letting loose a hearty laugh. Minutes later, he stepped into his rooms for a private discussion with his trusted aides. A messenger was soon dispatched to request the presence of Minister Fang.

The Fang Estate was not far from the Lü Estate, and his messenger promptly returned with an answer: "My lord, the family claims Minister Fang has recently come down with a foul disease, leaving him feverish and covered in a rash. They say he's unfit for company; they plan to send him to their villa in the capital outskirts to convalesce. This lowly servant saw the carriage they had ready and waiting. They were burning bed linens and clothing in the backyard."

"Did Minister Fang have any words for me?" Lü Chang asked.

"He did," the servant said respectfully. "Minister Fang asked this lowly servant to convey that he prays for your immediate success and hopes all your wishes come true."

Scoffing, Lü Chang waved a hand to dismiss him before stepping into his study. *Fang Qin, that sly old fox. His heart is filled with wicked plots, always ordering people about in the name of setting the nation to rights, but when push comes to shove, he shrinks back. He'll never be more than an inept advisor—why should I mind him. As it stands, our great undertaking is already more than halfway complete. All is ready save for the last push of the easterly wind.*[2]

Immediately after setting fire to his linens in the name of retreating to recuperate in the countryside, this rash-ridden "inept advisor" arrived in the northern capital outskirts via an inconspicuous little palanquin. It just so happened that Shen Yi, who had likewise snuck out of the capital, was also at the Northern Camp. He was shocked to hear that Minister Fang—whose esteemed buttocks, as far as Shen Yi knew, had yet to park itself on one side or the other—had come to call.

The newly appointed commander of the Northern Camp was formerly one of Tan Hongfei's lieutenants. Recognizing that the situation was a serious one, he said in a low voice, "General Shen, please withdraw for now; I'll go and meet with him."

Fang Qin spent nearly two hours at the Northern Camp. No one knew what he said. Only long after nightfall did Fang Qin finally take his leave in his tiny palanquin, shrouded in silence.

---

2   A reference to the fictionalized depiction of the Battle of Red Cliffs in Romance of the Three Kingdoms wherein Shu Han military advisor Zhuge Liang performs a ritual to summon an easterly wind, the final element necessary to ensure victory against the enemy Cao Wei army.

It was the end of the seventh month, and the Longan Emperor's Longevity Festival was imminent.

Li Feng hadn't properly celebrated his birthday since his ascension several years ago. The empress dowager had died young, and after the late emperor's passing, there were no elders suitable to tend to such affairs. Thus had he parsimoniously grown to such an age. This year, however, Li Feng had finally decided to mark the occasion.

Kite's Flight Pavilion had collapsed during the capital siege, and a new construction had been built on its ruins. Li Feng had always thought Moon-Shot Platform's appearance too inauspicious and the Great Yunmeng Outlook so extravagant it offended the heavens. He ordered that Kite's Flight Pavilion be rebuilt as the "Altar of Prosperity," doing away with the edifice's former function as a place of merriment and transforming it into a serious, no-nonsense altar of prayer. He even moved the Imperial Ancestral Temple to the new site. Whether the Longan Emperor simply had nothing better to do or whether he had been goaded by someone with a secret agenda was anyone's guess. Whatever the reason, he was determined to celebrate his birthday by ascending the newly built Altar of Prosperity to issue an imperial edict admitting his past mistakes, and to offer sacrifices to the heavens and his ancestors...

So it was that, while a gang of corrupt officials and scheming courtiers busied themselves gnawing away at the foundations of the country, Li Feng lived a life as bitter as Xiao Baicai,[3] unloved and uncared for. There was no one to cook him a bowl of longevity noodles on his birthday, which he spent publicly confessing his

---

3 Bi Xiugu, nicknamed Xiao Baicai or "Little Bok Choy" for her tendency to wear white robes with green trousers, was a beautiful young woman who was falsely convicted alongside her lover for murdering her husband. Her name has since become synonymous with miscarriages of justice.

errors in governance. The scene was profoundly depressing. Yet aside from a handful of bearded old pedants of the imperial court, no one whispered a single word of praise behind his back. This emperor was truly a walking tragedy.

When the Son of Heaven left the palace, it was customary for all the court officials to accompany him. The Imperial Guard cleared the way as the grand cavalcade processed to the Altar of Prosperity. A representative of the Imperial Astronomical Bureau stood by, attired in resplendent formal robes, as an ancient temple bell tolled throughout the city.

A stone staircase a thousand steps long climbed to the top of the Altar of Prosperity. In the center, there was a narrow "imperial road" reserved for the Son of Heaven. Two "noble roads," flanking it, used by members of the emperor's inner circle, ended halfway up to the altar at the five-hundredth step.

The collected ministers of the imperial court watched from the bottom of the staircase as the Longan Emperor stepped onto the imperial road and began his ascent. Along the left and right noble roads, he was accompanied by two major officials, one civil and one military, for five hundred steps. With both Prince Yan and Gu Yun presently out of the capital, Jiang Chong of the Grand Council and Shen Yi, the Southwest Army Commander who just happened to be in town, stepped forward in their stead.

Li Feng spent his days bustling about on official business. Upkeep of his riding and shooting skills had fallen by the wayside. Climbing a thousand stone steps wearing the heavy formal robes of the Son of Heaven was strenuous exercise. As he climbed, his thoughts drifted in the memories of his youth. He remembered the first time the young Gu Yun had returned with the old marquis' subordinates after quashing the bandit scourge in the south. Back then, Li Feng had still been the crown prince. He had welcomed the great army's triumphant return to court at his father's side.

When the boy general set out, he had been full of mettle, the immature softness of his face proclaiming his ignorance of the immensity of heaven and earth. Yet after returning from his first tour of duty, he seemed to have aged ten years in a flash. His features were as yet unsharpened by the whetstone of time, but his eyes had grown somber, their aura formidable as the blade of a windslasher. When he dismounted his horse and stepped forward, joining the military brass in shouting "Long live Your Majesty," his armor shimmered in the sun like the scales of a fish.

Li Feng was rarely allowed to leave the palace. Standing beside his father, he stared at the armored Gu Yun with envy. While the emperor spoke to the commander in chief, Gu Yun suddenly raised his head and threw a wink to the young crown prince who had yet to come of age. The two met each other's eyes and shared a smile.

Standing before the Altar of Prosperity, Li Feng couldn't help the quirk at the corners of his lips as he recalled those halcyon days. He pulled himself back to the present, glancing at the dense mass of bodies kneeling at the foot of the stone steps. All he could see looking out were the tops of their bowed heads. Likewise, the two officials who had accompanied him halfway up the slope, in adherence with custom, dared not offend the Son of Heaven by raising their heads...

There would probably never again be a young man who would lift his head to wink at him in this world. Li Feng felt a sudden wave of overwhelming loneliness.

The official from the Imperial Astronomical Bureau had finished preparations for the sacrifices to heaven and had just cleared his throat to speak when there came a loud disturbance from below the Altar of Prosperity. Li Feng had wished to formally admit his mistakes and reproach himself so as to establish his own reputation as a diligent and loving ruler. In furtherance of this, the capital had not been placed under complete martial law for the emperor's pilgrimage. Only the Imperial Guard had turned out to sweep the common folk out of the emperor's path. Countless citizens came out to watch the show, and the roadside was packed with onlookers. With so many crammed together, trouble was bound to break out at the slightest provocation.

A small group of masked men suddenly burst from the swarm of spectators, their movements swift as the wind. Each and every one was a master of martial arts; in no time at all, they had torn through the Imperial Guard's defense line, charging straight for the Altar of Prosperity.

"Look out!"

"Dongying assassins!"

The crowd of ministers at the foot of the steps devolved into chaos. Liu Chongshan, the captain of the Imperial Guard, cried out, "Protect His Majesty!" In his urgency, he dashed up the imperial road with his men in tow and fell to his knees two steps below Li Feng. "Your Majesty, it's too dangerous here," he said in a rush. "This humble general will escort Your Majesty away!"

Incensed, Li Feng lashed out at Liu Chongshan, kicking him in the shoulder. "Useless trash!"

Liu Chongshan looked up. His eyes flashed menacingly as the handful of Imperial Guards standing beside him drew their swords. A tremor shook Li Feng's heart as realization dawned—there were no Dongying assassins. This was a revolt. These tactics were identical to the ones the late emperor had used against the Black Iron Battalion at the behest of the barbarian concubine!

Torn between shock and fury, Li Feng stabbed a finger at Liu Chongshan. "Insolence! How dare you!"

Liu Chongshan chuckled as he rose easily to his feet. He brushed the dirt from his shoulder and stepped forward, closing in on Li Feng. "Your Majesty, please allow this humble general to escort you from this treacherous place. For your own good."

93

TREASON

THE MOMENT LIU CHONGSHAN finished speaking, a "Dongying assassin" broke through the Imperial Guards' line of defense and rushed brazenly toward the imperial road. Liu Chongshan drew his saber from his waist with a vicious smile and pointed it at Li Feng. "Worry not, Your Majesty. This humble general won't allow these wretched brigands to harm a single hair on Your Majesty's head."

Li Feng heard a blood-curdling scream. He whipped his head around in time to see an assassin leap out and kill the official from the Imperial Astronomical Bureau with a swing of his sword. Blood rushed from the dying man's throat, spilling across the stone steps. This scream seemed to act as a signal: Liu Chongshan promptly swung his blade downward. Li Feng had studied martial arts as a child, but unfortunately, he'd never had much talent. His skills were mediocre at best, and after years of neglect, whatever techniques his master had managed to impart had long since been returned in full. He frantically backed away to avoid the strike, stumbling on the stone steps in his haste. The hand with which he caught himself came away streaked with hot blood, the ceremonial robes he had donned for the occasion stained a bright and immediate red.

A more cowardly man would have already fainted from fright. But as luck would have it, the Longan Emperor's temperament was foul and inflexible as the most obstinate mule. Not only did he remain on his feet at such a critical moment, he had the gall to point accusingly at Liu Chongshan and seethe, "Traitorous scoundrel! Don't you know your family will pay for your sins with their heads?!"

The Son of Heaven wasn't some three-headed, six-armed god of war to begin with. With no one here to shield him, he was effectively stretching his neck out for his executioner's blade.

Liu Chongshan had missed with his first strike, but what little fear he had at the start had long since dissipated. Stalking his prey, he said, "In that case, to protect my family, I can only finish what I've started!"

Beneath the tip of a sword, the True Dragon and Son of Heaven was ordinary mortal flesh. Li Feng had nowhere to run as the bladed wind of death swung toward him—but as a scion of the imperial family, he refused to discard his dignity. He said not a word, but his heart filled with misery. He had managed to survive the attempts of his power-hungry brother to seize the throne and the chaos of the Far Western army's siege, yet now, just as the country began to recover, he was about to die ingloriously at the hands of a common traitor... He didn't even know why the man was rebelling in the first place!

A strong gust of wind whistled toward him, narrowly brushing the tip of Li Feng's nose. Liu Chongshan's steel sword, which had nearly drawn the emperor's blood, was knocked askew by a five-centimeter-long silk dart. Shen Yi, who had been left halfway down the slope, had finally rushed over.

The general accompanying the emperor up to the Altar of Prosperity was forbidden to carry arms and wore a suit of armor only for appearances. No one expected that Shen Yi's iron cuff was still loaded with a single silk dart.

Liu Chongshan had been seconds from tasting success, only for Shen Yi to thwart his plans. He cursed internally. Before coming here, Lü Chang had assured him that he had sounded out the Shen family and that they would pose no problem—they were sure to bury their heads in the sand and watch from the sidelines like that Fang bastard. Yet here was Shen Yi cropping up out of nowhere!

Shen Yi bent and helped the Longan Emperor to his feet. He and Jiang Chong, who had pelted up the steps with his robes hiked in his hands, took up positions to the fore and rear of their emperor. They were a lonely island before the onslaught. It seemed only in times of peril were a person's true colors revealed. Li Feng's heart filled with a hundred conflicting emotions. "My two dear ministers, your loyalty is greatly appreciated," Li Feng said, utterly exhausted.

Jiang Chong had not a scrap of martial training to his name, and looked around nervously. But Shen Yi had fought his way back to the capital at the head of the remnant army from the southwest. His face was impassive as he said, "Worry not, Your Majesty. The large crowd today was expected; to prevent any unexpected mishaps, many officials sent their estate guards to keep an eye on things from amid the throng. We have more than enough men to deal with these miscreants. And no matter how useless I may be, I still have it in me to handle these young-master soldiers and protect Your Majesty from harm."

Days ago, when Fang Qin had secretly visited the Northern Camp, he had brought with him a letter from his younger sister addressed to her mother. The contents were shocking. It seemed a young servant girl of Lady Fang, recently purchased and unfamiliar with the rules of the house, had accidentally intruded upon the master's study and been brutally beaten to death. This in itself wasn't terribly uncommon—but Lady Fang, a lawfully wedded primary wife, had also been placed under house arrest over this trifling incident. Thus, she had no choice but to write to her maiden family seeking help. The letter also mentioned that a number of guests had come by that day, including such prominent names as Liu Chongshan, the captain of the Imperial Guard.

The letter had been penned just after the Longan Emperor announced he would be venturing out of the imperial palace to make sacrifice to the heavens on his birthday. Considering the timing, one couldn't help but wonder what business these visitors had.

But this was little more than a vaguely worded personal letter. It couldn't be submitted to the emperor—if nothing happened, wouldn't such an accusation be tantamount to bringing false charges against an important minister of the imperial court? Li Feng loathed partisanship. This was exactly how the Imperial Censorate had embarrassed themselves before the emperor again and again—they had on multiple occasions attempted to impeach Prince Yan, but not once had their allegations been found true.

But absent an imperial summons, the troops of the Northern Camp were forbidden from entering the capital. If His Majesty really encountered some threat to his person the day he left the palace, they would be too far away to help.

Fang Qin proposed that they post troops from the Northern Camp just outside the nine gates. In the event of any mishap, they could force their way into the city to render assistance in the time it took a single stick of incense to burn. In the interim, they would borrow capable armed guards from the Shen family, the Marquis of Anding's estate, and other military families, and instruct them to blend into the crowd of civilian spectators. Should the worst happen, they needed only stall for a short while before the Northern Camp arrived with reinforcements.

Shen Yi had no particular love for Fang Qin, but he had to admit the old scoundrel was a meticulous planner.

Seeing Shen Yi so calm amid the chaos, Liu Chongshan was infuriated. "In that case," he sneered, "I would be much obliged if the general would allow me to test his skills!"

From behind him, the rebel Imperial Guards and assassins surged toward the emperor. The estate guards Fang Qin had planted among the crowd also made their move, charging up both sides of the Altar of Prosperity and engaging the insurgents.

Shen Yi pulled Li Feng behind him and yanked the wrist of a lunging assassin downward. With a tug, twist, and crack, he broke the assassin's arm and seized the oddly shaped Dongying sword in the blink of an eye. The heavy blade sprang lightly from Shen Yi's hand and sliced through the air, aiming straight for Liu Chongshan's face.

"Test my skills?" Shen Yi looked benign and inoffensive as he shook his head with a sigh. "I'm afraid Captain Liu isn't worthy."

Liu Chongshan and Shen Yi were both noble sons, fairly evenly matched in the privilege they enjoyed thanks to their well-connected families. They had taken the imperial examination in the same year. But while Shen Yi pursued a civic path and only stumbled into the army, Liu Chongshan had passed the examination as a bona fide military candidate. He joined the Imperial Guard by leaning into his family's connections and was once highly regarded. He had always considered the infamously shiftless Shen Yi beneath his notice.

But the Imperial Guard was filled with rich and powerful scions. After enduring so many years of service, Liu Chongshan had only recently been promoted to the measly rank of captain. Meanwhile, who the hell was Shen Yi? The man was a half-baked imperial artificer who happened to throw in his lot with the Gu family through sheer dumb luck. To think he would actually muddle his way into becoming a regional military commander.

Liu Chongshan laughed in anger, his eyes flashing with red light. He pursed his lips and let loose a long whistle. Another group of rebel soldiers rushed up the Altar of Prosperity as the commoners lining the streets struggled to flee.

"They say a mere thirty Black Carapaces were sufficient to decimate the Eighteen Barbarian Tribes. I wonder—how many of us can a Black Iron soldier like General Shen defeat with only his mortal flesh?"

The scream of iron machinery came from below as countless suits of rebel heavy armor tore through the perimeter, surrounding the emperor and the estate guards. They pushed Li Feng and his defenders back like the blades of a fan as terrifying streams of white steam rose into the air. The standards for the engines and armor used by guard details throughout the country had been established during the reign of Emperor Wu, and violations were dealt with strictly. Only the Imperial Guard was allowed to employ heavy armor units. Now, these ferocious imperial dogs had finally turned their fangs on their master.

Holding the Dongying sword he had seized vigilantly before his chest, Shen Yi prayed that the Northern Camp troops would hurry the hell up.

While Shen Yi was engaging Liu Chongshan, Li Feng had managed to catch his breath. He tossed aside his blood-streaked outer robe and stepped forward to interrogate his assailant. "Liu Chongshan, you have accumulated few merits over the years, and are unlikely to achieve any great accomplishments in your lifetime. In recognition of the Liu family's steadfast loyalty, we personally promoted you to captain of the Imperial Guard. We believe, after sincere reflection, that we have treated you more than fairly.

Do you intend to repay our kindness by colluding with foreigners and stabbing us in the back?"

Liu Chongshan had always held an inordinately high opinion of himself, believing his family's impotence was principally to blame for his unsuccessful official career. Filled with resentment and indignation, he had distanced himself from his own clan and instead thrown in his lot with the Lü family. Upon hearing that in Li Feng's eyes, he was scarcely worthy of his insignificant little captaincy, Liu Chongshan let out a brittle laugh. "What was it that Your Majesty said when you acknowledged the error of your ways? 'We lack the wisdom to understand the people and have no accomplishments in governance. In the nine years since we stepped onto the political stage, there have been many times when we blundered and brought disaster upon country and people'—you've explained things so clearly. So why have you not abdicated in favor of someone more worthy?"

Li Feng ground his teeth so hard they nearly turned to dust. "Please, enlighten us. In favor of whom are we to abdicate, exactly? To whom shall we pass the throne?"

Shen Yi and Jiang Chong both froze. Shen Yi knocked aside an assassin with a sweep of his sword, but his sudden spike of anxiety caused the Dongying blade, already ill-suited to his hand, to fly from his grip.

He should have known that Fang bastard was up to no good!

Once Liu Chongshan mentioned abdication, it was difficult to avoid thinking of Prince Yan. And once one went down that road, Gu Yun was sure to be dragged in too—why else would he choose to leave the capital at this particular moment? He and Prince Yan were traveling together. Were they acting in collusion or not?

All these questions flashed through Shen Yi's mind as he broke out in a cold sweat. He realized his thought process had been overly simple. Prince Yan had gone south to deal with Yang Ronggui; he would never get mixed up with such incompetent bunglers as the Lü family. Thus, whether for public or private reasons, Shen Yi would never allow Lü Chang's traitorous faction to succeed in their plot. But was Lü Chang truly the chief instigator of this insurrection?

It was only now that Shen Yi realized he had been had.

Assuming for a moment that Lady Fang really had been confined because her servant girl had inadvertently heard some tidbit unfit for her ears—how in the world did she, a well-bred young woman raised in the cloistered courtyards of nobility, manage to get word out? All the major noble families were inextricably entwined; this was common knowledge. They would rise or fall together. If the Lü family came to ruin, their in-laws would hardly be better off...but what if someone were to place justice before kinship?

In quietly bringing his younger sister's letter to the Northern Camp, Fang Qin had clarified his stance at the most critical moment. If His Majesty survived the assassination attempt without any major mishaps, he would have rendered a great service to the throne. So long as Lady Fang was willing to file for divorce, even if the entire Lü family was sentenced to death, she could still save her own skin.

Fang Qin looked helpless, but in reality, he was sacrificing a pawn to save a rook. He had set up the Lü family as a self-detonating cannon and aimed it directly at Prince Yan.

As Shen Yi stood there, shielding the emperor in the heart of the fray, he was suddenly at a loss for how to mop up this mess. Should he continue protecting the emperor and wait for the Northern Camp to arrive and eradicate the rebels, condemning Prince Yan and Gu Yun to certain death? Or should he privilege his personal loyalties, immediately defect, and send Li Feng to the King of Hell—thereby cementing Prince Yan's treason?

Old Maid Shen had never felt so trapped.

The instant the Dongying sword flew from his hands, Liu Chongshan pressed his advantage. Rushing forward, he swung his sword in three lightning strikes. Shen Yi staggered back to narrowly avoid disembowelment, the blade slicing a gaping hole through the front of his robes. As the rebel army's heavy armor closed in, a cannon went off, leaving the Altar of Prosperity suffocating under a cloud of billowing black smoke. Behind him, Jiang Chong cried, "General Shen!"

Shen Yi had barely managed to regain his footing. Whipping his head around, he saw a rebel heavy armor unit had slain three estate guards in rapid succession and now had its miniature cannon trained on Li Feng. It was about to blast the emperor sky-high—

The piercing shriek of a hawk sliced through the heavens, so shrill his ears ached. An iron arrow hurtled down, nearly brushing Li Feng's arm as it plunged into the gold tank affixed to the enemy heavy armor's breastplate. Jiang Chong threw himself at Li Feng, knocking him to the ground, as the heavy armor exploded like a firework bare meters away.

Shen Yi gasped in astonishment, his hands and feet numb as realization dawned.

After the Altar of Prosperity had completed construction, the capital's aerial exclusion field had been restored. Absent a decree from the emperor himself or an order relayed to the Lingshu Institute via the Black Tiger Iron Tally, how could this armored hawk fly into the city?

Could it be that...Gu Yun had returned?!

While Shen Yi's mind tangled itself into a knot, two more armored hawks swooped down from above. Making full use of their aerial advantage, they dispatched the assassins nearest the Longan

Emperor in short order. The leader alighted on the ground nearby and dropped to one knee to help Li Feng to his feet. With his iron visor lowered, it was impossible to discern his identity.

The shouting from without the city gates drew closer and closer: the long-awaited Northern Camp had finally arrived.

The Altar of Prosperity descended into chaos. As the Northern Camp soldiers fought the rebels, the armored hawks beside Li Feng quickly arrested the guards attempting to fish in muddy waters.

Shen Yi had an irrational faith in Gu Yun. Upon learning of the man's return—or at the very least, the Black Iron Tiger Tally's return, which meant the Marquis of Anding was aware of the situation—he calmed at once. Catching a windslasher tossed to him by one of the armored hawks, he promptly hacked off one of Liu Chongshan's arms before apprehending the traitor and dragging him before the emperor.

The Imperial Guard was no match for the troops of the Northern Camp. With the rebel army's leader captured, the dust soon settled.

Li Feng was no idiot. He knew someone stood in the shadows spurring Liu Chongshan to action. On his orders, the city gates were immediately sealed for a thorough investigation. The blood on his robes had yet to dry, and despite his narrow escape, his expression remained ugly. Li Feng raked his eyes over the bodies of rebels—still ironically dressed in the garb of the Imperial Guard—littering the ground. He thought of all the court officials who would be implicated in this incident, and of Liu Chongshan's recommendation that he *abdicate in favor of someone more worthy*, and felt as though a shaft of ice had pierced his chest.

At the moment, Li Feng hadn't the wherewithal to ponder such minor details as how armored hawks had entered the capital. His head was filled only with thoughts of betrayal.

High-ranking noble officials who had enjoyed generations of imperial favor had formed a faction and betrayed him. His most trusted Imperial Guard had betrayed him. Gu Yun, who had grown up with him and about whom he had only just been reminiscing, had betrayed him. Even his younger brother, who shared his blood—

Since taking his place in the imperial court, Prince Yan's bold deeds had shocked the whole of society. Following the establishment of the Grand Council, there had been an unending stream of memorials, regular as the rising sun, seeking to impeach him. Every one of them had been rejected by Li Feng. It was true that Li Feng had his concerns about his overly capable younger brother. He felt uneasy, hesitant—even envious—but he had never harmed a hair on Li Min's head. Could it be that, in acting with what he considered to be extreme benevolence and virtue, he had inadvertently raised a ravenous wolf that sought to bite the hand that fed it?

Noting Li Feng's odd expression, Jiang Chong said in a low voice, "Your Majesty, we are surrounded by untrustworthy eyes here. Please return to the palace first."

Li Feng looked at him blankly. He took two steps forward and suddenly bent at the waist. Clawing at the air with spasming fingers, he retched up a mouthful of blood.

Shouts of "Your Majesty!" rose from the crowd. Li Feng's ears were ringing. It was several moments before he realized he was clutching the armored hawk that had saved him moments ago, bloodstained fingers leaving smears of red on the soldier's iron-encased arm.

The new commander of the Northern Camp was standing some distance away. He failed to see that the emperor had just vomited blood and thus rather imprudently stepped forward, leading a captive, to make his report. "Your Majesty, this lowly general caught this man trying to sneak away through the south side of the city amid the chaos. He may have inside information about the insurrection."

The commander's prisoner was shaking with fright, glancing over and over at Lü Chang.

Another noble retainer standing amid the crowd below immediately called out, "Your Majesty, this lowly servant knows this man. He is Assistant Minister Lü's coachman. I've personally seen him waiting for Assistant Minister Lü after court sessions."

Lü Chang's face went ashen, and he fell to his knees with a dull thud.

Placing a hand on the armored hawk's shoulder to steady himself, Li Feng straightened as much as possible and said hoarsely, "Dear Minister Lü, why are you dispatching a messenger out of the city at a time like this? To whom are you sending word?"

The commander of the Northern Camp shoved the Lü family's servant to the ground and drew his sword, the blade ringing from its sheath.

The servant, a spineless individual, promptly pissed himself in fear. He pounded the ground with his head as he kowtowed frantically and said, "Your Majesty, please forgive me, please forgive me, this lowly servant had no choice... It...it was V-Vice Minister Lü! He secretly instructed this lowly servant that no matter the result of the attack at the Altar of Prosperity, I...I'm to take advantage of the chaos to bring news to Governor Yang on the city's outskirts..."

Shocked and bewildered, Li Feng asked, "Which Governor Yang?"

The servant swallowed a mouthful of spittle. "M-my master's brother-in-law... G-Governor Yang Ronggui..."

The hand clutching at the armored hawk curled into a fist as Li Feng raised his voice. "Yang Ronggui is the Governor of Liangjiang, a high officer of the frontier. He wouldn't dare enter the capital without an imperial summons. What nonsense!"

"Your Majesty, please have mercy!" the servant cried. "Governor Yang has secretly arrived at the capital's southern gate. He awaits my master's signal. I-if...Captain Liu had succeeded in his mission, he was going to..."

"He was going to what?" Li Feng demanded.

The man trembled. "He was going to lead the new emperor into the capital and install him on the throne!"

Darkness flickered across Li Feng's vision; if not for the timely support of the armored hawk, he would have collapsed on the spot.

Once again, Shen Yi found himself stupefied by the rapid change in circumstances. It had been possible still to exonerate Prince Yan by claiming Liu Chongshan's words from before were baseless posturing—but what now? Was there definitive proof? Had Gu Yun truly returned or not? Shen Yi's heart thundered as countless terrifying possibilities swirled through his mind. His cold sweat nearly caused his armor to rust.

Fang Qin bowed his head low, hiding the way the corners of his mouth hooked up in a smile.

Prince Yan was the emperor's younger brother. Unless he committed the high crime of treason, no one could touch him...yet now, hadn't he done just that?

"Bring Yang Ronggui and the *new emperor* that he would enthrone to us at once," Li Feng gritted out from between clenched teeth. "We want to see...we..."

94

INFIGHTING

S LI FENG BEGAN to stammer with rage, the armored hawk beside him finally lifted his visor, revealing a face that astonished everyone. "Your Majesty, the traitorous dogs have been apprehended. Please have a care for your health. Your Majesty spills blood, sweat, and tears working yourself to the bone for the sake of the nation. Why bring further harm to your body over these rebels?"

This voice couldn't be more familiar. Li Feng twisted his neck to look back in shock. The armored hawk holding him upright was none other than Gu Yun.

This man was supposed to be in the south—what was he doing *here*? His sudden appearance scared the wits out of half the crowd.

A loud droning sound reverberated through Lü Chang's head. Yang Ronggui had given him his guarantee—he would take every precaution; they would absolutely keep the Marquis of Anding in the dark!

Originally, his grand scheme was to be set in motion during Prince Yan's leave from the capital. That idiot yes-man Liu Chongshan was a pawn, so naïve that if one were to hand him a club and call it a needle, he would believe it true. Provided Lü Chang could provoke the man into killing Li Feng, there was no need for Yang Ronggui to risk his own neck. Lü Chang had instructed Liu Chongshan to push

Prince Yan into the spotlight. That way, whether Prince Yan willingly played along or was forced into the role by Yang Ronggui, the moment he showed his face, he would be found guilty of high treason.

Once the Northern Camp troops stationed in the outskirts realized what was happening, they would rush into the capital to suppress the rebellion and wipe out Prince Yan and Liu Chongshan's faction in one fell swoop. So long as Prince Yan and Liu Chongshan died in the chaos, well, dead men told no tales. The empire had no empress dowager, and the empress was an invalid who wilted at the slightest breeze. She barely had the strength to lift the phoenix seal.[4] As for the crown prince, he was a suckling infant who lacked the support to pose a threat. On the other hand, the eldest prince born to Consort Lü was already eleven years of age. It went without saying whose family would rule the nation.

Gu Yun was far away in Jiangbei. By the time he learned what had transpired, both the emperor and his "rebel" brother would be dead, and the dust would have long settled in the capital. Perhaps he would ignore the crisis on the borders and risk universal condemnation by rising in revolt to avenge two dead men—but even a vile character like Lü Chang doubted Gu Yun capable of such a deed. If Gu Yun intended to revolt, he would have done so during the Northern Camp Mutiny...if not earlier still, when he learned the truth behind the attack on the Black Iron Battalion. How else could that old fart Wang Guo drag out his ignominious existence to this day?

Their plan had two crucial pivots: First, it depended on Yang Ronggui's ability to cut lines of communication between the capital and his base of operations in Jiangbei, and to keep Gu Yun in the dark.

---

4   The phoenix seal confers upon its bearer the power to manage the imperial harem and symbolizes the empress's power as the legitimate wife of the emperor and the mother of the nation.

Second, it depended on Liu Chongshan's ability to successfully assassinate Li Feng.

Yang Ronggui had guaranteed the former on his family's lives. As for the latter, while it had been a foolproof plan at first, someone had clearly leaked word to outsiders. This had allowed so many skilled estate guards to hide within the crowd, the troops from the Northern Camp to arrive early, and Gu Yun himself to drop down from the sky.

However incompetent Lü Chang might have been, at this point, he finally realized one of his most trusted allies had betrayed him. It had to be either Yang Ronggui or Fang Qin. Yang Ronggui wouldn't benefit from this turn of events, which meant...

If it really was that Fang bastard, then he was beyond vicious. He had used the information Lü Chang provided against Lü Chang himself, leaking it to the Northern Camp and dragging Gu Yun back to the capital. The ensuing crisis would all be to his personal gain. Not only could he take credit for protecting the emperor, but with the Lü family gone, no other noble clan would be capable of challenging the Fang family's power and influence in the court.

As realization hit Lü Chang, he was struck by a sudden, paranoid thought: could it be that Fang Qin had been a member of Prince Yan's faction all along?

A few steps away, Minister Fang, who had just been arbitrarily labeled a member of Prince Yan's faction, also blanched at the sight of Gu Yun. He found himself suddenly unable to maintain his smile.

Fang Qin had thought, given Yang Ronggui's ability to conceal the truth of the epidemic, he would at the very least take proper advantage of Gu Yun's distraction on the front lines to accomplish his part of the plot. From start to finish, he had never accounted for the arrival of this god of slaughter. There was still Fang Qin's late-night visit to the Northern Camp and the merit he would accumulate for saving the emperor—in this regard, Gu Yun's appearance had little effect on Minister Fang's plans. But for some reason, Fang Qin had a dark premonition that things were about to spiral out of his control.

Every one of these people had their own secret motives. Among them all, Shen Yi alone heaved a genuine sigh of relief upon seeing his savior, Gu Yun. A cool gust of wind burrowed into Shen Yi's shredded court robes and swept over clammy, sweat-soaked skin. He shivered violently.

Unfortunately, he had breathed his sigh of relief too soon. The carnage had yet to conclude.

Gu Yun had handed Li Feng off to an imperial attendant who had rushed over during the lull. Now, he took a step back and dropped to his knees on the stone staircase.

Before Li Feng could question him, he seized the initiative and made a concise report: "Your Majesty. I left my personal guard with His Highness when I parted ways with Prince Yan and Commissioner Xu in Yangzhou. I then traveled with Lingshu Scholar Ge to inspect the Jiangbei Garrison. While there, I was surprised to receive a letter from a member of my personal guard. In addition to requesting aid, he reported that Yang Ronggui had secretly raised an army and seized Prince Yan.

"In a moment of desperation, I borrowed a detachment of armored hawks from old General Zhong and rushed to Yangzhou. There, I found that Yang Ronggui had set up a formidable defense around Yangzhou on pretense of putting down a rebel mob. My men and I investigated the surrounding area and eventually resorted to sneaking into the governor's estate under cover of night. Only then did I discover the heavy fortifications were but a smokescreen.

"Yang Ronggui had long since disappeared, and Prince Yan's whereabouts were unknown. My guard mentioned a treasonous plot in his letter; I feared the capital was under attack. Thus, I had no choice but to rush back with all haste. Please punish me, Your Majesty, for my inability to protect His Highness Prince Yan, and for my failure to complete my mission."

Gu Yun's speech shocked all who heard it into silence.

Fang Qin shot Wang Guo a surreptitious look. Catching his meaning, Wang Guo piped up: "Your Majesty, something puzzles this subject. If I may ask Marshal Gu... How can it be that Marshal Gu's armored hawks raced all the way from Jiangbei to the capital, yet still failed to intercept Yang Ronggui?"

Imperial Uncle Wang had outdone himself with this question. It seemed innocuous, but it aroused a host of suspicions in Li Feng. Was Yang Ronggui really so capable, or had Gu Yun allowed Yang Ronggui's people to slip by him on purpose? Had the Marquis of Anding truly flown like the wind to come to his aid, or had he always been in on the conspiracy and only switched loyalties upon seeing soldiers from the Northern Camp at the city gates? This was to say nothing of Prince Yan, whose whereabouts were supposedly unknown. If he really was among the insurrectionists outside the city walls, who was to say whether it was because he had been forcibly detained or for more nefarious reasons?

Everyone turned inscrutable eyes on Gu Yun, yet he seemed utterly oblivious as he responded evenly, "I am ashamed to say I had long lost track of Yang Ronggui by the time I was notified of the situation. I was also delayed significantly due to my search for Prince Yan within Yangzhou City and for the rebel army's tracks on my way back to the capital. As a consequence, I nearly bungled a matter of utmost importance."

These words clarified very little for most of the civil officials present. Zhang Fenghan, who was standing with the assistance of two attendants, inserted himself with a timely explanation: "Your Majesty and my esteemed colleagues may not know, but armored hawks fly at extremely high velocities while airborne. They are usually only employed to conduct searches along the front lines or within limited areas. Jiangbei is so far from the capital. Without knowing the path one's target has taken, and assuming the target itself isn't a massive army, with only three hawks, spotting Yang Ronggui on the road would be akin to fishing a needle from the sea."

But there was no turning back now; Fang Qin's faction couldn't let Gu Yun go so easily. Grasping at straws, Imperial Uncle Wang pressed, "Then, if Marshal Gu knew the situation was urgent, why not commandeer more troops from the Jiangbei Garrison?"

Gu Yun turned to glance at them. From Fang Qin's vantage, the curve of the Marquis of Anding's peach blossom eyes seemed particularly distinct, the outer corners of his eyes turned up like hooks. Combined with his cinnabar mole, it somehow gave the impression he was faintly smiling. Fang Qin's heart lurched—Wang Guo had put his foot right in his own mouth!

He had indeed outdone himself with his first question. This second question was right at Imperial Uncle Wang's usual skill level.

Gu Yun didn't usually pit himself against other officials of the court, but he was no fool. How could he allow his opponent the opportunity to recover?

"Imperial Uncle Wang, I'm afraid I don't quite take your meaning," Gu Yun began in a tone neither warm nor cold. "Is the Jiangbei Garrison my private army such that my word is enough to mobilize its troops? And what of our frontline soldiers who run short on supplies, and the foreigners who watch our shores with covetous eyes? If I may be so bold as to ask—aside from His Majesty, who in our nation has the ability to deploy troops stationed at the Jiangbei Garrison to the capital with a word? Please point them out to me so I may personally relieve the traitorous scoundrel of his head!"

The viciousness in these words pulled Li Feng back to his senses. He realized he had nearly been led astray by Wang Guo's half-baked logic. Gu Yun held the Black Iron Tiger Tally. If he wanted to launch a rebellion, he certainly didn't need to follow an idiot like Yang Ronggui and eat his scraps.

Gu Yun continued, "Your Majesty, for my slowness, I deserve a thousand deaths. By the time I finally managed to trace Yang Ronggui, I was approaching the capital. Prince Yan was likely in their custody; I dared not apprehend them for fear of alerting the enemy and bringing harm to His Highness. I planned to seek assistance from the Northern Camp. But to my surprise, I encountered their troops standing by just outside the nine gates. I realized at once that something might already be afoot inside the capital—thank heavens the Northern Camp received prior warning from Minister Fang. But we were pressed for time; I had no choice but to order the nine gates to temporarily disable the aerial exclusion field and allow the troops from the Northern Camp into the city. Luckily Your Majesty is blessed with great fortune and survived this harrowing incident without mishap. Of course, it was all thanks to Minister Fang's circumspection."

Fang Qin's face twitched; he could feel the eyes of the Lü faction practically burning holes through him. Feigning illness, acting under the veil of anonymity, even allowing Wang Guo to rush recklessly ahead...all of it had been in the interest of maintaining a low profile. The safest course was to let others take the lead. Ideally, Lü Chang wouldn't have even imagined he was involved in this matter. He'd never expected Gu Yun to so deviously skewer him and roast him over an open flame. Before, Lü Chang had only harbored wild suspicions. Now, his speculations had been substantiated. More than shock, what he felt most keenly was a desire to tear out Fang Qin's tendons and skin him alive.

This was the first Li Feng had heard that the Northern Camp's swift arrival wasn't because they had been especially quick to move out, but because they had long been lying in wait outside the nine gates. He became even more confused. "What's this about the Northern Camp?"

Fang Qin could do nothing but set aside the giant unforeseen disaster that was Gu Yun and, with the assistance of a deputy general of the Northern Camp, carefully relay the tale starting with the letter from his younger sister, Lady Fang. Fang Qin was confident his story would stand up to scrutiny; he'd been careful not to leave a shred of evidence that could be used against him. Under the blistering glare of Lü Chang, however, and with the paranoid mind of Li Feng considering his every word, the tiniest misstep would draw fire upon himself. He trod with utmost care.

The longer Li Feng listened, the worse his head ached and the more shocked he became. This was a far-reaching case, of a breadth and complexity unheard of in the Longan era. Civil and military officials alike fell to their knees, not daring even to breathe too loudly. The Northern Camp soldiers had blockaded the streets to prevent this business from spreading to the public. Before Fang Qin had finished declaring his whole-hearted loyalty, they had already taken Yang Ronggui's party into custody.

Yang Ronggui had been waiting for Lü Chang's report of success at the location they had agreed. But in the end, all he received for his efforts was a group of Northern Camp troops fencing him in. He realized immediately that the battle was lost. At first, he thought to at least use Prince Yan as a hostage. But the newly appointed commander of the Northern Camp was as impartial as he was incorruptible. After informing Yang Ronggui that Prince Yan had yet to wash himself clean of suspicion, he unceremoniously felled the rebel holding Prince Yan with a well-aimed arrow and proceeded to usher them all into the city.

Aside from Prince Yan, who was the emperor's kin and therefore received preferential treatment, everyone else was trussed up securely before being escorted up to the Altar of Prosperity.

Yang Ronggui had spent the entire march into the city figuring out how to save himself. Now, before his knees even hit the ground, he stunned his opponents by loudly proclaiming that he had been wronged.

Jiang Chong stepped forward. "You colluded with traitors and raised a rebel army," he said sharply. "Yet you're brazen enough to claim you've been wronged?"

Yang Ronggui knocked his head against the ground and wailed, "This guilty subject has been wronged, Your Majesty! This guilty subject has enjoyed imperial favor for so many years. How could I possibly turn my back on Your Majesty? From the very beginning, Prince Yan's faction has been slandering me and other officials in court. This guilty subject has no more than a hundred silver taels to his name. During our national emergency, I exchanged every cent of it for war beacon tickets. Accusations of corruption, of harming the country and people—these are complete nonsense! If Your Majesty does not believe my words, order your men to search my home; my devotion to Your Majesty will be proven for all to see. Please weigh this matter judiciously, Your Majesty!"

Li Feng's voice was so low it sounded like the words were being wrung from his throat. "Oh? Could it be that you traveled all this way north to the capital without our explicit approval in order to save us from these traitors?"

Yang Ronggui lied through his teeth. "Prince Yan, a member of the imperial court, hid the truth from the masses and deceived Your Majesty, formed a clique for his own personal gain, and committed all manner of evil. As for myself, I am innocent. My name was dragged into this conflict by a certain wicked individual. But even my younger brother-in-law, Vice Minister Lü, refused to believe I was uninvolved in these schemes. He wrote to me several times demanding an explanation, but that same wicked individual, an ally of the malicious prince, seized on his vulnerability and concern and goaded him into committing a huge blunder. I am stationed in far-off Jiangbei; by the time I learned what happened, it was too late. I was desperate. I had no choice but to take Prince Yan into custody and escort him back to the capital..."

Li Feng cut him off. "And who is this 'wicked individual'?"

Yang Ronggui raised his voice. "He is the Minister of Revenue, Fang Qin. It was he who proposed the scheme of 'donning the yellow robes' to my brother-in-law!"

"Your Majesty!" Fang Qin shouted furiously. "The traitors bear hatred in their hearts. They have no evidence to support their claims and are clearly making baseless accusations!"

Wang Guo promptly chimed in with support. "If Governor Yang has really come north to the capital to rescue Your Majesty, would he bring so few men with him? Just now, the Marquis of Anding reported that Yangzhou City is teeming with armed troops!"

Bitter tears streamed down Lü Chang's face as he wailed, "Your Majesty, I am innocent!"

Shen Yi's torrent of cold sweat had dried in the wind. Yet as he watched the greatest display of dog-eat-dog infighting the Longan era had ever seen unfold before him, a second wave of cold sweat drenched him. He was utterly flabbergasted. How on earth had his airheaded self managed to dodge these manifold political machinations and come out intact?

"Shut up, all of you!" Li Feng bellowed. "Bring Prince Yan!"

The long-forgotten Prince Yan and Xu Ling were pushed forward. Li Feng stared at the pair, eyes stormy, and said in a cold voice, "A-Min, we want to hear from you. What happened?"

Prince Yan hunched his shoulders and ducked his chin, his entire body quivering into a rounded lump. His handsome features and reserved aura had undergone a complete transformation; as he stood before them now, he seemed inexplicably wretched, like a terrified quail in human form. Before anyone else could react, Zhang Fenghan lost his cool. Striding forward, he shoved at Prince Yan's shoulder and said urgently, "Your Highness, please say something!"

It was then that the strangest thing happened. Prince Yan, a man who had once stood on the back of a Black Hawk and shot down the Dongying spy Liao Chi, toppled over from a push by the scruffy old geezer Master Fenghan. He staggered and crawled along the ground as one of his shoulders deformed.

The watchers were stupefied. Did Master Fenghan take a draft of violet gold, or had Prince Yan transformed into soft clay?

At last, the commander of the Northern Camp gathered up his courage and stepped forward. He reached a tentative hand toward Prince Yan's misshapen shoulder. "Your Majesty, this appears to be..."

"What is it?" Li Feng asked.

"This appears to be a shoulder pad!"

"Prince Yan" lifted his head. Tears and snot streamed down his face as his nose and chin moved in opposite directions, sliding to the left and right. The two halves of that handsome face seemed to clash with each other before splitting apart. This wasn't Prince Yan at all, but a monstrous demon of unknown origin!

Despite his shock, the commander of the Northern Camp promptly stripped the man of his outer robe. His shoulders, chest, and back were filled with remarkably realistic padding, and his shoes were also stuffed with five or six centimeters worth of insoles. The human skin mask as well as the fake nose bridge and chin came off with a sharp tug, revealing a short, shifty, repulsive-looking stranger.

Li Feng sucked in a sharp breath. Never in all his life had he seen such an astonishing transformation. "What the he—who are you?"

Shen Yi guessed that the emperor really wanted to ask, *What the hell is this?*

The man opened his mouth, but no sound came. It seemed his tongue had been cut out.

Upon closer inspection, the "Xu Ling" beside him also had a seam along his scalp where a human skin mask was attached.

Lü Chang and Yang Ronggui were speechless.

The pair cowering before them now were plainly two of the men Yang Ronggui had sent to guard Prince Yan and Xu Ling. Precisely when had they been relieved of their tongues and made up like this? And where was the real Prince Yan? Yang Ronggui thought—could it be that all this time, the real Prince Yan and Xu Ling had been hiding among his underlings?! He wrenched his head around to look. Sure enough, two men were missing from among the attendants who had been escorted into the city by the Northern Camp soldiers.

He had no idea when they had disappeared.

For a moment, even Fang Qin didn't know what to say. Minister Fang, whose heart brimmed with intrigue, couldn't help but wonder if Yang Ronggui had broken ties with Lü Chang much earlier than he'd thought.

Li Feng couldn't bear to watch anymore. He turned to leave, only to stagger on his very first step. At some point his legs had gone numb. If not for Gu Yun at his side, the Son of Heaven would have mopped the ground with his face.

"Your Majesty." Gu Yun spoke quietly into his ear. "Please allow this subject to carry you down."

Li Feng's heart tremored. He looked at Gu Yun, almost dazzled. It was as if, after all this time, the man beside him hadn't changed a bit. Naturally he no longer had the look of a half-grown teen, but that gaze was the same. Years later, the eyes of everyone else were adulterated by calculation and reserve. Only those familiar peach blossom eyes still seemed to hold the wild mischief of the boy who had once snuck him a smile amid a sea of armor.

He shook his head; he refused to show any sign of weakness before the staring eyes of thousands. Li Feng took Gu Yun's proffered arm and slowly descended, leaving that scene of carnage atop the Altar of Prosperity.

An imperial attendant raised his voice in a shrill cry: "Ready the imperial palanquin to return to the palace—"

The hazy glow of the setting sun lapped at the edges of the Imperial City, painting row upon row of glazed roof tiles bloodred before finally sinking beneath the horizon.

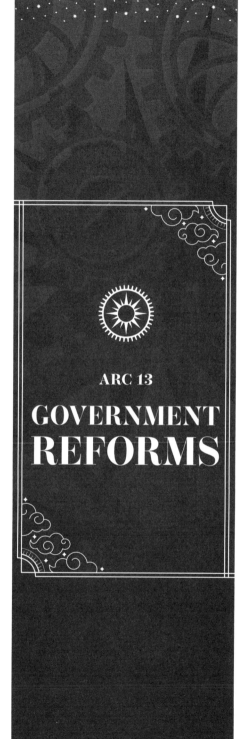

ARC 13

GOVERNMENT REFORMS

95
A SUDDEN CATASTROPHE

NO ONE SLEPT that night.

The Lü clan and their faction were swiftly snapped up and sent to jail to await trial. Fang Qin and his allies had performed a meritorious deed in saving the emperor. Though they had narrowly avoided any assignation of guilt, the results were far from what they had planned. They, too, were left in a sorry state. Meanwhile, Prince Yan, the eye of this hurricane, was still missing. No one knew whether he was dead or alive.

The grand assembly that had been set to meet the next day was canceled last minute as members of the Imperial Academy of Medicine scurried in and out of the palace like ants on a hot plate. Gu Yun and Shen Yi remained in the palace through the night. They didn't leave until early the next morning, shrouded in the cool morning dew of early autumn.

Gu Yun could still smell the medicinal brews that suffused the inner palace chambers. He had a sensitive nose and found joy in all sorts of scents: the sweet yet uncloying perfume of rouge and powder on a beauty's skin, the full and vivacious scent of greenery on a midsummer day, the fresh and peaceful fragrance of herbal incense on a certain handsome young man... The one scent he detested was the scent of medicine. Especially when it was stagnant, shut inside a room with doors and windows sealed, lingering obstinately in the air like a swamp that threatened to swallow one whole.

The two walked side by side. After such an ordeal, both were exhausted, and neither spoke. Shen Yi waited until they exited the palace gates to break the silence in tones of worry. "How are your eyes?"

Gu Yun shook his head.

Shen Yi didn't know if he was shaking his head to mean *nothing's wrong with them* or *not so good*. Figuring Gu Yun had no one at home to care for him, he instructed his driver to take them to his own estate. The curfew had yet to be lifted, and not a soul traveled the bluestone road with them. When Shen Yi lifted the curtain, the only sound was the clack of carriage wheels rolling over stone. Shen Yi heaved a weary sigh and adjusted the gas lamp swaying above their heads. The lamplight cast mottled shadows over Gu Yun's face—there were dark smudges below his eyes, and his cheeks were slightly hollowed. Gu Yun had crossed his arms and leaned against the side of the carriage to rest his eyes the moment he climbed inside. He didn't even ask Shen Yi where he was taking him.

When the carriage reached his home, Shen Yi finally nudged Gu Yun awake—he had fallen asleep during the brief ride. He opened his eyes groggily, only awakening fully after stepping out of the carriage into the cool dawn breeze. He squinted at the Shen Estate's gate. "There was so much going on last night; did I hear someone say Old Master Shen is ill?"

Shen Yi coughed awkwardly. He couldn't exactly spill the beans right there on the street, so he threw Gu Yun a meaningful look and twisted his face into a smile.

Gu Yun caught on at once. "I've come to visit someone on his sickbed, but I didn't even bring a gift..."

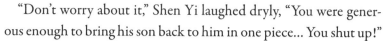

"Don't worry about it," Shen Yi laughed dryly, "You were generous enough to bring his son back to him in one piece... You shut up!"

This last was directed at the enigmatic door guardian hanging before the Shen Estate's gate. The myna was in a good mood today and hadn't planned on making any trouble. It was only stretching its neck to observe Gu Yun with curiosity but found itself scolded the moment it fluttered its wings. Overcome with avian rage, it began to welcome the guests with an ear-splitting screech: "Beast! Little beast! Bad luck written all over your face; die today, get buried tomorrow!"

This great ancestor was loyal only to Old Master Shen. Whenever it saw him, it was "Good fortune and wealth to the old master," yet it treated all other two-legged creatures like stupid bastards come to pick a fight.

Gu Yun was unfazed—this wasn't his first time getting cussed out. He curled his fingers, and with a well-practiced flick, a burst of wind smacked the bird across the beak. The myna tumbled off its perch, feathers scattering across the floor of its cage. Faced with a stronger foe, it immediately deflated. After a mute moment, it creaked out in a thin and woebegone voice, "Good fortune to my husband, may you rank in the imperial examinations!"

General Shen had half a mind to crawl into a very deep hole.

Gu Yun laughed as he stepped forward to enter the courtyard. As soon as his back was turned, the bird's attitude flipped as fast as the pages of a book. "Pah! Pah!" it spat.

By all the laws of common sense, a grown adult weighing several dozen kilograms had no reason to stoop to the level of a feather duster weighing several dozen grams. Unfortunately, the Marquis of Order bowed to no law. He swiftly stepped back, plucked the birdcage from the gate rafters, and prised the door guardian from its iron shelter. "Tell your old man I'm taking this brute with me; I'll gift him a new one another day."

Shen Yi had long detested the animal; he nearly shed tears of gratitude. "Of course, no problem, no thanks could be enough for this greatest of favors!" he assured him.

The terrified door guardian puffed itself into a ball. "A wife killing her own husband—*caw*!" Gu Yun had grabbed it by the neck.

The shriek awoke the old guard dozing by the gate. Rubbing his eyes to find Gu Yun standing before the house, he hurried over to welcome their guest in another flurry of activity.

Once they entered the inner courtyard, Shen Yi scanned the area and ensured they were alone. "Where is His Highness Prince Yan?" he finally asked in a low voice.

Slowly, Gu Yun shook his head.

"You don't know either?" Shen Yi was shocked.

"We lost contact in Yangzhou." Still grasping the bird in one hand, Gu Yun used the other to pinch the space between his brows so hard it left a mark. He briefly recounted their southward journey to Shen Yi. "He had Xiao-Cao impersonate him and meet with Yang Ronggui while he infiltrated the city in secret. One of the guards I left with him said he sought out a jianghu faction, looking for refugees to serve as witnesses. He sent a few lines assuring me he was doing well and not to worry, and said I should return to the capital. There's been nothing since. Yang Ronggui went and committed treason in his name, so what could I do but return to smooth things over for him? I left a few men behind and asked General Zhong to send some people to investigate quietly. But things are still..."

After all this ruckus, things were still up in the air.

Shen Yi didn't know what to say. He patted Gu Yun on the shoulder. "You know how capable Prince Yan is. Look, he didn't even bother to show his face during this mess; he must have been prepared for it. I'm sure all's well. He's been traveling the jianghu and running this way and that across the country with Zhong-lao and the others since he was young. What hasn't he seen by now? It'll be all right."

Gu Yun's furrowed brow showed no sign of smoothing.

Shen Yi tried a change of topic. "How is His Majesty?"

"He wasn't injured, at least," Gu Yun said with a sigh. "The imperial physicians say he made himself sick with fury and needs to convalesce—but let's be honest, I've heard the word *convalesce* so many times my ears have grown calluses. Don't these doctors have anything else to suggest? If we had the time to take it easy, who wouldn't?"

"Did he say anything when he called you in?" Shen Yi cautiously asked.

Gu Yun was silent a moment. "He did. He asked me, 'If rain pours in torrents and the river floods its banks, will a flood dragon grow horns?'"

Shen Yi's breath caught in his throat—a flood dragon growing horns foretold its transformation into an imperial dragon. The implication was crystal clear. "You..."

"I said, 'Flood or imperial dragons are always closely related in the folk legends. They can command the clouds, summon rain, and nourish the land; in this regard, they are alike. But though a flood dragon is a divine creature, if it caused the river to swell without regard for the banks just so it might grow horns and become an imperial dragon, would it not be merely another evildoer? Any dragon capable of it would surely be a wicked creature with a long record of crimes against the people.'"

"That's what you said to His Majesty?"

"Mm."

In truth, Li Feng had said more—the emperor was in his prime, but as he leaned against the head of the bed, he possessed the air of an aged man in his twilight years. He had abruptly asked Gu Yun, "What did the late emperor tell you before he passed?"

The late emperor had said quite a lot. To this day, Gu Yun could still remember every word. He thought it over for a moment before picking the safest excerpt. "His Late Majesty instructed this subject thusly: 'Doing too much is as bad as doing too little. Remember to appreciate your good fortune and know when it's appropriate to advance, and when to retreat.'"

Li Feng started in surprise, then turned to face the awakening light of dawn. He repeated the words *too much is as bad as too little* a few times, then said, seemingly out of nowhere, "A-Min told us he was abused by that barbarian woman as a child. Uncle, did you know?"

Gu Yun was a hundred and twenty percent on guard, yet he was still thrown by this remark. What was Li Feng driving at?

Outside the window, a little bird snapped a branch beneath its feet and fluttered off into the sky in fright. Pulled out of his trance, the dazed expression faded from Li Feng's exhausted face. He looked back at Gu Yun, gaze full of unspoken words, but in the end, said nothing more. Gu Yun was dismissed with a wave of his imperial hand.

Shen Yi sighed. "The heart of a ruler is inscrutable, and the hearts of people are inscrutable too."

At this, Gu Yun too came back to the present. "I'm tired."

"That's only to be expected." Shen Yi empathized very much. "Those with no regard for the law, the cornered dogs jumping desperately at the walls, those taking advantage of the chaos to fish in muddy waters...it's worse than fighting a war at the border passes. Honestly, I was most at ease when I was but an artificer in the

Lingshu Institute. Zixi, sometimes I feel like this capital city is a cavern full of man-eating demons, with danger lurking around every corner. Why don't we drop everything and run? We'll find ourselves a place to set up a little shop together, just enough to keep us fed. We won't have to bow to anyone's whims. What should we sell... hm, artificers' tools and engine oil. What do you say?"

"Are you daft?" Gu Yun rolled his eyes. "Dousing yourself in grease every day and serving a bunch of stinking customers as greasy as you are? I refuse. If I'm selling anything, it'll be rouge and powder. Now that wouldn't be so bad, watching a stream of beautiful women come in and out all day."

This immediately stirred Shen Yi's sanctimonious heart. "Does Prince Yan know about these grand ambitions of yours?" he asked with a fake smile.

Gu Yun chuckled along with him, but quickly found himself unable to laugh. He didn't expend much effort hiding his worries around Shen Yi.

Where was Chang Geng now?

Even if he returned unscathed, what should they say to Li Feng? After this incident, could these brothers continue as before, without any friction between them?

Looking on, Shen Yi saw how Gu Yun couldn't even feign nonchalance as soon as the topic turned to Prince Yan. He had never seen Gu Yun so serious about anyone. Shen Yi was shocked and a bit afraid to follow this line of conversation to its end.

Social customs had seen no little turmoil in recent years. In some places, people had become extremely open-minded, taking after the Far Westerners in throwing aside strict barriers between men and women. At the same time, many of the scholarly, aristocratic families clung more tightly to the old ways, howling about the collapse of social etiquette. The restrictions they placed on their own sons and daughters grew harsher still.

Somehow, Shen Yi felt both extremes were rather heartless. The former had couples growing fond of each other in three days and breaking apart in two more, brushing aside the directives of their parents and the arrangements of their matchmakers. And yet, who didn't have selfish concerns about the major affair that was their own marriage? Even if no one else tended to this matter, the bride and groom would run their own calculations. In the end, most ended up holding their noses and settling for someone well-matched to their own station.

The trouble with the latter went without saying. The compulsion to marry at an appropriate age was an obligation born of mindlessly following ancient rules of etiquette, forcibly binding two people who had nothing in common together for a lifetime. It was scarcely different from animal husbandry.

Finding true love and conjugal bliss was a stroke of luck as rare as a blind cat running across a dead mouse. There was only so much deep affection in the world. Madmen claimed some, and fools claimed some more. How could the handful of leftovers be enough for everyone to share?

A pair like Prince Yan and Gu Yun were truly a rare sight.

The two of them didn't flaunt their feelings around others, but Shen Yi understood Gu Yun. If Gu Yun could let go, he would never have overstepped the line of their godfather-godson relationship. The very thought alarmed Shen Yi. His mother hen instincts flared again. "Zixi," he began quietly, "I'm not trying to curse you. But have you considered what you'll do if something comes between the two of you in the future?"

Gu Yun was silent for a long while. This time, he didn't dodge the subject. Not until they had nearly reached the rear courtyard did Gu Yun finally speak, his voice so low as to be nearly inaudible. "I have. I don't know."

For once, Shen Yi didn't know what to say.

The grandest declaration of love in the world would have been less shocking to him than these five words.

They entered the rear courtyard to find Old Master Shen, supposedly still confined to his bed, up and lively as he ran through some boxing exercises. He showed no sign of being on the verge of death. The old man was overjoyed to see Gu Yun and promptly dragged him off to discuss his latest insights on healthy living. He even enthusiastically invited Marshal Gu to join him in a two-person tai chi pushing routine. Afraid his overzealous old father would be pushed straight into the grave by General Gu, Shen Yi hastily deflected this invitation and ushered Gu Yun inside to rest with cold sweat pouring down his forehead.

Gu Yun slept all the way through to the afternoon. He was still sleeping when Shen Yi barged inside and dragged him out of bed. "His Majesty has summoned you to the palace. It's urgent."

Thus Gu Yun rushed back to the palace. Upon arriving, he was shocked to find one of the guards he had assigned to Chang Geng's security detail. Travel-worn, injured, and bloodstained, the man had clearly withstood a long journey. Gu Yun's heart galloped in his chest. Stiffly, he wet his lips, mastered his emotions, and greeted Li Feng with a hasty bow.

"Please rise, Uncle." Face sallow with illness, Li Feng pushed himself up to a seated position and turned to the guard. "Repeat what you said about Prince Yan."

The guard bowed his head. "This subordinate acted on the marshal's orders to protect His Highness Prince Yan and Commissioner Xu as they went in secret to investigate the plague in Jiangbei," he said to Gu Yun. "The traitor Yang Ronggui intended us ill, and we were on our way to the Jiangbei Garrison with a message to that effect when we lost contact with Prince Yan. Later, when Yang Ronggui slipped away to head north, the marshal didn't know whether Prince Yan was detained or had escaped on his own, so he took a group of men back to the capital to head them off. We were instructed to remain in Yangzhou Prefecture and search for Prince Yan…"

This was the story Gu Yun had fed them ahead of time. In truth, Chang Geng had left the guards behind in Yangzhou Prefecture when he ventured into the territory of the Shahai Gang. Later, when Gu Yun sped north to the capital, he had left the guards in Yangzhou out of concern for Chang Geng, with orders to search for the lost prince.

Gu Yun frowned. He had a bad feeling about what they'd hear next.

"The man Yang Ronggui had was fake," Li Feng interjected. "Does this mean that you know A-Min's location?"

The guard retrieved a letter from his lapels. "Please read this, Your Majesty."

The envelope was marked in Chang Geng's handwriting. The strokes were sloppy compared to his usual neat script, and the paper was stained with blood.

Gu Yun's fingertips went numb. He suddenly understood what Chang Geng had felt when he had bandaged Gu Yun's injury at the capital gates and said, *I faint at the sight of your blood.*

Li Feng accepted the missive, his brow furrowing deeper the further he read. After a time, he sighed. He passed the letter to Gu Yun without a word.

Gu Yun must have used all the strength in his body to hide how anxious and terrified he was.

The letter was ordinary enough at the start, consisting of mostly nonsense—some fabulated tale about how Chang Geng had ingeniously escaped Yang Ronggui's clutches, leaving a double in his place. Later, he wrote, he had fallen into the hands of the Shahai Gang, where he discovered some of the Jiangbei refugees had been secretly detained and persecuted by Yang Ronggui while others had joined the local bandits. In order to gather witness testimony, Prince Yan had infiltrated the bandit gangs with Commissioner Xu... By now, Chang Geng must have that bookish fool Xu Ling wrapped around his little finger.

The second half of the letter was where things began to go awry.

Chang Geng recounted what he saw and heard in the Shahai Gang in a few brief strokes, including how Yang Ronggui had flouted the law to a truly astonishing degree. Yet just as he had convinced a group of the bandits to follow him back to the capital for an audience with the emperor, conflict erupted within the Shahai Gang.

Even if they had taken in helpless refugees, a bandit gang was a bandit gang. They had a natural hostility toward the government. Suspecting Prince Yan had in truth infiltrated the Shahai Gang to force their surrender, a few of the most ferocious bandits incited an argument that grew increasingly heated, until multiple factions within the gang were at each other's throats. Between the handful of instigators within the gang who loved to sow discord and the resentment many of the locals already had for the government, the situation quickly erupted into a full-on mob uprising.

In his letter, Chang Geng warned that although the mob looked threatening, they were limited in their engines and armor. They wouldn't hold out long against the proper army stationed at the

Jiangbei Garrison. However, to go that route would set the incident spiraling further out of control and intensify the antipathy of the people toward the emperor and his officials. Suppression by military force was the worst of all options; they should avoid bringing in the Jiangbei Garrison for as long as possible. Chang Geng closed by stating his intent to serve as a go-between in an attempt to win back the people and quell their anger.

Here, Gu Yun nearly flew into a murderous rage—*What the hell kind of rubbish is this? This is what he calls 'doing well'?!*

"Sir," the guard spoke up again, "His Highness gave us orders, so this subordinate dared not disobey. But the situation was growing increasingly tense. After Yang Ronggui left, the city defense troops under his command lacked a solid leader. The rebellious mob knocked them left and right. Many of the mob have friends who died at Yang Ronggui's hands; they hate the local government to the core. Their anger made them cruel, and they even tortured some of the captured soldiers to death. The situation was getting out of hand, so General Zhong sent me to bring an urgent report to the court and request imperial orders."

"Where is A-Min?" Li Feng asked.

The guard fell to his knees. "Your Majesty, His Highness Prince Yan...after His Highness delivered this letter through circuitous means, we never heard from him again. The one who snuck the letter out was a monk. His temple was burned down the very next day."

Gu Yun nearly choked on his next breath. Li Feng, too, was shocked stiff by this sequence of misfortunes.

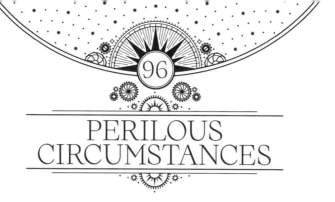

PERILOUS CIRCUMSTANCES

WHEN CHANG GENG opened his eyes, he found himself in complete darkness. The only nearby object reflecting a bit of light was Great Master Liao Ran's bald head. The instant he twitched, a bedraggled Xu Ling launched himself to his side. "Your Highness!" he bawled. "Your Highness, you're finally awake! Your Highness, do you recognize me? Your Highness..."

Within three sentences, Commissioner Xu had worked himself up to a sob. Like a filial son at an ailing parent's bedside, he mopped the tears from his face, only to find more taking their place. Unable to go on, he sat down a few paces away to wail and cry by his lonesome.

Chang Geng was at a loss for words.

This ear-piercing melody was cut from the same demonic cloth as his General Gu's flute. Chang Geng's ears buzzed from the racket. He felt more fortunate than ever that Great Master Liao Ran was mute. The monk not only didn't squawk, he was even so considerate as to console the tear-sodden Commissioner Xu.

Once Liao Ran had calmed Xu Ling, he stepped over to Chang Geng. "We are close to the Jiangbei Garrison; we should be safe here," he signed. "I've released a wooden bird, and Sun-dage's young helper was able to contact the Jiangbei Garrison with Your Highness's token.

Don't worry; as long as no other mishaps occur, General Zhong will be here soon."

This monk loved acting mysterious and hated to bathe, but he was after all an accomplished disciple of the Linyuan Pavilion. Of the more than three hundred sixty days in a year, there were always one or two when he could be relied on. Chang Geng nodded with some difficulty. After personally botching what should have been a straightforward mission, he couldn't help but laugh at himself.

He'd ditched his guards and entered the Shahai Gang with Xu Ling in tow. Unfortunately, luck wasn't on his side. He had shown up at the worst possible time—no sooner had they reached Boss Sun's branch within the Shahai Gang on their way to the main headquarters than they ran straight into the motley crew that was the rebel mob moving out in full force.

Chang Geng's heart had thudded in his chest, but he hadn't been overly nervous.

Given what he knew of Jiangbei, this rebellion was well within expectations. Cornered dogs would jump over walls and even trapped rabbits would bite. Everyone knew treason was a high crime that condemned the traitor's kin to the ninth degree. But if a person's kin were already dead, and they didn't know where they were going to get their next meal—if they were unable to scrape up even the most basic necessities for survival—what else could they do? Whether they died as a miserable wretch or a traitor, death was still death—so why not raise their banners in revolt? Even if they failed and found themselves beneath the executioner's knife, it wasn't as if they could be killed twice. At the very least they would die for a cause and leave their names behind in history.

The refugees who had fled captivity in Jiangbei had finally been pushed to the point of rebellion.

But Chang Geng was no deity. He could predict the refugees might revolt, but he couldn't pinpoint when and how they would do so. Thus, Chang Geng only thought he had come at a bad time. What kinds of turmoil hadn't Prince Yan experienced before? He never considered he might lose control of the situation.

Chang Geng had been confident that a rebel mob of commoners revolting out of desperation would be easy to resolve. First of all, both the government and the rebels understood that, in the era of violet gold, a handful of martial experts capable of killing a man every ten steps were not enough to carve out any real accomplishments in battle. Engines and armor were the key to victory. Even famed generals like Gu Yun would run out of tricks when their supplies ran out. No matter how large an operation jianghu bandits like the Shahai Gang ran, without engines, armor, and a violet gold supplier of their own, they were outmatched by the Jiangbei Garrison.

Revolt, then, was their way of demanding the government provide them a means of subsistence.

Chang Geng had been prepared to provide such means long before he arrived. The most ferocious, fearless person might still be swayed by a chance at survival. And once this chance was presented to them, who would choose to butt heads with the Jiangbei Garrison? No one wanted to be the egg casting itself against the stone.

On top of this, although Boss Sun, who had brought Chang Geng and the others into the Shahai Gang, was brusque and bad-tempered, he was a sensible man and not one to act on impulse. Seeing the way the wind was blowing, he made an immediate decision to conceal Chang Geng and Xu Ling's identities. Prince Yan dropping out of the sky into such a charged atmosphere wouldn't calm anyone; it would only incite the malcontents' rage. If some idiot lost his head and detained Prince Yan as a threat to the Jiangbei Garrison, they would lose any chance of bringing the situation to a neat conclusion.

Boss Sun's considerations were similar to Chang Geng's. Neither wanted to offer the lives of these unfortunate people as fodder for the Jiangbei Garrison's cannons, which ought to be pointed at the Far Westerners, just to make the government heed a desperate, exhausted cry for help.

Thus, with Boss Sun's aid and abetment, Chang Geng and Xu Ling maintained their guise as do-gooder merchants from the south. Liao Ran, who had been mingling with the refugees in Jiangbei as he performed his monkly duty of delivering all living creatures from suffering, also happened to be among the Shahai Gang at the same time. Leaning on his connections, Chang Geng and Xu Ling had successfully made contact with the leadership of the rebel mob.

Everyone knew Prince Yan possessed a silver tongue that could speak the language of saints and savages alike. Aside from its peculiar impotence against Gu Yun, it was an extraordinary weapon; there was no one he couldn't hoodwink if he put his mind to it. Within the span of a month, Chang Geng had more or less mastered the situation. Those who had been in an indignant fury when he arrived were able to sit down and weigh the pros and cons of potential actions after his intervention. The Shahai Gang had four bandit kings, including Boss Sun. Minus one thorny man who had an irreconcilable hatred for the government, Chang Geng had managed to persuade the other three to attempt negotiation with the government before reckless action.

It was then, however, that the Jiangbei Garrison, which had been searching for Prince Yan in secret all this time, began to move in the open. The atmosphere again grew tense. Chang Geng guessed the false Prince Yan must have reached the capital, and the entire plot had come to light. His disappearance in Yangzhou was now common knowledge. This matter involved a prince of the first rank; the Jiangbei Garrison had no choice but to make their position clear and switch from covert to overt investigation.

Chang Geng found himself placating the Shahai Gang's rebel army on one side, while on the other personally drafting a memorial imploring the Jiangbei Garrison not to make any rash move lest his plan fall apart on the cusp of completion.

But storms gather out of even the clearest skies. When someone ran into a spate of bad luck, they were liable to get something stuck in their teeth even while drinking cold water. Nothing had gone as smoothly as planned for Prince Yan ever since he infiltrated the bandits' nest.

When the Shahai Gang had begun to plot rebellion in earnest, they took after the crafty hare with three burrows and moved their main headquarters to a different location every half a month. At this point, the headquarters were located in the midst of a clump of hills in Jiangbei, backed against a mountain quarry. Such quarries weren't particularly rare in the Jiangbei region, and had Chang Geng had an astute artificer with him, they would have reminded him to take care—it was very likely that this type of terrain would pose a problem for wooden birds.

It was not unheard of for mountain quarries to cause compasses and similar devices to malfunction. Despite the Linyuan wooden bird's elegant exterior, its core was no more than a special magnet embedded in the creature's belly. The birds could avoid interference if they were already high in the air, but before these ones could be launched, a lap around the mountain quarries had caused the magnets in every wooden bird to fail. Since the birds couldn't get out,

Chang Geng was forced to resort to a cruder method—dispatching Liao Ran to deliver the letter in person. The lone letter he had sent this way was precisely the one Gu Yun's guard delivered to the capital.

But things went awry yet again.

None of the four rebel leaders had spent many days in school. Their aesthetic tastes were on the same basic level as old farmers who gathered in local city god temples to hear folk tales. They had named themselves after heaven, earth, humans, and ghosts, taking the titles "Heaven King," "Earth King," and so on, all exceedingly mortifying for their underlings to use. Boss Sun was the "Human King," and the "Heaven King" was the thorny one willing to commit every kind of cruelty to satisfy his ocean-deep grudge against the government.

This so-called Heaven King's words had originally held great sway. He'd had the whole gang ready to revolt with him when he was quite suddenly demoted from the big boss to an obstinate minority. After thinking carefully, he concluded that the Human King was the one to blame. Boss Sun had never been willing to fight the Jiangbei Garrison. Thus, the thorny fellow began nursing a grudge against the "spineless coward" Boss Sun and even bribed one of his enemy's confidantes in an attempt to dig up some dirt against him and send him to an early grave.

The bribed subordinate watched Boss Sun and his people like a hawk for the better part of a week but failed to get anything on Boss Sun. However, by complete and utter coincidence, he did see Liao Ran sneaking off in the middle of the night to liaise with government officials.

Would you look at that—these good brothers of ours were dogs of the court all along, thought the Heaven King in outrage. Whatever scant bit of trust he had in them collapsed entirely.

The moment Chang Geng discovered they had been exposed, he made a snap decision. He gathered all the people with any influence in the bandit gang and confessed his true identity before the Heaven King could interrogate them himself. Even if the timing was less than ideal, it was still a better option than allowing an outsider to incite the crowd by unmasking him. Of course Chang Geng could have killed the Heaven King, but the people of the jianghu had their own ideas of justice. This rough and tumble bunch wouldn't carefully weigh the situation like court officials, and any slip-up would blow up in his face.

At the Heaven King's provocation, the bandit nest erupted with furious accusations. Prince Yan pulled out a woodcarving knife and thunked it blade-first into the table. "Let's follow the usual rule, then. Three strikes, six holes—how many times should I stab myself to show my sincerity?"[5]

The vast majority were quelled by this. But one ferocious bandit decided to call his bluff. Emboldened by Chang Geng's offer, he grabbed the knife and stabbed Chang Geng without another word. Chang Geng knew there would be no getting out of this if he didn't take the blow—he didn't move. All the rebels—especially the rebel leaders—were struck dumb by the sight of this first blood. They knew they couldn't under any circumstances allow His Highness Prince Yan to die in the hands of the Shahai Gang. In that case, they would have no choice but to rebel, and no choice but to die. There would be no more room for negotiation. The three remaining kings rushed to smooth things over, which only enraged the Heaven King further. He declared he would take his people and quit the Shahai Gang on the spot.

---

5   A gang punishment for crimes that fall just short of calling for the perpetrator to commit suicide in atonement. The usual form would require them to stab themselves through the thigh three times, forming six wounds, hence the name.

With internal strife tearing the gang apart, the rebellion looked liable to end before it properly began. Boss Sun sent his men to escort Chang Geng and his party away that night, fending off several attacks from the Heaven King's underlings along the way. Most of the men Boss Sun sent with him perished on the journey.

Liao Ran, whose skills in combat stopped at getting himself stuck inside a suit of heavy armor, was little more than a burden. Xu Ling, meanwhile, was a burden through and through. For a martial expert, even throwing themselves into mortal danger alone was easier than fleeing for their life while hampered by two dead weights. Chang Geng was already injured; he hadn't been in such a sorry state in years. In protecting Commissioner Xu, he acquired yet another dangerous wound across his chest, so deep the flesh curled along the edges. It was only thanks to his training as half a disciple of Miss Chen that he managed to staunch the bleeding.

Liao Ran scooped some stream water into a leaf and offered it to Chang Geng, then produced some ointment and re-dressed Chang Geng's wounds. Chang Geng drank the water and sighed. He forced himself to alertness, and after gathering the energy to speak, patted the spot beside him. "Mingyu, come here, sit," he said to Xu Ling in a jovial tone. "When the old man lost his horse, how was he to know whether it was disaster or fortune? This may well be a blessing in disguise. Please, contain your grief until I've breathed my last."

Xu Ling gracelessly used his sleeve to wipe his tears, apologies tumbling from his lips. "This lower official has dragged Your Highness down," he choked out through his sobs.

Chang Geng chuckled. "When the Far Westerners besieged our city, Mingyu-xiong buckled down and secretly learned a foreign language. What are you planning to do this time? Study martial arts until you can smash boulders against your chest?"

Xu Ling blinked soggily at him.

"Look, Great Master Liao Ran isn't crying. He's perfectly calm."

"This humble monk has never done a day's labor in his life," the monk shamelessly signed, "and has relied entirely on Your Highness's protection. I promise to light an everlasting altar lamp for Your Highness when we return and top up the oil every day as I pray."

"You have my sincere thanks, Great Master. But if someone of your enlightened status prayed for me, I'm afraid I'd pay for the privilege with years off my life." Chang Geng struggled to find a more comfortable position, a bead of cold sweat slipping down his temple. He sucked in a few ragged breaths, then turned to Xu Ling. "About that...rumor...going around—even the bandits in the Shahai Gang were discussing it. Yang Ronggui committed treason in my name. Our consciences are clear, and there's nothing they could've found to use against us...but it's best not to tie one's shoes in a melon field..." he trailed off with a hiss of pain. "Great Master, you can't speak, but are your eyes also impaired?"

At this, the unobservant Liao Ran hurried up with Xu Ling to support Chang Geng from both sides and help him turn over, carefully avoiding his wounds.

"It's best not to tie one's shoes in a melon field...lest one be taken for a thief." Chang Geng finally finished through the pain. "Now that it's come to this, we can't give up halfway... Rather than hurrying back to explain ourselves to His Majesty, we may as well stay and fix things here for good. Afterward, these minor injuries will give me an excuse to step out of the spotlight for a while."

Watching blood seep through the freshly changed bandages on these so-called minor injuries, Xu Ling's admiration for Chang Geng reached unsurpassed heights. Perhaps even Master Fenghan back in the capital couldn't hold a candle to him now. He was about to sincerely profess his true feelings when a shift came over Liao Ran's face and he held up a hand for quiet. He pressed his ear to the ground, and after a moment, signed to Chang Geng, "A few dozen riders are approaching on swift horses. Whose people?"

They had no way to tell whether the newcomers were General Zhong's men or the Heaven King's mad dogs.

Bracing himself on Xu Ling's shoulder, Chang Geng struggled to his feet. Xu Ling was about to voice a shocked protest when Chang Geng cut him off. "Shh—"

The easy mask he wore dropped away. His eyes gleamed, his narrowed gaze like that of an injured king of beasts, fangs poised to deliver a fatal bite even as its blood pooled across the ground. Veins stood out on the back of Chang Geng's pale hand as he clutched a long saber stolen from some unknown bandit's hand. There was no hint of weakness from his injury; like this, his aura was all the more terrifying.

Xu Ling couldn't help but hold his breath.

Chang Geng suddenly cocked his head. A faint smile appeared on his dry, cracked lips. He tossed his saber aside and straightened the lapels of his disheveled clothes. "Go out. See which general is coming to meet us and welcome them in," he said to Xu Ling. "Extend them my invitation."

"Your Highness, how do you know..." Xu Ling was shocked.

"Are the hoofbeats and footsteps of the Shahai Gang this orderly? It must be someone from the Jiangbei Garrison." Chang Geng nonchalantly pulled his ratty outer robe to cover the grisly wound across his chest. "Forgive me for my breach of etiquette. I have been feeling unwell," he said, as elegant as ever.

Liao Ran was speechless. It seemed Prince Yan was truly Marshal Gu's protégé in acting skills as well.

Xu Ling could've prostrated himself in worship of Chang Geng. At this point, if Prince Yan so much as farted, he would trust it unconditionally. He immediately left to carry out his instructions.

Chang Geng felt for his leather sachet. In addition to pacifying fragrance, he also stored some emergency medicines inside. He extracted a hemp leaf with trembling fingers and tucked it into the palm of his hand. If he really couldn't withstand the pain, he would chew it as a last resort. Chang Geng declined Liao Ran's proffered arm and levered himself to his feet using the saber as support.

He heard Xu Ling outside. "Your Highness, it's..."

Before he could finish, the newcomer had burst inside accompanied by a horse's sharp whinny.

Chang Geng stared.

Striding toward him, silhouetted by the sun at his back, was someone who should have long returned to the capital—Gu Yun!

Chang Geng's feet slipped. The saber clanged to the ground as he fell forward into Gu Yun's arms. Prince Yan, who had moments ago been the perfect image of the saying "striding leisurely through foul winds and bloody rain," suddenly embodied "felled by injury like the collapse of a mountain." The calm and confident king of beasts became a delicate and sickly kitten. With one arm draped limply over Gu Yun's shoulder, he murmured in a voice thin as gossamer, "Zixi, it hurts..."

THE DUST SETTLES

IT WAS AS IF CHANG GENG had expelled all the injuries and pain in his body with this brief utterance. He felt like he'd been hollowed out, and nearly fainted on the spot. The instant he saw Gu Yun, his rock-solid spine turned to mush and drained away; he couldn't summon a spark of energy. Even so, he couldn't bear to close his eyes. He slumped against Gu Yun's shoulder and took a moment to gather himself, fingers unconsciously grasping at Gu Yun's clothes.

Chang Geng had lost too much blood. His entire body felt cold, and the hint of warmth and familiar medicinal scent coming off Gu Yun sent him into a dazed recollection of their very first meeting. He nearly forgot where he was. "...Is there any wine left?" he muttered.

Xu Ling finally caught up and sprang into eager action. "Marshal, I can..."

Liao Ran, who had unfortunately heard everything, grabbed the bookish idiot before he could get any further. The great master was a man who stood across the threshold from the mortal dust of the world—he had been shocked stiff by the implications of that name he heard Prince Yan murmur in his half-conscious daze.

Gu Yun said nothing. Holding Chang Geng securely in his arms, he lifted him into the carriage, a frown creasing his brow. "Send for a medic."

He pulled out his water flask. When armies were moving at a forced march or heading out on far-off expeditions, the soldiers didn't carry pure water in their flasks. Instead, they would mix in a bit of salt—this was something they learned from itinerant merchants in the desert.

Gu Yun let Chang Geng rest against him as he fibbed without blinking. "Here's your wine, open your mouth."

Chang Geng was only dazed, not completely insensible. If it hadn't been Gu Yun who showed up, perhaps he could have slaughtered his way through another band of bloodthirsty rebels. He cooperated and took a few sips before quietly chuckling. "Liar."

Lying was the least of it; Gu Yun was tempted to string him up and give him a sound beating. Maybe then Chang Geng would finally understand the adage, "wealthy sons sit not beneath treacherous eaves." But when he finally laid eyes on the man himself, Gu Yun's heart ached so much his chest went numb. How could he possibly lash out at him? No matter what avalanches Prince Yan had caused when he was out and about, Gu Yun had never before seen him injured so grievously. He sat there, stiff and expressionless, for a good while before carefully pulling aside Chang Geng's lapels for a look. He was immediately hit with the thick stench of blood. Gu Yun's chest heaved, and for the first time in his life, his hands began to shake.

Chang Geng seemed to sense his volatile mood. He had just gotten a taste of the benefits of pouting and acting spoiled; he wasn't about to stop now. Leaning into Gu Yun's ear to add fuel to the fire, he said, "I was scared I'd never see you again..."

Face drawn, Gu Yun closed his eyes. His hands were surpassingly gentle as he concentrated all the burning heat of his rage on the tip of his tongue. "Forgive my poor eyesight," he said icily, "but I fail to see how the indomitable Prince Yan is frightened."

Hidden within the carriage's curtains, Chang Geng nuzzled his cheek into the crook of Gu Yun's neck, his voice muffled. "If I really died, the last word you said to me would have been 'Out.' I wouldn't be able to rest in peace."

Gu Yun held his tongue.

The man in his arms was like a detestable climbing vine, stretching out a fatal little tendril to poke at his heart again and again. Hoofbeats approached outside, and a man called out in a messenger's booming voice, "Sir, the medic is on his way!"

Chang Geng looked as if he was in agony but was unwilling to show it. He sat unmoving and sucked in a slow and shallow breath, baring his alarmingly pale neck. Torn between anger and genuine concern, Gu Yun leaned down with a gloomy look and gave Chang Geng a kiss fueled by burning fury in the shadow of the curtain. His lips landed as gently as a dragonfly skimming the surface of a pond, but the expression on his face was like that of a man hunting his worst enemy.

Chang Geng's eyes flew open. His gaze, unfocused from the effort of remaining alert earlier, sharpened as he stared wide-eyed at Gu Yun.

Gu Yun breathed into his ear, "You'll be explaining yourself later." He ripped the curtain open and yelled at the medic jogging toward them. "Hurry it up!"

The medic had thought to dismiss any onlookers as he worked, but the instant he locked eyes with Gu Yun, he shivered in fright. Even if he borrowed two extra sets of guts, he wouldn't have dared to chase Marshal Gu off. He had no choice but to steel himself, sweating beneath Gu Yun's gaze and trembling with fright, and attend to the horrible pair of gash wounds marring Prince Yan's body.

Chang Geng would never voice his pain to outsiders. He merely twitched when the clumsy army medic tugged on his wound while wrapping it in gauze. Gu Yun's expression grew darker and darker. Suddenly, one of Chang Geng's ice-cold hands slid into Gu Yun's palm beneath his loosened robes. He seemed to sense Gu Yun's bad mood; Chang Geng didn't tighten his grip, but rested it there, maintaining contact as he snuck furtive glances in Gu Yun's direction until the medic finished and left.

Gu Yun looked at Chang Geng. A bead of cold sweat slid down Chang Geng's forehead, dangling from the tip of his eyelashes. In the next blink, it rolled off, leaving Chang Geng's gaze misty behind a haze of sweat.

In his youth, Chang Geng had been adept at acting spoiled. Now he clearly wasn't just adept, he had practically perfected the art. Gu Yun was helpless against him. If Chang Geng kept looking at him like that for another incense stick's time, he might actually climb up and fetch him the stars in the sky. Resigned, he wrapped his fingers around Chang Geng's and tugged him further into his embrace. "Close your eyes," he said softly.

Chang Geng obeyed without a word. With this venture, he'd quelled the chaos in Jiangbei like a sharp blade cutting through tangled hemp. A huge burden had lifted from his shoulders, and in that moment, he had not a single worry. With the sound of Gu Yun's heart thumping steadily against his ear, he wouldn't have a single regret even if he died that very second. He fell asleep, fully content.

The Shahai Gang, currently at war with itself, was no longer a threat. General Zhong had honored the promise he made Prince Yan and hadn't moved a single soldier. He wrote an earnest offer of peace to be delivered to the Shahai Gang. Chang Geng had dispatched a good portion of the Heaven King's men, and the allied forces of the other three bandit chiefs mopped up the rest. What had promised to be a bloody rebellion melted, just like that, into thin air.

Three days later, Yao Zhen arrived in Yangzhou. He had hastened from the Jiangbei Garrison to serve as acting governor of Liangjiang, with full authority to manage matters in Jiangbei. His first act was to detain all remaining members of Yang Ronggui's party while he took his subordinates to track down the locations of the imprisoned refugees. He freed each and every one of them, and after providing appropriate consolation, restarted the process of refugee documentation. He also specially assigned a group of officials to record and conduct searches for friends and family who had been separated. For those whose loved ones were found to have passed, he went in person to offer reparations.

Several days later, a large shipment of medicine arrived from the imperial court. Li Feng issued an edict calling for a portion of Yang Ronggui's confiscated funds to be returned to the capital and assigned the rest to provide reparations for the refugees. The Ministry of Revenue would complete the paperwork retroactively in the coming days. Xu Ling recovered his position as imperial envoy and took charge of investigating the Yang-Lü faction. In a brilliant display of his signature upright and incorruptible character, he cleanly stripped every inch of his targets' homes in search of evidence.

But it was just as Yang Ronggui said: his home hid very little gold, silver, or coin. All of it had been exchanged for war beacon tickets. At a loss, Xu Ling turned to Prince Yan for advice as the prince lay confined to his bed.

"I have a decent idea of how many war beacon tickets were distributed, and who bought them up," Chang Geng said. "That Yang bastard isn't the one propping up the national treasury. Investigate his associates among the civilian merchants—they're likely colluding with the officials. If you don't understand the account books or can't tell which records are real, don't worry. I've got someone who can help, and he should be here in the next few days. He's the son of the God of Wealth; he grew up holding an abacus. We are on good terms—he can be trusted."

Xu Ling nodded again and again.

"There's one more thing." Chang Geng leaned back against the headboard and looked up. The contours of those eyes, sharp and defined as if they had been carved with a knife, added a keen edge to his countenance that couldn't be erased even in the grip of his injury. "The court has declared that war beacon tickets are equivalent to silver and gold, and may circulate among the people. The exchange rates are set. There's no reason they can't be used as disaster relief funds. So what's the problem here?"

"Your Highness," Xu Ling said quietly, "the second batch of war beacon tickets have recently been distributed, but few have purchased them. Aside from the officials of the imperial court, the civilians who buy them are mostly members of large families with a bit of wealth to their name. None of these are short on silver to spend, so most leave the war beacon tickets sitting in their homes like some sort of prize. The tickets rarely circulate on the market, so truthfully, I don't know whether merchants will accept them. This..."

Chang Geng braced a hand against the edge of the bed to push himself upright. "I can't force people to spend them instead of stockpiling them in their homes, but refusing war beacon tickets as a legal tender is a serious crime. Starting tomorrow, inventory all the war beacon tickets in Yang Ronggui's estate and add them to your accounts. Use them to buy relief grain from the big grain merchants. I'd like to see if anyone dares treat the decrees of the court as scrap paper—requisition some men from the Jiangbei Garrison to accompany you, do you understand?"

Xu Ling understood. Prince Yan was instructing him to act like a common hoodlum. Using Jiangbei as an example, they would force the nation to accept that these "war beacon tickets" spent the same as silver and gold. They would hit the big merchants first—as the saying went, "those who wear shoes have more to fear than the bare-footed." None of these shoe-wearers wished to offend the court, so they would pinch their noses and capitulate. At that point, they'd either have to mutely eat their losses or find some way to turn these war beacon tickets into solid gold and silver—by putting their full weight behind their implementation.

"Let's light another fire under them." Chang Geng was still weak, and his voice was low. "Have Chongze-xiong issue this decree as the Governor of Liangjiang: if any merchant, large or small, refuses to accept war beacon tickets, anyone can report them to the Yangzhou prefectural government. If the report is verified, they shall be served a beating. Any who persist after repeat infractions will be jailed."

Xu Ling had been treated to a thorough demonstration of His Highness Prince Yan's methodology: conciliatory when the situation necessitated conciliation, and severe when the situation necessitated severity. He hurriedly assented and ran off to get to work. But before he reached the door, Chang Geng called after him. "Mingyu."

When Xu Ling turned, the stern look had dropped from Chang Geng's face. Within the blink of an eye, he was once more the graceful and elegant Prince Yan. "I'll be counting on you from now on."

"What do you mean by this, Your Highness?" Xu Ling was mystified.

"I'm afraid I'll be delayed here for some time," Chang Geng said. "I won't be able to return to the capital and debrief this mission with you. But I do have a memorial I'd like you to deliver to His Majesty on my behalf."

For a while now, Chang Geng had been pressing forward without pause. It was time to step back. He had to control his tempo, and his injuries were a perfect excuse to relinquish some of his power. Unfortunately, the straightforward Commissioner Xu clearly missed his point. He clasped his hands together in a very proper bow and said, "Of course. Your Highness's injuries are severe; you should take care of yourself and recuperate. I'll handle all the legwork. If there is anything I don't understand, I will be sure to ask for clarification."

Chang Geng chuckled. Xu Ling was hopeless; he left it at that and waved him off.

On his way out, Xu Ling ran into the Marquis of Anding on his way in. He snapped to attention to greet him. Gu Yun nodded politely. As the man brushed past him, Xu Ling started in surprise—Gu Yun was holding a fresh sprig of osmanthus blossoms tucked behind his back. The flowers bloomed a golden yellow, their sweet scent thick in the air.

Xu Ling watched blankly as the marshal carried that spray of flowers into Prince Yan's room, rubbing his perfume-filled nose in shock. *Marshal Gu really is so attentive to His Highness.*

Gu Yun stepped inside and hung the flowering branch in Chang Geng's bed curtain. "The osmanthus are blooming. I didn't want you to feel too cooped up lying inside—is the scent okay?"

Chang Geng's gaze attached itself to Gu Yun and refused to tear itself away.

Gu Yun met his eyes. "What are you looking at?"

Chang Geng reached out to tug at his clothes.

Worried he'd strain his wounds, Gu Yun hurriedly cooperated and leaned down. "Don't flail around!"

Chang Geng's pull was insistent, gripping Gu Yun's robes and drawing him close. "Zixi, it hurts."

After a lengthy pause, Gu Yun said expressionlessly, "Get out of here; I'm not falling for that anymore."

Since his injury, it seemed Prince Yan had no intention of preserving any dignity around Gu Yun. Whenever they were alone, he'd pipe up with an *It hurts, kiss me* any chance he got.

But bad habits, if indulged, would only get worse. This piece of wisdom always held true.

Gu Yun flicked his forehead with a finger, then turned to go change.

Chang Geng stared until he disappeared behind the folding screen. He plucked a tiny osmanthus blossom and carefully chewed it between his teeth. Then, grabbing a wooden cane from the bedside, he rose to stand. Chang Geng slowly edged his way to the table, not quite able to straighten his waist. He dipped his brush in a small pool of leftover ink and spread a sheet of paper to begin his memorial.

This was a physically demanding task for an invalid, and his forehead soon beaded with sweat. Suddenly someone snatched his brush from behind. Chang Geng had barely started to turn when an insistent pair of hands dragged him out of the chair and hauled him straight back to bed.

"Is the sky falling? Do you have to write it yourself?" Gu Yun snapped. "Lie down and behave yourself!"

"The Lü family and their entire faction are implicated in this case," Chang Geng calmly explained. "The Fang family hasn't gotten off scot-free either. It's the perfect time to push new policies. Even if I'm not acting in the open, I have to be prepared."

Gu Yun sat beside the bed. "Are you still considering special permits for violet gold usage? His Majesty will never agree."

"It's not that," Chang Geng said. "The time's not right. But the confiscated lands along the canal can still be used to resettle the refugees.

The most fertile land can be reserved for agriculture, and the rest used to build factories—Master Du and his chamber of commerce can split the construction costs half-and-half with the court. And the factories won't be the property of civilian merchants; they'll be officially run by the government. We can establish a dedicated department under the Grand Council, separate from the Six Ministries, to manage the allotment of violet gold and keep its distribution under strict control. Meanwhile, the chamber of commerce will be in charge of day-to-day operations. Sixty percent of the profits will go directly to the national coffers, forty percent to the merchants running the factory operations. This way, we can resettle the refugees without worrying His Majesty with leakage of violet gold. We can revitalize the national treasury at the same time, and provide incentives for altruistic merchants... What do you think?"

Gu Yun didn't say anything for a long time after listening to this speech.

It was obvious that Chang Geng had gone through countless drafts of this plan. He must have thought of it even before he came to Jiangbei. But if he had brought it up then, he would have essentially pulled a giant pile of lucrative jobs out of thin air. All the noble families would have been champing at the bit for a piece of the pie. Yang Ronggui and his ilk were not above snatching disaster relief funds to pad their own coffers; this level of profiteering was far from beneath them. In the end, this plan, intended to address a laundry list of problems, would have solved none of them: the national treasury wouldn't see a cent, the merchants would be hampered by the complex bureaucracy between major and minor court officials, and the refugees driven like livestock. Only the maggots would see their pockets stuffed.

It was for this reason that Chang Geng had deliberately intensified the conflict between the established nobles and the young upstarts in court, then used a convenient excuse to travel to Jiangbei and muddy the waters further. He drove a wedge between the deeply interconnected noble families and let them dig their own graves, then sat back and watched them brazenly flout the law. He advanced and arrayed his pieces, then retreated behind the curtain after a smooth endgame, removing himself from the spotlight. A few unexpected complications had arisen in the middle, but when all was said and done, he had achieved every one of his objectives.

Chang Geng blinked. "What is it?"

Gu Yun pulled his wandering thoughts back and smiled. "If I didn't know better, I'd think you really were some evil demon sent from the heavens."

His words seemed like a non sequitur, but Chang Geng somehow grasped his meaning. He scooted over to Gu Yun and clung to his shoulder. "Would you believe it if I said that the fate of Great Liang rises and falls with me?"

When Gu Yun turned to answer, Chang Geng picked the exact right moment to topple forward. Gu Yun's lips brushed against his cheek.

"You kissed me."

Gu Yun had no words. Weren't they talking politics?

Chang Geng looped his arms around Gu Yun's neck, insistent as he forced that mouthful of osmanthus fragrance between Gu Yun's lips. Gu Yun had no objections to fragrant beauties throwing themselves into his arms. Unfortunately, at times like these, His Highness Prince Yan absolutely refused to behave and play the part of the "fragrant beauty."

Romantics spoke of how a beauty's lips and tongue were sweet as honey, the taste of a beloved the finest delicacy in the world. Those who sampled this fragrance ought to start shallow before plunging deep, savoring every note. Chang Geng, however, never cooperated. Even if he began obediently, his ferocious nature would surface within moments; kissing him was less like an intimate moment of passion and more like he was trying to devour Gu Yun alive. Gu Yun felt this "delicacy" was a bit abrasive on the mouth; when the two finally parted, the tip of his tongue had gone numb. But still Chang Geng wasn't satisfied. Mesmerized, he ran his teeth lightly over Gu Yun's jaw and neck, as if looking for a place to bite—for all the world like he wanted to swallow him, blood and bone.

Gu Yun instinctively froze at the sensation of his vulnerable neck being assessed as a chew toy, but he wasn't willing to push Chang Geng away. Tense and ticklish at once, he didn't know whether to laugh or cry. "Were you bitten by a dog when you were younger?"

Chang Geng's gaze was searing. "The prohibition Miss Chen set for me is almost over, right?"

98

REVOLUTION

G U YUN'S HAND felt its way up Chang Geng's waist, enough to be teasing but not overly aggressive. The warmth of his palm seeped through the layer of cloth between them, a faint sensation against Chang Geng's side, as if he were lying next to a gentle flame.

Chang Geng had missed him too much. He had longed for this intimacy ever since their brief stay in the Jiangbei Garrison, but one thing after another had kept them apart.

Whatever grand ambitions he held in his heart, Chang Geng's body was still that of a man in his early twenties. It had been different before he had gotten his first taste—but to be cut off by Miss Chen when he had just had his fill was unbearable. If not for his too-busy workload that prevented him from relaxing fully, he would have long gone mad with want. He had no resistance to this teasing. One light touch from Gu Yun left half his body tingling. Chang Geng gulped down a few rapid breaths, his ears ringing. "Yifu, are you trying to kill me?"

"Your injuries don't hurt anymore?"

They did hurt, but not in the same way. Most of the time, His Highness Prince Yan's injuries hurt a normal amount. When he was pouting to ask for kisses, they "hurt a great deal." Right now, even if his wounds tore open and his blood flowed like a river, he would be as insensible to the pain as a man of steel.

"They don't? Perfect." Gu Yun caught Chang Geng's hand as it snaked into his clothes, fished it out, and tossed it to the side. "In that case, now's the perfect time for you to explain yourself," he said with a smile.

Chang Geng blinked.

Gu Yun pillowed one hand behind his head and reclined on the bed, his other hand still wandering over Chang Geng's waist. His tone was mild, but the words were enough to make one break out in cold sweat. "Tell me," Gu Yun said, "precisely what were you thinking when you decided to bravely charge into a bandit's nest with a helpless scholar like Commissioner Xu for company?"

"Zixi…"

"No need to *Zixi* me," Gu Yun said blandly. "You can keep saying *Yifu*."

Chang Geng laughed uneasily and offered an apologetic kiss. He had recently discovered that Gu Yun liked these sorts of clingy kisses. If he pecked him a few times, then stared at him with that beseeching gaze, Gu Yun would agree to practically any request…but today, this trick seemed to have lost its efficacy.

Gu Yun arched one brow. "You needn't be so polite; *my* injuries don't hurt."

Prince Yan, who usually had a whole deck of cards up his sleeve, was finally out of tricks. He had no choice but to properly answer the question. "I never thought they would actually rebel."

Gu Yun flashed Chang Geng an indulgent smile and caressed his cheek with the back of a hand before continuing his merciless interrogation. "Bullshit. You definitely considered the possibility."

Chang Geng's throat bobbed. "I... Commissioner Xu and I were on our way to their headquarters. I didn't think they would choose that time..."

"Oh." Gu Yun nodded. "Then you thought, 'Look, a one-in-a-million opportunity to seek my own death,' and off you went."

There was a note of danger in Gu Yun's voice. Chang Geng sensed the conversation was veering in the wrong direction; he immediately wised up and admitted the error of his ways: "I was wrong."

Gu Yun let his hand fall. His face was unreadable, peach blossom eyes half-lidded. Chang Geng couldn't tell what he was thinking, and he unconsciously tensed. But after the longest time, Gu Yun didn't unleash any of his anger. He only asked out of the blue, "Was it because I asked you when we could resettle the refugees and recover Jiangnan? Did I pressure you?"

When he spoke, a faint crease appeared between his brows, and an almost desolate look came into his eyes. Chang Geng had seen him with such an expression only once before—on that New Year's Eve so many years ago, aboard the red-headed kite. At the time, this same quiet, lonely chill had passed over Gu Yun's face as he honored thousands of deceased souls with three cups of wine. Then, it had seemed as if, even with every lantern in the capital lit as bright as day, nothing could illuminate his stark profile.

On the verge of panic, Chang Geng began to stumble over his words. "I wasn't... I... Zixi..."

When Gu Yun was younger, he had disliked opening up to others about his feelings. He felt that scrawling all of one's happiness, anger, sorrow, and joy across one's face was like peeling off one's clothes and showing people the bare skin beneath. It was indecent first of all, and who would want to see it? This preference had nothing to do with his inborn personality but was purely something endowed by his up-bringing. Normally, everyone sat together gnawing on hunks of meat and guzzling their wine in great gulps, with little difference between them. It was only when people were roaring drunk that such natural differences became apparent—some would cry and wail, while others would at most tap their chopsticks and break into song.

Though the timing wasn't quite right, the words were rolling back and forth on the tip of Gu Yun's tongue, bobbing up and down. When he spoke, it was tentative, as though testing the waters. "On the way here from the capital, I was..."

Chang Geng was an expert at reading others; he instantly sensed what Gu Yun was about to say. His pupils contracted, and he stared at Gu Yun in both panic and expectation.

Gu Yun had likely never spoken words so difficult in his entire life. He nearly lost his courage.

Holding his breath, Chang Geng prompted, "On the way here... you what?"

"...I was scared to death."

Chang Geng stared blankly.

When the Jiangnan Navy had been wiped out, when the Black Iron Battalion lost over half its number, when Li Feng summoned Gu Yun from the imperial dungeons, had Gu Yun ever said he was "scared to death"?

Gu Yun seemed eternally composed. He never panicked—and if he did, he was probably faking it. His strength was unnatural, which in turn made others uneasy—as if one day, he would up and collapse like the capital's nine gates.

These first few words seemed to open a long-sealed floodgate. The rest came in a rush. "If something had really happened to you this time...what would I do?"

Listening, Chang Geng hardly dared to breathe.

Gu Yun's voice was low. "Chang Geng, I really don't have the strength to...let another person into my heart."

Chang Geng was shocked.

This man had the strength to bring order to the northwest, the strength to spend sleepless nights locked in debate with old General Zhong over the organization of the Jiangbei Navy; if he perished before the nation recovered stability, he could never rest in peace. The one thing he didn't have the strength to do was love another person.

These past years, aside from Shen Yi, a friend with whom he'd braved mortal peril on countless occasions, Gu Yun had only a large and empty Marquis Estate. The scant bits of sincere personal affection he had managed to wring out were all spent on the youth the late emperor had entrusted to him years ago.

In the course of the endless exchange of favors that characterized the political sphere, officials often heaped praise on each other. And when they praised Marshal Gu, it was almost always in words that celebrated his selflessness in working to exhaustion for the good of the nation. But in actual fact, Gu Yun wasn't purely selfless, with no other desire than to work for the greater good. It was just that when it came down to it, he didn't have many selfish attachments to prioritize.

Gu Yun hadn't felt this loneliness quite so deeply when he was young. He was the Marquis of Order with the three divisions of the Black Iron Battalion under his command. Back then, even if he was bursting with grievance and indignation, downing a jug of wine would allow him to forget his troubles and crawl out of bed the next morning in high spirits as always. But as the years weighed on him, so too did his concerns grow heavier. Before he had realized it, the carefree disposition of his youth had been worn down to a nub. In recent days, he found himself tiring easily. And when he was fatigued in body, he often felt dejected in spirit as well.

If not for the oft-meticulous, oft-unbalanced Prince Yan acting as the target of his worries, there would really be no meaning to his life.

The fatigue and despondence on Gu Yun's face passed quickly, tucked away in the blink of an eye. He carefully settled Chang Geng on the bed, pulled over a thin blanket to drape across Chang Geng's body, and sighed. "Lie down. You can't even stand up straight and you're still thinking about that stuff? Can't you be serious for a single moment?"

Chang Geng grabbed hold of Gu Yun's hand. Gu Yun's hands were never warm. They always felt as if he'd just been holding a windslasher: dry, stiff, and cold. "Zixi, lie with me for a while?" he pleaded.

Gu Yun wordlessly removed his outer robe and lay down beside him. He wrapped his arms around Chang Geng over the blanket. Before long, he'd fallen asleep. Only then did Chang Geng quietly open his eyes. Every hair on his body was standing on end with the desire to drag this person over and ravish him, but Chang Geng couldn't bear to shatter the warm and peaceful atmosphere. He stayed stock-still as the flames of desire baked him alive, joyful in his suffering.

It had been almost eleven years since the day Gu Yun found him near Yanhui Town. Gu Yun had spent most of those at the border and on the battlefield. They were apart more often than they were together...but Gu Yun had never left his heart for a single day.

Sometimes, Chang Geng didn't know how he ought to go about loving him. He felt as if he could never repay what Gu Yun had given him even if he spent every day of the rest of his life trying. All of a sudden, he realized perhaps it wasn't that Gu Yun was the one good thing in his life worth looking forward to. Instead, it was as if everything he had suffered since birth was all to gather enough good fortune to meet this person.

At this thought, years of resentments miraculously melted away.

With Prince Yan injured and out of commission in Jiangbei, it was up to Xu Ling to resolve all matters, large and small, related to this case. Commissioner Xu was a beast of a man who bent to neither flattery nor intimidation, and he had also managed to dig up Du Lang, the God of Wealth's own son, from who knows where. Young Master Du was a man of few words, but he was difficult to fool and nearly impossible to bribe—his family was so wealthy even the emperor owed them a few debts. No one dared offer what trifling 'benefits' they could scrounge up to this man.

At the end of the ninth month, with the aid of Prince Yan's counsel and the concerted efforts of the Jiangbei Garrison, Xu Ling put a definitive end to the mob rebellion and resettled the local refugees. Yao Zhen stepped in as acting governor of Liangjiang, and Xu Ling returned to the capital to report on the completion of his mission, bringing Prince Yan's memorial with him.

Thus the curtain fell on a major case that had shaken the nation.

As for Prince Yan himself, he dawdled, taking his time convalescing while advancing toward the capital at a leisurely crawl. Though he had yet to show his face, his groundbreaking canal corridor plans had already put down roots. His memorial was held in the palace for only two days before passing in a single grand assembly with major support from the Grand Council and unusual silence from the Imperial Censorate and Department of Supervision. The noble families were occupied putting their own houses in order and had neither time nor energy to spare for outside affairs. Fang Qin, too, was lying low. The Longan Emperor approved the memorial the very same day.

The Grand Council, which had long expected this decision, moved with unbelievable efficiency. They produced a comprehensive plan within two days; one couldn't help but suspect they'd been prepared.

Within a month, the Grand Council had formed an independent Canal Commission distinct from the Six Ministries. The Canal Commission held plenary authority to represent the court in dealings with Du Wanquan and members of his chamber of commerce. In one stroke, the God of Wealth transformed from an independent man of business into a proper imperial merchant. The resources he had quietly readied flowed into the factory sites in an endless stream.

For a full month, the entire court worked tirelessly until a whole horde of civil officials who had only ever idled at their desks collapsed from exhaustion. The entirety of Great Liang was ablaze, as if striving to make up for two reigns overrun with sinecures all at once. In the end, they managed to gather all the refugees of the Liangjiang region beneath rudimentary factory shacks before midwinter.

It was then that Prince Yan finally arrived in the capital.

99

TURMOIL

LTHOUGH GU YUN had made a quick roundtrip between the capital and Jiangbei already, many things remained for him to do on the front lines. It was the perfect excuse for Chang Geng to take some time to recover, so the two only started heading back after Chang Geng had regained his usual mobility, making their way slowly toward the capital.

On the journey, they came across a busy scene along the canal banks.

A factory in the middle of construction was never a pretty sight. Dust swirled through the air, and every craftsman, laborer, civil official, and imperial merchant deployed to oversee the process was coated in a layer of grime. Yet it seemed, overall, to be an orderly process. The workers were provided two meals a day, and at noon, a bunch of young and sturdy refugees, who had so recently laid down the weapons they had raised in rebellion, fished coarse, multigrain buns from an iron cart.

Gu Yun had disguised himself in commoners' clothing to survey the site. The buns, made with good flour, were a solid weight in the hand and substantial when broken open. They were nothing compared to the banquets of delicacies served on jade plates in the Kite's Flight Pavilion of days past; such buns didn't even count as plain tea and simple fare. But it was still a comfort to see a group of men fresh off their shifts gathered with rations in hand, dipping them into a jar of sauce a foreman had brought from home, to share in a meal.

They approached the capital with Gu Yun on horseback following Chang Geng's carriage. When their conversation reached the topic of the factories, Chang Geng said with a smile, "Many of the craftsmen were invited from other regions to serve as foremen and lead the construction work. But Master Du recruited most of the remaining laborers from the refugees. Once construction's completed, they'll be able to stay at whichever factory they hauled bricks to build and will always have work. I hear Master Du requested an imperial edict from the Canal Commission to guarantee it. Unless the workers themselves want to leave, the factories won't drive anyone away. They'll have a place there for a lifetime."

No one wished to put down roots more than those wandering and destitute. Since the refugees were tasked with building their new homes themselves, they did the work eagerly and well, and few slacked on the job. Du Wanquan merely needed to provide meals. In exchange, he would save a great deal on labor and attract a flock of old ladies calling him "Philanthropist Du" and offering prayers to him along with the Buddha while he was at it. It was a brilliant maneuver by the God of Wealth.

"Good." Gu Yun thought for a moment. "It's a bit like the arrangement for military families, except without reduced rent for their dependents—but civilians don't match soldiers in discipline. What if someone shirks their work or breaks the law?"

"The Grand Council enacted a law," Chang Geng said. "I gave Jiang Hanshi instructions before I left, and it's been decreed alongside the imperial edict. There are thirteen articles in total, and each contains detailed rules and regulations. Specially designated criers

explain the law every evening after their shift ends. If there is sufficient evidence that a laborer has committed a crime, the local branch
of the Canal Commission has the authority to expel the offender...
Or are you worried about what would happen if officials and merchants colluded to take advantage of the laborers?"

Surprised, Gu Yun broke into laughter. "What, you have a plan
for that too?"

"We do," Chang Geng said. "If more than half of the veterans who
have worked in a factory for over ten years are willing to speak up on
behalf of the offender, that person can stay. In addition, the accused
can report the incident to a higher administrative level within the
Canal Commission—but even with all these contingencies, problems will crop up over time. We'll just have to slowly amend the
system as necessary; there's no sense expecting to get everything
right on the first try."

Gu Yun couldn't resist the urge to ask, "How long have you been
planning this?"

"I didn't come up with it alone," Chang Geng said with a smile.
"I had a vague idea when I first began speaking with Master Du, and
we've been laying the groundwork, having endless discussions and
making endless adjustments the whole time. We spent over a year
polishing it to this point. Master Du and his people have spent their
lives traveling the world and have even visited the Far West multiple
times. They have vast amounts of experience and are quick to adapt,
but they lacked an inroad. As long as I build that road, they can hold
up the rafters."

Scholars had their pedantic ways and lofty ideals, while merchants had their cunning and business finesse. Neither were inher-
ently good nor evil; it all depended how those in high positions
directed their efforts.

"Oh right, Zixi. Master Du said the Far Westerners have this giant carriage of tremendous length." Chang Geng stuck his head out the window as excitement crept into his voice. "It rides on iron rails and runs fast as the wind, but it's completely different from the great condor and giant kites. It can pull many more carriages behind it—wouldn't that allow you to transport as much cargo as you wanted? It's much better than using the canal, but it does require lots of land, and it'd be difficult to plan for long routes. While we're expropriating land to construct factories, it's a perfect opportunity to set aside the land needed for it. To tell you the truth, I've really got to hand it to the Yang-Lü faction for their eagerness in buying up properties. They've saved me a lot of trouble. Master Du plans to start in the canal region and build one as proof of concept. With the front line in Jiangnan at a stalemate, it's difficult to transport all the provisions, violet gold, and engines back and forth from the capital. If we could get it constructed one day..."

Gu Yun didn't have many opinions on the national economy or the livelihoods of the people, but he was extremely sensitive to matters of national defense and military affairs. He took Chang Geng's meaning as soon as he spoke. "Give me the details."

Chang Geng paused and beckoned Gu Yun close, as if he planned to whisper into his ear. Gu Yun urged his horse forward, drawing level with the window, and leaned over. "What, are there things you can't reveal yet?"

"It's not that I can't say it, but..." Chang Geng hesitated.

Gu Yun was bemused. He had just begun to wonder what reason there was for such secrecy when Chang Geng leaned out of the carriage and stole a kiss.

Gu Yun was at a loss for words.

Chang Geng peered around and confirmed they were blocked by the carriage; no one was looking their way. He quietly continued, "Let me do it again tonight and I'll show you the schematics."

Tugging on his horse's reins, Gu Yun leaned away. "How many times have I let you do it already? All you know is how to act spoiled because of your injuries or play shameless tricks—no way."

Chang Geng was a perfect specimen but for one thing: he was a control freak, especially when it came to Gu Yun. If he could, he'd be happy to dress and feed him as well. He usually kept himself in check to avoid making Gu Yun uncomfortable...but he had few such reservations in bed.

"Yifu," Chang Geng whispered, "if I'm not servicing you well, I can put more effort into my studies."

"...Son, you needn't go to such lengths."

They had by now passed the Northern Camp, so Gu Yun wasn't wearing his armor. Instead, he had donned a long robe in civilian style, with sleeves wider than the waist. Chang Geng snatched the corner of his sleeve with ease and mutely swung it back and forth.

In one of the small towns they passed through on their way, they had seen a three- or four-year-old child crying and tugging on his parent's sleeve, throwing a tantrum over a piece of candy. Ever since, who knew what screw had come loose in Chang Geng's head, but he copied the move in its entirety, and even seemed to be developing it into something all his own.

There was not a single sleeve on which he could tug as a child. Now, even though he had grown enough to hold up the skies unassisted, he seemed to still have some regrets and had decided to make up for them all via Gu Yun.

Gu Yun smiled as goosebumps prickled over his skin. "No means no; now hands off. Your Highness, have you no shame?"

Chang Geng held on tight. The way things were going, it appeared he didn't plan to stop till he had rendered Gu Yun a literal cut-sleeve in broad daylight.

Shen Yi and Jiang Chong had led a welcoming party to greet them outside the city gates. They saw from afar Prince Yan sticking his head out of his carriage to converse with Gu Yun as Gu Yun allowed his godly battle steed to proceed at a lazy stroll. A faint smile twinkled at the corners of his eyes, but his lips were pressed into a line as he intentionally ignored Chang Geng.

The first time Prince Yan spoke, Gu Yun rapped him across the back of the hand, forcing him to release his sleeve. Prince Yan refused to give up and spoke up again. This time, Gu Yun pulled down the curtain of his carriage, as if to put him out of sight and out of mind. When Prince Yan pulled the curtain aside to poke his head out and speak a third time, Gu Yun finally broke and began to laugh. He flapped a hand at him, seeming to concede.

Watching this exhibition, Jiang Chong was stunned.

Shen Yi sighed. "Thank goodness the marshal has no children of his own. He'd have spoiled them into absolute terrors to rival even himself. Just look how incapable he is of saying *no* three times in a row to His Highness. Even if he denies Prince Yan's first two requests, he's guaranteed to agree to the third."

Jiang Chong hadn't fully recovered from his shock. "I'd always thought, with how little time the marquis spends in the capital, he and Prince Yan were only godfather and godson in name. They seem to share quite a close relationship."

Shen Yi's musings went off the rails as soon as he heard the word *relationship*. He'd been just bemoaning how Gu Yun could never be a stern father, but now his train of thought took a sharp turn.

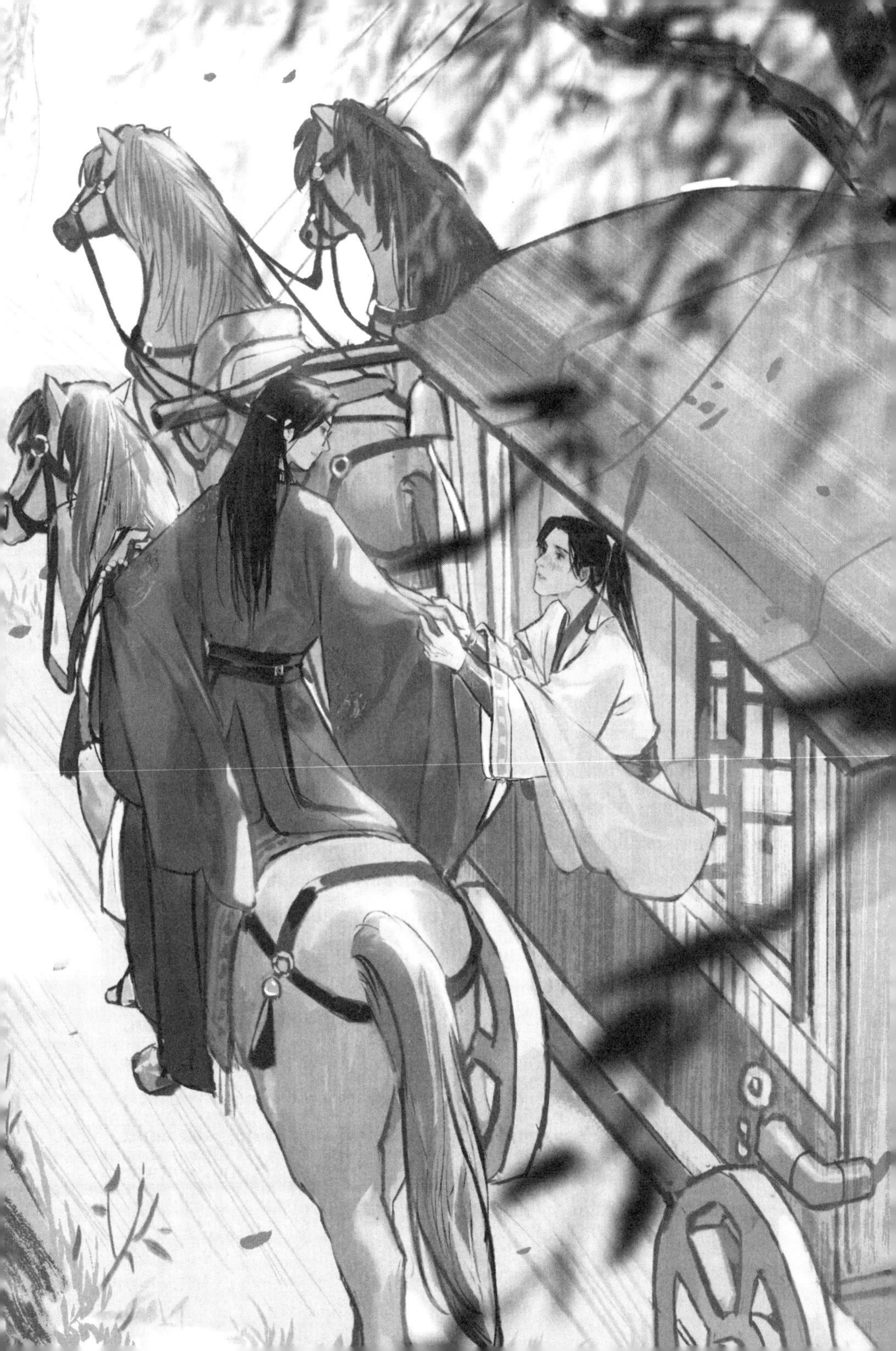

Gu Zixi has become addled with lust; he's never had a single moment of propriety his entire life. What the hell is he doing acting so shamelessly in the middle of the day?

The lust-addled lecher felt his nose begin to itch. When he turned to sneeze, he caught sight of Justice Jiang and Commander Shen observing them with looks, respectively, of *How reassuring to see harmony between generals and ministers* and *You awful influence, aren't you ashamed of yourself* written across their two faces.

As for Prince Yan, who had recovered his dignified bearing, he was whisked away to the palace before he even had the chance to step down from his carriage.

While Shen Yi was busy shooting Gu Yun a series of condemnatory glares, Gu Yun, who had just agreed to some truly shameful requests, was steeping in regrets. "What are you looking at?" he snapped at Shen Yi.

Commander Shen, the old pedant, laid into Gu Yun with all the power of his righteous indignation. "You're really too far out of line sometimes—I'm only pointing out what anyone would say."

"What did I do?"

"You're acting like a lecher bewitched by a fox spirit."

Gu Yun was speechless. This wrongful accusation was as absurd as warm thunderstorms in winter and driving snow in summer, yet he couldn't defend himself even with a hundred mouths at his disposal. He was sorely tempted to cut ties with this Shen bastard for good. Fortunately, before he could do away with Commander Shen, the man distracted him with business: "I figured you'd be here within a few days, so I didn't send anyone to bring you word. There're two urgent matters I need to discuss with you. First, the northern barbarians' Jialai Yinghuo sent an envoy."

A grim look came over Gu Yun's face.

After the Black Iron Battalion caught their breath and pacified the strife to their west, they had set their sights on the north. In the interim, they had greatly relieved the pressure on Great Liang's forces maintaining defenses along that border. The Black Iron Battalion was Jialai Yinghuo's lifelong nightmare. With the black crows watching the passes, the Wolf King of the eighteen tribes wouldn't make any rash moves. But the northern border had always been a barren region, and the people there relied on the mercy of the heavens merely to raise some cows and sheep. To fight this war, even Great Liang had emptied its coffers, to say nothing of Jialai Yinghuo, who had always neglected logistics like supplies and production in favor of his all-consuming desire for revenge. It was only natural that, as time went on, they would reach the end of their rope.

"Peace talks?" Gu Yun asked.

Shen Yi nodded. "It hasn't been brought before a grand assembly yet. His Majesty summoned us to discuss their conditions. You know what I'm thinking, don't you?"

Gu Yun's brow jumped.

"It's just like that time the old Wolf King increased the violet gold tribute and offered himself as a hostage," said Shen Yi. "The wording and tone are all too familiar, humble and earnest, and they're offering generous conditions too. Zixi, do you believe they're sincere?"

Gu Yun pondered a moment. His words, when he spoke, came slow: "Not really. The barbarians aren't like the Far Westerners. The Far Westerners are greedy, but the barbarians bear a generations-long grudge—especially Jialai Yinghuo."

"What are you thinking?" Shen Yi pressed.

"Ever since Jialai Yinghuo took command of the eighteen tribes, he's done nothing but pursue revenge against the Central Plains,"

Gu Yun said. "If they're coming for peace talks now, there are two possibilities: Either someone within the eighteen tribes has overthrown Jialai, or he's up to no good."

Shen Yi was hesitant. "We can't exclude the possibility that the eighteen tribes really are at the end of their tether..."

"No, it's not yet winter. I don't believe they've fully exhausted their resources already." Gu Yun sighed. "Listen, Jialai is a mad dog. Mad dogs don't care whether they eat meat or grass; all they want to do is bite. Right, what did His Majesty say?"

"His Majesty..." Shen Yi paused, then lowered his voice. "This was the second thing I wanted to tell you. His Majesty is doing poorly."

Gu Yun started in surprise.

"He's switched to holding grand assemblies every fifteen days, on the first and fifteenth of every month. Anything else that requires discussion is to be brought before a smaller assembly held by the Grand Council before it's passed up to the Western Warm Pavilion for His Majesty's approval. It seems to me His Majesty has less and less tolerance for listening to everyone squabble in grand assemblies of late." Shen Yi said quietly, "And listen—during the grand assembly on the first of this month, after the imperial attendant announced the dismissal, His Majesty trod on his own dragon robe when he stood. He would have tumbled straight down from his throne if the Imperial Guard on duty hadn't caught him. But he broke his leg..." Shen Yi pointed at his own calf. "Right here. He's still bedbound. I'm guessing that's why he summoned Prince Yan to the palace in such a hurry."

Gu Yun was shocked. "You can break a bone just from falling over? That's way too unlucky."

"The imperial physicians are all afraid to talk; they hemmed and hawed without saying anything. Later, they invited Miss Chen to examine him. She said years of overwork and improper diet have weakened him, to the point that his bones would break with just a fall. There're rumors going around that the late emperor suffered the same back in the day..."

No wonder the imperial physicians were so tight-lipped. Only Miss Chen, who frequently traveled beyond the pass, dared speak the truth.

This nation could grind people down to the bone.

Shen Yi glanced around. All the officials who had come to welcome Prince Yan had followed Jiang Chong away. Gu Yun had left his Black Iron Battalion guards in the Northern Camp, keeping only some personal guards from his estate. Shen Yi lowered his voice further still, whispering at a near-inaudible volume: "Even the noble consort was implicated in the Lü family's scandal. She was stripped of her title outright. It was never openly announced, but she's basically been shunned and sent to the cold palace.[6] The crown prince is still so young, and he can't count on much support from his mother's family. If His Majesty really... What do you think he intends, summoning Prince Yan to the palace so urgently? Is he going to entrust his children to him or..."

Gu Yun gave him a look, and Shen Yi's mouth snapped shut.

During the capital siege, when the Imperial City was on the verge of collapse, Li Feng had intended to abdicate—not to the crown prince, but to Prince Yan.

Then, the country had been a hairsbreadth away from falling into enemy hands. The young crown prince would indeed have been unable to hold up a nation ruled by the house of Li. But now, even if

---

6 Being sent to the "cold palace" was a severe punishment for members of the imperial harem, which involved being confined and isolated in a remote location within the palace. Historically, the "cold palace" was not a specific residence, but a term used to refer to any location used to carry out such a punishment.

their lost territory in Jiangnan had yet to be recovered, the northern barbarians had already sent a peace envoy. After a few more years of recovery, they would have the strength to fight. Would the emperor still choose to pass the throne to his younger brother instead of his son?

Gu Yun suddenly recalled the incongruous question Li Feng had asked him in the midst of the Imperial Guard's rebellion: "Did you know Prince Yan was abused by that barbarian woman as a child?" Li Feng wasn't the type to ask Chang Geng that sort of thing of his own initiative. It was far more likely the prince had broached the topic himself. What circumstances had led to such a conversation?

Chang Geng and Li Feng were brothers, but they weren't close. And Gu Yun understood Chang Geng, wolf pup that he was—if he wasn't close with someone, he wouldn't let them so much as stroke his fur. There was no way he would have taken the initiative to reveal his childhood wounds, and certainly not to garner sympathy. Unless... Understanding flashed through Gu Yun's mind as a plausible scenario occurred to him. Prince Yan had come of age years ago. Why had no one made arrangements for the major milestone that was his marriage? Even if Prince Yan's position made it awkward for others to bring up, it wasn't as if Li Feng would have simply forgotten.

That day, there must have been more to Li Feng's inexplicable words. Perhaps he meant to say, *Prince Yan is unable to overcome this barrier in his heart and unwilling to take a wife and have children*!

If Prince Yan had no heirs, then no matter what, no one could threaten the young crown prince's position. Thus, if anything should happen to Li Feng, he could perhaps entrust the heavy responsibility of caring for his children to Chang Geng.

What was more, Li Feng had always encouraged the young crown prince to spend time with Gu Yun. On the one hand, it was a way to improve his relationship with Gu Yun—but on the other, he must also have been seeking to secure his son's future.

These people and their plots...

"Do you think there's any chance His Majesty will pass the throne to Prince Yan?" Shen Yi asked.

"Shush—don't speak of this again," Gu Yun said. "Don't get involved; remember where our duty lies."

Shen Yi was quick to agree. But after a moment, he continued, "Actually, there was another thing I wanted to ask... Uhh, it's a personal matter."

Gu Yun looked at Shen Yi in surprise. "What is it?"

Shen Yi squirmed in embarrassment. "Are you...very familiar with Miss Chen?"

RISING WINDS

S TILL ABSORBED in the topic of the northern barbarian envoy and Li Feng's broken leg, Gu Yun didn't grasp his point right away. "Miss Chen?" he asked, mystified. "We're not very close—she isn't exactly the talkative sort. Why?"

Shen Yi was indignant. "She served as a medic in a hellish place like the northwest for you for so long without a word of complaint, and all you have to say about her is that you're *not very close*?"

The words *You absolute ingrate* were practically scrawled across Commander Shen's forehead.

"...Ah?"

Shen Yi stared him down in fury.

One absentminded, one incensed, both on completely different wavelengths. The two stared at each other for a long moment before Gu Yun began to catch on. He hummed knowingly, then looked Shen Yi up and down with a peculiar glint in his eye. "Why do you ask?"

Face tense, Shen Yi the blabbermouth abruptly went silent, as if prepared to guard this secret to his death. He bravely met Gu Yun's mischievous gaze, transforming himself into a mouthless gourd. Gu Yun raised an innocent eyebrow and reached out to poke Shen Yi in the chest. "Commander Shen, didn't the sages tell you to speak no evil? Is it at all proper for us two bachelors to discuss a young lady in broad daylight?" Recalling how Shen Yi hadn't held back a jot while scolding him, he jumped at the opportunity for payback. "Vile behavior."

Words failed Shen Yi.

Gu Yun was overjoyed to have obtained such prime blackmail material on Shen Yi for the low price of nothing. Suddenly his lower back wasn't sore anymore, and he even began whistling a tune that bore a striking resemblance to his flute playing as he urged his horse toward the city.

"Gu Zixi!" Shen Yi chased after him, gnashing his teeth. "You...you..."

You bastard!

Shen Yi used every iota of strength in his body to swallow these words back down lest he find himself cursing out his superior officer in front of the entire capital.

By the time Gu Yun'd had his fill of teasing Shen Yi, the two had left the estate guards far behind and were on their way into the Imperial City. At last, Gu Yun adopted a more serious expression. "I have no qualms about Miss Chen's character, and she's highly skilled—I bet she could beat up a few men like you without breaking a sweat."

It was quite the incendiary statement, but Shen Yi wasn't offended. Instead, he eagerly lapped up every last detail—especially when Gu Yun began to recount his first meeting with Chen Qingxu on the rebel ship in Jiangnan. Shen Yi wrung his hands and sighed, regretting he hadn't been there in person.

"As for her personality, likes, and dislikes...it wouldn't do for me to know too much; Chang Geng may be more familiar with her." Gu Yun paused. "But let me tell you a bit about her family background."

"The Shanxi Province Chen family, I'm aware," Shen Yi responded. "They produce miracle doctors every generation and practice their arts to serve the people of the world. Their family tenets are upright and honorable."

Gu Yun snorted. "I see you've done your research. Are you planning to approach them to propose a marriage?"

"Well, I'll be employing matchmakers and properly sending betrothal gifts, of course," Shen Yi said in full seriousness.

Gu Yun didn't know what to say.

This brother-in-arms of his was quite an oddball. He'd studied a basketful of books as a youngster and was poisoned by aristocratic traditions down to the marrow. But those old nobles only adhered to etiquette on the outside. They held others to high standards and did any dirty deed they wanted behind closed doors, where etiquette mattered not a bit. They were hypocrites one and all, and they knew it.

This son of the Shen family was the lone exception. He was notorious among outsiders for his rebellious tendencies—he had first abandoned the Hanlin Academy for the Lingshu Institute, then lowered himself to join the army. His friends, however, knew him as a truly honest gentleman who believed in the tenets of "see no evil, hear no evil." So upright was he that he'd managed to muck about with a bunch of army ruffians for over a decade and come out with his character completely unstained.

Chen Qingxu had remained in the capital for some time. After all that had happened, and given her position as the Chen family's representative in the Linyuan Pavilion, she must have crossed paths with Shen Yi on numerous occasions. But even after so many encounters, a certain someone was still afraid to talk to her face-to-face and had resorted to asking Gu Yun about her behind her back. The way he talked about her, it was highly likely he was totally unaware of the connection between the Chen family and the Linyuan Pavilion. He still thought Chen Qingxu simply unnaturally dedicated to serving her nation.

Gu Yun sighed. It was impossible to believe this block of wood called Shen Yi had risen from his command.

"Then I'll tell you something you don't know. Don't repeat this elsewhere—the Shanxi Chen family is no ordinary family of doctors. They're a pillar of the Linyuan Pavilion," Gu Yun said in a low voice. "Zhong-lao mentioned it once before; Miss Chen seems to be the family head of this generation. If that's really the case, she might not be free to marry into your family as a commander's wife."

Shen Yi was shocked.

Gu Yun considered for a moment. "How about this: I'll have someone pass a message for you and ask her thoughts on the matter..."

"No, not yet," Shen Yi hastily interrupted him. "That's too abrupt."

If Shen Yi himself wasn't yet concerned, Gu Yun felt like he might be worrying overmuch. But given Shen Yi's temperament, there was a good chance he'd remain wifeless until he died. As someone with plenty of experience in romantic affairs, Gu Yun took it upon himself to advise him. "Jiping-xiong, you have to treat these matters with urgency, or someone else will make the first move. It'll be too late for you to complain then."

But after another moment of thought, Shen Yi shook his head. "Even so, don't do anything for now. I need to think things through."

Gu Yun shook his head. He understood all too well. If a man began to hesitate after just a bit of unexpected information about a woman's identity and background, he was interested but not fully set on her. But it wasn't his place to comment on the feelings of the involved parties. He chose a rather neutral statement: "Fine, think it over first. Let me know anytime if there's anything I can do to help."

Shen Yi clearly wasn't listening, immersed in his own thoughts. "I was indeed unaware of this before. Now that you mention it, I agree it wouldn't quite work."

Still affecting neutrality, Gu Yun nodded. "Mm-hmm."

"There's no help for it then," Shen Yi continued. "I'll wait until this war is over, then I'll hand in my seal of command and resign my official position. I won't be a general anymore."

Gu Yun nearly fell off his horse.

Shen Yi prattled on, a faint look of worry stealing over his face. "But the war hasn't been won. Wouldn't it be bad luck to propose now? You know how it is for people like us. If we're too tied down, it holds us back on the battlefield, and that makes it more dangerous to fight. If something happens, won't I have made her a widow before she's a wife?" He sighed. "But neither time nor the object of my affections will wait for the war to end... It's a lose-lose situation. Zixi, do you think there's some way to keep the rabble off her?"

"...You don't need to worry about that. From what I understand, Miss Chen already possesses that particular ability." Gu Yun paused, then broke out into laughter.

Shen Yi was mystified. "What are you laughing at?"

Gu Yun shook his head. "I'm laughing at you. You passed the civil service examinations yet quit the Hanlin Academy the next day to joyfully throw in your lot with the Lingshu Institute. The moment you had some accomplishments to your name in the Lingshu Institute and people began to talk of you becoming Master Fenghan's successor, you left the Lingshu Institute and joined the Black Iron Battalion as a personal mechanic. And look at you now, with your brilliant military achievements. Step by step, you've walked what others would see as a road soaring into heaven. Breaking the siege on the capital, saving the life of the emperor... It wouldn't be strange if you were granted a title of nobility soon. Everyone thinks you're seeing a grand plan come to fruition, but here you are planning to quit your post and get hitched."

Shen Yi chuckled ruefully. Truth be told, he had no grand ambitions in the first place. He had simply run around all these years with a nanny's mindset, looking after this and that, following in Gu Yun's wake. The Marquis of Order lived in the eye of the storm—it just so happened that Shen Yi had achieved his own fame along the way. But he'd never sought it out, and he wasn't unwilling to part with it.

Some people were changeable by nature; they would become unrecognizable every five years. Others were static as still water, sticking to their original aspirations even after a journey of a hundred thousand kilometers.

Gu Yun looked at him as a multitude of emotions welled up in his heart. The pent-up frustrations that had risen as he'd listened to palace affairs disappeared without a trace. He slung a companionable arm over Shen Yi's shoulder and patted him a few times.

"If you need Miss Chen for anything in the future, how about I be your go-between," said Shen Yi. He remained absolutely ignorant of the Marquis of Anding's roiling emotions and still nattered on about his own worries. Before he knew it, he had slipped into rambling. "It's just...ah, do you think it'd be improper if I keep calling on her without anything official between us? Would she think I'm being indecorous? Ay, Zixi, just say something—actually forget it, you don't need to speak, you were never the decorous sort in the first place. I think..."

General Shen had entered the endless cycle of self-affirmation and self-doubt.

Perhaps there was no need for him to change his original aspirations, but it would be great if he could change his habit of blathering on without end.

After getting an earful from Shen Yi, Gu Yun's head was fit to split apart. Finally at the end of his endurance, he whipped Shen Yi's horse on the rear and took the chance to escape.

News that Prince Yan had been invited to the palace before he'd even made it to the city walls flew into every pricked ear in the capital as if on wings. Fang Qin was in his home, surrounded by advisors and members of his faction, when he got the news. After the chaos in Jiangbei, Minister Fang rather felt he had been conned into doing someone else's dirty work.

To Fang Qin, the Lü-Yang faction was like a rotten tooth—it grew in his own mouth but was constantly aching and inflamed. It not only did not assist him in chewing but became a hindrance. To have it pulled was no bad thing. But he hadn't expected Prince Yan to have so many tricks up his sleeve, and in the end, this pulled tooth had taken too much with it when it went. Even without a presence in the capital, Prince Yan had taken the first-mover's advantage before Fang Qin could react and bagged the entire canal region for his own ends.

The Canal Committee had been formed and factories were popping up like bamboo shoots after rain. It was too late to reverse the tide. Fang Qin was an old fox who had honed a keen nose from stalking the political hunting grounds for years. Reforms in farmland taxes, civilian trade, and other economic spheres were now inevitable. He had wanted to be the clever oriole lying in wait as the mantis closed in on its prey. He had never expected that while Prince Yan had been engaging him in a political dance, the prince was carrying out his true plans on the other side of the board. He'd plotted ten steps ahead with every maneuver; in the end, Fang Qin had fallen short.

When Fang Qin had first taken control of the battle-scarred Ministry of Revenue, he'd enjoyed a harmonious honeymoon period with Prince Yan's Grand Council. In those early days, a large tract of their nation had fallen to enemy hands, and they walked a tightrope with every step. They strove to rise from the ashes, and with a million things to be done, no one picked a fight with anyone else. All members of the court were compatriots in adversity, and they had worked tirelessly to buy the nation that precious bit of breathing room. They respected and admired each other's talent. No one knew their paths would diverge so soon.

Sometimes, Fang Qin couldn't help but envy Jiang Hanshi. Had their roles been reversed, he believed he could have done much better than Jiang Chong, Xu Ling, and the rest of them. If his surname weren't Fang—even if he were only a minor official of the seventh rank who'd earned his position through ten years of bitter study before a chilly window...

But fate was cruel. None of these musings were of use to him now. Prince Yan had set his mind on cleaning out the old guard within the capital, and with the turmoil in Jiangbei, he had flashed his butcher's blade. Now, they were as inimical as fire and water.

One advisor cautiously opened his mouth. "Minister, I heard that back when the Far Westerners attacked, His Majesty considered passing the throne to Prince Yan. Now he's gone and summoned him into the palace... Even if his intentions have changed now that we're at peace, he's sure to entrust the crown prince to him while the crown prince is young. Should we be making our own preparations?"

Coming back to the present, Fang Qin narrowed his eyes.

"His Majesty may be wary of the fourth prince after Yang Ronggui rebelled in his name," another person said. "But he used his injury to gain sympathy and took his opportunity to step out of the spotlight.

He faded into the background so thoroughly... His Majesty has likely set aside his suspicions by now. Prince Yan has obviously picked his moment to return to the capital and resume his post—he must be about to make a major move."

Fang Qin was doubtful. He stroked his whiskers. "The northern barbarians have sent an envoy, but we're still preparing for battle in Jiangnan. This war will continue for another few years. The revitalization of the canal region is ongoing, and the refugees have only just been settled. If we act against Prince Yan now, will it not injure the well-being of the nation? If so, we will be cursed by history."

"Minister," the advisor began with a smile, "your loyalty to the nation is admirable. But the imperial court will function with or without Prince Yan. Merchants are a lowly sort, and even these so-called 'altruistic merchants' are shackled by their nature—they will prioritize profit above all else. So long as we don't interfere with their profits, what do they care whose word holds sway within the court? Minister Fang cares so deeply for the nation and its people. We can settle the refugees and fight the war even without Prince Yan—and you must think things through. Prince Yan is ambitious. Sooner or later, he will use his lofty position to appoint members of his own faction to high places and subdue us. If we allow him to continue lawlessly devouring everything he sets his eyes on, it will be our lives on the line one day."

The rest voiced their agreement.

"Prince Yan is talented, yes, but he's too extreme in his methods. If we do nothing, he will bring disaster to the nation and its people."

"Minister Fang, you cannot retreat any further. If he gains any more power, he'll leave no room for us..."

Fang Qin sighed. He pressed his palm downward, signaling for quiet. "Bring him here," he said to the confidante beside him.

A long-brewing tempest was gathering once again.

Blissfully unaware, Chang Geng left the inner palace and returned to the Marquis Estate. Whatever Li Feng said to him, it seemed to have put him in an excellent mood. He attached himself to Gu Yun the instant he got home, refusing to let go, frisky even during their evening meal. Gu Yun didn't ask what Li Feng spoke to him about in the palace. It was evident simply by observing his behavior. Gu Yun used his chopsticks to smack Prince Yan's hand, which had wandered away from his own bowl to crawl up Gu Yun's thigh. Nonchalant, he asked, "When do you plan on returning to your position in court?"

Chang Geng rubbed the back of his hand and refilled Gu Yun's bowl in placation. "I'll go back after I rest for a few days," he said absently. "His Majesty said he's tired these days; he wants me to return to my position as soon as possible—Zixi, have some more."

Gu Yun waved him off. "Just a bit. I'll be uncomfortable if I eat too much so late. Did you hear Jialai Yinghuo sent an envoy?"

Chang Geng nodded, humming in affirmation. He pushed Gu Yun's hand aside as it reached for a teacup and served him a bowl of soup instead. "As for how we approach these negotiations, we leave it up to Marshal Gu."

"When a wild beast is mortally wounded, it will often pretend to be on the brink of death in order to lure its enemy into lowering its defenses. When the moment is right, it will lash out. One must be careful." Gu Yun gave Chang Geng a look. Then he blew the green leaves floating atop the soup to the other side of the bowl and downed it in a single gulp.

Chang Geng started in surprise. He had a feeling Gu Yun wasn't only talking about the barbarians—he seemed to be reminding him of something else.

101

FOG OF CONFUSION

T HINGS HAD BEEN GOING too well for Chang Geng for a while. First, he had flawlessly resolved the incident in Jiangnan, meeting every single one of his objectives. He also had Gu Yun's company on his return trip. Great Liang had been through one military crisis after another over the years. Aside from the time they'd spent in Yanhui in Chang Geng's youth, Gu Yun rarely had the chance to stay comfortably by his side for so long. The entire journey back, Chang Geng had felt as if they could stay that way until the sky was barren of stars and the earth grew old. The lonely chill of late fall melting into winter couldn't touch him at all.

Chang Geng had always been extremely anxious, paranoid about every detail and startling at the faintest sign of anything going awry. Although he was tense every moment of every day, he was also meticulous in his strategies and rarely ever made a misstep. But after so long spent sinking into the gentle warmth of a lover's embrace, it took these words from Gu Yun for Chang Geng to realize he had forgotten himself.

He pulled himself together and silently walked back over all that had happened after Li Feng summoned him to the palace. The scene gradually took on a different light—the supreme ruler of the nation reduced to an invalid, shut away in a room stifling with the scent of medicine, the heavy walls of the palace chamber and the silent servants all shrouded in gloom. The entire place was suffused with the bitter smell of death. But Li Feng was in his prime; he wasn't actually an old man. What could he be thinking?

Some people, when they realized their own helplessness, would fall into depression and cede their responsibilities of their own accord. Li Feng was absolutely not that kind of person. If he were so easily convinced to retreat, he would never have stepped out from the crowd when the Northern Camp rebelled, nor would he have stood atop that red-headed kite as an enemy army bore down on the city walls.

Gu Yun was reminding him of this.

Chang Geng shivered, and a bead of cold sweat rolled down the back of his neck. His look of unbridled joy relaxed into neutrality.

Gu Yun saw he understood. Chang Geng was far too sharp; oftentimes a single sentence was enough. Nothing more was required; he reached out and patted the top of Chang Geng's head. Chang Geng caught his hand and dragged it down to hold it in his own, and Gu Yun patiently waited for him to present his self-reflection. At the very least, he ought to say something along the lines of *What would I do without you?*

However, after clutching his hand for a time, Chang Geng elected to act unreasonably instead. "It's all your fault, you know. You made me lose my head."

Gu Yun was speechless.

He had been in the capital for less than a day and already been assigned the characters of both the perverted lecher and the seductive beauty. How busy his schedule was. His Highness Prince Yan had been so shy and introverted in his youth. How had he grown more shameless as he aged?

Gu Yun shook Chang Geng off—this boy was getting far too comfortable with him. He grabbed a nearby jar of wine, only for Chang Geng to leap up in one well-trained movement and snatch it. "It's freezing outside; don't even think about drinking cold wine!"

Tossing the jar from his left hand to his right, Gu Yun caught it as if it weighed no more than a feather. With his free left hand, he caught Chang Geng as he crashed into his arms, taking hold of his chin and lifting it for a kiss. Before Chang Geng could recover his senses and launch a counterattack, Gu Yun turned and draped his outer robe over his own shoulders with a smile. "I need to make a trip to the Northern Camp; you can sleep by yourself tonight. Recite your sutras twice before you go to bed so you don't lose your head again."

Chang Geng sputtered. What about his promise from earlier?! *The great and mighty Marquis of Order, going back on his word!*

Gu Yun was teasing him, but he really did have business to attend to. He should have stayed in the Northern Camp in the first place, and had only returned to the Marquis Estate to share a meal with Chang Geng out of worry. Now that he had a sense of the situation in the palace, he was on the move again, back to the Northern Camp. Not only did the Northern Camp oversee the capital's external defenses, it was also a relay station for emergency military dispatches from all over the country, which passed through it before being conveyed to the capital. The arrival of the northern barbarians' envoy was sudden, and Gu Yun was uneasy. In short, he went straight from worrying about private affairs to worrying about public ones.

It was late autumn in the capital, but the gloomy tang of midwinter already hung in the air when he walked through the door. The chilly nighttime breeze had the makings of winter's icy gales, yet Gu Yun had followed his usual habit in going out, wearing only a thin, unlined robe.

But today, when he mounted his horse and turned toward the gates, the winds inside the pass felt more biting than usual. He sighed to himself. In the end, he turned back, hung the jar of wine inside the stables, and asked Huo Dan to bring him a cloak. Only then did he finally hurry off.

Although Gu Yun had been running back and forth taking care of the uprising in Jiangbei and the traitors within the capital, he had never lost contact with Cai Bin, who was leading their forces on the northern border. If in Jiangnan the tears of those left behind ran dry amidst the dust kicked up by foreign hooves, he scarcely needed to ponder the conditions on the northern border. A vast distance of a hundred years, time enough for two or three generations to die out, might not be enough for the blood feud between the barbarians and Central Plains people to subside.

What did they mean by suing for peace now?

Cai Bin's letter arrived moments after Gu Yun reached the Northern Camp, before he even had the chance to sit and take a sip of water.

The letter was plainly phrased, but its succinct contents contained a wealth of information. After such a long standoff, both armies had installed scouts and spies among the other's forces. Cai Bin's agents in the enemy camp reported that Jialai Yinghuo seemed to have fallen ill that spring, and no one had seen him in public since. Even stranger, his eldest son disappeared from the public eye at the same time, claiming to be occupied with filial duties. Jialai's second son was left to handle all orders of business.

Jialai had three sons. All were born to the same woman, and he had followed Han tradition in naming the eldest son the heir. With their father gravely ill, it was no odd thing for sons to compete over demonstrations of filial piety. But was it really credible that the heir was so engrossed by his filial duties that he forgot all proper business, leaving his younger brother to manage the tribes in his stead?

Upon reading this report, the truth below the surface began to take shape: a second son—rich in talent and virtue, and frustrated with bowing to his brother's whims merely because he was born a few years later—had somehow managed to place Jialai and his heir under house arrest and usurp the throne.

"Sir, aside from those thirteen articles of the proposed treaty, the eighteen tribes are also willing to send Jialai's youngest son as a hostage to guarantee our continued negotiations." The newly appointed commander of the Northern Camp handed Gu Yun another memorial. "We received word earlier from General Cai that the young barbarian's convoy is preparing to enter the pass and have forwarded their documents to the capital to await the court's approval. This lower general was about to send someone to the Marquis Estate, so you've arrived just in time."

The memorial submitted by the barbarians was written with great sincerity and documented the identities of the third prince and all attendants in his convoy. The young prince was only fifteen, supposedly a weak and sickly child. He was accompanied by one special envoy doubling as a translator, ten young male and ten young female bondservants, and twelve guards serving as an escort. The name and origin of each individual were recorded in detail, and even the ages and responsibilities of the bondservants were meticulously described. They had followed Great Liang's immigration policies to the letter. Gu Yun read the whole thing from start to finish thrice but didn't find a single point to contest.

Shen Yi stood to the side, his arms crossed. "It looks like the rumors are true. The ambitious second prince imprisoned his father and elder brother, and now he's trying to rid himself of his younger brother by offering him up as a hostage so he can reign supreme over the eighteen tribes."

"What good does it do him to take over the eighteen tribes?" Gu Yun tossed the memorial aside. Despite sitting beside the furnace in the tent for so long, he felt cold. He unconsciously moved his hands closer to the heat and rubbed them together. "If they lose the war now, they'll only have a harder time opposing us in the future. They spend every year starving outside the pass, and whatever violet gold they dig up is surrendered as tribute. They couldn't even save their goddess or the Wolf King's daughter."

The feud between the barbarians and the Central Plains folk wasn't some recent development. The nomadic tribes of the north had established the custom of raiding their richer neighbors to the south every time they had a bad year several reigns ago.

The north possessed a ferocious spirit, every citizen born with the capacity to make war, whereas the south had a solid backbone that produced famed generals generation after generation. The two were locked in an endless cycle: one side pressed south to loot and plunder, then the other side raised armies in retaliation. For a hundred years, neither nation had come out on top—until Great Liang beat their adversary to developing steam technology.

It had been the golden age of artificers, glimpsed today only through the annals of history. Great Liang, with its vast tracts of fertile soil, had been like a great beast awakening from slumber. Endless varieties of engines and armor sprang up like bamboo shoots after rain: light pelt armor, heavy armor, giant kites, armored hawks... Steam billowed like the rising tide, iron puppets flooded the capital city, and the maximum range of cannons, both long and short, was exceeded by the day.

At first, the narrow-minded barbarians looked down on Great Liang's decision to open maritime trade and pour its energy into the development of engines and armor—*These southerners and their obsession with luxuries and magic tricks*, they thought. The Wolf King of the north trusted too much in his own claws and fangs, and his pride cost him the first-mover's advantage. He failed to get a seat atop the billow of violet gold smoke ascending into the heavens and lost so soundly to the Central Plains that he had no chance of turning the tide for decades. Not only was he forced to surrender all the violet gold excavated within his borders as tribute, he was unable to acquire armor technology of his own no matter how hard he ran to catch up. Even now, the north still leaned on the Far Westerners to supply them with technology.

The eighteen tribes ignored this bloody lesson at their own peril. They couldn't simply watch as factories sprouted up all over Great Liang. With the restrictions set by the Token of Mastery Law lifted, the country seemed to be approaching a second golden age of engines and armor. If things continued along this trajectory, if they allowed Great Liang to survive this winter and come back to life, the northern barbarian tribes might truly have no chance of survival.

"I can't speak to the second prince's character," Gu Yun said, "But I know Jialai Yinghuo. That old bastard would rather die than allow his fate to fall into the hands of another. Forget the son; even if they sent the father, we would still have to be on our guard—go fetch me my seal."

That night, a dozen war beacon decrees left the Northern Camp, a military mobilization on the same scale as when the Far Westerners launched an attack on Dagu Harbor. Additional troops were dispatched to every relay station between the northwest and the capital, as if preparing to meet a great enemy force. A team from the Lingshu Institute rushed to the encampment of the Northern Border Defense Corps to inspect their engines and armor, preparing for war to break out at any moment.

Great Liang marched into winter under these foreboding clouds.

On the cusp of the new year, the court was extraordinarily quiet— Prince Yan held control of the Grand Council, situated at the eye of the storm, and every corner of the court watched his return with interest. But Prince Yan bucked everyone's expectations. He didn't do as Fang Qin had imagined and begin hacking away at old policies with newly penned reforms the instant he returned. Instead, he took things easy and interfered little, as if carefully cooking a small fish.

After Prince Yan's return to the capital, he abandoned his habit of running around so busily he practically tripped over his own feet. He first lazed about in his home for nearly half a month before quietly appearing in the Grand Council. He spoke little both in grand assemblies and in smaller meetings, and in all ways returned to being the invisible man he was before the war. He spent his time handling rote business in the Grand Council, wrote summaries and visited the palace as necessary, fulfilled all his responsibilities with meticulous care, and did nothing that might attract negative comments or place him under suspicion of neglecting his duties. Aside from that, he wasn't interested in managing a single extra thing.

Prince Yan was no longer spotted among the members of the Grand Council who worked by candlelight deep into the night. He strolled around the premises by day and left precisely on the dot in the evening. He came and went on schedule, took all his breaks, and refused guests when there was no business to discuss. He even acquired a little garden on the outskirts of the capital. Whenever Gu Yun was occupied at the Northern Camp and refused to come home, Chang Geng would stroll over to tend the flowers and play with his birds. Within half a month, he had trained the Shen family's terror of a myna bird into a honey-mouthed creature that complimented everyone it saw...though its tail was now mysteriously bald. He had the servants make a toy with the feathers and gave it to the little crown prince to play with.

One day, after Li Feng's leg had healed enough that he could manage a limping walk, he thought to visit the boy and went down to the crown prince's study with the aid of a palace attendant's supporting arm. The crown prince was a well-behaved child and never slacked off during his studies. Li Feng didn't disturb him and merely stood at the back door for a while, holding on to his attendant. His gaze was drawn to a little ornament on the crown prince's desk.

It was no ordinary piece of earthenware, but had rather a light metal frame. A thin trail of steam emerged from the end of the object, and a delicate little carriage inset with a Western clock ran in circles on a pair of rails that looped around a tiny flowerpot in the center. The pot was empty, revealing the drainage hole bored in the bottom. The crown prince probably hadn't decided what to plant yet.

Li Feng walked slowly over and picked up the device to inspect it. Startled, the crown prince shot to his feet to bow then snuck a glance at his father, fearing he was about to be scolded for dallying with material pleasures and forgetting higher ambitions. But Li Feng must have been in a good mood; no anger appeared on his face. He simply asked, "The Department of the Imperial Household has been instructed to increase income and reduce expenses. Haven't they been forbidden from importing these kinds of opulent toys? Where did you get this?"

Afraid to even breathe too loudly, the crown prince carefully replied, "Father, this wasn't purchased by the Department of the Imperial Household. Fourth Uncle gave it to me."

Li Feng frowned. "I haven't seen A-Min in some days. This is what he's spending his time on?"

The attendant stepped forward. "Your Majesty, didn't His Highness Prince Yan recently ask you to bequeath him a garden? He hasn't been as busy with official affairs lately, so he set up a greenhouse in the garden to cultivate rare flowers and grasses. He's invented all kinds of intricate pots with Scholar Ge. It's almost the new year, and everyone wants flower arrangements. His Highness's novelty arrangements can hardly be bought for a thousand gold. See, you put water inside this little carriage, and it will water the flowers at a set time every day. If it's placed in a well-lit area, after it makes a few laps, you can even see a little rainbow when beads of water are sprayed."

The crown prince piped up, speaking quietly. "Uncle said he used normal plant and flower seeds, the type you can buy by the handful for a single coin in the countryside. He merely potted them and cut them into shape. He said it's perfect for fooling the uncultured rich."

"How absurd. What does he mean by this?" Li Feng snapped. "We told him to guide the crown prince; did he take that to mean teach him how to garden, walk birds, and scam people?"

Seeing his father's face darken, the crown prince was thoroughly cowed. He stood where he was, quiet as a cicada in winter.

Li Feng set the flowerpot down heavily, a look of vexation on his face. "We asked you to learn the ways of governance from Prince Yan. What has he taught you? Let us hear it."

The crown prince risked a glance up. Nervous as he was, he didn't dare neglect the question. He responded in a thin voice, "F-Father, Fourth Uncle taught this subject that governing a great nation does not require tireless work day and night nor driving oneself to exhaustion. The most important principle is to utilize every resource and person to their fullest. Laws and institutions are the foundation of a ruler's governance. As long as a comprehensive system of laws and institutions is in place, all civil and military officials perform their duties, and the national treasury is well funded, uh..."

The creases on Li Feng's brow smoothed slightly. "What?" he couldn't resist asking upon hearing his son stutter.

The crown prince plucked up his courage and continued, "...then with a single determined effort you can ensure a life of leisure and spend the rest of your time mooching off the imperial coffers."

Li Feng blinked slowly.

The crown prince pressed his lips together, afraid his father would fly into a rage at these heretical and roguish notions. But after waiting a good while, the fury and punishment he expected hadn't arrived. He timidly raised his head to find a look of calm upon the unyielding face of the emperor. After a long moment spent lost in thought, he finally sighed. "He's right. A-Min sees more clearly than we do."

The crown prince looked at him in confusion. He felt his father was in an uncommonly good mood today.

Certain fools within the court saw Prince Yan's retreat into the shadows somewhat differently. In their minds, he seemed to have lost imperial favor after Yang Ronggui's rebellion and was now too fearful to act. They submitted bold memorials censoring the prince, presenting a plenteous list of crimes, and thereby earned themselves a scolding from the Longan Emperor during one of his rare appearances at a grand assembly. His words and delivery made abundantly clear his intention to protect Prince Yan.

And that wasn't all. The next day, the emperor, a famous miser, broke his own rules and approved an excess expenditure by the Department of the Imperial Household. He became a scam victim and paid an exorbitant price for a whole pile of novel and intricate metal flower arrangements from Prince Yan's garden to gift to all the palaces, dipping into his own purse to support his brother's business.

No one quite understood what was going on with the Grand Council anymore.

Fang Qin and his allies wrote up critical memorials and revised them again and again. The new year was soon upon them, yet they still hadn't found a chance to submit them. Even Fang Qin couldn't help but wonder—was it really possible for someone to relinquish their position and walk away after taking up such heavy responsibility in a time of crisis? Did Prince Yan have absolutely no ambition?

These peaceful days continued until the twenty-third of the twelfth month, when the hostaged northern barbarian prince arrived at the capital.

PALACE BANQUET

A T THE START of the year, Gu Yun had still been on the northwest border. The entirety of Great Liang had been blanketed in an ominous pall, the people prepared to lose their nation at any time.

By the year's end, the entire country had burst back to life with a shocking vivacity. Even if the resplendent days of song and dance were no more, the mischievous children lining up to buy candy on street corners and in alleyways had begun to don new clothes, fire-crackers popped throughout the day, and every household was busy preparing their new year's goods.

The fallen city walls rose again, and the reconstructed aerial defense field atop the Altar of Prosperity opened its watchful eye. Rows of parhelion bows and silent iron puppets observed as their uninvited guests entered the city flanked by soldiers from the Northern Camp. Their escort stopped outside the nine gates in rigid formation, their keen spirit, honed by blood and flame, clear in their bearing as they waited amid a pin-drop silence.

It had been a year of bitter turmoil. Prince Yan had brought the nation back from the brink of death—this single accomplishment ensured his place in the annals of history.

The barbarian third prince's entourage rolled slowly down the long streets. The biting breeze lifted a corner of the curtain, revealing a brief glimpse of a thin, wan face. A hand emerged from inside the carriage and drew the curtain closed, blocking prying gazes from within and without.

Gu Yun sat in Southward Tower, dressed in civilian clothes, a glass monocle perched atop the bridge of his nose—this wasn't the one he used in a pinch when his eyes were failing, but a type of field scope used for sighting across long distances on the battlefield. Chang Geng and Shen Yi sat on either side of him. After a moment, the door of their private room swung open, and a figure darted inside—Cao Chunhua, who had disappeared after their misadventures in Jiangbei.

Cao Chunhua dipped in a shallow bow, then plopped down in a chair. "I'm parched."

As readily as if he'd done so a thousand times before, Chang Geng grabbed a wide bowl and poured it full of wine. Cao Chunhua accepted it without the slightest hint of embarrassment and drained it in a gulp, as though the contents were merely cold water. Even Gu Yun, alcoholic that he was, boggled at the sight. He felt he had met a wine flask come to life.

"Another," Cao Chunhua sighed in satisfaction. "After I parted ways with the marshal in the capital, I went straight back to the north. I've followed them through every kind of wind, frost, rain, and snow on the way here; I haven't had an easy time of it, I tell you."

Cao Chunhua had been skilled in the art of disguise since his youth. He had a perfect memory for learning foreign languages and could achieve fluency in a new one with half a month of study. Chang Geng had sent him on a long-term undercover mission to the northern border, and only summoned him back because he needed a perfect body double for his investigations of the case in Jiangbei.

Cao Chunhua hefted his second bowl of wine and threw a

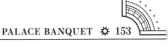

flirtatious glance at Gu Yun, who was watching with a hint of envy. The look successfully awakened Gu Yun's unfortunate memories of this young man undulating his hips until they were level with his waist while wearing Chang Geng's face. Gu Yun quietly rubbed away the goosebumps on his arms and averted his gaze, face ashen.

"What happened?" Chang Geng asked.

"I don't want to talk about it. Every single member of their party is a martial expert, slaves included. I couldn't get within half a kilometer of them, and I was tripping over myself trying to keep up. Ay, I won't lie to you," Cao Chunhua trilled in high, lilting tones, "when I was on the northern border, I once managed to infiltrate Jialai Yinghuo's personal guard. I even disguised myself as one of the second prince's favored female bondservants and hovered around him a whole day and night, and I was never caught. After over a year undercover, the only one I was unable to approach was this third prince. I've never even seen his face."

"You couldn't catch a glimpse from afar when he went out?" Chang Geng asked.

"He never goes out. Everyone in the eighteen tribes says the third prince suffers from a terrible illness and can't be exposed to the wind." Cao Chunhua sighed, "Aside from Jialai Yinghuo himself, no one sees so much as a hair on his head. Not only that, the third prince is a taboo subject within the eighteen tribes. His residence is surrounded by three layers of guards. I infiltrated the outermost layer once, but I couldn't manage the second. Those people are like iron puppets. They don't say much, but every one of them is a top-tier martial expert willing to sacrifice their lives. I tried a number of methods to no avail and nearly alerted them to my presence in the process. I had to give it up as a bad job. Your Highness, have you seen that special envoy accompanying them?"

Cao Chunhua pointed with the tips of his chopsticks. Everyone looked out the window and watched as a middle-aged man turned to speak to the guards. Though his face was unremarkable, there was an indescribable aura about him, steely and immovable as a mountain peak.

"That's the captain of Jialai Yinghuo's personal guard," Cao Chunhua said. "He is one of his closest confidantes. He's a formidable man, I wouldn't mistake him."

Everyone at the table was shocked. Shen Yi frowned. "If what you say is true, then General Cai Bin's information may not be accurate. Perhaps the reported coup is a show of internal unrest for our benefit, and the hostage prince has come bearing some ill intent."

Gu Yun stayed silent. He suddenly had an ominous premonition.

Great Liang and the eighteen tribes were at war. It was obvious the hostage prince and special envoy wouldn't receive a warm reception upon arrival. Not a single person of note had come out to welcome them. The exact orders Li Feng had given to the Imperial Court of State Ceremonial were, "Do as you see fit." The Minister of State Ceremonial had grasped the emperor's intent and opted to leave the barbarian hostage prince sitting around in a relay station for Great Liang's diplomats. He had also upgraded the capital's defenses the very day they arrived. The newly reorganized Imperial Guard surrounded the relay station three layers deep, changing shifts every hour and patrolling the area twelve times a day, around the clock.

But it was also then that Chang Geng fell ill at an extremely inopportune time. He seemed to have caught a cold at Southward Tower that day and began running a fever as soon as he got home.

Chang Geng was diligent in his practice of martial arts and knew how to maintain good health; plus, he was only in his early twenties. Under normal circumstances, even gale winds wouldn't break him. But for some reason, the fever overtook him like a raging wave that day. By the time Gu Yun hurried back from the Northern Camp in the middle of the night, Chang Geng had already drunk his medicine and gone to bed, his cheeks inflamed with heat.

Gu Yun felt his forehead, then lay down beside him fully clothed. Whether Gu Yun came home or not, Chang Geng only ever took up half the bed. Even when ensnared by nightmares, he was a well-behaved sleeper and never rolled about. Afraid Chang Geng's fever would worsen in the night, Gu Yun didn't allow himself to sink into a deep sleep; he woke immediately when the person beside him moved. Reaching out, he found Chang Geng's body hot as coals, his breathing quick and shallow.

Often, Chang Geng was beset by nightmares in his sleep, and Gu Yun had long gotten used to them. Most of the time, he had only to groggily reach out to hold and soothe him, and Chang Geng would calm down on his own. But tonight, perhaps because of his illness, a pained look came over Chang Geng's face, and he instinctively grabbed Gu Yun's wrist, fingers clenching tight. A groan escaped his lips, but he wouldn't wake no matter how Gu Yun tried to rouse him. At a loss, Gu Yun pulled out a silver needle from the medicine pouch near the head of the bed, held Chang Geng down, and carefully pricked a certain spot on his wrist.

Chang Geng awoke with a violent shudder. Gu Yun sucked in a breath—*Twin pupils.*

But compared to the catastrophic confusion of his last wu'ergu attack, Chang Geng was much more restrained this time. He made no aggressive movements, and merely stared dazedly at Gu Yun, the rims of his eyes gradually going red.

On tenterhooks, Gu Yun carefully called his name. "Chang Geng, do you recognize me?"

Chang Geng blinked rapidly, beads of cold sweat dripping down his lashes. "You're...back?" he asked, his voice hoarse.

In the space of this brief exchange, the twinned pupils in his eyes slowly merged into one, and the redness faded as well. It was as if Gu Yun had hallucinated the entire episode. Gu Yun kissed him, wiped his sweat away, and coaxed him back to sleep.

Early the next morning, still worried, Gu Yun sent someone to the palace to request sick leave and went himself to fetch Chen Qingxu.

"It's nothing major," Miss Chen declared after her examination. "Your Highness is in good shape, but the weather over the past few days has been unusually changeable, and you caught a slight cold. A few doses of medicine will see you better."

"That's what I said, but he refused to believe me," Chang Geng said with a smile. "He insisted on making a big deal of it and dragging you out here."

Miss Chen never wanted to see such a pleased look on His Highness Prince Yan's face ever again—brides who had just birthed their first child were less smug than this man. When she reached the limits of her tolerance, she bid these two goodbye in her usual otherworldly manner, and Gu Yun personally saw her to the door.

As they passed through the long and lonely corridors of the Marquis Estate, Gu Yun suddenly spoke in quiet tones. "I didn't ask Miss Chen to come here to treat a cold. When his fever spiked last night, I saw twinned pupils in his eyes. I was concerned."

Chen Qingxu immediately adopted a more serious expression, a frown creasing her brow. "Please elaborate, my lord."

Gu Yun explained how Chang Geng had taken a sudden turn for

the worse before immediately regaining clarity. "What do you think is going on with him?"

She pondered, her eyes lowered, as if carefully recalling what she had just read from Chang Geng's pulse. She thought for so long that Gu Yun had grown nervous by the time she finally spoke. "His Highness has a strong will. It is truly admirable."

Gu Yun understood at once. "You mean his current lucidity is entirely due to his own self-control, and some cracks showed because he was muddled by fever last night?"

Chen Qingxu nodded. "His Highness has been tormented by the wu'ergu since he was a child. He's accustomed to it, and usually remains partially alert even while asleep. It's just that...he is young and strong now, with energy to spare. But as the years pass and his strength wanes, I worry whether he can keep it up indefinitely."

But Gu Yun was struck by a different concern. "If that's the case, then his symptoms will manifest if he's ill or injured, or accidentally consumes some drug that induces confusion?"

"That would be the logical assumption, yes. It depends on the severity of the ailment."

"But..." Gu Yun thought for a moment. "A while back, he was injured in Jiangbei. He was unconscious for a whole day and night from blood loss, but he was very calm the whole time. He never suffered a wu'ergu attack; he wasn't even woken by any nightmares."

Chen Qingxu froze in shock.

"Miss Chen?"

"Impossible," Chen Qingxu muttered. "Was it the qi and blood all along... Was I on the wrong track entirely?"

It was quite an alarming statement—but Chen Qingxu made no move to explain. As if struck by some epiphany, she turned to leave without another word.

"Hey...Miss Chen..."

"Let me think about it." With these parting words, Chen Qingxu glided off as if her feet didn't touch the ground. She was a dozen meters away in the blink of an eye and soon disappeared from sight.

Shen Yi, who happened to have come calling, was giving Huo Dan an earful about all of Gu Yun's faults—he'd started straight after walking through the gate and had been going for fifteen minutes without taking a breath. Captain Huo, meanwhile, was fretting over how to politely rid himself of this chatterbox. Yet as he was still racking his brains, Shen Yi's mouth snapped shut of its own accord.

Huo Dan looked up to see a white figure sweep across his field of vision like a fluttering ghost as General Shen turned into a towering wooden plank of a man beside him.

"Miss Chen." Shen Yi greeted her.

Chen Qingxu wasn't the talkative type and responded with a succinct greeting of her own. "General Shen."

After this exchange of salutations, the two stared awkwardly at each other for a long moment before Shen Yi realized he was blocking her way. He scrambled to the side in a panic. "After you, Miss Chen!"

Chen Qingxu had thought he'd been about to speak to her. She shot him a mystified glance, then drifted off like a flurry of snowflakes in a winter storm.

In fact, Shen Yi had come to see Gu Yun on official business.

"His Majesty has left the barbarian envoy languishing in that relay station for days now. He plans to formally receive him at the annual palace banquet as a show of strength. But the barbarians have their shamanic skills, and he's afraid some agents left behind by the barbarian women may have escaped the purges. To avoid a repeat of what the Imperial Guard attempted on the Altar of Prosperity, the guard detail in the palace will be jointly arranged by the Northern Camp, the Palace Guard, and the newly reorganized Imperial Guard so each can provide checks on the other. He's asking you to supervise the proceedings in person."

Gu Yun nodded. Li Feng was once bitten, twice shy.

This year's palace feast was magnificent to the point of decadence, an unsubtle display of Great Liang's wealth and power. Guards stood in intimidating ranks on either side of the hall, every soldier armored with a blade at their hip. Even their own people felt rather like they were walking into a Hongmen banquet, and might see some famed minister of state murdered before their eyes.[7]

It was also Gu Yun's first time seeing the barbarian third prince, rumored to be so fragile he would keel over dead at the slightest breeze. The youth was fourteen or fifteen years of age, elegant in appearance but with a wan complexion and a decidedly wooden expression. He kept his eyes glued to the ground and did nothing without prompting from his attendants, who led him forward to greet the emperor as if he lacked the ability to move on his own.

"May the emperor of Great Liang forgive us," said the special envoy. "The third prince was born with congenital deficiencies. If he violates any rules of etiquette during this banquet, I beg that Your Majesty forgive him on account of his youth and inexperience."

Li Feng waved a hand and ordered them to rise, but the young man acted as if he hadn't heard a thing—he seemed not to understand the language. The special envoy leaned down and murmured a series of coaxing words into his ear. Still wearing a vacant look

---

7   A banquet with the aim of murdering the guest. Refers to a famous episode in 206 BC when future Han emperor Liu Bang escaped an attempted murder by his rival, Xiang Yu, during a sword dance at a feast held in his honor.

of confusion, the third prince was half-supported and half-hauled upright by the special envoy and hustled back to his seat.

Gu Yun's keen ears pricked: he heard the people nearby whisper among themselves in low tones, "Is this third prince an idiot?"

What did Jialai Yinghuo mean by sending an idiot son to the capital as a hostage?

Gu Yun locked eyes with Shen Yi, who was standing not too far away, their expressions identically grim. Perhaps he was overthinking things. Still, Gu Yun sensed something ominous about that young man.

As Li Feng's bureaucratic exchange with the barbarians neared its end, the barbarian envoy made a seemingly innocuous remark. "Before I departed my homeland, I heard that the emperor of Great Liang has under his command two subjects one simply must meet. One is the great hero Marquis Gu who's never lost a battle, and whose acquaintance I've already had the great fortune to make today. But the other...seems not to be in attendance?"

"Of whom do you speak, Envoy?" Li Feng asked.

"The young man who heads your Six Ministries," the barbarian envoy said with a smile. "His Highness Prince Yan. He has quite the connection to my tribe as well."

Gu Yun's eyelid twitched.

Li Feng swept his gaze around the room to find that Chang Geng was indeed absent. "Where is A-Min?"

103

ENCOUNTER

A S THE REVELRIES at the palace were reaching their peak, Chang Geng was in Miss Chen's temporary residence in the capital, helping her pick herbs.

His cold had come quickly and gone just as fast. After a couple doses of medicine, he was well on the way to a full recovery. Even so, Gu Yun had advised him to avoid the banquet. First, on account of the sensitive matter of his parentage, and second, because of Chen Qingxu's new lead on the wu'ergu. Thus he had begged off sick to meet the doctor instead.

"You mean to say the wu'ergu flows within my blood?"

Chen Qingxu's hands were occupied flipping through a whole spread of yellowing books, pausing here and there to snatch the fragile pages that fluttered loose before they fell. Her hands were a flurry of movement, but her words were as measured as ever. "Wu'ergu acts on the mind, so I always thought this poison would be rooted in the brain. If not for the marquis's remark, I would never have considered this angle. See here—the earliest records the barbarians have of the wicked god Wu'ergu say this: 'Treacherous at birth; he consumed the flesh and blood of his brother to fuel his own growth. He had four legs, four arms, two heads, and two hearts. Oceans of blood flowed within his chest, and he was brutal to the extreme.' I'd always thought 'oceans of blood' was only a metaphor, but it's actually a clue to the mechanism behind wu'ergu attacks."

Only when Chen Qingxu spoke on this kind of topic could she spill so many words in one go.

"Flesh and blood." Chang Geng fell silent a moment, then shook his head with a wry laugh. "Miss Chen means to say my entire body is suffused with poison, and the only recourse is to scrape my flesh clean from my bones like the heroes of legend?" The prospect somehow seemed even worse than having something wrong with his head.

Chang Geng sorted the herbs into their different types and placed them into containers one by one. The medicine rack's gears clicked against each other as the filled compartments slowly ascended, revealing new empty compartments underneath. This was precision work that took a patient and steady hand.

Chen Qingxu looked at him with no small admiration. In recorded history, no one afflicted with wu'ergu had made it to adulthood with a clear mind, much less maintained such a tranquil temperament. Was it because he was naturally strong-willed, or because he had a Gu Yun while others did not?

"I won't lie to you," Chang Geng said. "I've been feeling unwell lately. The wu'ergu has been acting up more and more frequently."

"The marquis told me," Chen Qingxu said without thinking.

"He…" Chang Geng blinked in surprise.

Gu Yun had always treated the wu'ergu as merely a strange barbarian poison, and never seemed to take Chang Geng's "little problem" seriously. He rarely spoke of it, and never showed any concern in front of Chang Geng.

So he…was actually worrying about it all this time?

Chen Qingxu paused, realizing she had said too much. She tried a casual change of topic. "Your Highness, if you have no other instructions, I plan to make a trip back to the Chen family residence in Shanxi soon. Treatment will be much easier now that we've discovered the root cause. We're sure to find a solution."

Chang Geng hummed in acknowledgment and cupped his hands in a bow. "Thank you for your trouble. But about the cure for Zixi..."

Before he could finish, they were interrupted by a messenger from the palace.

A young medical apprentice led in the palace attendant, who made a polite bow to Chang Geng. "Your Highness, His Majesty heard you were ill and ordered this servant to pay you a visit. He also sent an imperial physician, but the imperial physician felt it improper to set foot inside Miracle Doctor Chen's courtyard. He is waiting outside."

Chang Geng frowned. "My thanks to my brother for his attentions. It was but a cold, not any major ailment."

"Yes, this servant can see Your Highness is in fine spirits," the attendant said with a smile. He hesitated for a moment before continuing, "Your Highness, a banquet is being held in the palace this evening to welcome the barbarian third prince and the diplomatic delegation. The special envoy from the eighteen tribes specifically mentioned Your Highness to His Majesty, and His Majesty ordered this servant to convey a verbal decree: if you are feeling unwell, you needn't put yourself to any trouble. But if you are able, come out for some fresh air."

Startled, Chen Qingxu shot Chang Geng a glance—it would have been one thing if no one commented on his absence. But given that the barbarian envoy had mentioned him by name, it wouldn't do for Chang Geng to refuse him outright. There was a layer of awkwardness here: the northern barbarians were Great Liang's enemy, but they were also His Highness Prince Yan's maternal family.

He obviously shouldn't associate with them too willingly, yet it was also improper for him to intentionally avoid them. It was a delicate balance.

The envoy had asked after him, but the key factor in Chang Geng's decision would be Li Feng's attitude. If there was one thing he could use as an excuse to keep to the shadows, it was this.

Chang Geng good-naturedly produced a pouch from his lapels and handed it to the attendant. "If it isn't too much trouble, what did my brother say?"

The attendant hefted the weight of Prince Yan's gratitude in his hand and smiled until his round face went completely red. He sputtered out a string of courtesies. "Oh I could never, I could never... ah, Your Highness, you overwhelm this servant with your generosity, this... It's more than I deserve..."

Whether he deserved it or not, he happily tucked the cash away and finally got to the point. "Your Highness is a man of considerable status; you needn't show those bloodthirsty barbarians any particular respect. His Majesty said if Your Highness is willing to make a social call, you should visit the palace to make your New Year's greetings; you oughtn't stay cooped up in your home. You can leave after sitting down a few minutes, no need to dance attendance on those insignificant others. His Majesty would be gratified to see you, especially as it's so close to the end of the year."

Chang Geng understood. "Allow me to freshen up and change. I'll come to the palace at once."

"In that case, this servant will go and prepare your carriage," the attendant cheerfully agreed.

A faint smile remained on Chang Geng's face as he watched him leave, but his expression cooled as soon as he turned back into Miss Chen's workroom.

Chen Qingxu followed him inside. "Can I help?"

Chang Geng shook his head. "Security's tight at the palace banquet this year, and Zixi is there too. Everyone who enters or exits has to pass several rounds of inspections. Aside from the third prince and the special envoy, all the rest of the barbarian entourage has been detained at the relay station. Even if that barbarian third prince is packed full with violet gold beneath his skin, he can't make much of an explosion—I only need you to lend me a room to freshen up."

Chen Qingxu didn't make a habit of meddling in politics, so she didn't insert herself further. She instructed the apprentice to lead Chang Geng to a spare room. He walked to the doorway, hands tucked behind his back, before suddenly pausing and turning around. "Miss Chen, would you happen to have a silver knife?"

Wang Guo sat among the civil officials, listening to a group of Great Liang's silver-tongued civil servants vent their national enmity and personal grudges upon that barbarian envoy in a litany of criticism. The envoy's tongue wasn't quite so silver, but he managed to keep up with the flow. Whenever the conversation got a bit too heated and he was unable to respond, he would simply smile. It rather sold the story that he was indeed here to endure humiliation in order to ensure the success of their suit for peace.

Imperial Uncle Wang's gaze lingered on the third prince, who was still silent, his head bowed. But his attention was quickly diverted—he had no interest in that idiot. He had planned a much better show.

Wang Guo wasn't like Fang Qin and his influential allies, who always kept the livelihood of the nation and its people hanging on their lips. He was well aware of his state of disgrace; he knew everyone looked down on him. Even Minister Fang and his people only addressed him with respect when they needed him; behind his back, they called him the "eunuch imperial uncle" just like the rest. They all whispered that he was so devoted to his responsibilities as imperial uncle that he'd even taken over the job of head eunuch managing general palace affairs.

Wang Guo had used to be a minor figure who ran errands for the late emperor. He was destined to be an obsequious subject, a scapegoat for the throne. Since the situation between the late emperor and the barbarian consort erupted, he had lived every day in terror. It wasn't that he had anything against Gu Yun or the Gu family. There were no benefits to be gained for him there, as Great Liang's civil and military officials had few dealings. As long as neither side's ambitions exploded to the point of wanting to take full control of the court, they would never compete over shares of the same pot no matter how they strove for power. Not to mention, if one were to compare Wang Guo and Gu Yun's families, the Gu family was the true noble clan. It was only that they were not blessed with many children and happened to be in a rather unique spot in terms of marriage alliances.

Wang Guo had even fewer disputes with Gu Yun when it came to personal opinion—he had few thoughts on consequential matters of state, and his only insights were on how to make the emperor happy. The court was full of accomplished civil and military bigwigs with their own ideas and agendas. There had to be a few people with whom the emperor could relax after the time he spent testing his intellect and courage in the political arena, hadn't there? If possible, he'd have never raised a hand against the Gu family even if he was out of his mind with boredom.

But fate was impossible to scry, and an ordained ruler's orders impossible to disobey. The old emperor was dead and gone, out like a candle's flame—yet he had clung to the very end to his misguided beliefs that if a ruler ordered his subject's death, the subject must bare his neck for the blade. Wang Guo was left behind as the scapegoat and target of everyone's disdain.

Right now, the Longan Emperor was still willing to protect this useless trash heap of an uncle out of nostalgia. He would allow Wang Guo to struggle forward on his last legs and beg a mouthful of sustenance to fill his meager bowl.

But what of the future?

Wang Guo had nothing to fear from any farm tax or civilian commerce decree Prince Yan proposed. What he feared was what Prince Yan would do with him if he took the throne. Prince Yan had been close to Gu Yun since youth, but he was also the son of the late emperor and the barbarian consort. A child couldn't prosecute their parents' crimes. But when the time came, the first move Prince Yan would undoubtedly make to curry Gu Yun's favor and gain the military's support would be to sacrifice the unfortunate Wang Guo to the Gu family's ancestors.

Minister Fang and his ilk worried about Prince Yan shuffling the cards of the court, but what did that amount to? They risked only their salary, status, good name, and the prospects of their family. Imperial Uncle Wang's very life hung in the balance; he worried constantly about the head sitting atop his neck. High status and a generous salary were no good to him if he were dead.

The barbarians had been on their best behavior since their arrival in the capital. They hadn't naively attempted to toss bribes around. Besides, the capital was filled with princes, dukes, and nobles; no one was poor and short-sighted enough to risk committing treason for such a measly profit. The special envoy from the eighteen tribes sent out only one tentative feeler once the palace banquet was almost upon them—and the one he contacted was precisely Imperial Uncle Wang, this man who seemed nothing more than an insignificant sycophant.

The special envoy swore upon the Eternal Sky and made two promises to Wang Guo: one, that Prince Yan would never again be the sword hanging over his head, and two, that whether their efforts succeeded or failed, they would never reveal Wang Guo's part in the plot. If, in the future, Wang Guo should ever find himself in mortal danger, the eighteen tribes were willing to save his life.

The unruly mob that was the eighteen tribes was uncivilized, cruel, bloodthirsty, and far too fond of playing with poisons, but there was one good thing about them: they took their oaths seriously. And what they asked of Wang Guo was as easy as a lift of the hand. Prince Yan was likely to keep clear of the banquet to evade suspicion. Imperial Uncle Wang was to ensure he would make his appearance.

The barbarians hadn't explained what they planned to do. Wang Guo intended to quietly watch events unfold—but in case they failed, he had a backup plan prepared. He had to hand it to Minister Fang for making it all possible. In order to unseat Prince Yan, Fang Qin had been secretly sheltering a certain man in a courtyard belonging to the Fang family. Years ago, when the barbarian consort fled the capital, a large group of palace servants, guards, and imperial physicians had been implicated in the case. Many of them were wrongfully put to death, while the true culprits had planned their escape routes ahead of time. The old imperial physician in the Fang family's courtyard was one such person. He had fled in guilt.

Years later, however, his son had accidentally killed a man. To pay the blood debts of the younger generation, he was forced to sell a secret: back when the barbarian consort had fled carrying her un-born child, Commandery Princess Xiu, who had fled along with her, had also been pregnant out of wedlock.

Xiu-niang, also known as Huge'er, had colluded with the barbar-ians in their invasion of Yanhui Town. She hated Great Liang to the bone. Had she really been content to raise the son of her enemy? Was the boy Gu Yun brought back from Yanhui Town really the late emperor's son—or was he Huge'er's bastard by an unknown father?

Fang Qin had taken that imperial physician in but done nothing rash. He had learned his lesson from the last time he failed to defeat Prince Yan. This time, he planned to strike true on the first attack. He was slowly brewing a plan in the shadows. But Wang Guo had no intention of waiting for him any longer. Lords and ministers had their ways, but petty villains had their own paths to walk. He didn't need to take the high ground, and it didn't matter how low he struck as long as it drew blood.

When the envoy asked to meet Prince Yan, Li Feng hadn't replied right away. Upon finding that Prince Yan was ill, he ordered an attendant to run an errand and check on him in his stead. Li Feng's exact words were "Bring an imperial physician to check on A-Min and tell him to get some rest. If he's feeling better in a few days, he oughtn't stay cooped up in his home; he can visit the palace to pay us New Year's greetings. No need to dance attendance on insignificant others."

With that, the Longan Emperor had fulfilled his obligation to appear at the palace banquet and took his leave.

But Imperial Uncle Wang wasn't the "eunuch imperial uncle" for nothing. He had bribed a whole crew of seemingly unimportant errand-runners. As long as the messenger skillfully distorted Li Feng's words just a touch, Prince Yan would come without a doubt.

And when he did...there would be Prince Yan, running to the palace immediately after the emperor had left the scene to greet the barbarian delegation despite his illness. How would he turn the tide after his muddy origins and attempts to soil the imperial bloodline were exposed before the eyes of all?

Li Feng's departure marked the peaceful passing of the majority of the palace banquet. Seeing the end in sight, Gu Yun let out a breath of relief and picked up his cup of wine to moisten his lips. But he had hardly registered the taste of the alcohol when a palace attendant entered to report Prince Yan's arrival.

Gu Yun's heart thudded in his chest as he reeled at this sudden twist.

Fang Qin looked mildly surprised. Wang Guo lowered his head. The envoy turned toward the door to the hall with a faint smile on his face, but the barbarian third prince, who had been quietly tucking into his meal in the corner, suddenly froze where he sat.

Chang Geng noticed the throne was empty the moment he stepped into the grand hall. He knew at once he had walked into a trap, but it was too late to turn back now. Chang Geng's gait didn't stall, and his face remained serene despite its mild pallor. His usual gentle and elegant smile played on his lips as he strolled inside, removing his cloak as he went. Using the movement of turning to hand it to a servant, he swept his gaze around the room—the attendant who had lured him here had already disappeared.

A noble sitting nearby, though uncertain why Prince Yan had appeared, seized the opportunity to cast the first stone. "Your Highness Prince Yan, didn't you excuse yourself from today's palace banquet?" he asked with an unkind chuckle. "It seems the words of our guests from the eighteen tribes are weighty indeed. They've summoned Prince Yan from his sickbed with a single word."

Another picked up where he left off. "You ought to penalize your-self with a drink for that. Perhaps you could find fault were it anyone else, but we're graced with no ordinary guests today. The eighteen tribes are His Highness's maternal family; of course they ought to receive special treatment."

The sleeves of his wide court robes trailing nearly to the ground, Chang Geng calmly parried. "His Majesty went to the effort of sending someone to ask after me, so I've come to the palace specifically to give His Majesty my New Year's greetings. But it seems I've come at a bad time. Has His Majesty already left?"

"His Highness Prince Yan has come at a bad time, but we came at just the right one. It is our fortune of three lifetimes to be able to meet the twin jades of Great Liang's court today. Our prince would like to offer His Highness a toast!"

The envoy from the eighteen tribes stood, dragging the third prince up by the arm.

Gu Yun shot Shen Yi a look. Several guards hidden within the shadowed corners of the great hall suddenly revealed their killing intent, locking onto the envoy and the third prince. The third prince stepped out from amid the banquet seats. He seemed extremely ner-vous, his hand trembling so much around his winecup that he spilled half the contents before he got anywhere close to Chang Geng.

As the youth approached, a wave of restless heat rose in Chang Geng's body. The fever that had broken last night came back with a raging fury and his ears roared, all the blood in his body roiling like burning violet gold.

Every hair stood on end. All the countless pairs of eyes in the hall, alight with schemes or malicious glee, presented less pressure than a look from this slight young man. Chang Geng exhausted nearly all his strength to suppress his extreme discomfort and maintain the dignified bearing befitting a prince of the first rank as he forced his lips to smile. "Do the princes of your tribe always present toasts without saying a word?"

The northern barbarian envoy began to chuckle. He retreated a slow step behind the third prince. All of a sudden, a calm came over the trembling young man. His pallid hands, frozen in midair, seemed to give off a corpselike glow. He lifted his chin and met Chang Geng's gaze. Bloodshot eyes bored into Chang Geng like a stake of ice, revealing a pair of glacial twinned pupils.

The young man was a wu'ergu!

No one knew what would happen when two such "wicked gods" faced off. There was no record of such an event—how lunatic a thing was the wu'ergu? How vast a hatred, how great a convergence of fortune was required to create even one such creature? How turbulent did an age have to be to allow two wu'ergu to come face-to-face?

The two seemed to share some indescribable connection. In a split second, the vastness of the great hall scattered like ash before Chang Geng's eyes and pain erupted in his chest, as if in the next moment he would combust.

Delusion and reality swirled into a mess before him, and the terrible poison he had kept suppressed within his blood and bones for years exploded outward like hot oil tossed over a raging blaze... All the irreconcilable hatred and fury in Chang Geng welled up in his heart; every nightmare squirming in the depths of the abyss poured from its lair, gaping maws open wide to swallow him whole.

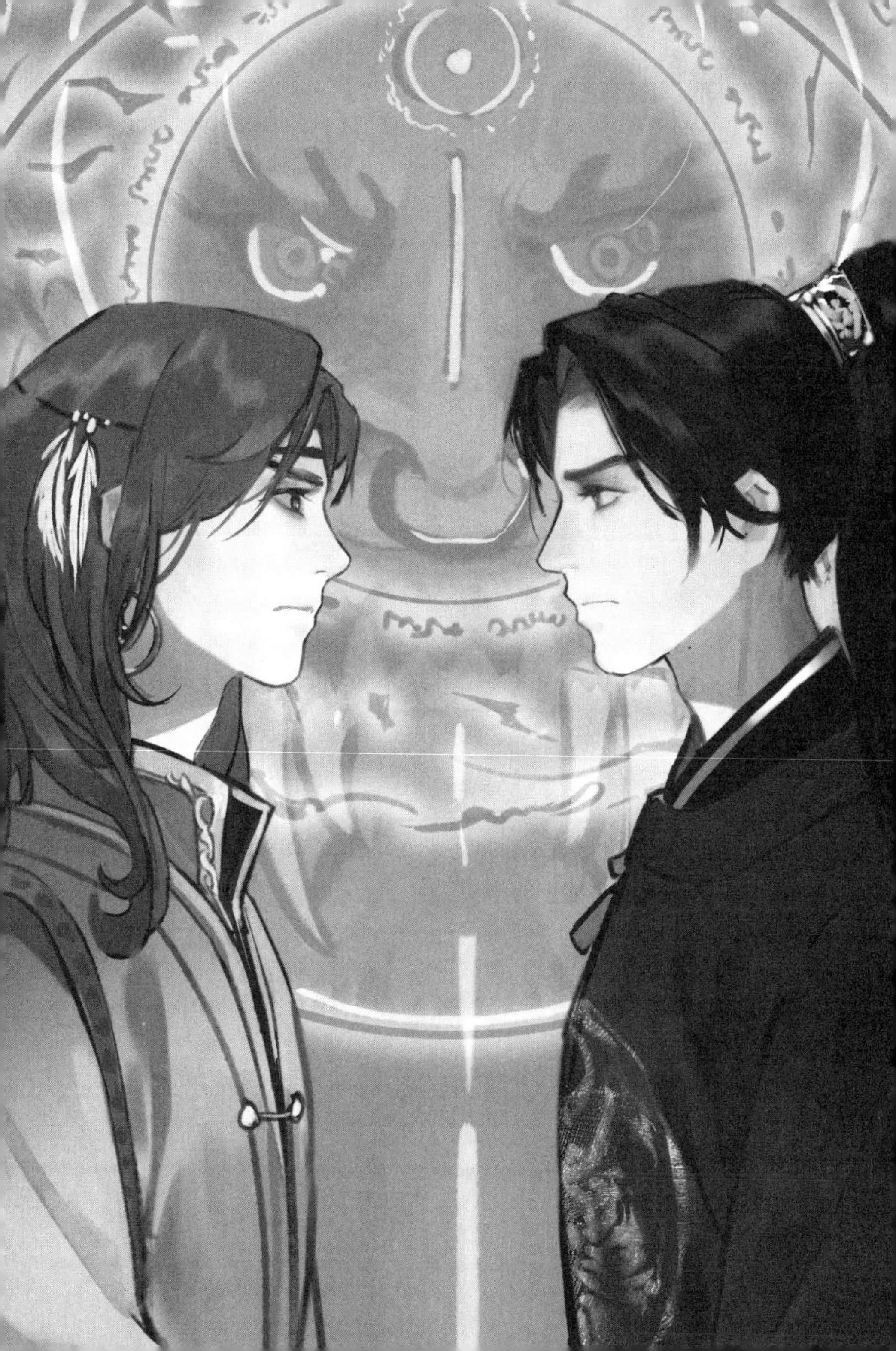

104

INCITING WAR

THE BARBARIAN envoy's smile contorted in Chang Geng's
eyes, mysterious and sinister as the expression Huge'er wore
as she filled his ears with her malevolent curse on the brink
of death. It was the poisonous resentment of the eighteen tribes,
built up like silt over thousands of years striving against heaven and
earth, striving against fellow humans in a desperate fight for survival.
Chang Geng's field of view narrowed in on the silver cup in the third
prince's hands. He felt as if he had been locked in a set of manacles
weighing a thousand kilograms, yet to the eyes of a casual observer,
he seemed merely to pause a moment before he spoke.

Chang Geng lifted one hand under the crowd's watchful gaze.
Although his lips were nearly devoid of color, he was elegant and
composed as ever as he accepted a cup of wine from a nearby palace
attendant.

Anyone with eyes could see that Prince Yan had just recovered
from illness. His hand was as pale and bloodless as his cheeks, and
his fingers shook around the cup. He dropped his gaze and lightly
tapped his cup against the one the third prince held. "Your Highness,
please do as you will. I've been taking medicine and cannot tolerate
wine, so I'm afraid I can't drink this toast," he said coolly. "We can
have a proper drink together when the eighteen tribes deliver this
year's tribute."

The third prince stared at Chang Geng through those twinned pupils. Chang Geng touched the wine to his lips, then tossed the silver cup aside and strode past the barbarian envoy without a sideways glance. To everyone else, it appeared His Highness Prince Yan was simply taking a cold attitude with an enemy diplomat. But Gu Yun could see the aggressive discomfort he was repressing from the ghostly pallor of his face.

There was indeed something amiss with that third prince. Gu Yun's heart sank, and he shot Shen Yi a look. Understanding the unspoken command, Shen Yi slipped quietly from the great hall. Gu Yun pushed aside everyone in his way and walked toward Chang Geng. "Your Highness, please come inside to rest," he called out.

He was still a few steps away when his sensitive nose caught the faint scent of blood. Remembering Miss Chen's vague remark about "qi and blood," he was immediately unsettled.

At the same time, the barbarian envoy was stepping forward. As if he had entirely failed to read the atmosphere, he said, "Thinking back to how the goddess of our tribe perished in a foreign land, I never imagined I would meet the heir to her bloodline one day. Surely this is a blessing imparted to us by the Endless Sky."

"Prince Yan is a rightful member of our Great Liang's imperial house," Xu Ling coolly retorted. "Envoy, your remark is inappropriate."

The barbarian envoy stared into Chang Geng's eyes, as if searching for something in their depths. The longer he looked, the more shocked he grew. A wu'ergu was difficult to refine for several reasons. Not only must its maker have the resolve to resort to such cruel extremes, it also required exactly the right combination of time, place, and person. The host must possess a tenacious temperament in order to give the bloodline of the wicked god sufficient time to ripen. If they lost control too early, their mind would remain immature, their cognitive development never progressing beyond that of an idiot child.

The third prince was an example of such a failure. This innocent child had been born with a twin brother, the lives of both boys forfeited to their father's hatred. The child's mind had failed to withstand his first wu'ergu attack; he was already ruined. His only remaining use was as a "sacrifice" to another wicked god. By comparison, this Prince Yan standing before them was a specimen of the highest quality. He had maintained clarity of mind this whole time and upheld his veneer of calm even when face to face with the sacrifice. How indomitable was his will to accomplish this?

The wicked god Wu'ergu was born through an act of devouring. When one wu'ergu approached another weaker, incomplete specimen, the stronger's base instincts would be triggered; they would lose their senses. This was why the failed wu'ergu was called a sacrifice. If a person with the right knowledge was there to provide ample guidance and take control of the stronger's mind when they lost themselves, with the aid of some medicine, the puppet master could compel the wicked god to obey their every command until the wu'ergu broke down entirely.

Xiu-niang herself probably never imagined the wicked god she gave up on halfway through would be this strong. Unfortunately, this creature had been whisked away by the unknowing Central Plains people. Not only had it failed to reach its true potential, it had become a keen blade turned back on the eighteen tribes themselves.

"My king once met Your Highness in the little town of Yanhui. Back then, he still thought you were Huge'er's child born of her violation. He was extremely rude to Your Highness then. He ordered this subject to deliver his apologies in the course of these peace talks." The corner of the barbarian envoy's lips curled up as he seamlessly wove the words that would trigger the wu'ergu into his speech. "Your Highness, has Huge'er ever said anything to you about the eighteen tribes?"

The words "Huge'er...said" surfaced from the nonsense small talk, whipping up a tempest within Chang Geng's mind with no one the wiser. The image of this sturdy barbarian envoy overlapped with the mysterious and beautiful Huge'er, and the curse that woman wailed with her last breath erupted like a peal of thunder in his ears. An unidentifiable scent emanated from the third prince's body and poured into his lungs—slightly metallic and slightly bitter, it yanked on Chang Geng's nerves with its full might to summon the bloodthirsty urges within him.

The door flew open on memories he had sealed away, drowning him in a crashing torrent of fragmented recollections.

Huge'er's nightmarishly beautiful face, the corpses strewn about the bandits' mountain, the great fire that formed his first memory, the inescapable stench of blood, endless curses and beatings... every old scar beneath his beautiful court robes came alive with a vengeance, diving into his flesh like bloodsucking leeches. As if his mortal frame was unable to bear the vast power of the wicked god, Chang Geng's chest, limbs—his very bones—felt lacerated by blades. It was the pain that signified an oncoming wu'ergu attack.

Even worse, these words from the barbarian envoy, which had such a monstrous effect, were perfectly calculated to make their victim appear to be overreacting to a perfectly innocuous remark.

Wang Guo immediately joined the pile on. "Envoy, is it entirely appropriate to bring up Princess Xiu, Huge'er, on this august occasion? While Princess Xiu did a meritorious deed in raising His Highness Prince Yan, she was also guilty of exacerbating the hostilities between our nations to the point of nearly inciting a war nine years ago...not to mention, I've heard that Princess Xiu was quite the troublemaker. She plotted against the Black Iron Battalion, then convinced the noble consort to flee with her when her plans failed. From what I heard, she even got herself mixed up with some unknown man. Did you never hear the rumor that came out from the Imperial Academy of Medicine? They say Princess Xiu was pregnant out of wedlock. A woman like this does not deserve the title of commandery princess of our court, nor the goddess of your tribe."

Even the densest listener could discern the veiled meaning within these words. At the sight of Wang Guo so boldly brandishing his hidden blades against Prince Yan himself, all those who had been chiming in with their agreements turned mute, waiting for the next development in bewilderment.

When they turned back to Prince Yan, they saw that, whether out of discomfort from his illness or something else, beads of sweat were rolling down his forehead. He seemed to be struggling to stand.

Fang Qin's brow creased in a frown. He saw the bigger problem at once: Wang Guo and the barbarians had allied at some point without his noticing!

He could spare no time delighting in Prince Yan's plight. He was on the verge of a breakdown. Internal strife was one thing; it was expected that people would jockey for position within the court. Whether any winner emerged to ink their name in the history books or whether it was naught but an endless struggle with no victors, it was all domestic affairs. But what was Wang Guo thinking bringing these foreign tribes into it while their borders were yet unrecovered, and a great swath of the country still lay in enemy hands? If he were to be exposed—no, he didn't even need to be exposed. If Wang Guo managed to successfully insinuate that Prince Yan had muddied the imperial bloodline, what would the rest think once they recovered from their shock? No one would believe the Fang family innocent. Fang Qin's faction was publicly aligned with Wang Guo, and the guilty old imperial physician who had spilled the secret was even now living in the Fang family's courtyard. He would never wash his hands of this.

Fang Qin was drenched in cold sweat. Wang Guo had not only used him; at this rate, he was going to have him strung up as a traitor to the nation!

Minister Fang didn't think he lagged behind anyone in talent or cunning. But just look at Prince Yan—the young man had a right hand in Jiang Chong, an ally righteous in speech and action in Xu Ling, over half the Lingshu Institute in his pocket, and commanded the loyalty of the Northern Camp with whom he had once fought shoulder to shoulder. He even had close ties to the Marquis of Order, the commander in chief of the Southwest Army, and other military top brass.

And Fang Qin? He was surrounded by the Lü faction, Wang Guo, and their ilk, venomous serpents and petty miscreants, people whose failures well outnumbered their accomplishments.

For a moment, an ice-cold fatigue flooded Fang Qin's heart. He experienced the full weight of that thing called "fate," unerring as the tide. Was it truly impossible to resist by human will alone?

Listening to Wang Guo's attempts to stir the pot, the barbarian envoy sneered disdainfully. He watched as Prince Yan's pupils dilated. It wouldn't be long before they split entirely, and Prince Yan sank into hallucinations. At that point, he would become deaf to the outside world save for certain key words and spells—he would transform from a man of mortal flesh and blood into a true wicked god.

The barbarian envoy reached out as if to offer Chang Geng a supporting hand. "Your Highness, are you not feeling—"

Before he could say *well*, a voice exploded furiously from nearby, "Insolence!"

The envoy's pupils contracted. A stiff breeze whistled past his ear, its cold, deadly aura seeping into his pores. Every hair on his body stood on end, and before he could react, he felt a chill at his neck and found a steel blade pressed against it. Before the astonished eyes of the court, Gu Yun held a sword he had drawn from a guard's waist in one hand and pulled Prince Yan into his embrace with the other. Chang Geng leaned into him with a muted groan as if he had lost the strength to stand. Yet the twinned pupils the barbarian envoy watched for did not appear. Chang Geng was clearly still lucid. He followed Gu Yun's lead and struck back at the envoy in a wisp of a voice. "The barbarians'...shamanic poisons..."

Xu Ling cried out in alarm. "Your Highness, what have they done to you?!"

Blood dripped down the sleeve of Chang Geng's court robes. The cloth was swiftly soaked with red.

Every guard in the hall drew their weapons.

Wang Guo was unprepared for this development. But after a moment of shock, he pressed on, refusing to let his efforts go to waste. "Marshal, you... If you have something to say, speak civilly. There's no need for violence... What has happened to His Highness? Summon the imperial physicians. Where are the imperial physicians?"

Gu Yun's head whipped around. He said not a word, but a killing intent as keen as a black-iron windslasher fixed on Imperial Uncle Wang. Wang Guo's legs immediately went soft, and he collapsed onto his rear with a cry of shock.

As soon as Wang Guo uttered the words *imperial physician*, the corner of Fang Qin's eye twitched violently. He couldn't sit by any longer—if he was to draw a line between himself and

Wang Guo, it was now or never. He had to find a way to push the blame onto that sniveling rat bastard; otherwise, he could resign himself to infamy for the rest of history.

Fang Qin whispered furious orders to his attendant, instructing him to silence that guilty old imperial physician as soon as humanly possible. Then he calmly stepped forward. "How audacious these barbarians are, to act so brazenly in full view of the imperial court. They clearly mean us ill. Detain them!"

Unfortunately, aside from a few palace guards, the soldiers on duty were all members of the Imperial Guard or the Northern Camp. These men would never defer to a civil official like him. They stood still as stone, waiting for Gu Yun's order.

Fang Qin choked—but now wasn't the time to be scrambling after his own dignity. He gathered himself and turned his flattery on full bore. "Marshal Gu, there's something very queer about all this. The palace attendants ought to have known His Majesty left the banquet; why would they ask Prince Yan to come to the palace tonight? And if they did, they ought to have brought His Highness to see His Majesty directly, not to the banquet. I propose we detain these criminals for interrogation, then report to His Majesty. We must carefully investigate the exact course of events this evening; perhaps barbarian spies are involved... Uhh, why don't you first take Prince Yan to rest and summon the imperial physicians..."

Gu Yun coldly interrupted his guilty rambling. "Please don't put yourself to the trouble."

Never had Fang Qin encountered such a stubborn mule since the day he'd left his mother's womb. He forgot his lines.

A guard in the uniform of the Northern Camp ran inside. "Sir, we've surrounded the relay station and detained all members of the barbarian diplomatic delegation."

Fang Qin stared in shock. Did Gu Yun intend to start a war?

"Report this incident to His Majesty at once." Gu Yun gave his orders with swift efficiency. "The imperial physicians have no understanding of these dirty barbarians' tricks. Summon Miracle Doctor Chen to the palace."

Now that Gu Yun had taken charge, the situation would be handled in a brisk and orderly fashion even if the sky fell on their heads. Both Chen Qingxu and the Longan Emperor were notified of the incident straight away and hurried to the scene. Li Feng hastened over to examine Chang Geng as Fang Qin stepped forward without any prompting from Gu Yun to relate the night's events and his own suspicions.

The Longan Emperor was furious. He commanded every single servant and palace attendant be detained. Chen Qingxu he allowed inside to attend to Prince Yan, while her apprentice stayed behind to help identify the suspect.

The servants faced interrogation outside, but Gu Yun, disinclined to watch them lash out at each other, remained by Chang Geng's side. His hand was slick with blood; even the wooden beads the late emperor had given him were dyed scarlet. His complexion looked terrible, even worse than the injured party.

"It's all right, this wound is self-inflicted." Chang Geng looked at him and said, "I had it well in hand..."

"Like hell you did!" Gu Yun bit out. "You really had to come here and see what the barbarians looked like for yourself? I seriously..."

Chen Qingxu spoke quietly as she prepared salt water for Chang Geng. "Marshal Gu, please calm yourself. The body of a wu'ergu is unlike ordinary people; a minor injury won't do him much harm. Your Highness, what did you encounter that forced you to bleed yourself?"

Chang Geng let his lashes flutter closed. When he opened them again, his eyes were even clearer than usual. If not for the fact that Gu Yun had yet to wash this man's blood from his hands, he would have suspected Chang Geng faked everything.

Wary of listeners, Chang Geng answered in sign language. "They tricked me into the palace. I had thought, even if the eighteen tribes came with hostile intent, it would be foolish of them to play any tricks. Regardless of whether they're sincere about negotiating peace or simply stalling for time, our entire army is on high alert. I never expected the barbarian envoy to be so bold as to act against me in the open... Not to mention, given Fang Qin's cautious nature, I reasoned he probably wouldn't risk anything truly treasonous."

"Probably?" Gu Yun snapped.

Eager to deflect Gu Yun's rage, Chen Qingxu pressed Chang Geng. "Your Highness, could you explain in more detail?"

Chang Geng cast Gu Yun a cautious glance, then briefly described the third prince's abnormalities and the strange scent he remembered. Chen Qingxu managed to staunch the bleeding while still sparing an eye to follow his hands. Slowly, a frown creased her brow.

"It wasn't necessarily Fang Qin who lured me here." Chang Geng offered his analysis of the situation. "He's not stupid enough to let the barbarians use him, and his eagerness to jump in may have been an attempt to clear himself of suspicion... But on reflection, the envoy from the eighteen tribes merits further investigation."

Just looking at Chang Geng upset Gu Yun right now. He turned to face the window instead, putting him out of his sight. One of his hands unwittingly hovered at the hilt of the sword sheathed at his waist, and the vicious gloom lingering about him had yet to disperse. He had come to similar conclusions even before

Chang Geng's explanation. The one who bribed the palace attendant was more likely than not Wang Guo, who had been so impatiently champing at the bit just now. Gu Yun had always considered
Wang Guo and his kind to be mangy dogs following shamelessly
at the late emperor's heels. He had never felt the need to stoop to
their level and confront them. But now, it seemed his restraint had
given certain imperial uncles the false impression he had a good
temper!

Chang Geng squeezed the back of Gu Yun's hand with an
ice-cold paw, the picture of an aggrieved and pathetic patient. "Zixi,
I feel terrible. Look at me."

Now it was Chen Qingxu pretending she could ignore the things
happening right in front of her if she simply averted her eyes.

Gu Yun's heart hurt so much his chest was stuffy with it, but he
had no outlet for this feeling. He wished for nothing more than to
don his armor and leave the capital this very instant to pluck off
Jialai Yinghuo's head. It was a long, silent moment before he suppressed his rage sufficiently to continue the conversation. "Perhaps
they wanted to assassinate His Majesty at first, but found the capital's defenses were tighter than they imagined and made you their
target instead. Or else they were here specifically for the wu'ergu.
The barbarians must have a way of controlling the curse. During a
wu'ergu attack, the host has immense strength, surpassing the lim-
itations of the human body. The guards in the great hall would be
afraid to hurt you. If the barbarians used you as a shield, the guards
may not have been able to stop them. I can think of only one reason
they would have gone to such trouble: this diplomatic delegation is
here not to broker peace, but to incite a war."

"If Jialai Yinghuo wants a war, he could mobilize his army. Why
go to such convoluted lengths to start one?" Chang Geng countered.

"But perhaps General Cai's intelligence isn't entirely without merit. There must be something going on within the eighteen tribes—"

"Forget the eighteen tribes for now," Gu Yun interrupted him. "You heard what Wang Guo said in the great hall. He's getting desperate; we don't know what he'll try next. Why don't you focus on meeting his attacks first?"

105

CASTING ASIDE THE BOW

CHANG GENG was silent a while, eyes dim as he mindlessly rubbed at the prominent joints of Gu Yun's fingers. Finally, he sighed. "There's nothing I can do. No one can testify to the circumstances of his own birth."

Besides, the truth was he had never fully accepted his own identity as royalty, even after he became Prince Yan and stood near the pinnacle of power. Chang Geng felt like he could hold up the skies—but he couldn't say for sure who his parents were. On top of that, he had Gu Yun now. He wasn't particularly eager to chase after his exact origins.

Unfortunately, his lack of interest didn't mean others felt the same.

Chen Qingxu stopped the bleeding and bandaged Chang Geng's wound with great efficiency, then wrote him a prescription to pacify the spirit and calm the heart. She didn't insert herself into the conversation nor let any emotion show on her face, but an unspeakable sorrow and fury welled up in her heart.

Chen Qingxu had opposed giving the Linyuan tablet to Prince Yan because of the wu'ergu. Her single vote against him had no effect on the final outcome, so she could do nothing but watch over Chang Geng all this time, taking note of his every action to the extent of her abilities. Since they had begun rebuilding the battered capital,

Prince Yan had reassembled the mangled court bit by bit. He had rushed all over the nation, infiltrated deep into a rebel faction and nearly perished in the process, and questioned lines of profit no one else dared touch. His actions made him the target of open condemnation and whispered ire from every corner of the court.

These unmatched accomplishments ought to have secured his place in history for a thousand years—could they really be erased by a few questions about his origins? If he really wasn't the late emperor's son, did the war beacon tickets, the Canal Commission, and even the hundred thousand refugees happily settled and hard at work in Jiangbei count for nothing?

Chen Qingxu had spent years braving the jianghu. She was no naïf; she understood all the logical reasons behind this mode of thought. But there were still moments here and there where she shivered at the coldness of this world and the beliefs of its people.

"Oh right, Miss Chen." Chang Geng's voice drew her back from her thoughts.

She blinked. "What is it?"

"If His Majesty asks, I'll be troubling you to help keep my secrets."

Chen Qingxu quickly gathered herself and nodded.

Gu Yun stood up, pinching the bridge of his nose. "Okay, you two can keep chatting—you've pissed me off to no end, but I really can't stay. I need to at least go back and check on the situation."

With a hum of acknowledgment, Chang Geng reluctantly released his hand. He stared imploringly at Gu Yun until he managed to catch his eye, then showed him a brilliant and ingratiating smile.

Gu Yun stood firm, face stoic as he returned Chang Geng's gaze. "What are you smiling at?"

Chang Geng beamed back at him. If he had a tail, it would've been wagging so hard by now it was about to go bald. Finally, Gu Yun

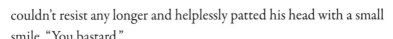

couldn't resist any longer and helplessly patted his head with a small smile. "You bastard."

He turned and walked off, leaving a smug-looking Prince Yan and a faintly green Miss Chen.

The Northern Camp, once summoned into the capital, rounded up the barbarians with the greatest of ease. The delegation was separated and imprisoned in the imperial dungeons to await interrogation. Meanwhile, the patrolling Imperial Guard captured a palace attendant attempting to sneak out amid the chaos. Chen Qingxu's apprentice recognized him on sight as the one who had falsified an imperial edict to trick Prince Yan into coming to the palace banquet.

The servant was merely a lowly subordinate running what he'd thought was a small errand. The severity of the proceedings broke him before they'd even begun the interrogation proper.

He started out hollering, "Your...Your Majesty, my lords, please judge this situation with clear eyes. This servant did not falsify anything; this servant conveyed His Majesty's verbal edict word for word. It was His Highness Prince Yan who insisted on entering the palace to meet with His Majesty..."

He was still defending himself when Jiang Chong waved for someone to summon Doctor Chen's assistant. The little medical apprentice, though young, already exemplified the admirable characteristics of the Chen family. Upon seeing so many powerful figures gathered in one room, the youth showed no sign of panic, and displayed a perfect memory by repeating the attendant's conversation with Prince Yan word for word.

How could this band of cunning politicians fail to understand the implications?

Before Li Feng could lash out, Fang Qin launched the first volley in a towering fury. "Who instructed you to say this?"

Struck by inspiration mid-crisis, the palace attendant immediately chose to save his own skin: "It was Imperial Uncle Wang! Imperial Uncle Wang often instructs the servants on how to better serve our ruler, and he said...he said...since His Majesty asked after His Highness at such a time, that meant he intended to summon him to the palace, and that I should take initiative and make sure he gets the message..."

Li Feng turned the ring on his thumb and sneered. "Is that what we intended? Perhaps even we don't know anymore."

Wang Guo crashed to his knees. He'd known from the moment his people failed to locate the old imperial physician that Fang Qin had abandoned him. Fang Qin was gracious on the surface but vicious at heart. He cared not a whit for personal relationships or impersonal justice, and could turn on someone in the blink of an eye. Wang Guo should have known—that Fang bastard and the Lü faction had been so cozy they practically walked about in the same pair of pants. Yet didn't Fang Qin sell them out and betray them with a snap of his fingers all the same?

The attendant screamed his innocence, but only managed a few more wailed pleas before he was gagged and dragged away. Fang Qin spoke next. "Your Majesty, Imperial Uncle Wang is the beloved uncle of our nation. This subject refuses to believe him capable of committing treason and colluding with foreigners. Your Majesty, you must investigate carefully and prove his innocence."

The defense ready behind Imperial Uncle Wang's lips was shoved back down his throat by Fang Qin's words. He had been prepared to decry this malignment, betting the emperor still had some goodwill for this uncle of his, or would at least hesitate to put an old subject to death. Perhaps he would find it in his heart to let him off. Wang Guo had at worst committed the serious crime of falsifying an imperial edict and deceiving his liege. But if the Longan Emperor himself was unwilling to pursue the case, he could plausibly give out that Imperial Uncle Wang was getting on in years, and that, in his muddled old age, he had misheard an imperial edict. Perhaps he had rambled to the servants, as he was prone to do, and merely caused a misunderstanding.

But Fang Qin was entirely too ruthless. Now that he had spoken, it would be impossible for Li Feng to protect Wang Guo even if he wanted to—to do so would be tantamount to admitting the imperial uncle's guilt. If Wang Guo was truly innocent, he would welcome a thorough investigation. The problem was that he was not at all innocent!

Would the barbarians protect him? Would the "gift" he hadn't managed to get his hands on in time protect him? Would those traitorous palace eunuchs protect him?

Wang Guo steeled himself—the only option left was to try muddying the waters even further.

"This old subject deserves a thousand deaths," Wang Guo said, loud and clear. "It's true that I was impatient to see Prince Yan and distorted His Majesty's intent."

Li Feng narrowed his eyes. "We never realized Prince Yan had become such a precious sight. He is a constant presence in the court, and we have never seen Uncle particularly friendly with him. Pray tell, why was Uncle overcome with the need to see him after just a few days of leave?"

Courage bolstered by malicious conviction, Wang Guo kowtowed with his forehead to the ground, face tense with resolve. "Your Majesty, this is a long story known to very few. Several days ago, while visiting Minister Fang's residence, this subject became drunk and lost his way. Wandering the residence, I accidentally encountered a man I found somewhat familiar. Only later in the course of our conversation did I realize I had seen this man many years ago—Your Majesty, you were still young at the time. He was the most renowned imperial physician of the Imperial Academy of Medicine and very close to the barbarian noble consort. In fact, he was implicated when she disappeared, and he fled in guilt..."

Internally Fang Qin scoffed, but he affected an outward look of confusion. "Imperial Uncle Wang, what do you mean by this? Are you claiming I harbored a fugitive of the imperial court in my home? Your Majesty, this is absurd!"

Li Feng leveled them both with a cool look.

Wang Guo acted as though he hadn't heard a thing. "At the time, this subject was terribly shocked. After speaking a few words with the man, I learned that this old imperial physician had ended up at Minister Fang's door when his son ran into some trouble."

"Absolute nonsense. I would never violate the law for personal gain!" Fang Qin cried.

Wang Guo sneered. "Of course, Minister Fang was unmoved at first. But in exchange for Minister Fang's protection, the old imperial physician offered up a fascinating secret: the barbarian Princess Xiu was in fact with child when she left the palace. What Minister Fang made of this, who can say? Minister Fang is so cunning; perhaps he already silenced that old imperial physician and his entire family, and dead men tell no tales. But Your Majesty, we all know Princess Xiu colluded with Jialai Yinghuo to breach our borders in Yanhui Town. Certain generals were personally on the scene. Although I have no evidence, those barbarians are certainly aware of this as well. You have only to interrogate them to prove the truth of my words!"

It was an outright declaration that Prince Yan's parentage was in doubt, made in front of the whole court. Li Feng slowly sucked in a breath.

Has this old dog Wang Guo gone mad? Fang Qin thought. *He'd sacrifice himself just to drag me into the muck?!* He called out, "The barbarians are devious foes, eager to see our Great Liang fall into eternal turmoil. How could you suggest His Majesty trust their wicked words? Imperial Uncle, it seems to me that the one who has conspired with barbarians in secret is *you!*"

Wang Guo threw everything he had into this gambit. He knocked his forehead against the ground again and again. Accompanied by the firecrackers popping away in every street and alleyway, the sharp crack of his head against the floor was enough to scare the nian beast[8] away for good. "This old subject will swear his loyalty on the heavens and earth. But the imperial bloodline cannot be muddied. Ever since I met that old physician, I held suspicions in my heart. After all this time, I found them unbearable—this is the only reason I chose the ill-advised course of inviting His Highness Prince Yan into the palace—"

"All because you thought you could obtain evidence from those barbarians that His Highness Prince Yan is not a descendant of the late emperor?" Fang Qin cut him off. "Imperial Uncle Wang, how concerned you are for the stability of the nation! Your Majesty, let's imagine His Highness Prince Yan is indeed a spy sent into the palace by the barbarians to muddy the imperial bloodline. Does that mean the one the Marquis of Anding retrieved from Yanhui Town on the late emperor's orders was a false prince, a fish eye passed off

---

8   *The nian beast or new year's beast is a creature in Chinese folklore said to terrorize villages at the beginning of the year. It fears the color red and loud noises, which is said to be the reason Chinese people wear red, light firecrackers, and play drums during New Year's celebrations.*

as a pearl? Why not summon Marshal Gu and General Shen here and get to the bottom of this? Let's discover exactly what these two famed generals of our nation intended!"

As if on cue, an attendant arrived to report the Marquis of Anding's arrival.

"Send him in," Li Feng ordered, face stormy.

Gu Yun had caught Fang Qin's words on his way in. He didn't bother with niceties but knelt down and got straight to the point. "Your Majesty, back then, this subject searched for the fourth prince on the late emperor's orders. We reported his physical characteristics, age, and the jade token he carried to the late emperor and returned him to the capital with His Majesty's express approval. The late emperor personally claimed him as his son. What's more, this subject recalls Your Majesty once mentioning that His Highness Prince Yan suffered considerably in his youth and was abused by his adoptive mother. That barbarian woman had no sincere feelings for him and must have reluctantly raised him solely because she was unwilling to part with her sister's only child. Though the tiger is vicious, it does not eat its own young. Had she really carried His Highness Prince Yan in her own womb, would she have treated him this way? What mother in the world could bear to do so?"

Gu Yun could talk circles around anyone the instant he opened his mouth. Fang Qin's mouth twitched into a smile.

After finishing this speech, Gu Yun turned toward Wang Guo. "This subject has another question for Imperial Uncle Wang. What advantage do I gain by muddying the imperial bloodline? Allow me to speak frankly: the Black Iron Battalion has been stationed in the northwest for years. If I were plotting with the barbarians, the gates of our nation in the northwest would have swung open a hundred thousand times by now. Imperial Uncle, you've spent so much time worrying over the affairs of others. But have you managed to clear your own name of suspicion for colluding with those barbarian women to slaughter loyal subjects twenty years ago?"

Wang Guo was genuinely afraid of Gu Yun, and his fright was mixed with guilt. He was cowardly by nature and had only made it as far as he had today through sheer desperation. Now that Gu Yun was here before him, he couldn't even speak properly, let alone manage another impassioned tirade. Cold sweat poured down his back.

Lowering himself to speak these few words to Wang Guo seemed to have exhausted Gu Yun's sparse patience. He turned away and stepped forward to address the emperor directly. "Your Majesty, the barbarians have gone too far. This subject has been in the capital over half a year, and my windslasher is covered with two fingers' worth of rust. There is no need to hide our blades any longer. This subject requests deployment to the northern border!"

Gu Yun had considered this request over and over on the way here. The barbarian envoy's tricks, combined with the rumors relayed by General Cai's spies, suggested that Jialai Yinghuo was likely facing rebellion in his own backyard. Gu Yun needed to go to the northern border as soon as possible to verify this information. If the northern barbarians really were caught up in internal strife, this would be the ideal time to attack. Even if the northern lands had nothing else to their name, they were rich in one thing—violet gold mines. If Great Liang used this war to fuel the next, perhaps an engagement with the north wouldn't exhaust them but bolster their strength instead.

Li Feng, however, frowned. In his opinion, Gu Yun's request was too abrupt. He was caught between a rock and a hard place.

An attack on the capital and an invasion in Jiangnan both amounted to losing half their nation to the enemy. But to the princes, dukes, and nobles of this city, being forced to move the capital and beat a hasty retreat was vastly different from having foreigners squat on some faraway riverbank where the emperor's influence was weak. The latter seemed much less urgent a concern. After all, the skeletons scattered about a ghost village where the peoples' tears ran dry amidst the dust kicked up by foreign hooves weren't the ones beneath their silk and satin robes. Right now, real gold and silver were slowly filling the national treasury, and a great batch of refugees had recently been settled. The nation had enjoyed only a few peaceful days. With all this in mind, Li Feng wasn't particularly keen on restarting the war right now.

On the other hand, although Li Feng's ambitions had been losing their edge, he still had his temper. If an investigation found that the barbarians had indeed come to slap him across the face, he couldn't bear the insult.

These two conflicting interests fought to a stalemate in his head. He waved Gu Yun's request off for the time being. "Imperial Uncle, please rise. Mobilizing the army is not a decision made in haste. We will discuss this again after the interrogation—guards, strip Wang Guo of his official's robes and detain him for questioning. The Imperial Court of Judicial Review will take charge... Detain that despicable servant too."

Li Feng rose and, without giving Gu Yun another chance to speak, said, "We will check on A-Min."

After watching Prince Yan deal so skillfully with Gu Yun, Chen Qingxu had figured the brute would pull through. She was preparing to leave when she ran into Li Feng on his way in, and hastily dropped an unpracticed curtsey.

Li Feng had met her when he broke his leg. "We have troubled Miracle Doctor Chen," he said politely. "How is Prince Yan?"

Chen Qingxu fabricated a likely tale on the spot. "The barbarians used a rare poison that confuses the mind. Perhaps they wanted to kidnap His Highness and use him as cover to escape. Fortunately, His Highness reacted swiftly and slashed himself to bleed out the poison. He's much better now."

Li Feng didn't quite follow the rest of it, but frowned at a certain detail. He turned to Chang Geng and asked evenly, "What did you use to cut your arm? You really were too vicious with yourself."

On the surface, he appeared worried about Chang Geng's injury, but his real question was clear: Why did Chang Geng come carrying a knife?

Chang Geng, the very picture of a weak and sickly patient, slowly got down off the bed and knelt, using the headboard for support. "When this subject received Brother's imperial edict, I was at Miss Chen's residence. I enjoy working with herbs and medicines in my free time, and I was helping her organize her medical ingredients. The palace servant was impatient, and in my haste, it seems I took her silver knife with me... I merely used what I had on hand in the moment."

So saying, he produced a knife shorter than the length of a finger from a nearby tray. It was a tiny thing, only useful for cutting medicinal herbs, and the blade wasn't even sharpened, duller than a cutlery knife. It wasn't any sort of weapon at all. The violence with which Prince Yan had used it on himself was evident as well—his strike had left the small blade bent out of shape.

Chen Qingxu felt terribly conflicted. She could see the hidden needles within this conversation, as well as the seamlessness with which Chang Geng's plan fell into place. She bade them farewell, leaving Li Feng and Chang Geng alone in the room.

Li Feng studied Chang Geng's face. He was very handsome, but his features weren't the perfectly proportioned lines of wealthy nobility.

He had a pair of deep-set eyes, passionate and expressive, matched with heartless and fickle thin lips. He had just bled, and his cheeks retained an unhealthy pallor. Upon closer inspection, his brows and eyes bore a slight resemblance to the former barbarian consort, while the straight ridge of his nose resembled the late emperor. Yet put together, he didn't look like anyone at all. The young man had the face of one born under an unlucky star, destined to walk alone, with neither friend nor family beside him.

Li Feng quietly averted his gaze. "There are some rumors going around. Don't take them to heart. Just focus on healing from your injuries. That old bastard Wang Guo has been coddled beyond all reason these last few years; I promise I'll see him give you what you're owed."

Chang Geng knew Li Feng had indeed taken them to heart as soon as he told him to do otherwise. "Are they saying I'm not the child of the late emperor?" he asked of his own volition.

With a smile, Li Feng parroted Gu Yun's argument. "You're thinking too much. The late emperor personally acknowledged you as his son. Who would dare doubt his claim?"

"No one can really be sure of such things," Chang Geng said after a moment's consideration. "If it's come to this, will you allow me to temporarily step down from my position as head of the Grand Council to avoid suspicion?"

Li Feng narrowed his eyes and didn't respond right away.

Chang Geng chuckled without much humor. "The new reforms in governance have just been established. Even if I stay, I don't know what further contributions I can make. I'll only be attracting others' hatred. I hope Brother will sympathize with my situation."

These words plucked right at Li Feng's heartstrings.

An emperor's best weapon was balance. When the Lü-Yang faction and the Imperial Guard rebelled, he had been forced to crack down on Great Liang's noble families of old. At the same time, the newly promoted officials had charged their way onto center stage with the support of the major merchants, and were poised now to become even stronger.

Li Feng could tolerate these young sprouts, and he was happy to see them push back against those arrogant noble families. But he absolutely could not allow them to grow into towering trees that tore through the rafters of his home. This faction was growing far too quickly—even the imperial uncle of the nation couldn't keep himself out of the fray. This time it was Wang Guo—who next? Would the emperor be forced to cleanse every prince and duke in his court? What would the surname of the nation be then? If the government reforms sought to carve out a fresh and bloody path, some would inevitably be sacrificed to the new order.

He looked at Chang Geng. "All right. You have suffered much in recent days; it's only right for you to take time to convalesce."

The skies changed overnight.

An imperial uncle who had enjoyed the highest of favor throughout two reigns was consigned to the dungeons. Countless attendants in the palace shared connections with him; they were dragged out for interrogation one by one. Fear reigned behind the many-layered palace walls, and a whole pile of minor misdemeanors was ferreted out like mud brought up with a radish pulled from the ground. The old case of the attack on the Black Iron Battalion was unavoidably dug up once again, and like monkeys scattering from a fallen tree, the court scrambled to draw a line between themselves and the

Wang family. Everyone was afraid the tiniest stain would drag them into collective punishment.

The barbarian envoy who had instigated the scandal was secretly detained. The Northern Camp patrolled in shifts, on high alert.

But even Fang Qin couldn't have predicted the conclusion of this episode. Prince Yan, that constant thorn in his side, resigned from his official position—and the Longan Emperor allowed it.

Despite his age, this was the first time in Fang Qin's life he had truly experienced the unpredictability of the world. Back when he brought every plot and scheme against Prince Yan, the man was perfectly untouched, while Fang Qin nearly sacrificed himself in the process. This time, he'd had no intention of getting involved. He was merely anxious to distance himself from Wang Guo and hadn't hesitated to stand on the same side as his political enemy to do it... yet somehow, he'd gotten exactly what he wanted.

No wonder the ancients said, "Even demons and deities cannot speak to an emperor's intent."

A heavy fall of snow that night glazed the plum blossoms in the Marquis Estate in a crystal-clear layer of frost, suspending their color elegantly in ice.

The passengers returning home instructed their carriage to stop at the entrance. Snow capped the tops of the gas lamps dutifully casting their patches of light from where they hung over the twin gates. With a long sigh, the iron puppets guarding the door creaked around, and steam drifted into the air as the gates swung open.

Gu Yun jumped down and waved Huo Dan off, lifting the hanging screen himself. "Give me your hand."

The wound Chang Geng had given himself with the silver blade looked frightful, but it hadn't hit anything vital. Even if Chen Qingxu hadn't treated him, it would have quickly scabbed over thanks to his wu'ergu-reinforced constitution. There wasn't a damn thing wrong with him at this point. But he couldn't resist making the most of his injuries around Gu Yun.

Chang Geng put on a great show of clinging to Gu Yun as he exited the carriage, then used his momentum to bonelessly throw himself into Gu Yun's arms. He clung to Gu Yun's shoulders and refused to let go, his grip so tight Gu Yun couldn't toss him off if he tried. Gu Yun had to wonder what kind of injury granted a person such an increase in strength.

Gu Yun knew Chang Geng was faking his weakness, but he also felt Chang Geng had truly been wronged. He didn't have the heart to reprimand him. He merely smacked Chang Geng lightly on the back, then bundled him into his cloak and strode off toward the gate.

The chilly breeze that followed them into the room roused the bird hanging in the cage at the window. Rudely awakened from its pleasant dreams, the bird shivered at the chill and lashed out in anger. "Bastard, you're freezing Daddy to death... *Squawk...squawk squawk...* good fortune to you! Beautiful flowers beneath a full moon! May the money come rolling in! May all your wishes come true!"

Gu Yun was speechless.

Man and bird stared at each other until finally, the myna lifted one wing to hide its face in shame. It seemed to know its obsequious attitude was an embarrassment and could no longer bear to be seen.

Beside him, Chang Geng snickered. General Gu was truly beyond words.

"Your face is red from the cold." Gu Yun touched Chang Geng's chin. "You're so happy to have stabbed yourself and lost your job, huh? Hurry up and go change."

"Giving up all those official duties is a weight off my shoulders." Chang Geng chuckled, then turned to find a clean and dry set of robes. Once changed, he took a seat by the window and snatched up the bird to stroke its feathers. The myna trembled under his attentions, nearly perishing out of fright on the spot. "Hey, Zixi, if I really am Huge'er child, who do you suppose was my dad?"

"Don't think about such nonsense."

Chang Geng laughed lightly. "That person definitely wasn't a barbarian, or they would have left with Huge'er when she fled. But they must have had a close connection with the barbarian women; they may have even helped plan the consort's escape. And they probably took control of the forces the barbarian women left behind in the capital and the palace...only showing themselves once the capital was besieged."

He was speaking of course of Great Master Liao Chi, the same candidate as Shen Yi's initial guess—the man Chang Geng had shot to death with his own hands.

Gu Yun didn't much care. "You mean that Dongying man? Dongying people don't grow as tall as you. But if you really start showing signs of that crow-beaked old monk's ugly mug in the future, I won't want you anymore."

Chang Geng shook with silent laughter.

"I'll get someone to brew some ginger tea. Don't catch a cold."

Leaping to his feet, Chang Geng stuffed the bird back into its cage. He tossed a large black cloth over top as a hint of mischief slipped into his tone. "There's no need for tea to drive away the chill. Allow me!"

ARC 14

DIVERGENT
PATHS

106

THE NORTH

FTER A ROUND of interrogation, the barbarian envoy was escorted into the heavily fortified imperial dungeons.

As the guards shoved him into that place of total darkness, he glanced back at Shen Yi astride his horse. Their eyes met, and Shen Yi's heart constricted. The barbarian envoy flashed him an eerie smile and crooned the first bars of a lilting folk song: "The purest spirit of the grasslands, even the heavenly winds seek to kiss the hem of her skirt..."

The Celestial Wolf Tribe had resided in the grasslands since time immemorial; their people were naturally blessed with beautifully resonant voices that rang clear across the plains of their homeland. The man's voice was deep and low as it echoed in the snow and wind, suffused with the unique, soul-stirring grief of a wolf that had reached its final days. Even when the prison doors closed behind him, the man's song lingered in the air. Listening, Shen Yi frowned—this was the sound of change that came with the swift flow of time.

Heavy-armor units patrolled the imperial dungeons. Violet gold burned quietly in their gold tanks, casting a subtle purple halo, and steam drifted across the snowscape, dissipating in an instant. The grasslands, the galloping horses, and the sharpened swords, spears,

halberds, darts, and pikes all faded away, frozen before the dark
and sturdy silhouette of that heavy armor, which stood like an iron
puppet on guard.

Shen Yi was overcome by a vivid feeling that he was watching an
era draw to a close before his very eyes.

But he didn't spend much time lamenting. If Gu Yun's speculation
was correct, there was a good chance the eighteen tribes were already
at each other's throats. Shen Yi shook off his distraction—this was
an opportunity they couldn't afford to let slip. All signs pointed to
war resuming on the northern front.

Finishing his tour around the imperial dungeons, Shen Yi turned
to leave when he noticed a white shadow flit past a short distance
away. It was so fast anyone might think it merely a blurring of the
eyes. Had Shen Yi not spent so many years on the battlefield honing
his senses, he wouldn't have detected it at all.

Shen Yi flashed a hand signal to the oblivious soldiers standing
nearby, then led the way into the imperial dungeons with his windslasher strapped to his back. His apprehension grew as he walked;
incredibly, there were no footprints on the ground. The cavernous
imperial dungeons were as silent as a grave. The two prison guards—
one sitting, one standing—were stock-still: upon closer inspection,
they had been quietly knocked out.

A slight breeze brushed Shen Yi from behind. Throwing himself
forward on instinct, he drew his windslasher in a wide backward
swing—and missed his target entirely. There was a soft *clink* as his
windslasher met something light but unyielding. Shen Yi didn't
turn; he lunged forward, vaulting up the room's corner and kicking
off the wall in a clean flip. He grabbed the edge of the intruder's veil
and yanked down, exposing a familiar face.

Chen Qingxu.

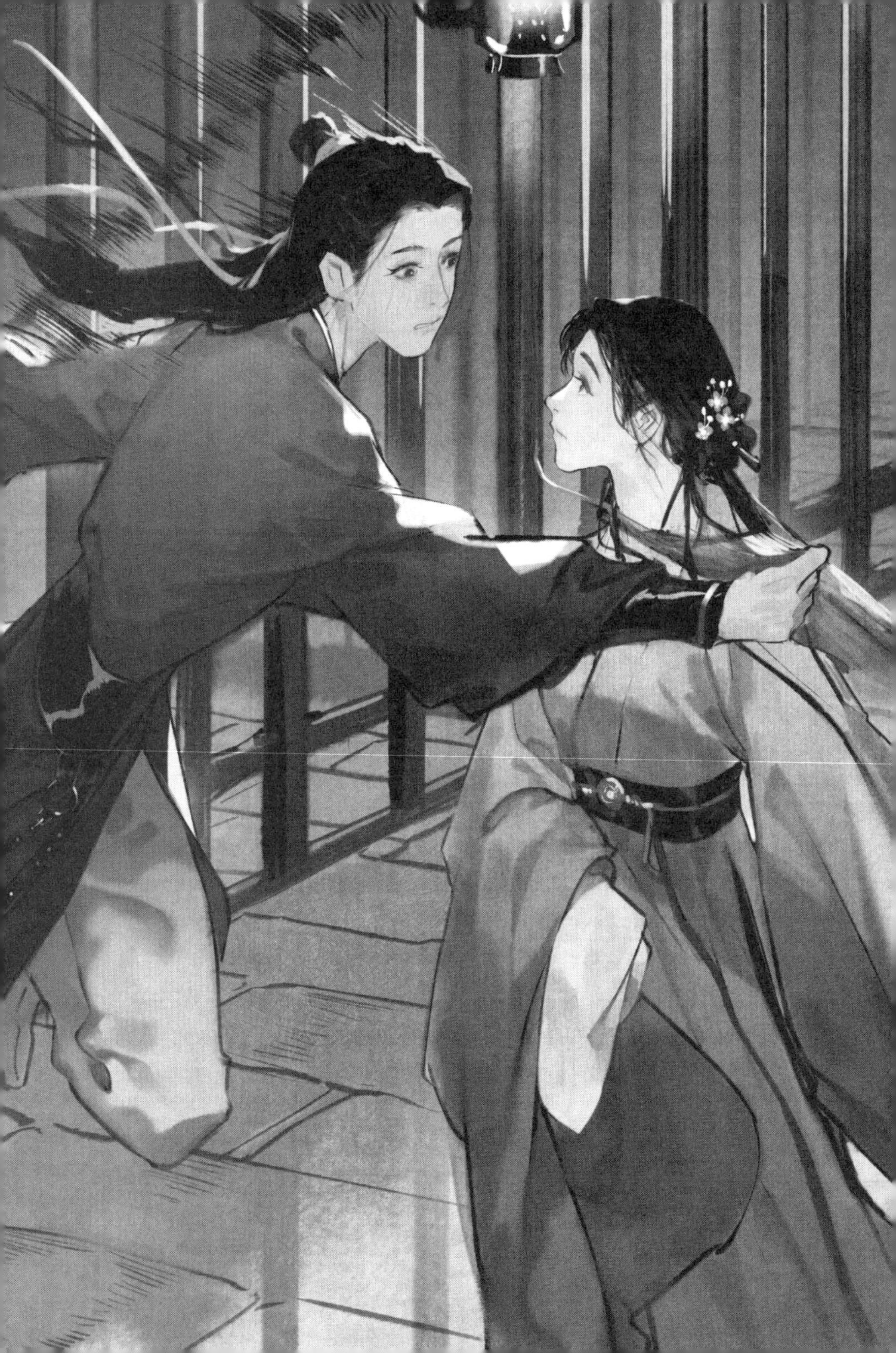

Shen Yi's voice abandoned him. He had no idea how he managed to land and nearly sprained his ankle gaping like an idiot.

The brisk patter of footsteps sounded behind him—the Northern Camp soldiers who had followed him into the imperial dungeons. Shen Yi came to his senses. He shook his head at Chen Qingxu before pushing her into a dimly lit corner. Then he calmly sheathed his windslasher and strolled back out.

"General Shen, is something the matter?" asked one of the soldiers.

"It's nothing," Shen Yi said blandly. "Just my eyes playing tricks on me. That barbarian is skilled in treachery. Tell our brothers to stay vigilant."

No one questioned him. The soldiers promptly split into teams and spread out to patrol. Shen Yi stood in place for a long moment, taking several deep breaths to gather himself. He felt his heart was about to leap out of his chest. Half an age later, after wiping the second wave of cold sweat from the palms of his hands, he turned toward Chen Qingxu's hiding place and whispered, "Miss Chen, what are you doing here?"

Chen Qingxu had come to see the barbarian envoy. She was loath to pass up any potential clues about the wu'ergu and had informed Chang Geng of her plans before coming. At first, Chang Geng had wanted to ask the guard for help, but after brief consideration, Chen Qingxu rejected the offer. She wasn't attempting a prison break, just slipping into the imperial dungeons by night; it shouldn't pose much difficulty. Better to keep the number of people who knew about the wu'ergu to a minimum.

But she hadn't expected to be caught, much less by an acquaintance. She cupped her hands and said somewhat awkwardly, "Many thanks, General Shen, for your lenience. I came to the imperial dungeons hoping to verify a few things with the barbarian envoy—here, please read this."

She took out Chang Geng's letter, which was stamped with Gu Yun's personal seal. This was the back door Chang Geng had prepared for her, borrowing a bit of Gu Yun's influence. Chen Qingxu hadn't planned on using it, but now she thanked her stars for Chang Geng's foresight. Otherwise this would have been impossible to explain.

She had kept the letter in her lapels, and it was still warm from the heat of her body. Shen Yi accepted the document with trembling fingers and looked it over as if in a dream. The words were like mist dissipating before his eyes; not a single splotch of ink made it into the burnt sludge of his brain. Standing in that tiny side room with Chen Qingxu, Shen Yi didn't dare lift his head to look at her.

Noting his long silence, Chen Qingxu pointed out, "It's stamped with Marquis Gu's personal seal."

"Ah..." Shen Yi awoke from his reverie. "Oh, right. In that case, please be careful. Uh...after you."

Chen Qingxu breathed a sigh of relief and strode forward to enter the imperial dungeons. But after a few steps, she found Shen Yi had not followed her. "General Shen, if you're concerned, you can come with me."

Shen Yi nodded, tight-lipped, as if every word spoken was precious as gold. "Mm, I'll be troubling you then."

He followed Chen Qingxu in silence, lagging five steps behind and scarcely daring to breathe. This man was quieter than the lifeless iron puppets standing guard. Luckily the imperial dungeons were black as pitch, so Chen Qingxu didn't notice the pathetic way

Shen Yi's face turned as red as a monkey's bottom. In fact, she was rather surprised—didn't people say birds of a feather flocked together? How had the Marquis of Anding befriended such a rigidly old-fashioned individual?

The two walked all the way to the barbarian envoy's cell without exchanging a single word. At long last, Shen Yi opened his esteemed mouth: "This is Chikuyou, the Wolf King Jialai's trusted aide," he said succinctly, doling out his words one by one.

Hearing him suddenly speak up like a corpse jerking back to life startled Chen Qingxu so badly she nearly drew her weapon. Seeing her fingertips gleam with silver, Shen Yi shut his mouth in chagrin, now more reluctant to speak than ever.

Just as Shen Yi was about to crawl into the cracks of the dungeon walls, he was saved by their foe. Upon hearing Shen Yi's brief introduction, Chikuyou calmly responded from where he was confined within the cell. "Others might call me a traitor to the Wolf King. The general is certainly perceptive."

The instant Shen Yi turned to Chikuyou, his stiff lips seemed to loosen. "A traitor? So the rumors of your tribe's second prince seizing the throne are true."

Chikuyou shook his head. At this point, there was no reason to hide it. "The second prince is but a child," he said calmly. "He has no such ambitions as of yet. There are three princes beneath the wolf banner of the eighteen tribes. They've detained the crown prince, and the third prince... Ha ha, he's an idiot who requires the aid of his attendants for the most basic tasks. The second prince is the only one fit to serve as their puppet."

Shen Yi astutely noted the word *they*. The cogs of his brain whirred fast as the wind when they weren't stuck on Miss Chen. He realized at once—the northern barbarians were sometimes known as the Eighteen Tribes Confederacy, but they were never a single entity to begin with. Aside from ensuring everyone's bellies were filled, any man who wished to lead as king of the wolf pack must have fangs sharp enough to snap his challengers' necks.

Shen Yi narrowed his eyes. "And? The Wolf King is willing to tolerate such treatment?"

Chikuyou laughed grimly. "Even the greatest heroes grow old. How else could wild dogs seize the opportunity to lead?"

So. Jialai Yinghuo was either gravely wounded or deathly ill, and had already lost his grip on the eighteen tribes. Shen Yi unslung his windslasher; with the blade sheathed, it was the perfect length to prop against the ground. Chikuyou's pupils shrank—the Black Iron Battalion would always be a shadow looming over three generations of the eighteen tribes.

Leaning on his windslasher, Shen Yi's speech took on the erudite tones of a Hanlin scholar. "The Wolf King of the eighteen tribes has a volatile temperament. I'm sure your tribesmen have struggled to get by in these war-torn years. At present, my nation's great army guards the northwest, while the fierce warriors who serve the Wolf King may lack the strength and will for another fight. Please forgive me if this is an obtuse question, but why would your esteemed self go so far as to infiltrate this diplomatic mission and disrupt peace talks? Are you not also implicating the third prince, who is an innocent child?"

Chikuyou glanced at him, eyes placid. "General, your words are quite sensible. I fear many within the eighteen tribes think the same. However, this is not what my king desires. I once swore to the Eternal Sky that I would remain loyal to him above all others. Even if I bear the brand of a traitor, I will do what I must to fulfill his wish."

"Please enlighten me, then," Shen Yi said.

"A wild beast ought to act like a wild beast. Rather than following men who would grovel before their adversaries, allowing Great Liang to tame them into dogs that know only to dig for violet gold, it would be better for the eighteen tribes to be wiped out on the battlefield tomorrow." Chikuyou gazed at Shen Yi. "General of the black crows, let me ask you this: would you rather scrape out a pitiable life or die in a raging fire?"

This Chikuyou spoke like a zealot. Chen Qingxu thought Shen Yi would find the question beneath his dignity, but to her surprise, he gave Chikuyou a thorough answer: "For myself, I would prefer to die in a raging fire. But I understand that even the lowliest insects cling to life. I'm a soldier who guards my nation's borders; it's my duty to protect those who have a greater desire to live. To my mind, there's nothing pitiable about a peaceful life spent fishing, farming, studying, or woodcutting. And if any of my people do lead truly pitiable lives, is it not the fault of the weapon-wielding higher-ups who sit in positions of power?"

After saying his piece, Shen Yi felt he had more or less learned what he wanted to know. He stepped back and politely waved Chen Qingxu forward. "Prince Yan sent this young lady here to ask you a question, so let's save the small talk."

At the mention of Prince Yan, Chikuyou's expression grew slightly queer—yet it held, too, a touch of reverence. He spoke before Chen Qingxu could open her mouth. "Are you here to ask about the wu'ergu?"

Chang Geng had sent Chen Qingxu with a message to pass to Chikuyou: *Hand over the barbarians' shamanic secrets and we'll give you what you want.* Chen Qingxu had been baffled by these words. But after listening to Chikuyou's bewildering conversation with

General Shen, she had muddled out some semblance of understanding. Thus, she relayed the message.

A rare pensive expression came over Chikuyou's face as he responded politely, "Regarding the wu'ergu, I only know how to activate and control it. As for how to create and refine it, that information is privy solely to the leader of the eighteen tribes and the goddess herself. It's a closely guarded secret. Please forgive me if I'm unable to give you an adequate answer."

"Then what about the cure?" Chen Qingxu asked.

Chikuyou stared at her blankly. "What did you say? The cure?" He sighed and pursed his lips. "Central Plains woman, the wu'ergu is nothing like the inferior poisons you Central Plains folk use where, if it doesn't kill you immediately, you can take an antidote and live another day. Those who have been refined into wu'ergu are simply wu'ergu. They have been wholly reborn; they are no longer human. To force them back into their original form would be no different from stuffing a newborn pup back into its mother's belly and forcing her to birth a rabbit. It's impossible."

Chen Qingxu wasn't so easily fooled. "Save the 'wholly reborn' nonsense for laymen. If you genuinely want to demonstrate your sincerity, try something else."

Chikuyou's eyes flicked to the side, and he flashed her a cunning smile. "How unfortunate that I'm just such a layman. Huge'er has been dead for years. Before she passed, she entrusted the goddess's secret techniques to my king. He personally refined the third prince into a wu'ergu... Granted, its abilities are limited by the host's poor aptitude. It cannot be considered a complete specimen. But if you want to know the secret of the wu'ergu, you may seek him out—assuming of course your black crows can cut their way through the wild dogs holding the Wolf King captive."

The barbarian envoy was cunning—he was obviously trying to provoke an all-out war—but he had confirmed one thing: if the third prince was a genuine wu'ergu, then Jialai Yinghuo had complete knowledge of the goddess's secret techniques. This was a lead.

Chen Qingxu wasted no more words; she turned to leave.

The next day, Chen Qingxu left a note and departed the capital. Shen Yi nearly went mad. If he could, he would have glued wings to his back and flown at once to the northern front. He proceeded to harass Gu Yun day and night until the marshal grew so annoyed by Shen Yi's antics he visited the palace thrice in two days.

Finally, on the third day of the new year, Li Feng relented and ordered Gu Yun to the northern front in secret. He was to exercise utmost caution in his investigation of the eighteen tribes and expressly forbidden from rashly mobilizing troops.

Prince Yan wasn't fit to travel to the front lines. He saw Gu Yun off from the Northern Camp, an inexplicable frisson of anxiety unfurling in his heart.

Chang Geng glanced back at the overlapping eaves of the palace complex and instructed his coachman in a low voice: "Take me to Southward Tower."

107

UNEXPECTED COMPLICATIONS

O N GU YUN'S FIRST NIGHT out of the capital, he was putting on his glass monocle when the frame inexplicably snapped in his hand. The lens rolled along the bridge of his nose, struck one of his black-iron pauldrons, and cracked. For a general's personal belongings to break just as he was about to leave on campaign was a terrible omen. The personal guard on duty was scared out of his wits, afraid Gu Yun would take this superstition to heart.

Gu Yun rubbed at his nose. "Tsk, have I worn my armor so long my body finally turned to steel?"

His quick-witted guard immediately declared, "This means that you'll have a 'smashing' new year. Give me a moment, sir, I'll fetch you another."

This guard looked after Gu Yun's daily necessities in the field and knew he kept spare monocles in his pack. As he rifled through his commander's effects this time, however, he came across a thick envelope tucked into a stack of Gu Yun's robes. Sealed with wax, it was inscribed with the words, *For Marshal Gu's eyes only.*

The Marquis of Anding tended to countless important matters every day. Surely he wasn't in the habit of writing long letters to himself. No matter how the guard looked at it, wrapping something like this in a person's clothing was an intensely intimate act.

Who would help Gu Yun pack his clothes?

Aside from the old servants of the Marquis Estate, the only answer was his lover.

The wax on the envelope was intact; Gu Yun probably hadn't found it yet. Eager to prove his usefulness, the clever little guard bounded over to Gu Yun with the monocle and envelope in hand and whispered conspiratorially, "Sir, I found an important letter in your clothes. Quick, take a look. Be careful you don't delay responding."

Setting the monocle on his nose, Gu Yun glimpsed the familiar handwriting on the envelope. A subtle shift came over his expression. He glanced back up at the young guard, who threw him a bawdy wink. "What are you looking at?" he chided with a laugh. "Scram!"

With a final snigger, the guard pulled a face and ran off.

The envelope was hefty in Gu Yun's hand and as thick as a tome. If it was a love letter, Prince Yan must have started writing it when he was in diapers. As Gu Yun tore through the seal, he gave free rein to fantasy. *Is it a deed to a house? Or a plot of land? War beacon tickets? Money? Or perhaps the secret to immortality?*

But even after all his wild imaginings, the envelope's contents, when he finally pulled them out, still stunned him. Inside was a thick stack of schematics drafted on soft yet durable billow paper. This kind of paper was impervious to fire and water, but even so, the material in some places had begun to yellow and curl with age. The documents had clearly been in the making for quite some time. The ink on the paper varied in hue, a telltale sign that the writer had annotated these documents time and again rather than drafting the whole thing at once.

At the top of the stack was a giant map of Great Liang that would cover the expanse of the room's floor if spread flat. The three sections of the Yangtze River, the five lakes, the former territories of the Chu and Ouyue Kingdoms...all things big and small were labeled on this sheet of paper. In addition to landmarks, the map was covered in a dense layer of annotations penned in minuscule script—the places they ought to cut into a mountain and the places they ought to build factories; the most fertile land for planting and fishing and the ideal ports to expand toward global trade; harbors that could accommodate a fleet of proper seafaring dragon warships and passages that could be developed into a dedicated channel for the transport of violet gold...even regions that required expansions to the official highway system and areas that would eventually be linked by the giant kites and improved great condors. And more lines, crawling over the entire country like so many arteries—these were railways, the tracks for the Western steam locomotives Chang Geng had mentioned to him once upon a time, which sped across the land like the winding coils of dragons, capable of traveling a thousand kilometers in a day.

Attached to the bottom of the map was another sheet of paper containing schematics for the steam locomotives themselves, marked with Master Fenghan's expert annotations and the God of Wealth's calculations on transport capacity and construction costs.

Below these, the thick stack of billow paper contained a strategic plan for the future direction of Great Liang's government. The Grand Council and Canal Commission had already come to fruition, but there were listed several other organizations Gu Yun had never even heard of, their highly efficient hierarchies succinctly delineated.

On and on the documents went, their pages innumerable.

Had Gu Yun seen such a thing five years ago, he would have thought it the exaggerated plot of some wild tale told by commoners.

Now, though many of the plans sketched here had yet to be actualized, they were a stone's throw away from becoming reality. These ideas were no longer the stuff of fantasy.

At the very bottom of this stack of marvelous schematics was a painting. The brushstrokes were somewhat crude—it was clear the artist was no master of this craft—but the subject was unmistakable. Sparse lines depicted a young child playing with firecrackers by the roadside. Behind him stood a tree painted with large swaths of bright color—flowers, or some sort of unidentifiable fruit—on its branches. Far in the distance, an overlapping landscape of mountains and rivers smudged its way to the edges of the paper. It was an idyllic scene, festive and peaceful. There was no artist's signature or poem; only four words, *The world at peace*, laid over the image like a stray annotation.

Their vast nation seemed to unfurl like a length of silk brocade beneath brush and ink.

Warmth sparked in Gu Yun's chest; he pressed a hand to it and realized he'd been holding his breath. He couldn't help but bring his fingers to his temple and laugh soundlessly. Little Chang Geng with his childish appeals for affection was pathetically adorable, but it was Prince Yan, shaping the state through the power of his pen, who truly moved him.

In the blink of an eye, Gu Yun and Shen Yi arrived on the front lines of the northern border. Taking a small detachment of soldiers from the three Black Iron divisions, they regrouped at the rear of the Northern Border Defense Corps' encampment. The commander in chief of the Northern Border Defense Corps had been killed in action during the barbarians' initial onslaught. But the northern border was a strategic location; its forces had to be led by an experienced senior

officer. General Cai, originally the commander of the Central Plains Garrison, had stepped in as interim commander.

Cai Bin was getting on in age, and the years had taken their toll. When Gu Yun had worked with him not so long ago to eradicate the bandits in the Central Plains, the old veteran's back hadn't yet been so hunched, nor had his hands shaken so badly as they did now.

In all truth, how many years did a young man have to press forward with indomitable spirit? How much hot blood could he carelessly spill before it began to cool? In his twenties and thirties, he might become highly decorated, weaving through the battle-ground unhindered—but over time, as he grew old and weary, even if his iron-wrought soul was steady as ever, he must work harder and harder just to keep up. Those days of burning youth were no less ephemeral than a beauty's fresh and lovely face.

The fighting on the northern front had been deadlocked for some time, but the rhythm of the war was different here than on the Jiangbei front, which saw enemy combatants separated by the Yangtze River. Though the barbarians didn't dare attempt any large-scale maneuvers, minor skirmishes occurred on a daily basis, and small- to mid-scale battles broke out once a week. The entire army, from the most highly ranked commander to the lowest foot soldier, slept with their spears beside their pillows. They patrolled around the clock, never letting their guard down for a moment. Thankfully, most of Cai Bin's children had come of age and could shoulder some of the old general's burdens. Even his youngest—a pair of boy-girl twins—were nearly twenty. The "Cai Family Army" looked quite promising, and ensured that at the least the man wouldn't die from exhaustion.

On the way to the northern border, Gu Yun and Shen Yi had seen the nearby villages and towns almost completely abandoned. The region was a poor one to begin with, and now, with the war ongoing and bandits rampant on the roads, it was either lose your home or lose your life.

"Things have calmed slightly since the barbarian envoy departed for the capital." Cai Bin coughed a few times before continuing. "Our scouts report that the barbarians are assembling the annual violet gold tribute in accordance with the terms proposed in their overture of peace. We're expecting the delivery within the next few days. If the reports are true, they must be somewhat sincere in their desire to end the conflict. Is this why the marshal came to the border? For the violet gold tribute?"

News of the barbarian envoy's imprisonment in the capital had been quickly suppressed, and Gu Yun's party had traveled with all due haste. Even if there was a leak, it had yet to trickle to the front lines. Cai Bin had no idea the peace talks had broken down.

Gu Yun exchanged a glance with Shen Yi. As the commander in chief of all Great Liang's fighting forces, he kept abreast of all developments on the battlefronts. Nevertheless, he asked the general for a detailed account of the eighteen tribes' present circumstances.

"Right," Cai Bin said. "The north has suffered terrible storms this year. They lost most of their livestock, and there isn't enough meat. The harvest from last year's planting isn't sufficient to feed their people, much less support the war effort. When the marshal took control of the Western Regions, the barbarians' supply chain was broken as well. Granted, I hear the Far Westerners haven't had an easy time of it in Jiangnan either. Even if the Westerners could still supply the barbarians, I doubt they'd have the energy to spare."

"I've gotten information that the second prince of the Tianlang Tribe had no intention of seizing the throne," Shen Yi spoke up, "but rather that some internal strife has arisen within the Eighteen Tribes Confederacy."

After a moment of thought, Cai Bin nodded. "General Shen's report makes sense. Actually, at the start of winter this year, some barbarians were secretly mining violet gold to exchange for food. The quantity of violet gold seemed too much for the work of a few civilians. At the time, I thought perhaps it was a sign of discord between tribes, and that the alliance might dissolve. It was shortly after this that the second prince placed his father and elder brother under house arrest."

Shen Yi glanced at Gu Yun, who nodded in response.

Sensing something amiss, Cai Bin asked in confusion, "Marshal, what is it?"

Only then did Shen Yi divulge the events that had precipitated the barbarian envoy's detention in the capital.

There was a stunned silence. Cai Bin shook his head, his face grave. "Marshal, General Shen, even if there's infighting within the eighteen tribes, why go to the trouble of sending someone to infiltrate the capital? Whether Jialai Yinghuo hopes to reunite the tribes against a common enemy, or whether he's insane enough to destroy his own people along with us in the name of revenge, this method is too indirect. Even charging in and setting fire to our encampment here on the northern border would be more effective. Aside from a lone personal guard, is there really no one else he can deploy?"

Shen Yi shook his head. "It would certainly be more convenient to attack directly, but it's likely that the people holding actual power within the Tianlang Tribe will simply scapegoat a few unfortunate souls and leave it at that."

The eighteen tribes had been unified under the Wolf King's banner for centuries, and held the ruling family in high regard, similar to the imperial family of the Central Plains. It was not impossible that even those who opposed Jialai lacked the courage to make a move against him in the open. Perhaps this was why they had come up with such a convoluted plot to raise the second prince as a figurehead.

The poisoning of an imperial prince wasn't an insult Great Liang could let stand. If Chikuyou had succeeded in activating the wu'ergu in the middle of Great Liang's imperial palace and seized control of Prince Yan, Great Liang's troops would have no choice but to fight their way deep into the eighteen tribes' territory and demand the Wolf King hand over the antidote. Jialai's plan was clear: he wanted to force the traitors' faction to either meet Great Liang in a head-on battle, or shed all pretenses of cordiality and openly bear the disgrace of betraying their king.

Cai Bin frowned. "Jialai Yinghuo is a mad dog, but it's hard to believe he's descended to such a degree of insanity. He's always been a man who can restrain himself when necessary. Even if he foments new conflict now, who will do the fighting for him? The starvation victims of the eighteen tribes?"

Shen Yi was stumped by his question, but Gu Yun rose and walked over to the sand table. He stood for a spell with his hands clasped behind his back. "He does have someone who will fight for him—if we assume the foreigners occupying Jiangnan wish us to divert our attention to the northern front."

Cai Bin and Shen Yi both started in surprise.

Gu Yun swept a hand over the sand table. "Their supply chain is broken. They lack food and ammunition; dragging out this conflict will lead to their ruin. Now they may either surrender or make a desperate last stand—that is, unless their southern allies join them in a coordinated attack that allows us no reprieve. If we're forced to spread ourselves thin across both fronts, they could slip behind our lines, catch us when we least expect it, and re-establish their supply routes to the south. Fighting this way is their best chance. If I were Jialai Yinghuo, I might choose such a perilous path out of desperation...on condition that the Far Westerners are willing to cooperate."

"Then the marshal is saying..." Cai Bin began, puzzled.

But Shen Yi had grasped his meaning. "In the time the Westerners have occupied the south, they've funded their war effort with plundered goods and done everything they can to rob our people of their hard-earned wealth. They even forced our captured citizens to labor in the mines, all to ship valuable resources back to their homeland and drum up domestic support for the war. They seem to be biding their time and gathering their strength. But lately, General Zhong has been making changes to the deployment of our navy, and the Lingshu Institute delivered a new batch of sea dragon warships to the Jiangbei front line. The foreigners are growing uneasy. The pope has likely tricked Jialai into staking it all on one final gambit. He's shoving the eighteen tribes to the forefront as a diversion; the moment we shift our focus north, we'll be vulnerable in the south. Once we're at their mercy, the pope only needs to signal his intention to open peace talks. Even if the officials of our imperial court must hold their noses, they'll have no choice but to accept his conditions. Everything south of the Yangtze will fall into their hands without a drop of their own blood shed!"

Bowled over by this revelation, Cai Bin turned to Gu Yun. "Marshal, what should we do?"

Gu Yun smiled. "Just wait. The foreigners aren't the only ones who know how to use a diversion."

Three days later, the Black Iron Battalion soldiers Gu Yun had secretly assembled appeared without warning on the front lines of the northern border. The ambiguous "peace-talking" atmosphere immediately grew tense. The instinctive fear the eighteen tribes had of the Black Iron Battalion was seared into their bones. This wasn't something they could ignore; they sent a messenger speeding over on horseback to inquire about the situation the same day. Gu Yun ordered his men to detain the messenger, then announced with great fanfare the news of Chikuyou's attempted uprising. At the same time, he employed the authority of the Black Iron Tiger Tally and ordered the Jiangbei Garrison to seal off the waterways and halt their daily patrols. Finally, he recalled the majority of the Lingshu Institute specialists that had been sent to the south, creating the false impression that Great Liang was withdrawing from the southern front and ready to host peace talks with the Far Westerners.

The barbarians had their own informants in the south. It took only a few days for news of what had passed along the shores of the Yangtze River to reach the northern border.

The eighteen tribes went berserk. General Cai's undercover operatives within the territory sent word that the Eighteen Tribes Confederacy had broken into conflict twice in a single day. The Wolf King's yurt was tightly guarded; no one was allowed to approach. The very next day, the barbarians sent a pair of severed heads and a hastily assembled shipment of violet gold to the northern front. Gu Yun accepted the offerings, tossed out the envoy, and ordered the Black Iron Battalion to advance five kilometers, making his position clear—he wouldn't let this go so easily.

Whatever internal strife roiled within the eighteen tribes was about to come to a head.

Yet Shen Yi began to panic. Bursting into the commander's tent, he demanded, "What about Miss Chen?"

Gu Yun had been speaking with He Ronghui and Cai Bin. At Shen Yi's urgent question, he lifted his head, the picture of calm despite the chaos swirling around him. "Which Miss Chen?"

Marshal Gu believed in sharing gossip—He Ronghui and Cai Bin had evidently heard everything. He Ronghui snickered under his breath, while old General Cai shook his head in exasperation. Shen Yi didn't have the means to deal with them. "Stop pretending! Miss Chen has probably already reached the eighteen tribes' domain. Things are such a mess over there..."

He was interrupted by the entrance of a figure in a conical bamboo hat.

Shen Yi fell silent.

Chen Qingxu brushed aside her veil. "Does General Shen mean me?" she asked, puzzled.

Members of the Linyuan Pavilion were never without their wooden birds. Chen Qingxu had received word of the situation en route and headed straight for the Northern Border Garrison.

The senior officers in the tent burst into uproarious laughter. He Ronghui snorted so hard his face turned red. He moved to sling an arm over Shen Yi's shoulders, a belly full of jibes prepared. But at that moment, a Black Hawk dropped out of the sky. The man stumbled upon landing and crashed to the ground, sending up a cloud of dust and nearly knocking over half the commander's tent. If not for the armor's internal supports, the soldier would have been smashed to paste by such a fall.

Black Hawks were highly disciplined and extremely well-trained; it was rare to see this sort of accident. After a beat of silence, the officers burst into guffaws once more, many of them asking to which scouting team this fresh recruit belonged. He Ronghui's face flushed so red this time it nearly turned purple. Deeply embarrassed, the Black Hawk commander released Shen Yi and turned to dress down his subordinate.

Before he could begin, the grime-covered Black Hawk lifted his head. He Ronghui blinked in surprise—this man was a veteran from Scout Team Three who'd once served under He Ronghui's own command.

"Marshal." The Black Hawk scout ignored the officers' mockery as he pulled out a mail canister from his lapels. "Emergency dispatch from the Grand Council!" he said, rapid-fire.

Dispatches from the Grand Council were by and large sorted into four categories based on the colored streamers attached to the ends of the mail canisters. Yellow signified an imperial edict, green marked transcripts describing major upheavals in court, and black denoted ordinary military affairs. Red was used for emergency military dispatches only—for instance, when enemies had invaded their borders, the war beacon decrees Gu Yun sent to all corners of the country were marked with this red tag.

The sight of the red streamer evoked a shiver of dread in all present. Gu Yun jumped to his feet as his heart missed a beat. His steady pulse seemed to have suddenly tripped over an obstacle before haphazardly picking itself up to pound out a messy rhythm, and his mouth had gone inexplicably dry. He Ronghui didn't dare delay official business; he took the canister and presented it to Gu Yun with both hands.

How many words were contained within that red-tagged canister, no one knew. Gu Yun stared at the letter long enough to burn through an entire stick of incense. Everyone craned their necks, their imaginations conjuring wild thoughts of a second siege on the capital, until Gu Yun finally lowered the dispatch.

He Ronghui wasn't a patient man. He was first to ask, "Marshal, that's a red tag, isn't it? What's going on?"

108

JIANGBEI

I
T WAS THE NINTH year of Longan, the second day of the second month: the Dragon Head-Raising Festival.[9]

The Jiangbei Garrison sent an emergency dispatch to the Grand Council—during a routine patrol, General Zhong Chan fell from his horse. All the field medics in the Jiangbei Garrison had rushed to his tent, but the prognosis was bleak. After urgently verifying the situation, the Grand Council hadn't even time to send word to Gu Yun before a second letter from the Jiangbei Garrison arrived.

General Zhong Chan was gone.

He had died on the front lines, but he had not fallen in battle. He had passed like any of the thousands of ordinary old men in the world, in a moment that was as fleeting as it was peaceful.

A death like this left a sense of desolation. There was no enemy to hate, and thus no hatred to vent. Nor was it the expected consequence of a drawn-out, chronic condition. Suddenly, between one second and the next, a person was gone. It was an uncomfortable thought. After staring at that red-tagged emergency dispatch for an entire incense stick's worth of time, Gu Yun released a slow breath

---

9   Held on the second day of the second lunar month, the Longtaitou (lit. "the dragon raises its head") Festival celebrates the Dragon King, the deity that presides over all bodies of water and is the dispenser of rain, to ensure a good harvest in the coming months.

from his frantically beating chest and returned to his senses—
this was no dream.

For a moment, a hush settled over the commander's tent. Then,
though no one knew who started it, condolences rose in a flurry of
murmurs.

"Sir," Shen Yi said quietly, "the old general was seventy-six this
year. His long life should be celebrated rather than mourned. You
shouldn't take it to heart."

"I know." Gu Yun sat in silence for a while, then waved a hand.
"I know, I'm fine. It's just that the situation in Jiangbei is delicate. To
lose the commander in chief there now is a heavy blow. Chongze has
only just taken up the post of the Governor of Liangjiang. He can't
attend to the responsibilities of both. I fear the situation will change
for the worse. Hm...let me think..."

But curiously, though he said *Let me think*, his mind went completely blank, as if all of his thoughts had fled. He couldn't quite
figure out where to begin. Seeing the detached expression on his
face, Shen Yi spoke up in hushed tones once more, "Sir, the Jiangbei
Navy was personally assembled and trained by old General Zhong
and Governor Yao. I'm afraid no one else can lead effectively when
it comes to naval warfare."

With Shen Yi providing this lead, Gu Yun finally snapped out
of his daze. He promptly added his own voice to the conversation.
"Yao Chongze and Zhong-lao's deputy should be able to handle
things for now. But it's been less than half a year since the Yang
Ronggui incident..."

It wouldn't do to blather on in the presence of so many others,
so Gu Yun closed his mouth on the rest. The political situation in
Jiangbei had finally stabilized after extensive efforts. The refugees,
merchants, and local officials had just settled into their new roles,

and many of the factories had just been built. The people there had barely made themselves at home in their new abodes. Meanwhile, Prince Yan had recently resigned his official post—who would take over management of the Jiangbei Canal?

Were they in for yet another bloody power struggle? Would all their efforts thus far be in vain?

Just as some people were born at the wrong time, some people died at the wrong time. And old General Zhong's death had truly come at the most unfortunate time of all.

"I need to go check on things down south." Gu Yun hesitated. "The situation here..."

"Please rest assured, Marshal," Cai Bin responded immediately. "With Generals He and Shen here, we won't have any trouble on the northern border."

Gu Yun nodded. He instructed his personal guards to pack up and quickly smoothed a sheet of paper to begin penning a letter to the imperial court. After entrusting the missive to a courier, he spent a long while sorting out the logistics involved in handing over his command. He was still in the process of laying out his instructions to Shen Yi when the lamps were lit. "Jialai Yinghuo is usually a formidable opponent, but sometimes he's like a mad dog. The current unrest within the eighteen tribes may result in certain consequences—do you take my meaning?"

Shen Yi nodded. "The barbarians will fall into decline."

Since Pangu[10] separated heaven and earth, how many clans and bloodlines had vanished into the mists of time? Whether through natural disasters, the turmoil of war, or gradual assimilation through intermarriage... Some met their demise in a momentous crash like

---

10 A primordial god who separated the clear from the turbid, forming Heaven and Earth out of the Chaos, thus creating the world.

the collapse of Mount Tai, while others faded like the gradual gust of wind over sand. Shen Yi finally identified what he'd felt as he listened to Chikuyou's song that day in the imperial dungeons. It was the sound of the barbarian tribes coming to the end of their road. Even if they mounted a final desperate struggle, an invisible hand nudged them toward obscurity.

Today, it was the barbarian tribes. If the capital had fallen back then, perhaps Great Liang would be the one falling to ruin.

"As long as you're aware," Gu Yun said. "Those lunatics Jialai Yinghuo and Huge'er were both willing to turn their own children into wu'ergu. No one knows what they're capable of when backed into a corner, so don't lower your guard under any circumstances. Cai-lao is getting on in years and He Ronghui is too hotheaded. Jiping, you're the only one I can count on here."

Gu Yun indulged in idle gossip and silly jokes in his spare moments, but he wasn't one to ramble on when it came to serious matters. This degree of instruction was incredibly long-winded by his standards—he was well and truly worried.

"Understood," Shen Yi said. "Leave it to me. If something happens on the northern border, you can have my head."

"What would I want your head for?" Gu Yun quipped with a laugh. "I don't eat pig heads."

Shen Yi had no words. Before he could explode with rage, Gu Yun escaped beyond his blast radius. He grabbed a windslasher and slung it diagonally over his back with a flourish. "I'm off, then."

"Wait, Zixi!" Shen Yi called out. "Take Miss Chen with you."

After receiving the news of old General Zhong's death, Gu Yun had written a memorial to the imperial court, methodically arranged for the handover of military affairs, and given verbal instructions to each and every one of his subordinates. He'd even cracked a few jokes.

From an outsider's perspective, his attitude was so calm it bordered on callous. Shen Yi was buzzing with worry by comparison. Yet back when Gu Yun had extracted those clues about the old attack on the Black Iron Battalion from Jialai Yinghuo's mouth, he had initially been just as calm.

"Why would I take her with me?" Gu Yun didn't turn as he spoke. "Don't tell me you genuinely believe the Chen family peddles magical elixirs that can bring the dead back to life."

With that he was gone, racing into the distance as if in a rush to be reincarnated.

All walls had their cracks; there was no such thing as an absolute secret.

Despite the best efforts of Great Liang to keep it quiet, it was impossible to conceal from their enemy the fact that their commander in chief on the southern front had fallen. At the same time Gu Yun was forgoing several nights' sleep to speed back to the Jiangbei Garrison after receiving the news, the Far Western navy's encampment in Jiangnan was likewise brightly lit around the clock.

Mister Ja accepted a bowl of medicine from an attendant. "I'll take this to His Holiness. Tell the others he's not to be disturbed."

The attendant withdrew with a respectful bow.

Mister Ja heard the sound of the argument before he reached the door.

"Absolutely not. You ask too much." The pope spoke hoarsely between coughs. "I cannot endorse this plan. We cannot, in our greed, swallow an entity larger than our stomachs. If we do not curb our appetite, we court disaster!"

A second man in the room responded, his voice like the slithering hiss of a snake. "Forgive my bluntness, Your Holiness. This isn't greed, but plucking the fruit within our reach. If I dreamt of swallowing a star, that would be greed. But if I only reach for an extra pastry that happens to be sitting next to my hand..."

Frowning, Mister Ja rapped on the door, then pushed it open without waiting for an invitation. "Pardon the intrusion. It's time for His Holiness's medicine."

The man shut his mouth at once. He stroked his mustache and lifted a shoulder in an insolent shrug. This emissary from the Holy Empire had been in Great Liang for over half a year and seemed to have no intention of leaving. It was an open secret that the king and aristocracy of the Holy Empire had sent him to oversee the Far Western force's activities.

The ruler of the Holy Empire, impatient to consolidate his territory and power, was eager for the pope's downfall. It was therefore no surprise that the holy emissary he sent had initially done all he could to prove the war a complete and utter mistake. Yet as the plundered treasures and mineral resources shipped back to the homeland piled high, the grumbles of discontent gradually ceased. The Holy Empire's voracious appetite for the mysterious and richly endowed East had been well and truly whetted, and the nobles who had wished to see the pope crawl back with his tail between his legs slowly changed their tune. Now eager to open their little mouths and swallow this colossal creature whole, they had become the most vigorous proponents of the Far Western occupation of Great Liang.

It was the holy emissary who conceived the plot to divert Great Liang's focus to the northern front and make their move while the enemy had their hands full dealing with the eighteen tribes.

The pope had spoken vociferously against this plan. Between the northern and southern fronts lay the vast lands of the Central Plains. Since lines of transport and communications had been severed with the loss of their foothold in the Western Regions, his army's ability to coordinate with their allies in the north had been severely impaired. When the pope first rallied Great Liang's power-hungry enemies to attack the nation on all four borders, he had exploited just such a communication blockade to hinder Great Liang's response. He knew too well the transient nature of opportunity in war. And that was to say nothing of Jialai Yinghuo himself, whose bone-deep madness and volatility, in the pope's opinion, made him completely unfit for long-term collaboration.

Unfortunately, though the pope had military authority to command his troops, any authority vested in him belonged first to the sovereign families of the Holy Empire. And while other supplies could be plundered, the same could not be said of violet gold. There was not a single drop of the precious fuel in Jiangnan; thus he had no choice but to rely on deliveries from the homeland. In this, he was at their mercy.

And now, Gu Yun had turned their own trick against them and provoked the barbarians into infighting, accelerating their northern allies' defeat.

As reluctant as the pope was to work with Jialai Yinghuo, he couldn't allow the Black Iron Battalion, still stationed in the northwest, to move southward. There was also the problem of the eighteen tribes' vast violet gold resources—the moment Great Liang obtained these, the Far Western Army in Jiangnan would lose any advantage they had.

It was at this juncture that they received news of the passing of the Jiangbei Garrison's commander in chief. Thus the holy emissary proposed yet another rotten idea.

Mister Ja set the medicine bowl on the table and said, perfectly respectfully, "You may have been unaware: though the Central Plains folk continue to bolster their numbers in Jiangbei, they seem reluctant to engage in a pitched battle. They too desire a moment of respite. If we wish, opening up peace talks are not out of the question. Why act recklessly and risk the lives of our valiant soldiers?"

The holy emissary scoffed, turning back to the pope. "Your Holiness, your assistant is talented enough, but he's still wet behind the ears. Both parties must come to the table to sign a treaty, but the difference between the terms for those who have the upper hand and those who do not is as vast as the distance from the Holy Empire to the Central Plains. Need I spell it out for you? The commander of the Jiangbei Navy is dead. This opportunity is a gift from God. If we are too gutless to seize it, we will certainly come to regret it."

Mister Ja's expression never changed. "You are correct; the commander of their navy is dead—but Gu Yun yet lives. He will surely come."

The holy emissary shot him a dark look. "In that case, we can use this period of transition to launch a surprise attack and take care of Gu Yun once and for all. Did Your Holiness not say Gu Yun has fooled the Celestial Wolf Tribe into thinking we've turned our backs on them? Then why not prove ourselves through our actions? Perhaps our allies will surprise us."

Ridiculous, thought Mister Ja. But he could only choke on his words for lack of an adequate retort.

The pope gulped his medicine as though drinking poison and wiped his mouth with a handkerchief held in a shaking hand. "Your Excellency, it's impossible for the deaths of one or two people to make a difference in a war of this scale. The Jiangbei Navy has spent the past year establishing itself. Have you considered what would happen should our surprise attack fail?"

The emissary's smile cooled. "Indeed, the deaths of one or two are insignificant in a war of this scale. In that case, why are you so scared of Gu Yun?" Without waiting for a response, he jumped to his feet. "There is always a possibility things will go awry. But even if worse comes to worst, we will have at least made our intentions clear, which will spur our northern allies into action. There is much more we can gain from this fight—Your Holiness, your caution is unwarranted. Our naval supremacy along the banks of the Yangtze River is undisputed. So what if the Central Plains folk have rebuilt their navy? It's been how long—a year? Two? This navy of theirs is an infant suckling at its mother's breast. If I were commander here, I would never have allowed Liangjiang to fall silent this long. I wouldn't have allowed the Central Plains folk time to rebuild their navy in the first place!"

The corner of Mister Ja's eye twitched. Never had he witnessed such a brazen display of egoism and avarice.

The pope also rose to his feet. "Your Excellency, this is an incredibly irresponsible plan," he said gravely.

The emissary folded his hands together and lifted his chin. "Your Holiness, authority over violet gold allocation is mine. The mission entrusted to me by the Holy Empire allows me to execute orders on your behalf when necessary!"

Mister Ja took a furious step forward, a hand on the sword strapped to his hip. "You!"

The emissary's vicious gaze swung to fasten on Mister Ja as the pope grabbed his assistant by the sleeve. They stood deadlocked until, finally, the holy emissary turned back to the pope. "I've never doubted Your Holiness's wisdom and prescience," he said, his mouth curved in an insincere smile. "Please consider my suggestion carefully. Now, if you'll excuse me."

He picked up his top hat, set it on his head with an arrogant sneer, and swept from the room.

"Your Holiness, why did you stop me?" Mister Ja asked. "If I killed him..."

"If you killed him, the troops loyal to the king and the nobles will mutiny." The pope shot him a glare. "Do you really think your soldiers hold their commander in the same high regard as those of the Black Iron Battalion?"

Mister Ja was taken aback. "Then what should we do? Compromise?"

The pope went quiet. "We must pray for God's blessing."

Pray the Jiangbei Navy truly was in its infancy like the holy emissary said. Pray Jialai Yinghuo was mad enough to pin down Great Liang's army on the northern front. Only then could they reach a favorable destination via this treacherous path.

While the Western troops were arguing among themselves about their newest scheme in Jiangnan, Gu Yun was speeding to Jiangbei. Within minutes of arriving, he gave orders: he reinforced the defensive perimeter, ensured the soldiers on the watchtowers changed shifts every four hours, and saw that the entire army was fully suited up and at the ready. He made a round of the camp to boost morale and reorganized the troop formations, sending commanding officers who had been reshuffled back to their original positions. Governor Yao, after all, was a civil official; he could hold down the fort, but he couldn't command the same strict obedience as Gu Yun, nor did he work with the same degree of efficiency.

After rushing about from noon till nightfall, Gu Yun finally had a moment to take a sip of water. He felt smoke was about to rise from his throat and could practically taste the metallic tang of blood on his tongue. He couldn't be fussed with brewing a fresh pot of tea; picking up a bowl of cold water, he downed the contents in a single draught.

Spring was late to arrive in Jiangbei this year. Sleet had fallen just a few days prior, leaving a lingering chill that sank to the bone. That bowl of cold water froze Gu Yun through and through. He shivered violently and thought to himself in a daze, *What else do I have to do again?*

Just then, Yao Zhen reappeared. "Marshal, when we sent the emergency dispatch to the court, they said they would dispatch someone immediately. I received word just now—Prince Yan will be arriving in the next day or two on behalf of His Majesty."

Prince Yan had resigned his official post, but his noble status remained intact. Not to mention, he had once himself been a disciple of old General Zhong. As a gesture of the emperor's favor in honoring the old general, sending Chang Geng to represent the imperial family was more than reasonable.

"Mm, it's right that he should come." Gu Yun finally remembered what he had forgotten. "Hey, uhh...Chongze? Where's the mourning hall? I'd like to pay my respects."

Yao Zhen led the way.

The mourning hall was several degrees colder than the rest of the encampment. Zhong Chan's coffin sat in the center, surrounded by winding streams of incense smoke.

Gu Yun's footsteps came to an abrupt stop on the threshold. He had been so busy these past few days, rushing from north to south, worrying over all sorts of things big and small. In the midst of it all, he had instinctively blocked this new reality from his mind. The realization struck him in the chest without warning.

He thought, *My teacher is gone.*

Yao Zhen glanced back at him, puzzled. "Marshal, what's wrong?"

Gu Yun took a deep breath and shook his head. He stepped into the mourning hall and lit a stick of incense for Zhong Chan. "Go do whatever it is you need to do. I'll stay with him for a while. Just call me if anything comes up."

"To be born, to grow old, to get sick, to pass away—such is the fate of mankind," Yao Zhen said, voice low. "Nevertheless, you have my deepest sympathies, Marshal. The commander's tent has been cleared for you. When you're done here, please get some rest. I'll leave someone at the door. If you require anything, please let them know."

Gu Yun nodded absently, but it was impossible to know how many of Yao Zhen's words he registered. Only when he was finally alone did he slowly turn his gaze upon Zhong Chan's face. Old General Zhong had died a peaceful death. His expression showed no signs of distress, but neither was it particularly serene. The faces of the dead always seemed covered in a layer of dust, as though the skin had been molded from wax, subtly different from its look in life. Absent the soul, a body was just a body—cold and empty.

Sitting at the side with an elbow propped on the coffin, Gu Yun cast his mind quietly back to his childhood days, when Zhong Chan was his teacher.

Back then, the General of the Flying Cavalry was not yet stooped with age. An awe-inspiring and valiant warrior, his eyes seemed to hide a pair of knives, their keen edges only revealed when he fixed his gaze on a target.

"Young Marquis Gu, memorizing a book on military strategy doesn't mean you can fight a war. Did you not heed the ancients' warnings against becoming an armchair strategist? Grow complacent and I'm afraid you'll be lucky to win a brawl against street urchins."

"Young Marquis Gu, there are two things one must keep in mind when it comes to martial arts. One is 'effort,' and the other is 'pain.' The old marquis and princess are both gone. You are of their noble blood: aside from His Majesty, no one dares harm a hair on your precious head. No one can force you to progress if you'd rather wallow in comfort. Please think carefully about the kind of man you wish to become."

"Glory, splendor, wealth, and rank have no place in the life of a military leader. The nation is at peace. If His Majesty insists on casting his generals aside like a bow once the birds have gone to roost, he may do as he wishes. This humble general can no longer accompany you, Young Marquis Gu, so please take care in the future. Just as the mountains and rivers cross by chance, may we meet again!"

In the flow of the Yangtze River, the waves behind drove those that came before. Even the most brilliant men of their generation grew old.

Gu Yun's hearing gradually faded, and his vision began to blur. He narrowed his eyes beneath the candlelight, immersed in past memories. For a great general to live well into his seventies and die from old age was a blessing. Many would envy such an end; indeed, it was worth celebrating. Whether what he felt was grief, Gu Yun couldn't say—there seemed to be something stuck in his chest.

Chang Geng, too, had rushed all the way to the Jiangbei Garrison. By the time he arrived, the sky was dark. He didn't bother to unpack his things; upon hearing Gu Yun was paying his respects to General Zhong, he dismissed his attendants and headed over straight away. The personal guard standing at the mourning hall's doors recognized Chang Geng's figure even from a distance. Quick-witted, he darted in to inform Gu Yun before Chang Geng could call out to stop him.

"Sir, His Highness Prince Yan has arrived."

There was no response from Gu Yun. Perhaps he'd been so busy he'd forgotten to take his medicine. Chang Geng gathered up the hems of his robes to step over the threshold, waving a hand. "It's fine."

The guard reached out and cautiously patted Gu Yun on the shoulder. "Sir?"

Gu Yun, half-blind, started in surprise. Before he could determine the identity of the newcomer, he was lurching out of his seat, thinking some new emergency had arisen. The stuck feeling in his chest resolved into a sharp stab of pain.

He bent and threw up a mouthful of blood.

109

TEN YEARS

T HE GUARD WAS SO TERRIFIED his soul nearly fled his body. Chang Geng shoved the stupefied man aside, hair standing on end as his limbs turned colder than the chilly Jiangbei weather.

At first, all Gu Yun felt was the ache in his chest. Now that he had spat out this mouthful of filthy blood, he actually felt much better—yet he couldn't seem to stop coughing. The front of his robes was quickly stained red. Blind to his surroundings, Gu Yun waved a frantic hand. "Don't tell anyone...*cough*, I'm fine...*cough, cough*..."

Chang Geng dragged himself back from the edge of complete mental breakdown and was about to pick Gu Yun up when the man slurred out his name: "Chang Geng..."

He sucked in a breath and pressed his ear to Gu Yun's lips. "Hm?"

Nose filled with the stench of blood, even Gu Yun's keen sense of smell abandoned him, leaving only his mind struggling weakly for clarity. He muttered haltingly, "Chang Geng... Prince Yan will arrive soon—don't disclose what happened here, especially not...to him..."

Chang Geng's heart nearly cracked open. "Call the medics!" he shouted as the rims of his eyes turned red.

The guard turned on his heel and ran.

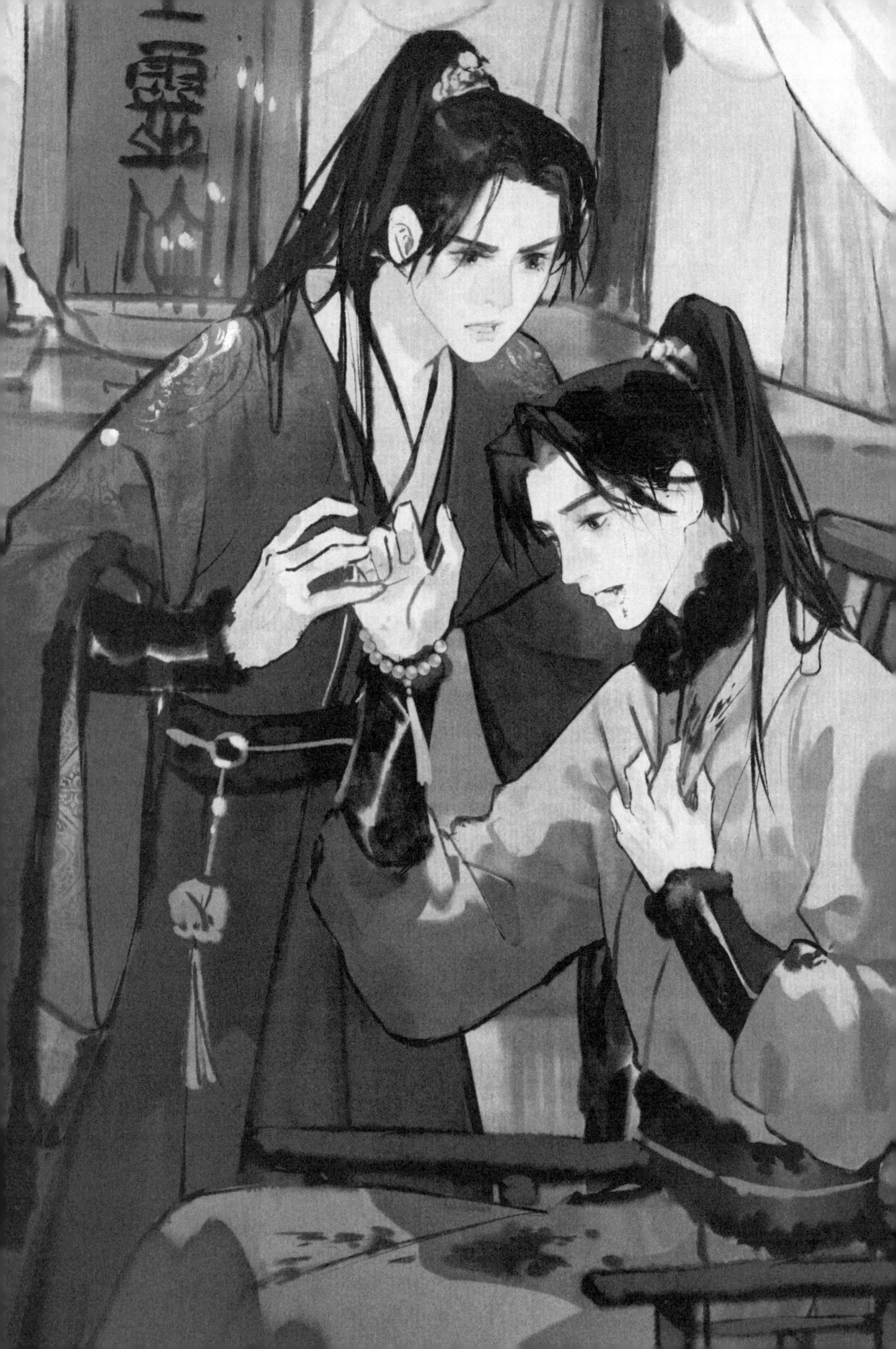
靈

Yao Zhen was about to keel over from exhaustion. He was starting to suspect the Jiangbei Garrison's location had terrible feng shui. They had lost their first commander just days ago, and now a second had collapsed—this one an indispensable figure they could not afford to lose under any circumstances. Yao Zhen turned to Liao Ran, who had arrived with Chang Geng, and asked weakly, "Is the great master here to conduct burial rites for Zhong-lao? There's no rush on that front; perhaps you can recite some scripture to expel malign energies from the Jiangbei Garrison first?"

Great Master Liao Ran gazed at him in sympathy and signed, "The mute cannot recite scripture."

Chang Geng had thought the time he spent studying with Miss Chen was sufficient to render him half a doctor. Only now, in crisis, did he realize there was one patient who would always leave him helpless. The instant he saw Gu Yun's blood, his mind went blank, as if all the medical texts he'd memorized had been returned wholesale to Miss Chen. He could forget about practicing any actual medicine.

The best field medics of the Jiangbei Garrison clustered inside the freshly cleared commander's tent, every one of them crackling with nerves. Chang Geng sat right beside Gu Yun, holding his hand in a vise grip, not caring if he was in the way. All the medics trembled with fear in his presence. Liao Ran stood outside the door and gazed at Prince Yan in worry. Stories of how Chang Geng had transformed into a needle-covered hedgehog in the aftermath of the capital siege had reached his ears as well. If Chang Geng had a flare-up here in the Jiangbei Garrison, no one could subdue him.

But to Liao Ran's surprise, Chang Geng was perfectly calm. He didn't show even the slightest sign of madness. Gu Yun's slurred instructions forbidding his subordinate from informing Chang Geng were like a stabilizing force pinning his soul firmly into his body.

244 ☼ STARS OF CHAOS

He suddenly felt that he had been demanding too much of Gu Yun. Without realizing, he had grown more and more insatiable, to the point that not a day went by without him giving Gu Yun some cause to worry. On the other hand, Gu Yun had kept Chang Geng firmly in the dark as to the origin of the myriad injuries—both new and old—on his body. Chang Geng could visualize clearly all the times Gu Yun had compounded old hurts with fresh wounds and instructed on-lookers to silence, all to protect Chang Geng from concern.

"Your Highness." One of the medics cautiously stepped forward. "The marshal's collapse is due partially to accumulated fatigue from overwork. Also...the uhh...various untreated injuries he's acquired over these past few years while fighting on the front lines have dam-aged his lungs. That blood he spat up has been stagnating in his body for a very long time. Though it was a frightful sight, the fact that he expelled it may be a positive sign."

Chang Geng pressed his fingers against Gu Yun's wrist in silence and tugged his tangled thoughts into order. But after feeling at length, he still couldn't detect anything from Gu Yun's jumbled pulse. He had no choice but to trust the doctors' diagnosis and murmur his acknowledgment. "What about medication? Have you settled on a prescription?"

The medic hesitated. "Um...given the marshal's condition, it would be best for him to refrain from overmedicating. What he needs most is simply rest."

The moment these words left his mouth, the medic knew he had asked the impossible. He glanced cautiously at Chang Geng's hand, which was clutching Gu Yun so hard veins were bulging along the back of it. Terrified that Prince Yan was about to bite his head off, he trembled in fear. But in the end, Prince Yan said nothing and merely sat in a daze. Eventually, he politely cupped his hands. "You have my sincere gratitude. Thank you all for doing your utmost for the marshal."

Surprised by this unexpected consideration, the team of medics filed out of the commander's tent, newly energized. When they had gone, Liao Ran stepped quietly into the tent. He stood before Chang Geng for a while, face creased with worry. Feeling he ought to help somehow, he touched a hand to Gu Yun's furrowed brow and silently invoked the Buddha's name as a meager contribution.

Chang Geng sighed. "Please don't, Great Master. He has an acrimonious relationship with the Buddha. Are you trying to wake him in a rage by reading scripture in his presence? ...Do you have your wooden bird? Send a letter to Chen Qingxu."

Liao Ran looked up at him.

His face was expressionless. "Ask her how many things she's helped Gu Zixi hide from me."

"Your Highness, are you all right?" Liao Ran signed.

Chang Geng's shoulders quivered and for a moment, Liao Ran thought he would break down. But Chang Geng did no such thing. He gazed at Gu Yun for a time before instead doing something that nearly scared Liao Ran out of his wits. Holding Gu Yun's hand in that unforgiving grip, he leaned down and pressed a kiss to Gu Yun's forehead, there before Liao Ran's very eyes. This kiss was as earnest as it was devoted, nearly reverent.

Liao Ran gaped, dumbstruck.

Chang Geng's eyes never left Gu Yun. When he finally spoke, it was difficult to say to whom his words were addressed. "I'm fine. Don't worry."

Stricken, Great Master Liao Ran fled the tent, silently chanting the words *Lust is an unworthy pursuit* and leaving Chang Geng to sit his vigil in silence.

During the latter half of the night, Gu Yun sank from blank unconsciousness into deep slumber. He tossed and turned, as though caught in some nightmare. When Gu Yun had suffered a fever after his stint in the imperial dungeons, he had also been restless in sleep—but if he sensed someone by his side, he would settle. When Chang Geng recalled this, he leaned against the side of the bed and gathered Gu Yun into his arms.

Over in General Zhong's mourning hall, the candles glowed throughout the night. If the old man lying beneath the Nine Springs could see his disciples now, who knew what he would say to Gu Yun when he visited him in his dreams.

Chang Geng tightened his embrace, cradling Gu Yun in his arms. For the first time, his heart was absent both the dependence he felt toward his little yifu and the desire he felt toward the man he loved. Instead, he held Gu Yun as one would hold a precious, frail child.

In the days he had desperately pined after Gu Yun, Chang Geng had wondered on countless occasions how different their relationship would be if only he had been born ten or twenty years earlier. Now, in the damp cold of the Jiangbei front line, that impossibly wide span of ten years shrank down to bare centimeters, easily traversed by a single step.

Unfortunately, no matter how many years Chang Geng matured overnight, it did little to hinder the Far Westerners' schemes.

That evening, the conflict between the holy emissary and the pope resolved in the emissary's favor. They agreed to mount a sneak attack on Great Liang's naval forces. The assault was slated for night-fall—but before they could move out, the watchtowers sent word that Jiangbei had tightened their defensive perimeter and entered the highest state of alert.

Mister Ja charged onto the battle-ready flagship with the news. "Your Holiness! Gu Yun arrived too quickly. Great Liang's navy is no suckling infant; the enemy has already raised their guard. Meeting force with force like this goes against all—"

He was still speaking when the holy emissary barged in after him, an ugly expression on his face. "No one will be changing the plan!"

The holy emissary was a highly trusted and brilliant noble young master, arrogant with youth and status. He had the powerful backing of the king and aristocracy, and the authority to contend with the Holy See and the army. Mere days ago he had been tooting his own horn, declaring Great Liang's navy and Black Iron Battalion insignificant threats. He'd never expected to eat his words so soon; regardless of all else, the holy emissary's ego couldn't bear the humiliation.

The pope had also lost his patience. "Set aside your personal feelings on this matter. There is no place for petty grudges in the middle of a war!"

"No one is taking this less than seriously, Your Holiness." The emissary flushed with anger. "What if it's a bluff? In that case, this is our best opportunity to attack!"

"And if it's not?" Mister Ja countered.

"Impossible." The holy emissary shot him a venomous glare. "That puny fleet lacks any real combat ability. You're afraid to take risks—"

"What utter nonsense." Mister Ja spat.

"Mind your words, good sir," the holy emissary said coldly, turning away and pulling out a roll of parchment. "Gentlemen, I am not here for a discussion. As the representative of the highest authority in the Holy Empire, I signed the troop mobilization order half an hour ago. This is a copy—please read it carefully."

Mister Ja's face flushed with rage, but before he could voice his objections, the sea monster flagship rumbled with a long, low sound like a sigh and began to move.

"Have you lost your mind?!" Mister Ja burst out. He drew his sword without thinking. "Stop this, immediately!"

The holy emissary unsheathed his own gold-and-gem-encrusted cavalry saber. "It is our honor to lay our lives on the line fighting for the infinite glory of our king. We did not come to the front lines to hole up in our harbor and pray on our knees!"

"What are you—"

"Enough!" Mister Ja was cut off by the pope's furious shout.

"Apologies, does Your Holiness have further instruction?" the emissary scoffed.

The pope's face twitched uncontrollably. The flagship was already leaving the harbor, and he had reached the end of his patience. He relented. "If you insist on seeing this ridiculous plan through, at the very least allow my people to command on the battlefield."

This was what the holy emissary had hoped for all along. On the infinitesimal chance this operation failed, the pope was a ready-made scapegoat. Sneering at Mister Ja, he sheathed his sword and shouted his order: "Full speed ahead!"

That night, the Far-Western sea dragon warships donned their disguises and dispersed along the extensive Liangjiang battlefront. They slipped quietly past the Jiangbei Garrison and prepared to make landfall bathed in the glory of God.

Thousands of kilometers away in the north, the eighteen tribes had sent their second group of envoys to negotiate with Great Liang.

Cao Chunhua had also hurried to the northern border. Like Chen Qingxu, he had traveled extensively in the wild northern grasslands and knew the Tianlang Tribes inside and out; his expertise was essential in navigating the delicate situation on the northern front. He joined Shen Yi and met with the barbarian envoy just beyond the Black Iron Battalion's defensive perimeter.

Through the field scope, Cao Chunhua watched the envoy's party approach trailed by a baggage convoy—they had once again come bearing gifts. And judging by the wagons' exteriors and the depth of their tracks, it seemed this gift was violet gold.

A young man in his mid-twenties rode at the center of the group. At first glance, he appeared to be their leader—but upon closer inspection, the young man's face was deathly pale, tight with obvious panic. Wedged between several other horses, he seemed more like a captive than anything else.

Shen Yi didn't have the nerve to whisper to Chen Qingxu. He quietly asked Cao Chunhua, "Who is that man?"

Cao Chunhua peered through the field scope. "Jialai Yinghuo's second son."

"What?" Shen Yi frowned. "Are you sure?"

Cao Chunhua batted his eyelashes at him and tapped him on the chest with gracefully curved fingers. "Aiyo, General Shen. Shen-xiansheng, there are two things in which my memory has never failed me: I never forget a face, and I never forget a voice. Trust me on this."

Shen Yi had taught Cao Chunhua to read as a child. Back then, he had seemed like a perfectly ordinary little girl. Who would've imagined that when he grew up and "recovered" his male identity, he would transform into someone like this. Shen Yi, a pedantic old bachelor, couldn't stand, much less enjoy, being the subject of

Cao Chunhua's bold flirtations. He prickled with gooseflesh and took a subconscious step in Chen Qingxu's direction, shying away from those wily fingers.

Raising her eyes, Miss Chen parted her noble lips to coolly admonish Cao Chunhua. "Xiao-Cao."

Of all the members of the Linyuan Pavilion, the individual everyone most feared offending was Miracle Doctor Chen. Cao Chunhua snapped his mouth shut. Straightening up on his horse and in a great show of decency, he explained his analysis to Shen Yi: "General, it seems to me that the eighteen tribes have come to negotiate in earnest. Handing over the Wolf King would be far too humiliating; perhaps they're hoping to shift blame for the incident in the capital to their puppet ruler, the second prince, to keep the peace."

Shen Yi tapped his fingers lightly on his horse's bridle. "Hold on, let's not get ahead of ourselves. Somehow, I feel the barbarians have given up too easily."

He had confronted the people of the eighteen tribes too many times to be unfamiliar with their nature. These shepherds were incredibly tenacious and would give up only when death stared them in the face. The Black Iron Battalion had advanced to this point by leveraging threats; they had yet to cross their enemy's defense line, much less launch an actual attack. If Shen Yi wasn't mistaken, the eighteen tribes should still have the strength to resist for quite a while.

Cao Chunhua looked again at the wagons, presumably full of violet gold. He licked his lips. "Then, what should we do? Should we let them in or not?"

Shen Yi opted for vigilance. "Archers, stand by with parhelion arrows at the ready. Allow no barbarians to approach our perimeter. Send for the gold valuators; have them inspect all the wagons."

Cao Chunhua's expression was solemn as he turned to meet Shen Yi's gaze. Both remembered the giant kite packed with barbarians that had flown into Yanhui Town all those years ago. If their adversary were anyone else, they could at the very least be trusted not to harm their own children—but Jialai Yinghuo didn't bow to ordinary logic. He was more than capable of using his son's life to dupe the enemy into opening their gates.

At Shen Yi's orders, the Black Iron Battalion soldiers readied their weapons. Killing intent surged toward the northern barbarian delegation. The second prince was shaking so badly he was about to topple from his horse. Soon thereafter, a group of highly trained gold valuators approached the barbarian delegation and began to open and inspect their wagons.

As Shen Yi and the rest watched, several huge wagons full of enough violet gold to make one's heart burn with envy were revealed to their eyes.

The gold valuators dared not cut corners; they checked each and every wagon for quality and dipped specially made rods into the sealed compartments to verify the volume of violet gold within.

When these violet gold-covered rods were delivered to Shen Yi, their gradations showed the wagons filled to capacity with the precious fuel. The gold valuators gave their report: "Sir, there are no problems with the purity. It meets the standards established for annual tributes."

Shen Yi murmured his acknowledgment, but his doubts remained. He glanced up at the second prince. A grubby purplish mark like a lash from a whip marred the young man's forehead. His face was covered in tears and snot, and though his mouth gaped as if he were screaming, he made no sound.

Chen Qingxu spoke quietly. "General Shen, that purple mark— I heard about it during my travels. It's a shamanic technique used to silence its victims. That man's body is stiff as a board; he's probably been tied to his saddle and can't even cough. In another hour, the mark will blacken, and he will collapse and die. Even if an autopsy is conducted, the coroner will only find that he suffered sudden, intense heart palpitations and died of fear."

Shen Yi didn't have time to blush from shyness; he shouted, "Wait! Stop them right there!"

A Black Hawk circling overhead called sharply, "Halt!"

The barbarian second prince seemed to lose his balance as his horse jerked to a stop. He tipped forward, his stiff riding boots striking the edge of one of the violet gold wagons. A resounding *clang* reverberated into the distance.

The corner of the wagon was hollow.

Shen Yi's pupils contracted. "Retreat!"

The order was still ringing in the air when a member of the barbarian delegation lunged at one of the violet gold wagons and was shot and killed by an arrow from a sharp-eyed Black Hawk overhead. The Black Iron Battalion soldiers silently and swiftly drew back. Shen Yi grabbed the bridle of Chen Qingxu's horse and wheeled the animal around before slapping it on the rear and sending it to the back of the column.

A skinny Tianlang youth was hiding under the wagon. One wave of the firestarter in his hand lit the hidden fuse tucked beneath the cargo. He bared a terrifying smile heavenward.

Sparks shot into the sky like a flash of lightning.

The first violet gold wagon exploded, turning the boy to ash. A shock wave swept outward from the center of the blast as a tower of purple flame rose dozens of meters into the sky. The air seemed to boil as ripples of heat rolled over the Black Iron warriors bringing up the rear, scorching the ice-cold backplates of their black armor a vivid red, melting through their gold tanks, and setting off a chain of fatal explosions.

110

SWORDS DRAWN

TANGLED IN ENDLESS NIGHTMARES, Gu Yun missed a step and tumbled deeper into the darkness. His body spasmed as he awoke in a sea of pitch black. He was alert the moment he opened his eyes, his mind snapping to attention as he recalled where he was and what tasks still required his attention.

An ice-cold cheek was suddenly pressed to his forehead. Gu Yun started in surprise—no one in the Black Iron Battalion would dare to treat him so intimately, much less the soldiers of the Jiangbei Garrison. He detected the scent of pacifying fragrance, and as his half-blind eyes adjusted to the gloom, a fuzzy silhouette materialized. His clammy skin had scarcely dried before he was drenched in a second wave of panicked sweat. *What is he doing here?*

A twist of Chang Geng's fingers lit the simple gas lamp above the cot. He silently took a handkerchief from the basin beside the bed and wiped away the sweat beading on Gu Yun's forehead. Gu Yun's body felt boneless; an invisible wound seemed buried deep within his chest, aching dully with the slightest strain. Flustered, Gu Yun fumbled through the blankets and closed his fingers around the frame of his glass monocle. "I can do that myself..."

Head bowed, Chang Geng ignored him, catching his wrist and pinning it down with ease.

An inexplicable feeling of guilt rose in Gu Yun. He licked his lips nervously. *No one talked, right?*

Chang Geng wiped down his body with quick, efficient movements, then gathered Gu Yun's lapels tightly together and tugged the blankets over to bundle Gu Yun up. Finally, he lifted his head and met Gu Yun's eyes.

Gu Yun flashed him a hasty smile.

Chang Geng gazed back at him, expressionless.

Tugging his hand weakly out from beneath the blankets, Gu Yun reached out and laid a hand on the back of Chang Geng's neck. After gently kneading his nape a few times, he ran a finger down the line of Chang Geng's jaw. "You've just seen me and you're already pulling a long face? Has your yifu's beauty faded so fast?"

Struck by a sudden, perverse urge to see how long Gu Yun could keep up his act, Chang Geng asked icily, "And what exactly is the matter with you?"

Through narrowed eyes, Gu Yun read Chang Geng's lips and responded without a change in expression. "I caught a cold."

Chang Geng was speechless. He'd expected Gu Yun to fob him off; he never imagined he would be so half-assed about it.

Gu Yun was determined to cheerfully muddle his way through this interrogation, so he patted Chang Geng's cheek. "Come here, let me see if you've lost any weight."

Chang Geng slapped away his hand. "Gu Zixi!" he snapped, furious.

Immediately, Gu Yun switched tactics. Scowling, he summoned an imperious air that seemed to declare, through sheer intensity of his furrowed brow, a martial law as immovable as the mountains. "Whose tongues have been wagging? General Zhong has scarcely passed, yet the Jiangbei Garrison has grown so undisciplined?"

Chang Geng took a deep breath. "Back at the mourning hall—"

The hypocrite Gu Yun cut in to sling the first accusation. "Which little bastard was standing guard at the mourning hall? Get Yao Chongze in here, I need to ask him whom I ought to court-martial!"

Chang Geng gently ground his teeth.

Gu Yun shook his head, as if he weren't lying like a cheap rug. "The Jiangbei Navy is young indeed. This would never happen in the Black Iron Battalion."

"Is that so?" Chang Geng smiled thinly. "Well, I'm the little bastard you're looking for. So is the marshal going to court-martial me?"

Marshal Gu, ever-versatile master of *The Thirty-Six Stratagems*,[11] had never truly experienced what it meant to be reduced to silence until this moment.

Chang Geng had a belly full of questions, but he knew Gu Yun would never answer them honestly; besides, he couldn't bear to see this idiot work himself into a lather fielding his inquiries. Although the words gathered on the tip of his tongue, he shoved them back down again and again.

He was saved from his dilemma by a sudden disturbance outside the tent. One of Gu Yun's personal guards called urgently. "Your Highness! Prince Yan!"

Frowning, Chang Geng stood up and stepped outside. "What's going on?"

He was still speaking when the ground began to quake. Chang Geng's expression turned grim—these were the tremors of naval long guns shelling the near shore.

Suddenly, Chang Geng realized the Jiangbei Garrison was ablaze with light. The rumble of approaching hoofbeats filled his ears as cold light glinted from iron armor. A copper squall blared overhead, the sound heavy in the humid Jiangbei air, reverberating into the

---

11 A sixth-century essay detailing a series of stratagems used in war, politics, and civilian life.

distance like muted thunder and startling the north bank awake. Gas lamps blinked into existence one by one aboard the sea dragons anchored offshore, their chilly gleam piercing the thick mist as they readied themselves to cast off, while the white beams of the watch-towers swept across the breadth of Jiangbei.

They were under attack.

Even without his hearing, Gu Yun recognized the shaking earth and the flashes of light spilling into the tent. His first act when he arrived was to strengthen the defensive perimeter, but that had only been to bolster morale. He hadn't actually expected the usually imperturbable Far Western fleet to launch a surprise attack on the Jiangbei Navy at a time like this.

Sometimes, no matter how desperate one's efforts, they were still bound by the plans of heaven. Gu Yun had exhausted his mental re-serves countering the Westerners. How was he to know his enemy was dealing with a fire in their own backyard—one that had mysteriously resulted in the appointment of a commander whose battle tactics were completely antithetical to those of his predecessor. Gu Yun had no time to examine this sudden shift. Throwing on his outer robe, he rose from the bed and stumbled as his legs nearly gave out on him. It was as if he had taken five kilograms of muscle-weakening powder.

A Black Hawk screeched down from the sky, landing directly before the commander's tent. Before the soldier could open his mouth, a red-tagged emergency dispatch tumbled from his hands, rolling over the ground until it came to a stop under Gu Yun's out-stretched foot. Gu Yun clutched at the headboard and bent down with great difficulty to retrieve it, opening the mail canister under the light of the gas lamp as the Black Hawk quickly gave his report. "Sir, the eighteen tribes used their surrender as a pretext to bring a caravan of six wagons full of violet gold to our border. The leaders were all suicide fighters. They set fire to the violet gold and used the explosion to break through our defensive lines. Right after, an army of elite troops numbering in the tens of thousands turned out in full force. They seem intent on fighting to the death."

Gu Yun looked up from the letter in his hands. "What is the current situation? How many have we lost?"

"This subordinate left too quickly and does not know."

After a moment to collect himself, Gu Yun gritted his teeth and scraped together enough strength to grab the windslasher hanging at the head of the bed. "Bring me a suit of heavy armor," he ordered. Right now, only a heavy armor's built-in support could compensate for his physical weakness.

Raising a hand to stop the guard from leaving, Chang Geng turned to Gu Yun. "Zixi, you stay here and oversee the main force. I'll go," he said, voice low.

Gu Yun gazed at him steadily, his mouth pressed into a tight line. Chang Geng recognized this expression—it was a sign that he was about to say *no*.

Before he could, Chang Geng spoke up. "You don't trust me?"

Gu Yun sighed. "I..."

Chang Geng extended a hand. "Give me the windslasher; I'll go in your stead. If you trust me, don't set one foot outside this tent."

The distant flames of war danced in Chang Geng's eyes. His pupils seemed to catch fire, burning with the intensity of Great Liang's desperate fight for survival.

Taking cautious hold of one end of the windslasher, Chang Geng slowly but firmly pulled it from Gu Yun's grip. The task was not a difficult one—Gu Yun's wrist was shaking, drained of strength. Chang Geng slung the black-iron weapon across his back. "Please allow me to be the marshal's pawn," he said, dipping in a shallow bow.

Gu Yun stared deep into his eyes before spinning to face the Black Hawk. "Bring me a sand table," he instructed. "You'll act as my runner."

Chang Geng strode from the tent, windslasher in hand.

The Western sea monster that had traversed oceans to arrive on these shores slowly surfaced in the fog-shrouded river. In its massive shadow, countless Western dragonets sliced through the water in parallel formation, closing in fast as tiger sharks. Gu Yun's defensive line reacted immediately. Warning sirens blared, and the Jiangbei Garrison's light cavalry, which had been standing at the ready, split into three groups and sped toward key strategic positions along the northern bank.

They ran head-first into the Far Western navy secretly attempting to make landfall. Blood streamed down the river as artillery fire twisted across the water's surface in a brilliant sea of fireworks.

"Cannons, maintain barrage fire." Chang Geng called orders from horseback. "Parhelions, provide covering fire while they reload. Black Hawks, stand by—I need you suited up and beyond the parhelions' firing range in five minutes. We control the skies; keep the enemy's armored hawks grounded on that sea monster flagship. Pin them down and take them out!"

"Tighten the right flank!"

"All sea dragons, load gunpowder and prepare to get underway!"

For a moment, the runner beside Chang Geng thought he'd misheard. "Did Your Highness say *all* the dragons? Are we engaging the enemy on all fronts?"

Chang Geng glanced down at the soldier from his seat astride his horse. "Correct. It's time to show these foreigners that Great Liang has a navy as well."

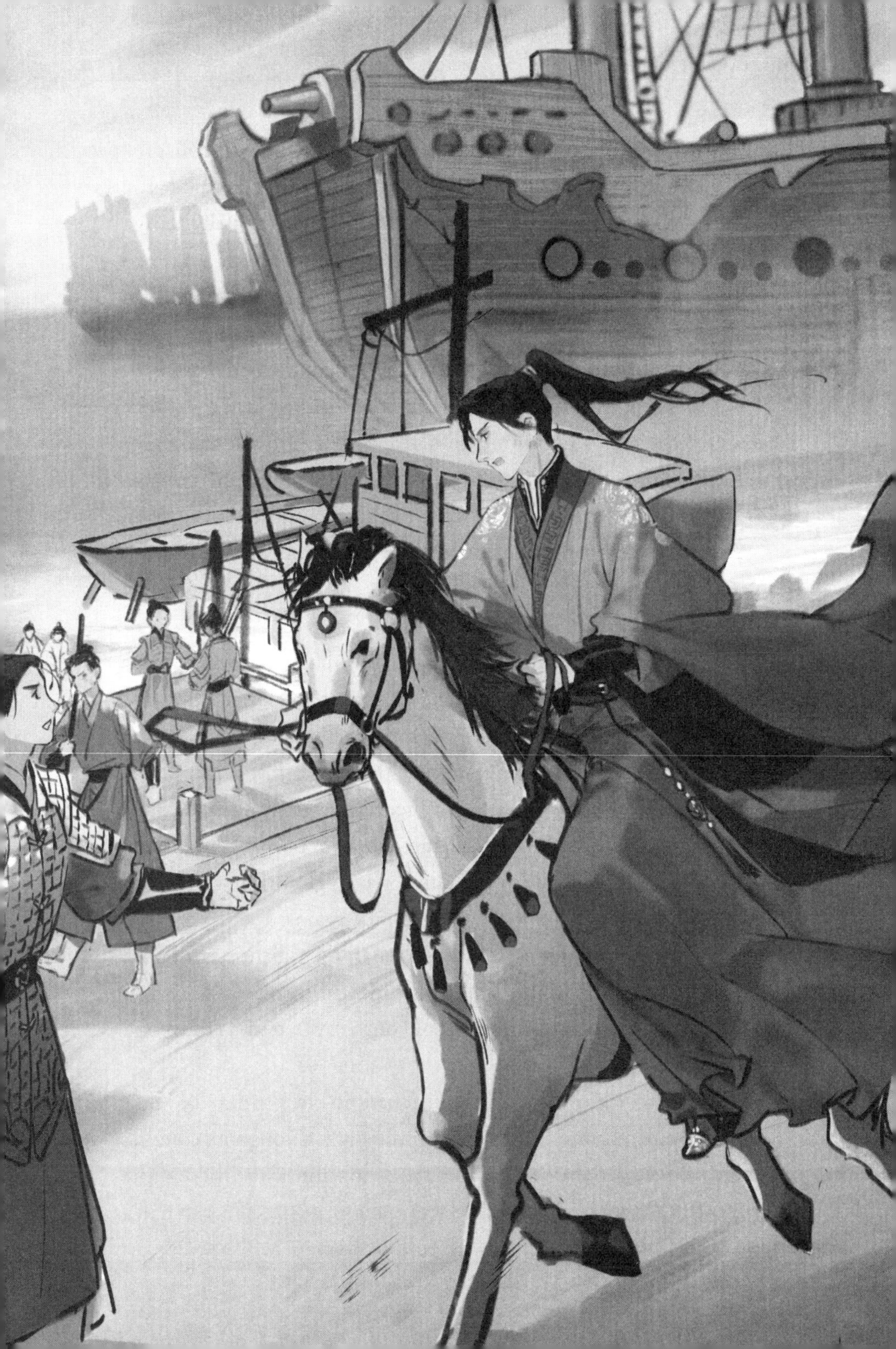

Once upon a time, Great Liang's navy was so weak it collapsed from a single blow; even its commander had perished in that battle. In the aftermath, it had fled northward in a panic, hastily reorganized by a civil official who could barely ride a horse. Scattered survivors of the navy joined forces with their brothers-in-arms from military branches all over the country who had likewise lost their command structure to war. They formed the most oddly assorted band of soldiers imaginable and returned to the place they once suffered their greatest humiliation. The former ground troops got seasick, completely disoriented the moment they stepped onto a boat. They struggled to make sense of the complicated navigation systems—systems that lagged far behind their enemies' advanced sea dragon warships...

All of that seemed like a lifetime ago.

The Jiangbei Navy had undergone two major reorganizations since its establishment. The Lingshu Institute had worked in the shadows overhauling the navy's warships three times, even sending over a replica of the Far Westerners' lightning-fast "tiger shark" dragonets. Now, as a rare northerly breeze blew over the twin banks of the Yangtze River, the altar lamps in the mourning hall flared with bright light, setting the hanging screens aglow. The white cloth fluttered like soul-summoning flags, stark against the darkness of the Jiangbei encampment. It was as though the valiant spirit of old General Zhong still walked among the living.

The blade had been forged; it could only be whetted on the blood of its enemies.

Unable to see or hear, Gu Yun relied on the tremors beneath his feet to determine the distance of the fight. Though he couldn't monitor the battlefront in person, he didn't appear worried in the least. The Black Hawk at his side was stunned to find Gu Yun had a map of the Jiangbei Navy's defenses laid out in his head. The strong and weak points in their formation, the places where the enemy was likely to break through... He predicted them all without fail.

He had already given Chang Geng his command of the front line, and now he magnanimously gave him his unreserved trust as well. He issued no orders, allowing Chang Geng to marshal Jiangbei's three divisions as he saw fit. Gu Yun kept one eye on the breadth of the battlefield, gauging the distribution of violet gold and ammunition to the various squadrons. At the same time, he considered the red-tagged emergency dispatch, splitting his attention between the northern and southern fronts to encompass every theater of war across Great Liang.

The Far Westerners' assault tonight was a performance put on for the barbarians; they fought not for total victory, but for the upper hand at the bargaining table. If Great Liang could hold the northern front, these Far Westerners would become little more than a band of buffoons. But if the north should fall...

As the smoke of endless cannon fire wrapped Jiangbei in a hazy fog, the silver snowscape of the northern border boiled into a searing heat.

Jialai Yinghuo had sacrificed a band of suicide fighters and his own son to blast his way clear with precious violet gold. An army of northern barbarian warriors rushed out in the wake of the explosion, hell-bent on slaughtering all in their path.

Shen Yi immediately pulled the Black Iron Battalion, which had advanced deep into enemy territory, back half a dozen kilometers and led their adversaries on a wild chase through the snow. That the soldiers of the Black Iron Battalion were of the highest caliber went without saying. They proceeded to stretch the barbarians' offensive line over a vast area, reducing deep columns of soldiers to a single man.

The barbarians had flipped on their adversaries as fast as a scholar might flip the pages of a book—but the soldiers of the Northern Border Garrison were accustomed to their good neighbors' volatile moods. Upon seeing the Black Iron Battalion's signal, they moved out at once. He Ronghui and Shen Yi had worked together for years, and their collaboration was seamless. The Northern Border Garrison reinforcements soon tore through the enemy's overextended offense.

But no one anticipated that Jialai Yinghuo would empty his coffers to the last cent. The barbarian light cavalry fell away to reveal a small formation of war chariots he had painstakingly stockpiled over the years. Several hundred suits of heavy armor turned out in full strength, using their considerable firepower to push forward like a giant net smashing directly into the dark whirlwind that was the Black Iron Battalion. The battlefield lapsed into stalemate.

Less than an hour later, the northern barbarians' reinforcements arrived—neither human soldiers nor steel armor, but rather a large convoy of wagons filled with violet gold. Wave after wave was set afire as the northern front transformed into a sea of scalding steam. Even the blizzard winds couldn't dispel the blistering heat. The temperature rose dramatically, and swaths of ice and snow melted into hot springs that seeped into the parched earth. White mist swallowed the plains in every direction as purple fire painted a singular, tragic scene.

A suit of armor needed only get a little too close for its steel surface to cook its wearer. The barbarians seemed determined to hollow out the north. Working without cease, they gave everything—their chariots, their people, even the heart of their earth—as fuel to burn out a path in a dazzling pyrotechnic display.

By nightfall, the Black Iron Battalion had no choice but to retreat once again.

111

ETERNITY

THE BATTLE ON THE NORTHERN border devolved into chaos. Jialai Yinghuo, last of his family line, seemed increasingly unhinged, preferring to die in a fight to the death rather than allow his enemy a single drop of violet gold. Wherever his troops fell short in terms of strength, he ordered his subordinates to set alight their violet gold wagons and carve a fiery path through their adversary's defenses. Brandishing hellfire, he fought the Black Iron Battalion to an impasse. As for Great Liang's troops, they could do nothing but resign themselves to these bizarre tactics. Through this sort of back and forth, the battle dragged on to the third day.

Cao Chunhua no longer bothered with his appearance. His mink fur hat had been pressed into service as a fan as hot sweat dripped from his temples. He glanced enviously at Shen Yi, who was stripped to the waist. "Good heavens, has it ever been this warm during the second month on the northern border? You must be feeling nice and cool, General Shen."

Shen Yi shot him an irritated glare. *Like hell I'm feeling cool!*

His back was mottled with burns. He hadn't had time to deal with them on the front line, so it was only now when He Ronghui relieved him that Shen Yi could finally catch his breath, remove his armor, and treat his wounds. The blisters from the burns had been rubbed raw against his armor, leaving his back a bloody mess. He looked as if he had been skinned alive.

Seeing Shen Yi's shoulders tight with strain, Chen Qingxu hurried to ask, "General, am I pressing too hard?"

Shen Yi flushed and shook his head. Even the searing pain of the burns couldn't distract him from the humiliation he felt in that moment. Exposing his chest and back to a young woman like this—it was so improper, so distasteful, he could barely speak to Miss Chen for shame.

Chen Qingxu assumed the redness of his neck and ears was due to the heat. She felt a bit conflicted. She had been in the thick of many jianghu gang fights and had worked in a field hospital for some time. In these situations, she had always come and gone with ease. She had little firsthand battlefield experience. The current clash was worlds different from Gu Yun's cunning takedown of Prince Wei's attempted insurrection all those years ago. When two armies composed of tens of thousands of seasoned troops met in pitched battle, the screams of soldiers and horses, the roar of cannons…all of it blurred into an overwhelming pandemonium. It was too easy to lose one's way at the slightest distraction. Never mind remaining calm and collected as the commander in such a battle, the fact that these soldiers could follow their superiors' orders in the midst of such a din was a testament to their stringent training.

On a battlefield like this one, no matter how capable or skilled one was in martial arts, their ability to enact tangible change was limited. Even the most indomitable stone pillar would soon be overcome by the sea of soldiers and wall of artillery fire.

When Chen Qingxu worked at the field hospital, she had treated soldier after soldier who had lost an arm or a leg and suffered the most horrifying physical trauma imaginable. Now she saw with her own eyes how those wounds came to be.

Like a cave of demons that consumes human flesh, Chen Qingxu thought as she trimmed necrotic flesh from Shen Yi's body with nimble fingers before carefully cleaning and applying medicine to his burns. When the two armies clashed, Shen Yi attended to all corners of the battlefield—yet despite being pulled in every direction, he had still made a point of looking after her. Grabbing the bridle of her horse, he had stared intently at Chen Qingxu for a moment before telling her somewhat stiffly, "Stay with me."

For some inexplicable reason, that look had left an impression on her more profound than even the towering flames of war.

"General, you mustn't wear light armor anymore," Chen Qingxu said. "It's too heavy and will chafe against your wounds. You will be much worse off if these fester and you get a fever."

Shen Yi was drenched in sweat. Rationally, he knew Chen Qingxu didn't mean anything by her quiet urging, but he still broke out in gooseflesh. His body tugged itself apart in disorder as his skin tried to decide whether to sweat or shiver.

He was saved by a messenger bursting in. "General Shen!" the soldier cried, gasping for breath. "Old General Cai was grazed by a barbarian cannon just now and fell from his horse. The enemy is rallying its troops there to break through our defensive line!"

Shen Yi lurched to his feet. The motion caused the burns on his back to flare with such agony he nearly howled to the heavens—but as interim commander in chief standing before the young lady he fancied, he couldn't do it.

"Report—General! An emergency dispatch from Jiangbei!"

When Gu Yun had gone south years ago to catch the runaway Chang Geng, it had taken him several days to fly from the Silk Road in the Western Regions to Jiangnan in Black Hawk armor. Since then, the Lingshu Institute had upgraded the gold tanks on Great Liang's military scouts and significantly increased their maximum velocity. Now, in an emergency, they could traverse the distance between Jiangbei and the northern border in less than a day.

Gu Yun's name was like a pillar of support for Shen Yi amid the chaos; upon hearing this, he immediately relaxed. His entire body swayed in place, and he nearly fell over. Shen Yi reached out on instinct and grabbed something to steady himself. Only when he returned to his senses did he realize Miss Chen had lent him her hand.

Miss Chen's hand was like the rest of her—slightly cool to the touch. Her fingers were so slender as to be almost bony, yet possessed the firm strength of a master of her craft.

Mortified, Shen Yi snatched his hand back and turned to the messenger. "What did the marshal say?"

The Black Hawk blurted his message in a single breath: "The Far Western army launched a surprise attack on the Jiangbei Garrison. The marshal told me to inform all the generals here: should the northern border fall, prepare to beg for forgiveness before your ancestors!"

Shen Yi felt a weight as heavy as Mount Tai fall on his shoulders with a thunderous crash, the word *ancestors* smashing into him with such violence he nearly spat blood. He wanted to cry, but he had no tears. Shen Yi had never envied Gu Yun's glory as the leader of the three divisions of the Black Iron Battalion. Now, he wished for nothing more than to weep and beg Gu Yun to return from Jiangbei and relieve Shen Yi of his command.

Didn't he say he'd be back after checking on the southern front?

Didn't he say appointing Shen Yi commander in chief was a temporary measure?

Shen Yi felt the greatest tragedy of his life was his poor judgment of character when it came to making friends. He couldn't make sense of it—he was simply an ordinary man with an overabundance of compassion and a complete and utter lack of ambition. He had zero interest in toadying up to powerful officials, nor did he wish his achievements to be remembered for all eternity. So how exactly had the astronomical burden of the northern border landed on his unassuming head?

He Ronghui rushed in, bringing a wave of heat. "Jiping, Cai-lao's troops can't hold the barbarians much longer. I'm going to back him up!"

Shen Yi snapped back to his senses. He pinched hard at the space between his brows before accepting Gu Yun's token of authority from the messenger with a solemn expression. "You can't leave—the Black Hawks are all that's suppressing the barbarians' movements right now. Let me think..."

"General Shen, this humble general is willing to go!"

Shen Yi raised his head, seeking the source of the voice, and spotted a young man standing in the corner. He looked like he had yet to come of age, his cheeks still childish and round. Cao Chunhua reminded him quietly, "Old General Cai's youngest son. He's been fighting in the vanguard here on the northern border this entire time. He's only nineteen, but he's crossed swords with the barbarians several dozen times."

Seeing he had Shen Yi's attention, the young man took another step forward and repeated himself in resolute tones. "This humble general is willing to go. I'll die before I allow the barbarians to advance another step!"

Shen Yi started in surprise—for an instant, he felt he was seeing Gu Yun in his youth.

More than a decade ago, when news of rebellion in the Western Regions reached the capital, the late emperor and his courtiers, drunk on the illusion of peace and prosperity, had stared at each other aghast. Pandemonium had broken out in the grand assembly the next day. Some officials had gone so far as to suggest distributing wanted posters among the common folk in hopes of finding and recalling old General Zhong Chan from retirement. It had been the orphan of the Gu family who calmly brought the frenzied arguing to an end.

At seventeen years of age, Gu Yun had yet to shed the fearless arrogance of youth. "This subject is willing to go. Our enemies in the borderlands near Xiliang are no more than a band of bungling clowns. Do they think the windslashers of the Black Iron Battalion are too rusty to part the heads of scoundrels like themselves from their necks?"

Now, little General Cai sniffed and said without batting an eye, "The mad barbarian dogs are merely mounting a last-ditch struggle. This humble general may be young and inexperienced, but I have strength enough to hoist my father's blade. I will ensure none of them come out of this battle alive!"

The older generation of famous generals had either died on the battlefield or lost their edge with age. Yet the mountains and rivers remained unchanged; there would always be youngsters who were fearless in their naivete as they donned their armor, drew their parhelion bows, and rose above the rest.

When a decade passed, another decade would come. After a century passed, another century would follow—and so ever onward, for all eternity.

Shen Yi's frantic thoughts went still all at once. He handed the token of authority to little General Cai. "Very well, my good brother. Go on."

When he was gone, Shen Yi opened Gu Yun's emergency dispatch. The oral proclamation the Black Hawk relayed had been harsh and uncompromising, but Gu Yun's letter was perfectly reasonable.

The barbarians are a cornered beast fighting for its life. This will be their last stand. The eighteen tribes have already been rocked by internal conflict; they can't drag this fight out for long. The first few days will be the most difficult. But so long as we hold our ground, we can expect their morale to slowly and steadily decline. When the time comes, call for a ceasefire. Dispatch an envoy to sow further dissension among the eighteen tribes. In the days that follow, perhaps we can settle things on the northern border once and for all. Be careful, but do not fear. I may not be with you in person, but I march with the Black Iron Battalion in spirit.

Shen Yi's eyes stung. "Relay my orders to all units: pin the enemy down—we don't give them an inch!"

Unbeknownst to Shen Yi, the man who boasted so easily about his spirit marching with the Black Iron Battalion was not at all relaxed when he penned this letter. It took great effort for Gu Yun to steady his hand, and by the time he finished stamping his personal seal, a stack of battlefield reports had gathered on his desk. Perhaps to keep Gu Yun from worrying, Chang Geng had appointed a special team of light cavalrymen to ride between the front line and the commander's tent with the latest developments on the battlefield. All his life, there had rarely been a military engagement that did not require Gu Yun to personally step onto the field, so this was quite a novel experience. Inside the commander's tent, no extraneous information disturbed his thought process. He didn't need to worry about evading overt or covert enemy attacks, nor deal with the violent emotional upheavals of combat. On the contrary, he was practically a bystander as he observed the entire battlefield with a bird's eye view.

The opening stages of this battle were a test of the tightness of the Jiangbei Garrison's formations and their navy's vigilance. Old General Zhong and Gu Yun had laid a strong foundation that allowed their troops to easily withstand the Far Westerners' bombardment. Once this foundation had been blasted away and the two armies' strengths were evenly matched, however, their commanders' skill and experience would determine the rest.

Gu Yun's back prickled with cold sweat when he heard the Black Hawk's battlefield report. The enemy commander had laid out his troops with a shrewd ruthlessness; whoever he was, the man was a true expert at naval strategy. Even if Gu Yun personally took to the field, he would have to proceed with utmost caution.

A Black Hawk darted in to report the latest developments. "A small group of enemy ships in the southwestern quadrant has fallen behind the rest of the fleet. Prince Yan has adjusted the vanguard's course to break through the enemy line."

Gu Yun's heart stuttered in his chest as he jumped to his feet. Unlike the vanguard, who were required only to be brave above all else, a commander's blood might burn hot, but it was critical that their mind remain cool when confronting the enemy. Commanders who lacked experience and got caught up in the killing could easily get carried away by their troops' bloodlust.

He promptly broke his promise. "Bring me my armor and prepare my horse!"

For Chang Geng, this battle had proved extremely draining. During the capital siege he'd needed only concern himself with defending the area above and below a small section of the city wall— not to mention, he'd gone into that fight expecting to be killed in action. This time, he fought with the entire northern half of the nation and tens of thousands of Jiangbei troops at his back.

The sailors of the Liangjiang navy weren't fitted with hawk armor, and the Jiangbei Garrison's Hawk Division was even greener than its navy. When it came to combat, they were more difficult to command than the armored hawks of the Northern Camp, let alone the Black Hawks. Meanwhile, the enemy utilized that impregnable sea-monster warship as their center of operations. After weathering Great Liang's first wave of attack, they steadily seized the tempo of the battle. Chang Geng searched anxiously for any weakness in their ranks—if his forces couldn't break through, they would have to remain on the defensive. The instant his vanguard tore a hole in the enemy's left flank, he instinctively directed the main battleship fleet to press their advantage. Chang Geng was by nature extraordinarily calm and perceptive; the chase had barely begun before he sensed something amiss.

By then, it was too late. The Far Western corvettes had swarmed forward at full speed and surrounded their enemy, severing Chang Geng's path of retreat.

"What should we do, Your Highness? Should we attempt to return to port?"

Chang Geng's palms turned clammy with sweat as Gu Yun's words echoed in his ears—*On the battlefield, whoever clings to life is the first to die.*

"Don't be absurd. Full speed ahead," Chang Geng said coldly. "It's but a swarm of flies on our tail. Ignore them and stick to the plan— puncture the enemy's left flank!"

He would transform this entire fleet into a fearless vanguard that didn't flinch in the face of death. Was their enemy hoping to catch a turtle in a jar? In that case, he'd simply shatter the jar.

The messenger shivered at the ruthless edge in his voice. "Yes, sir!"

The fleet of sea dragons was like a spinning windslasher. They dove into the heart of the enemy formation, fighting at close quarters. Chang Geng knew if they took too long smashing through their adversary's defenses, they would find themselves hemmed in on all sides once the troops on their tail caught up.

The Jiangbei Navy's long guns and short-barrel cannons loaded their ammunition. Firelight sparked in the darkness over the sea dragon warships like scattered stars—it was the glow of the cannons' gold tanks. Chang Geng wiped sweaty palms on his filigree sachet stuffed full of pacifying fragrance and opened his mouth to give his next orders when something strange happened.

The enemy ships blocking their path suddenly and inexplicably melted away.

Chang Geng stared. What new ruse was this?

But there was no way to pull the brakes on a fleet that was sailing full-bore. Great Liang's navy plowed straight through the enemy fleet, emerging at their adversaries' rear unimpeded. Through night vision field scopes, a signalman on the enemy command ship could be seen frantically waving his flags, bidding the errant ships to come back around. The retreating Far Western corvettes ignored the order completely, openly defying commands as they cut through the water and refusing to lure the Jiangbei Navy's cannon fire.

Chang Geng was baffled, but there was no time to waste. He ordered the cannons to switch targets, redirecting all their firepower to their rear with a blast that parted the Yangtze River. The high-speed tiger sharks chasing them had no time to evade; they were struck head-on. As the small vessels took fire, their high-efficiency gold tanks detonated in a chain of explosions. The surface of the water seemed to boil as Great Liang's ships shot out from the fray. Having somehow survived the trip through enemy lines without mishap, they retreated to a safe distance.

Aboard the Western flagship, Mister Ja was fuming. "Bastard! He dares disobey orders in the middle of battle?!"

The lines of the pope's face were so severe they seemed carved by a knife.

The left flank that had bolted were the warships led by the holy emissary. Just then, the man in question was likewise gnashing his teeth—his small fleet had been meant to provide backup, but after several changes to formation, the dastardly old pope had shoved his squadron to the van!

Only when Great Liang's warships were bearing down on him did he realize he'd been set up as cannon fodder. Even the king couldn't fault the pope if his emissary was tragically killed in action. The holy emissary refused to take the fall; he withdrew without a second thought, caring not a whit that doing so would scupper the Far Western navy's battle formation.

Chang Geng was like a venomous snake; the moment he had the opportunity to turn the tables, he reared up and barraged the enemy mercilessly in retaliation for the fright he'd suffered a moment ago. The Westerners now found themselves on the back foot.

The momentum of the battle had shifted. On the riverbank, a light cavalryman raced to the commander's tent to relay his report to Gu Yun.

Gu Yun had already donned his armor and mounted his horse. Upon hearing the news, an odd expression stole over his face. He thought somewhat helplessly that maybe it wasn't too far-fetched to claim that Great Liang's fortunes rose and fell with Prince Yan—that maybe it was actually true. Reining his horse around, he headed back without a word to the main commander's tent, where he stowed his armor and ordered his men to keep quiet about the fact he had stepped out.

After Chang Geng sank their left flank, the Western navy was like a man with a lame leg. But even at such a substantial disadvantage, the pope had a fearsome command of the seas and remained a formidable opponent for the young and inexperienced Prince Yan. The battle dragged on till dawn.

Gu Yun reached up and turned off the gas lamp. Then, he picked up his brush and penned three letters in rapid succession: The first was an order for the transport of violet gold. The second was a request for armor and engines from the nearest branch of the Lingshu Institute. Last of all was a military brief to be sent to the capital.

When he finished, he rubbed his stiff neck and instructed the Black Hawk standing by, "Tell His Highness Prince Yan—there's no need to pursue if the Westerners retreat."

The Black Hawk started in surprise. Before he could ask Gu Yun how he knew the Westerners would retreat, a messenger burst into the tent. "Sir, the enemy flagship is withdrawing south!"

Gu Yun showed no sign of surprise; he merely waved a hand toward the Black Hawk. Not daring to delay, the soldier took to the sky to deliver the message.

Freed of dividing his attention between the various acute crises that developed in battle, Gu Yun could instead devote himself wholly to analyzing the entire field. He had determined the depth of the enemy's violet gold reserves hours ago. After fighting through the night, their adversary had more or less reached their limit.

When their violet gold tanks ran empty, their enemy would have no choice but to return to their encampment empty-handed and tally their disastrous number of casualties. Conflict in the ranks was sure to follow. Rather than continuing to advance, it would be more effective for Great Liang's navy to apply pressure from afar.

Less than an hour later, the Western navy ordered a general retreat, just as he'd expected. The night raid was declared a great failure; they hadn't even made landfall on the northern bank.

To show he was a man of his word, in lieu of stepping out of the commander's tent, Gu Yun stood at the door to greet Chang Geng. He paid no mind to the blood staining Chang Geng's clothes as he spread his arms to embrace him.

Only then did Chang Geng realize he was utterly spent. He swayed on his feet as he wrapped his hands around Gu Yun's waist and mumbled into his ear, "I don't want you to go to war ever again."

112

URGENCY

IS VOICE WAS LOW and muffled. Even with his mouth pressed to Gu Yun's ear, Gu Yun couldn't make out his words. Tilting his head back to look at Chang Geng in confusion, he asked, "What did you say?"

Chang Geng met Gu Yun's eyes, half-obscured by his glass monocle. He was exhausted, but his blood was still racing, his body burning so hot his throat felt dry and cracked. For a fleeting instant, he wanted to pull Gu Yun tight against him right there in the open—but as he scanned their surroundings, he spotted Great Master Liao Ran standing in the distance with a mien that declared his total indifference to worldly temptations. Chang Geng couldn't help but laugh as he realized he had nearly gotten carried away. He released Gu Yun's waist and picked up his hand instead, calming himself to the beat of the man's weak but steady pulse. "It's nothing. I saw a courier heading north just now. Did you send a memorial to the capital?"

"I did." Gu Yun nodded. "This time, the initiative lies with the imperial court to send someone to the foreigners. We've been passively reacting all this time. Now, we can make this move with confidence."

"Are we going to sue for peace?"

"Of course not," Gu Yun said, serene. "Can a man allow others to sleep in his own bed? And that's not even reckoning the debts of blood yet to be paid. Just thinking of those animals occupying the fertile lands of Jiangnan makes me sick to my stomach."

Chang Geng grasped his meaning immediately. "You intend to drag this out until we can recover the occupied territories."

The plan unfolded in his mind: Signal an interest in opening peace talks. Let the enemy feel they'd caught a break after failing to achieve their objectives yet leave room for discord to brew in their ranks. Make unreasonable demands to keep them talking while instigating small-scale skirmishes that would slowly push back the enemy's front line and provide opportunities to train Great Liang's navy. Finally, once the northern bank had completed its preparations and the young Jiangbei Navy had matured, take the south in one fell swoop.

Gu Yun murmured in agreement. He allowed Chang Geng to take his wrist and pull him into the commander's tent before reaching up to wipe Chang Geng's cheek. "Your Highness, your face is filthy," he said with a smile.

Chang Geng felt half his bones melt in response to Gu Yun's sudden tenderness. Yet he quickly grew wary—he couldn't help but suspect Gu Yun's gentle attitude portended bad news. Sure enough, Gu Yun sat down and took Chang Geng's hand, squeezing it fitfully before breaking the silence. "There's one more thing."

Arching a brow, Chang Geng gazed down at him, his face absent emotion.

Still holding Chang Geng's hand, Gu Yun covered it with his other palm and ducked to press a kiss to Chang Geng's cracked fingertips. "I plan to stall the Far Westerners while I wrap things up on the northern front."

"You're going back to the northern border?" Chang Geng asked.

Gu Yun nodded.

"When?"

A pause. "Soon."

When Gu Yun said *soon*, he meant he might leave at any time. If he felt the situation in Jiangbei was more or less stable, he would leave that very night. If there were a few adjustments or mobilization orders that still required his authorization, he would sort them out tonight and leave first thing in the morning.

"What will you do then? Rush back and forth between the two fronts?" Chang Geng asked.

Gu Yun said nothing—a tacit confirmation.

He suddenly felt he had failed Chang Geng. Years ago, on the road to the Western Regions, he had solemnly vowed to Chen Qingxu that even if Chang Geng went mad, he would take responsibility for him to the bitter end. Yet in recent days he had begun to quietly worry he wouldn't be able to make good on that promise. Gu Yun had no fears when it came to his own mortality. Old General Zhong's mourning hall was right there. When he thought about it, it seemed his elders, whether malignant or benign, teachers and tormentors alike, had nearly all passed on. He knew even peerless heroes couldn't escape the ultimate fate of mankind; there was no need to agonize over it. He was just afraid...that he couldn't always be there to protect this little lunatic—that he would end up adding to his burdens instead.

Gu Yun's sudden show of silent, deep regret left Chang Geng at a bit of a loss. When he finally saw it for what it was, he was struck by a feeling like someone had torn a hole in his heart. Blood poured out in an endless stream with nowhere to go.

His heart ached unbearably, but he forced himself to smile. "All right," Chang Geng said, his tone light, if not excessively so. "Don't worry, just go. Did you see the schematics I tucked in your bags?

Believe it or not, soon—maybe by the time you've mopped up the barbarians—I'll be done laying down the first tracks for the steam locomotive."

Soon he could build a Great Liang respected in all corners of the world. When the time came, perhaps the three divisions of the Black Iron Battalion would merely guard the entrance of the Silk Road and help maintain order among the merchants. Or perhaps they could be deployed to the border regions to help clear the land for agriculture. Whether his general wanted to drink grape wine on the frontiers or pick fights with pet birds in the capital, Chang Geng would accept it all. No longer would Gu Yun have to rush constantly from one corner of the nation to another; he wouldn't be compelled to do anything ever again.

"You've participated in one little skirmish and you're gasping for breath," Gu Yun said with fond exasperation. "Maybe you should figure out how you're going to get back into the Grand Council first."

Chang Geng leaned in. "How will you reward me if I succeed?"

"What do you want?" asked Gu Yun, ever magnanimous.

After a moment of consideration, Chang Geng pressed closer and whispered something into Gu Yun's ear. One could only guess what shameless filth Prince Yan relayed in secret; even the half-deaf Gu Yun couldn't bear to listen after a time. Laughing, he cursed at him, "Fuck off."

This obscenity landed directly on the ears of Governor Yao, who had come to report on the battlefield. Utterly bewildered, he asked, "Where would the marshal like this lower official to fuck off to?"

Chang Geng clasped his hands behind his back, unhurried. Standing there with an unfathomable smile on his face, he looked as poised as any famous beauty. Yet as Gu Yun turned his full attention to his discussion with Yao Zhen, Chang Geng's satisfied smile faded, and his countenance gradually turned solemn.

I'm running out of time, Chang Geng thought to himself.

Gu Yun stayed until the second day. He accompanied Chang Geng to burn a stick of incense for General Zhong Chan and ate a bowl of congee personally prepared by Prince Yan in the commander's tent. As per usual, he was displeased by the sight of the greens in his bowl and alluded to his displeasure with a declaration that he had no desire to live like a goat. As per usual, he was ignored. But even persnickety goats had to eat; Gu Yun had no choice but to swallow the hateful things whole.

Bright and early the next morning, he set out for the northern border.

When Gu Yun arrived in a flurry of activity, he was gratified to find Shen Yi had successfully held the line along the northern front against the rampaging barbarians.

The deeper Jialai Yinghuo's insanity, the closer the eighteen tribes drew to their final days. Just as Gu Yun predicted, after putting up a fierce fight for four or five days, the northern barbarian offensive slowed considerably. During one overzealous pursuit of the retreating enemy, little General Cai had captured one of the barbarian strongholds. But upon charging in, all he found was a bit of leftover violet gold. All the people had long pulled out.

Cao Chunhua gestured wildly as he spoke, spit flying. "If Jialai can act now, he must have purged—or at the very least suppressed—the rebel faction. But he still needs able bodies to fight a war; he can't kill everyone. At most, he's executed some of the ringleaders from the major tribes as a warning to the rest. It's not impossible that the rebel faction could rise from the ashes."

"They only need an opportunity," Shen Yi said.

"Exactly," Cao Chunhua agreed. "A while back, General Cai mentioned a group of barbarians secretly came to trade violet gold for other goods. General Cai was cautious; he monitored the exchanges carefully and recorded every transaction. He even had portraits made of the traders who came frequently. Well, I took a look at the sketches and spotted a familiar face."

As he spoke, he pulled a simple scroll from his sleeve and spread it open on the small table. He pointed at the figure in the painting: "This is Jialai Yinghuo's stable boy. I know this guy. He works for Jialai Yinghuo's steward and spends his spare time lording the connection over others... After so many years, their people are tired of war. The ambitious families of the eighteen tribes aren't the only ones with resentment toward Jialai Yinghuo. I see an opening here."

"How confident are you about this?" Gu Yun asked.

Cao Chunhua shot him a flirtatious glance, his tongue curling around his words as he purred, "That depends on what the marshal can offer in terms of monetary assets."

If this kid had stayed with me a little longer, I would have beaten these terrible habits out of him at any cost, Gu Yun thought. He dismissed the affectedly delicate Cao Chunhua with a wave; out of sight, out of mind.

Shen Yi was about to ask about the specifics of the operation when Gu Yun's personal guard announced Chen Qingxu's arrival.

Gu Yun clicked his tongue in amazement as he watched that idiot Shen Yi straighten from his messy slouch, his face tensing as if he'd encountered a formidable foe. Gu Yun had never seen him so solemn before, even in audiences with the emperor.

Chen Qingxu had come to say goodbye. She was set on leaving with Cao Chunhua to find what Jialai Yinghuo knew about the

barbarian goddess's secret poison. Alarmed, Shen Yi shot Gu Yun
a look. Gu Yun feigned ignorance, his eyes darting away. He had
come to understand the temperament of the Chen family fairly well
over the years. Miss Chen was notifying them of her plans to be
polite; she wasn't soliciting their opinions.

Since Gu Yun had failed him, Shen Yi could do nothing but
rally his half-paralyzed tongue and take to the field himself. "A miracle doctor like Miss Chen is invaluable. She shouldn't be on the
front lines in the first place. It would be beyond reckless to let her
go behind enemy lines! If anything should happen to her... Right,
marshal?"

Gu Yun responded accordingly. "Mm, indeed, Jiping has a point."

"My reason for coming north was always to find Jialai Yinghuo
and learn about the barbarians' shamanic arts," Chen Qingxu said.
"If I can provide some assistance along the way, isn't that for the
better? I'm aware of my own limits. Thank you, General, for your
concern."

Gu Yun sighed. "I really am sorry for making you run around like
this on our behalf, Miss Chen."

Chen Qingxu was suddenly reminded of the inquisitorial letter
from Chang Geng lying on her desk. "The marshal needn't apolo-
gize—but I would appreciate if you could mention my efforts in the
presence of Prince Yan," Chen Qingxu said, her face a bit wan.

Shen Yi was speechless.

Just a second ago, this Gu bastard agreed he had a point—what
was this nonsense about Miss Chen running around on their behalf?! This asshole was as mercurial as ever!

Shen Yi wracked his brain for more reasons to forestall her. *It's
dangerous behind enemy lines?* Given the skill and courage Miss Chen
had displayed sneaking past members of the Black Iron Battalion

to break into the imperial dungeons, this reason seemed rather specious.

Then...*the field hospital needs you?* Previously, she had stayed to help out only as a favor. It was perfectly reasonable if she wanted to leave. The field hospital had its own medics, and their work consisted mostly of crude procedures like dressing wounds and performing amputations. Truth be told, Miracle Doctor Chen was wasted there.

Chen Qingxu had never been much of a conversationalist. When Shen Yi lapsed into flustered silence, she assumed the discussion was over. She cupped her hands and turned to leave.

"Miss Chen!" Shen Yi stood up in a panic, nearly upending the table.

Gu Yun quietly lifted a hand to cover his face.

A thousand words queued up on Shen Yi's tongue, eagerly awaiting their turn to divulge all his innermost feelings to the room. But when they reached his lips, they found this final gateway refused to open. The lot of them backed up in his throat; in the end, all Shen Yi managed to spit out was an awkward, "Is Miss Chen doing this for Prince Yan's sake?"

What, am I dead to you? Gu Yun marveled.

Shen Yi wanted to slap himself the instant the words left his mouth—seriously, what was he saying?

Thankfully, Chen Qingxu wasn't the type to overthink. "Prince Yan holds the Linyuan tablet," she said with utmost seriousness. "He is an important figure burdened with great responsibility. As a member of the Chen family, I'm duty-bound to help cure him of the wu'ergu. Besides, the secret shamanic techniques of the eighteen tribes are largely unknown in the Central Plains. Countless strange poisons in this world lack antidotes—yet many life-saving cures may be merely hidden in a pile of old books. Since I have the opportunity,

I must try. If even a little of what I learn can be passed down to future generations, my efforts will not have been in vain."

Shen Yi felt a chill lance through his chest as he listened. While he was daydreaming about living a simple life surrounded by a wife and children, Miss Chen was concerned with the welfare of future generations. The distance between them seemed greater than between the capital and the northern border. It was a span uncrossable even by a suit of Black Hawk armor pushed to its limits and trailing white smoke.

He gazed into Chen Qingxu's pale face and found himself lost for words. He produced a tiny signal flare from his lapels and held it out to her. "This recently arrived from the Lingshu Institute. You don't need to light it; just toss it into the air. As long as you throw it high enough, it'll light automatically and be visible within a fifty-kilometer radius. In case something happens...I...you..."

Merely listening to him made Gu Yun's teeth ache.

Chen Qingxu held the tiny signal flare, still warm from the heat of his body. No matter how oblivious she was to such matters, by now, even she had noticed something. She glanced at Shen Yi, eyes unreadable. Shen Yi couldn't bear the burden of her gaze. He wanted nothing more at that moment than to dig a hole to bury himself; he quickly made up an excuse and took his leave, scampering off at top speed.

Gu Yun rose and turned to Chen Qingxu, his features serious once more. "If the barbarians make any unusual moves, do not hesitate. Light the signal flare and we'll come to your aid. You must be careful... And when you return in triumph, we'll have Shen Jiping sing you a song."

Chen Qingxu had been nodding along, but the longer she listened, the stranger his words became. "Sing what song?"

That paragon of impropriety Marshal Gu beamed. "How does it go? *The mountains have their trees, and the trees have their branches, I love you so, yet you don't know.*" [12]

That night, Chen Qingxu and Cao Chunhua crossed the northern barbarians' defense line and snuck into the eighteen tribes' Grand Capital.

Although it was called "grand," it was in reality merely a mid-sized tribal settlement. Aside from the occasional barbarian warrior passing through, most of the civilians lining the streets were dressed in rags.

The emaciated body of a dead child lay unattended by the roadside, slobbered over by wild dogs. A dull-eyed woman loitered nearby for a short while before seemingly accepting her fate and drifting away like a walking corpse. Stern-faced shamans in heavy armor patrolled the lavish yurts of noble families as goshawks wheeled overhead in the company of armored hawks. The stench of blood and rotting flesh filled the air, where it blended with the subtle fragrance of violet gold.

Beneath the Wolf King's banner at the center of the settlement, an unremarkable-looking man entered the Wolf King's living quarters with a bowl of medicine cupped in his hands. The guards flanking the entrance greeted him respectfully, "Steward."

The steward didn't look up, grunting a response as he brought the medicine into the Wolf King's yurt.

A haggard young man came out to greet him. Taking the bowl, he said, "I'll do it."

The steward seemed to see something in his expression. "Your Highness, how fares our king today?"

---

12 Lines from "Song of the Yue Boatman," a famous love song.

"Same as usual." The crown prince shook his head and accompanied the steward deeper into the yurt.

Thick felt parted to reveal a wheelchair equipped with a gold tank, bathed in a beam of light from a skylight overhead. Within it sat a massive skeleton. Hearing the shuffle of feet at the door, this skeleton slowly turned its wheelchair toward the newcomers and cracked open terrible eyes. Those eyes had yet to cloud over—rather, they were terrifyingly bright, as if all the man's essential energies had gathered in his ferocious gaze.

It was Jialai Yinghuo in the flesh.

Last winter, the Wolf King Jialai Yinghuo had suffered a stroke and fallen into a coma. When he awoke, he could barely speak and remained bedridden for months. Presuming him done for, the leaders of several of the eighteen tribes joined forces to oust him. They placed the crown prince under house arrest and pushed the cowardly and weak second prince onto the throne, then made a frantic attempt to appease Great Liang by sending an envoy to negotiate a peace.

Even the captain of his royal guard had betrayed him—no one expected the Wolf King to turn the tables. Rather than roll over, he secretly commanded said captain to infiltrate the envoy's party. Nor had anyone known of his trump card: leftover heavy armor units sent by the Far Westerners, intended for use in the tribes' vanguard at the start of the war. Some of the desperate tribal chiefs had secretly raised private funds to deal with Great Liang, and using this as pretext, he arrested the rebel faction and purged the confederacy under the Wolf King's banner. Then, in one brazen move, he gathered fifty thousand kilograms of violet gold and launched a counterattack on Great Liang's northern border.

The steward bowed his head in deference as the Wolf King spoke to the crown prince, not daring to meet Jialai Yinghuo's eyes.

Every strand of this terrifying man's hair seemed suffused with the stench of blood.

Without warning, Jialai hurled the bowl at the crown prince, soaking him in medicine. "Incompetent trash!"

The steward shook with fear.

"Father," the crown prince said cautiously, "we are running out of supplies. Half the children and elderly of the tribes have died of starvation; everywhere you look there are corpses yet to be collected..."

"Useless garbage. If we're out of violet gold, delve deeper into the earth. If we're out of supplies, steal them from the Central Plains! If that's not enough, make those noble leeches donate the rest!"

His tongue was still clumsy, and the words he bellowed were stiff and slurred. The rims of the crown prince's eyes turned red. "Father, the Black Iron Battalion guards the border to the Central Plains; we cannot break through. And as for the nobles, they have nothing left to give. They..."

He was once again furiously interrupted by Jialai Yinghuo. News of the fresh outbreak of hostilities between the Far Western navy and Great Liang's troops had spread north, but with lines of communication cut, they had yet to learn of the navy's defeat. Jialai Yinghuo staunchly believed that once they and their Western allies surrounded Great Liang from the north and south, a rapid victory would follow.

He was vicious as ever, but his viciousness was increasingly indistinguishable from madness.

The steward watched in silence as the Wolf King abused the crown prince, receiving a bruise from a teacup lid thrown at his own head for his efforts. He quietly withdrew. Back in his yurt, representatives from several noble families as well as the honored guests from the Central Plains were awaiting his news.

113

RESISTANCE

T HE STEWARD WALKED FASTER and faster until he was nearly running back to his own yurt. The residual heat of the burning violet gold had faded, leaving the northern border as frigid as ever, yet the steward found himself sweating profusely. He wiped his face as he ran until his entire sleeve was drenched. Heart hammering with worry, he waved off the female bondservants who stepped forward to attend him and entered his heavily fortified yurt.

He glanced around carefully. Only after making certain there were no others nearby did he seal the entrance to his yurt and step into the inner chamber with a heavy sigh of relief.

A voice sounded from within. "How is he?"

The steward jumped in fright. He froze in the entryway of his own house for a handful of breaths, as though his heart was about to stop. Only when an elderly noblewoman stepped out of the darkness and revealed part of her familiar face did he suck in a sharp breath. He waved a hand, feeling he was overly paranoid, and followed the old woman in.

In the north, the days were short and the nights were long. Those who dwelled here usually did what they could to maximize light within their residences. The people in this room, however, insisted on covering the windows and sitting around a shabby gas lamp in the gloom. The most respected families of the Eighteen Tribes

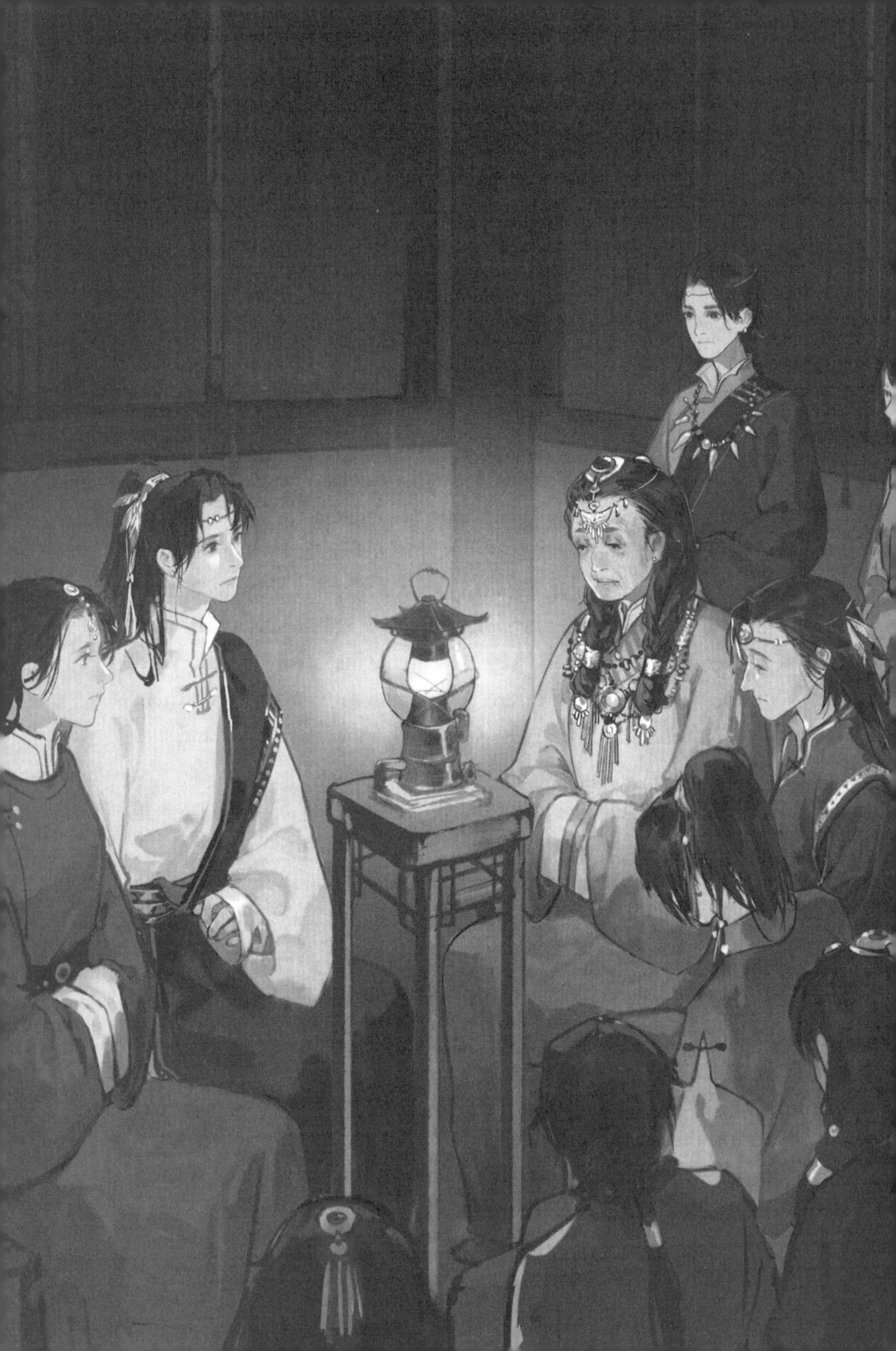

Confederacy had all sent representatives, and a few seats down from them sat a man and woman from Great Liang.

Though the two were dressed in the style of the eighteen tribes, they were obviously foreign. Regardless of noble status, the harsh wilds and bitter cold of the north were reflected in the faces of those who lived here—those rough planes were nothing like the smooth and pampered skin of Great Liang's citizens.

The guests from Great Liang were of course none other than Cao Chunhua and Chen Qingxu, who hadn't put much effort into hiding their identities. After crossing the border, they used Cao Chunhua's connections to make the acquaintance of some of the eighteen tribes' nobility. Claiming to be emissaries from Great Liang's Northern Border Garrison seeking a truce, they bribed everyone they spoke with from top to bottom, requesting an audience with the Wolf King Jialai.

They spent money like water and gave gift after lavish gift. Yet the greater their generosity, the more certain Cao Chunhua became that no one would make the introductions they sought. To these barbarian nobles they were a pair of money trees, but the moment the mad Wolf King learned of their existence, he would almost certainly pull them up by the roots.

Thus, they continued to urgently express their death wish to see Jialai Yinghuo while navigating the ever-fluctuating moods of the eighteen tribes. Less than a month later, with Cao Chunhua's silver tongue paving the way, these nobles had finally mustered the courage to gather and discuss the Wolf King in the dark.

Meanwhile, after scouting the Wolf King's yurt several times under the cover of night, Chen Qingxu had more or less nailed down its guard rotation. It was almost time to reel in the net.

Someone poured a bowl of kumis for the steward, who accepted it with trembling fingers. The fermented milk seemed to revive him.

After downing the whole bowl, he collapsed into his seat in a limp sprawl and said hoarsely, "Do you need to ask? Even the crown prince suffered his temper. The Wolf King is determined to fight."

Cao Chunhua affected an expression of artless naivete. "Our imperial court has already sent an envoy south, where the fighting is at a standstill. It's meaningless to continue this war. Could it be that the steward did not convey this information to the Wolf King?"

The steward struggled to speak. His body was like a vessel that had sprung a leak; he lifted a hand and found it once more drenched in sweat. "Young man, had I relayed that message today, I'm afraid I would never have arrived for this meeting."

The representatives of the eighteen tribes said nothing, so Cao Chunhua shook his head and spoke up, unhurried. "In that case, there's nothing to be done. I'll be honest. The reason we've asked everyone to gather here today despite the risk is this: We have received word from Marshal Gu. He blames us for the lack of progress and says if we cannot produce results, he will dispatch troops to conquer by force. The two of us will be fine—at worst, we can look forward to a reprimand from our superiors and the loss of a couple months' salary—but I know you here have no desire to fight again."

The steward's face was pinched as a bitter melon.

Chen Qingxu spoke next. "Let's go. We've done our best."

She exuded a sense of authority that brooked no argument. It was one thing if she said nothing, but the moment she opened her mouth, she had the final word on the issue. Before Cao Chunhua could react, the nobles erupted in protest. Panicked, the old woman sitting at the head of the table grabbed Chen Qingxu's sleeve. "Wait!"

Chen Qingxu shot her a cool glance.

The woman's wrinkled face twitched slightly, her features twisting with a witch-like benevolence. "Young lady, please give us a few more days," she said with an ingratiating smile. "Our king may be obstinate, but I am still his elder. I will try speaking with him; please don't leave so soon."

"Ma'am, you must understand, it's not that we're unreasonable," Cao Chunhua said with a deep sigh. "But we are also under orders; we daren't act on our own initiative."

Chen Qingxu tugged her sleeve free and responded with indifference. "The Wolf King intends to satisfy his own personal grievance with a fight to the end; I doubt speaking to him will do much good. If it backfires, you will be the one to get burned. It would be best to leave it, ma'am."

These words resonated with everyone present.

When the various tribal chiefs first joined forces in rebellion, they had kicked up a great fuss about the improperly close relationship between Jialai Yinghuo and the goddess in their youth. The goddess had been dead over twenty years; there was no way to verify whether anything unspeakable had truly passed between them. But once the seeds of doubt had been planted, how could they be so easily removed?

Jialai Yinghuo had been using Great Liang's debt of blood and his people's immense feelings of shame and humiliation to incite them to sacrifice for his cause. Yet it was an inherent weakness in human nature to forget past pains once the wounds had healed. He could stir the people to momentary fury, but when supplies ran low and one's belly was empty, how could a decades-old humiliation compare to the agony of seeing one's child die from starvation?

When a woman who had died so long ago lingered over the eighteen tribes like a vengeful ghost, bringing only war and bloodshed... was she truly a pure goddess of the Eternal Sky? Or was she a false idol of monstrous origin?

Having said her piece, Chen Qingxu ignored the expressions on the faces of the barbarians. She tipped her head in a simple nod and headed for the door with Cao Chunhua in tow.

The old barbarian woman seemed to come to a firm resolution; she slammed her walking stick against the ground. "Two days. I humbly ask that you delay your departure for two more days. I have lived over seventy years. I put my time on this earth down as guarantee—we will give you a proper answer in two days!"

This old woman was highly respected within the eighteen tribes; even the Wolf King called her *Auntie*. Now that she had spoken, no one present dared voice their objections. Only the steward, sick with anxiety, attempted to open his mouth before cowering under her disdainful glare.

Cao Chunhua exchanged a glance with Chen Qingxu, furrowing his brow and affecting a look of worried indecision. Finally, and with great reluctance, he said, "Very well. Since Lady Hongxia has given her word, we must at least try. We will await your good news. Until then, goodbye."

Only after the two foreigners left through the secret passage in the rear entrance did the room explode into an uproar.

The steward turned to Lady Hongxia, practically in tears. "Third Granny, didn't you hear what I said just now? The king is determined to fight to the end! He even struck the crown prince! Look at this bump on my head...right here... The king said, if we're out of violet gold, dig deeper into the earth. And if we run out of supplies, he wants you to empty your wallets!"

Before Lady Hongxia could respond, a middle-aged man interrupted, face red with anger. "Why does he still cling to delusions of victory? Does he expect us to trample the Black Iron Battalion's defense line and plunder the Central Plains, or does he think that the Far Western monkeys will deliver food to our door? For twenty years we prepared, gathered a hundred thousand brave warriors and countless armor and engines, stocked up mountains of dry provisions and meat—we joined hands with foreign nations to assault Great Liang on all four corners. And with all that, have we set one foot in the Central Plains?! He's lost in his fantasy of conquest—and for what? For the starving children who fill our streets? We could scrape the marrow from our bones and still not satisfy his appetite."

His voice rose, resonant as the folk songs their people sang as they herded their flocks. Several of the nobles sitting beside him paled in fear as they cautioned him to silence.

The man sat heavily back down and sneered, "Third Granny, your promise is as good as broken. You think to throw caution to the wind and lean on your seniority—but even if you hung yourself before his eyes, that lunatic Jialai wouldn't so much as blink."

Lady Hongxia knocked her walking stick harshly against the side of the table. "Shut your mouth, you useless fool. What use is barking your head off within the confines of this room?!"

The man scoffed in indignation.

Lady Hongxia's face moved not a jot as veins bulged along the backs of her wizened claws like the roots of an ancient tree. She continued evenly, "Last time, the Wolf King had a card up his sleeve that allowed him to remove a handful of our leaders. What do you all think? Does he have a second card of this nature?"

A hush settled over the room, its occupants horror-struck by the old woman's audacity. After an extended pause, the steward finally said, voice trembling, "Th-Third Granny, the blood beneath the wolf banner...has yet to dry."

"Rebellion means death, but allowing this war to continue also means death. In the end, what difference does it make?" the old woman's voice rasped in the quiet. "Our ancestors' bodies flowed with the blood of wolves. Have you all been trained into dogs? Would you rather watch your families starve or fall in battle so you can drag out your miserable existence a few more months?"

She lifted her head and swept rheumy eyes over the barbarian nobles, each with their own secret agendas. Some looked stern, others thoughtful; some appeared hesitant, while others shook with fear. Laughing grimly, she continued, "I know we are not of one mind. Some of you are already thinking of betraying this old woman to Jialai the moment you step out of this room. Let me put it this way for you cowards: if we succeed, we will have saved you from certain death. If we fail, we won't implicate those who choose to stand back. As for the vermin who think to inform the Wolf King of our plans— do you really imagine Jialai, that glimmering deceiver, that killing star, will remember your service? Or will he merely think you too close to this band of suicidal old fools and suspect your motives as well?"

The man who had just been ranting in righteous indignation jumped to his feet. "Well said, Third Granny! I'm with you!"

The noble families of the eighteen tribes had suffered too much under the tyranny of Jialai Yinghuo over the years. The nobles hated him, yet they also feared his oppressive policies. Now that someone was willing to lead, the outraged members of the group were quick to line up behind them.

Lady Hongxia turned to the steward. "We can speak of this till we're blue in the face, but no plan will work without your help and support, Steward."

The steward froze in his seat, as though he might evaporate under the heat of their gazes and fill the sunless room with a haze of steam. At last, he gritted his teeth and slapped his thigh. "I'm at your command, Third Granny!"

Bloody power struggles were inevitable when a nation was at stake. Whether it was Great Liang, the Eighteen Celestial Wolf Tribes, or even the foreigners mired in Jiangnan, all had to find new ways to survive upon hitting rock bottom. It was a treacherous path relying entirely on chance. Leap one step ahead, and home and country would prosper; fall one step behind, and it might mean the extinction of an entire people.

In the eighteen tribes, a violent current churned beneath the surface as the major noble families began to silently organize their forces.

The next evening, a black shadow flitted up one of the eighteen tribes' watchtowers like a sparrow. These watchtowers had been built with Far Western funds and depended on them for maintenance as well. Now, with the Far Westerners busy fighting their own war, most of the machinery in these watchtowers had ground to a halt and served only as decoration.

The men standing watch had been quietly knocked out. Moonlight revealed the face of their assailant—a reticent servant boy who worked for the steward. He scrambled nimbly to the top of the watchtower. When he saw who awaited him, the "servant boy" stopped in his tracks and wiped away his mask, revealing that flower of many faces, Cao Chunhua.

"We're clear," Cao Chunhua whispered, "The steward dosed Jialai Yinghuo's medicine with a sedative."

"They're not going to poison him directly?" asked Chen Qingxu.

"It's not that easy," Cao Chunhua said. "Jialai is a master of shamanic knowledge. The slightest misstep could leave him on high alert. But he often uses sedatives in his own medicine; this way, even if he notices something, he won't become suspicious. Members of various noble families are already among the guards of the king's yurt. They'll do the deed quietly in the night—Jialai Yinghuo will die in his bed without a sound, and they'll push the crown prince forward to succeed the throne first thing in the morning. Once the steward confirms Jialai has taken his medicine, he'll make an owl's call—that's the signal. All we have to do is wait. Have you notified the marshal?"

Tucked between Chen Qingxu's fingers was a tiny ball that glowed faintly with silver light—the signal flare from Shen Yi. The little gadget had been hidden in her sleeves all this time. As she took it out now, Chen Qingxu suddenly found herself reluctant to part with it.

Cao Chunhua knew nothing of her thoughts. Sighing with great feeling, he said, "A fiercely ambitious man, unmatched in his generation, yet his followers slay him without even allowing him his last words. How does such a thing happen?"

"He inspires too much fear." Chen Qingxu stood atop the watchtower, a field scope affixed to the bridge of her nose, and gazed down at the king's yurt. "I forgot to ask—how did you convince Lady Hongxia to step forward?"

"Her son died on the battlefield," Cao Chunhua said casually, tucking a stray lock of hair behind his ear. "All she has left is her grandson, who will soon turn sixteen. Jialai has declared all boys from noble families over the age of sixteen must enlist to fight in the war—reprehensible, I know. When I infiltrated the barbarian tribes before, I saw her son a handful of times. So a few nights ago, I made a mask of his ghostly likeness and visited his mother on his behalf... The mask might not've been totally accurate, but between the dim lighting and her poor eyesight, it got the job done. I held her, we cried disconsolately into each other's arms, I told her I couldn't bear the thought of my beloved son following his father to the grave... Look, my eyes are still swollen. I've been covering the redness up these past few days—Miss Chen, would you happen to have any special medicine to help reduce swelling?"

Chen Qingxu didn't know what to say.

Cao Chunhua shook his head and gazed up at the moon, voice full of self-pity. "How many tears have I shed wearing the face of another? Ay, it really is—"

"Shhh." Chen Qingxu cut him off. "Did you hear that?"

The hoot of an owl cut through the cold night—the steward had made his move.

Chen Qingxu pushed open one of the watchtower's windows. A near-invisible silk thread shot out from the tips of her fingers to anchor in the ground below, and she flitted down with a tap of her toes.

Cao Chunhua produced a small pot of violet gold from his lapels and splashed it straight down, as if the neglected mechanisms in the watchtower had sprung a leak. In the next moment, he set the structure on fire. Curling flames snaked down like a dragon, bathing the tower in a glow as bright as daylight. Chen Qingxu tossed the signal flare high into the sky, where it split in two halves that shot apart with a flash like a bolt of lightning. This white flare was another singular invention of the Lingshu Institute. It wasn't at all blinding when one stood nearby, its glare easily eclipsed by the flames of violet gold. Yet at a distance, that beam of light pierced the darkness.

The instant Shen Yi spotted that bright flash through his field scope, he jumped up from where he was lying in wait. "Marshal! They've made their move!"

Gu Yun gave a lengthy whistle, and the Black Hawks took off into the night, skimming close to the ground like a flock of bats, discernible by sound but invisible to sight.

Shen Yi charged out impatiently with the rest only to be struck by a thought. Turning back, he said, "Zixi, you just got back from Jiangnan yesterday and haven't had time to rest. Are you sure you're up for this?"

Gu Yun blinked in surprise, then burst into laughter. "My word, how do you come up with all these different ways to worry? Don't fret about me; go find Miss Chen. Seeing that bastard Jialai Yinghuo get his just deserts is a more effective tonic than any miracle cure, I assure you."

There were also those secret shamanic techniques the old lunatic had hidden away. Gu Yun didn't dare speak the words aloud, nor did he dare to hope—but after everything, he still wanted to personally go and take a look.

What if...

What if there really was a cure for the wu'ergu? Gu Yun came to a quiet resolution: *If such a thing exists, I'll go light a stick of incense for those bald donkeys in the National Temple.*

Chen Qingxu's skill in qinggong[13] was without peer. Seconds after leaping down from the watchtower, she vanished into the darkness. The rebel army wished to kill Jialai Yinghuo swiftly and silently, but she wished him to speak a few last words first—otherwise, who could tell her about the goddess's secret shamanic techniques?

Cao Chunhua struggled to keep up with the fleet-footed Chen Qingxu. Midway through his pursuit, he heard the roar of parhelion arrows leaving the string and glanced up to see flames rising into the sky in the south. The Black Iron Battalion had arrived; it was only a matter of time before they broke through the northern

---

13 Literally "lightness technique," the martial arts skill of moving swiftly and lightly through the air.

barbarians' defenses. By the time Cao Chunhua looked back down, in the space of this brief lapse in concentration, Chen Qingxu had already disappeared.

Compared to Chen Qingxu, the guards assigned to the Wolf King's yurt were mediocre at best. On top of that, nearly half their members were in on the plot; it was the work of moments to blend in among their number. She alighted atop the yurt in the shadow of the Wolf King's banner and waited for a handful of armed rebels to pass before dropping lightly to the ground and joining the group with no one the wiser.

The rebels marched obliviously toward the main yurt. Halfway there, Chen Qingxu realized something was wrong. The Wolf King's yurt was almost deserted—it should be missing a portion of its regular guard tonight, but not this many. Heart racing, Chen Qingxu grabbed for her dagger just as the rebels arrived at Jialai Yinghuo's yurt.

There came a soft rustle as all four entrances of the yurt flew open, bristling with cannon muzzles and arrows nocked and ready to fire. Hundreds of barbarian royal guards and soldiers poured out from the darkness to outflank their prey, surrounding the unsuspecting rebels on all sides.

DESTRUCTION

C HEN QINGXU SHRANK back at once, practically blending into the surrounding vegetation as she suppressed her presence. From the blind spot behind the thick black velvet banner flapping above the king's yurt, she watched with the cool eyes of a bystander as this unexpected development unfolded beneath her.

The door of the yurt opened, and a violet-gold-powered wheelchair glided out, trailing tendrils of steam. The Wolf King Jialai Yinghuo sat curled in its seat, wrapped in a heavy cloak and seemingly on the verge of death. He swept a chilly glare over the rebels caught red-handed outside his yurt.

"Third Auntie," he murmured, his shriveled lips splitting in a smile. "My mother died when I was young, and you raised me in her stead for five years. You treated me like your own son, but now...will you, too, draw your sword against me?"

Lady Hongxia was the ringleader of this rebellion, but at the end of the day, she was a feeble old woman. She could lay a plan, but she couldn't personally take to the battlefield and cut a man down. Jialai Yinghuo's mutterings dissipated into the air, unanswered. Whether it was enmity or hatred, happiness or delight, his grand plan of establishing hegemony or the long path toward vengeance, this ferocious wolf king, last of his line, had borne it alone. His parents, brothers, children, relatives, and friends...he had lost them all.

He treated his fellow tribesmen like pigs and dogs, and they repaid him with vicious betrayal.

A few of the rebels' hands were shaking, as though they could barely hold their weapons. One dropped his sword with a clatter, the sound ringing clear in the silent night.

"You've all betrayed me; you all want me dead." Jialai barked out a bitter laugh. He raised one claw-like hand and swung it down in a slicing motion. "Well, you can all go to hell first!"

At his command, the air filled with volleys of arrows. Surrounded front and back, the rebels had nowhere to run and no choice but to fight; what should have been a silent assassination became a bloody brawl. The disturbance spread outward, rousing the entire settlement as the Eighteen Tianlang Tribes' Grand Capital descended into chaos. Some ran to the watchtower to help put out the fire, while some rushed to the side of their king to quell the rebellion. Others steeled their hearts and joined the rebel faction. Most stood in a daze, unsure what to do.

The crown prince and the steward were bound and shoved forward. The steward had long since wet himself from fear. He glanced at the terrified crown prince beside him and thought, *The Wolf King only has one son left. Perhaps he'll spare him, but the same can't be said of me.*

Slowly, his expression of petrified despair turned into one of resolute determination. His eyes bulged from his sockets as he flexed his jaw and ground his teeth. Seconds later, his face drained of color as his body stiffened and crumpled before everyone's eyes—the steward had crushed the poison capsule hidden in his mouth and committed suicide.

Amid the confusion, Cao Chunhua had begun to panic. He'd considered the possibility that the assassination would fail and concluded it didn't matter. As long as pandemonium broke out in the northern barbarians' Grand Capital, Gu Yun and the others could exploit it to break through their defenses. When the mantis stalked the cicada, it mattered little which insect triumphed over the other; the oriole would always be waiting to swoop in at the end. But he'd never considered Chen Qingxu might run ahead and get sucked into this weltering maelstrom.

The fight between the rebels and the royal guards was reaching its peak when a barbarian stumbled haphazardly into the king's yurt. "Report—enemy attack! It's an enemy attack!"

These words were like a tossed stone that raised a thousand waves. The area around the king's yurt fell briefly still as the captain of the royal guard shoved aside the motley crew of combatants and sprinted over to Jialai Yinghuo. "Sire, someone's set fire to one of the watchtowers. A large force of demon crows has taken advantage of the chaos to make their move—they're approaching as we speak!"

Jialai Yinghuo's eye twitched as his face revealed a hint of what might have been joy. "Who's approaching? Is it Gu Yun?"

The captain's brow was covered in sweat; he had no idea why Gu Yun's arrival would be cause for celebration. In the next moment, he looked on in astonishment as Jialai, who had been paralyzed for nearly half a year, dug his claw-like hands into the wheelchair's armrests and rose to his feet with a low shout.

"Sire!" the captain cried.

"Gu Yun... Gu Yun..." Jialai mumbled. His eyes were terrifyingly bright, as if his three immortal souls and seven mortal forms were burning under his skin. One couldn't help but doubt the rumors from before—perhaps it wasn't the dead goddess who was the object of his obsession, but rather Gu Yun. "Bring me my armor!"

The captain had never seen such a novel method of suicide, and for a moment, he thought he misheard. "Sire, what...what are you saying?"

"My armor! My armor!" Jialai roared.

The captain of the guard staggered back in fright—Jialai's face seemed on the verge of cracking open with rage. But the guard didn't dare disobey; he hastily dispatched someone to fetch the Wolf King's heavy armor.

A snow-white iron monster nearly the height of two men arrived on the backs of four burly men, who set it down with a resounding *thud*. Jialai Yinghuo was shaking like a leaf in the autumn wind. He clutched at the armor with emaciated hands as he dragged his leaden feet over and slowly shoved himself inside.

The unique internal support system of heavy armor made it much easier to operate than a light pelt. Still, it wasn't something a half-paralyzed old man could handle. After crawling into the suit, Jialai Yinghuo strained, red-faced, to open the valve at the soles of his armored feet. A furious jet of steam erupted from the armor's back as its powerful propulsion system rumbled to life, as if ready to charge wildly into the plains.

But the man within was no more the peerless young hero who once slaked his thirst with the blood of his enemies.

After a single step, Jialai was already an arrow at the end of its flight. He listed to the side, unable to maintain his balance. The hundred-kilogram iron giant fell with a deafening crash, marking the ground with a deep pit.

The captain paled with fear and rushed forward.

No one could see the expression on Wolf King Jialai's face. The man's body, withered to skin and sharp bone, was hidden within the massive suit of armor like a shriveled insect secreted inside a walnut.

In that moment, everyone, even his enemies who knew him as a heartless lunatic, was struck by a feeling of sorrow. This hero had reached his end.

The shrieks of Black Hawks drew closer and closer. The Black Iron Battalion was a highly mobile force. Only their enemy's reckless burning of violet gold had allowed the current stalemate to drag on for so many days. If not for that, the demon crows would have ended the fight long before now.

With the Grand Capital in chaos, the three divisions of the Black Iron Battalion stormed into the settlement as though marching through a barren land.

The captain of the royal guard rushed forward to open the heavy armor and hoisted the pathetically trapped Jialai out and onto his back. "Sire, I fear the Grand Capital will fall tonight. We'll escort you away at once..."

Jialai sprawled over the captain's back, eyes unfocused. At length, he pointed into the distance. "That way."

Chen Qingxu dodged a stray arrow and dropped down from behind the black banner. A sudden thought had occurred to her. A flick of her fingers sent a handful of fine needles flying, and several nearby barbarians crumpled silently to the ground as she chased Jialai Yinghuo's entourage into the darkness.

The team of royal guards escorting Jialai sped away from the king's yurt and headed westward. As they distanced themselves from the rabble, there were fewer and fewer places to hide. Chen Qingxu struggled to keep pace, risking discovery as she followed in their wake. She had chased them for over half an hour when she realized she had tailed Jialai to an abandoned temple.

The temple was palatial, so tall it seemed to breach the clouds and wrought entirely from stone. Its main gate was carved from giant boulders, the thick piece of felt hanging over the door densely mottled with an indecipherable script. The surrounding area was overgrown with weeds—no one had been here in a very long time. A lone crow, disturbed by the arrival of humans, took to the sky with a flutter of dark wings.

Chen Qingxu wasn't the only one baffled by their destination; even the royal guards looked at each other in confusion. No one had set foot in the Temple of the Goddess since its namesake fell from grace.

Jialai threw off the captain's steadying hand. "Leave me."

Startled, the captain took several steps back.

The Wolf King slowly lowered himself to the ground, his knees so stiff he nearly fell flat on his face. The captain hurried forward to help him up only to be unceremoniously slapped. "Fuck off! Stay away from me!"

It took Jialai an extraordinary amount of effort to kneel properly. Struggling, he straightened his hunched back and pressed his palms together. The pig-liver redness of his face—the shame, anger, and violent pique—gradually faded as his expression took on a peculiar calm. After a moment, he shuffled forward, like an old dog with one foot in the grave. Having been struck once already for his efforts, the captain of the guard dared not put himself in the way of another thrashing. He merely watched in bewilderment as his king hobbled along.

Jialai crawled in this manner until he was beside the giant stone door. Once there, he lifted the ragged felt and ran his fingers over the raised incantations.

Realizing this long-abandoned temple might be pivotal to her mission, Chen Qingxu crept closer as she watched Jialai with unblinking eyes. Suddenly, Jialai pressed down on something and shoved his arm forward. The ground began to quake. While Jialai's

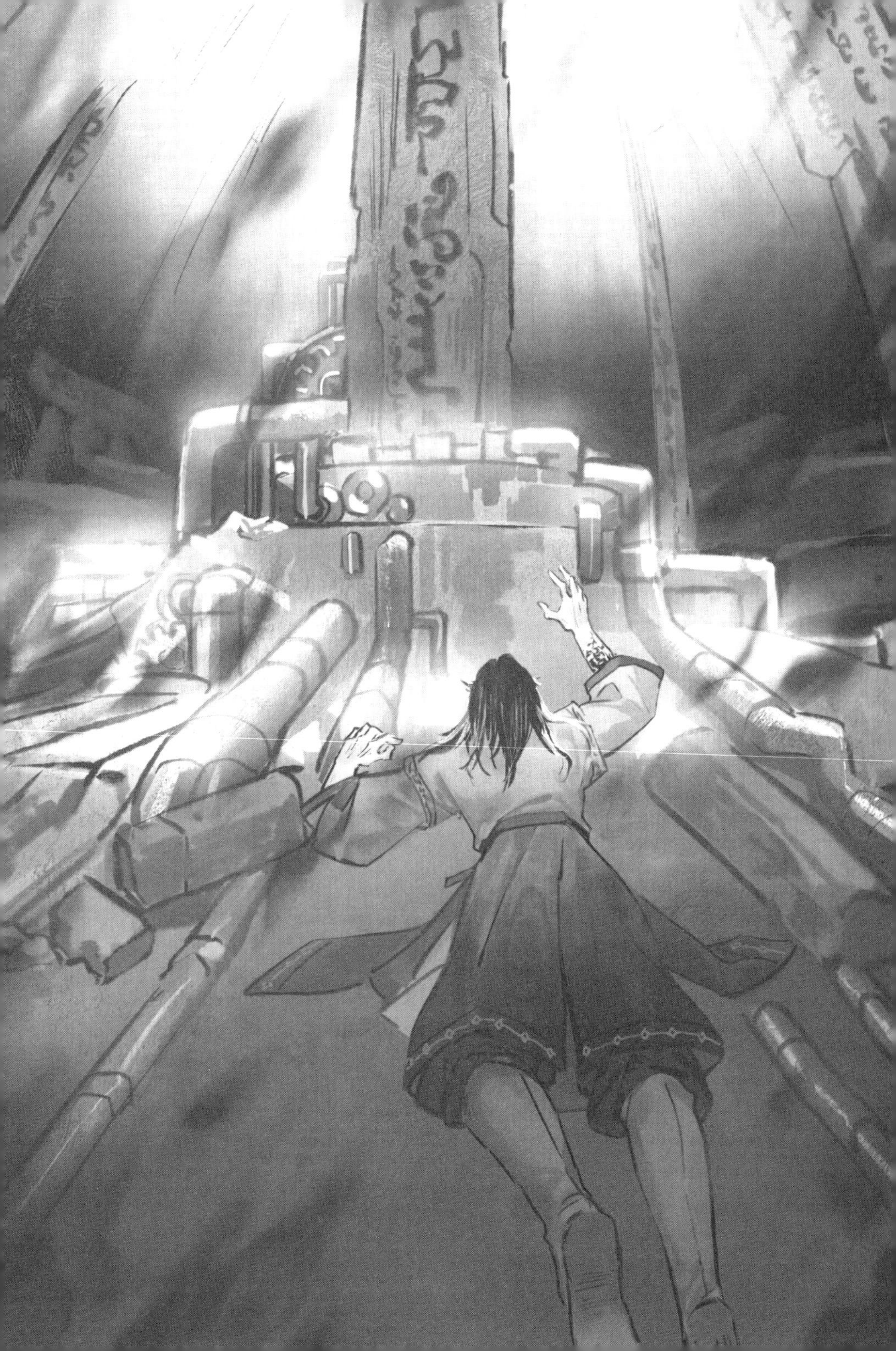

guards blanched with fright, Chen Qingxu darted after him without a second thought.

The rocks around the temple shuddered as giant interlocking gears rose through the earth one after another. Countless rusted steel pipes extended in all directions, surrounding the temple in a closed loop. The pipes locked in place, and metal plates spread outward from both sides with a hiss, forming in rapid succession a series of fire pinions that quivered in the breeze. Chen Qingxu thought with some astonishment that this contraption looked remarkably like one of Great Liang's kites.

The entire temple looked as if it would be able to rise straight up into the sky with just a bit of violet gold. Chen Qingxu was stunned. *Isn't it said the barbarians were only flattened by the Black Iron Battalion all those years ago because they lacked their own engine technology? Then what on earth is this? Is this barbarian planning on using this thing to flee or send himself to heaven?*

Her mind was still racing when she heard a soft *click*. A plume of burnt-smelling smoke poured from the circle of pipes, followed immediately by a series of cracking sounds. Stored deep underground for so many years, the bubbling violet gold had long become contaminated with untold impurities. The flames beneath the fire pinions flickered as the acrid stench of adulterated violet gold slowly filled the air.

Time seemed to slow—but in truth, from the moment the first crack formed until the entire temple caught fire, everything happened in the blink of an eye. If Chen Qingxu had been a mechanical expert like Ge Chen or Zhang Fenghan, she would have recognized that though this temple indeed resembled a giant kite, its construction was far from complete. It seemed elaborate, but its creator had simply blindly copied the kite's fire pinions and the pipe-shaped gold tanks.

They had done nothing to address the hull of the ship, which was the greatest obstacle to the giant kite's flight. Even if this vessel were to burn the enormous quantity of fuel required to achieve lift, it would disintegrate long before reaching cruising altitude. Now, years of disrepair had exacerbated whatever inherent flaws it had to begin with—this iron creature seemed completely disinclined to take to the skies and had instead self-destructed in protest.

The giant kite buried beneath the temple and the goddess who had once prayed to the Eternal Sky were destined to be nothing more than the last elusive dream of the dying Celestial Wolf Tribe.

Scared witless, the captain of the guard cried out, "Sire! Get away from there!"

As if rocked by his yell, the massive stone gate collapsed, crushing a formation of tubes that had risen out of the ground. The gas from burning violet gold exploded outward with a thunderous *boom* as a roiling fireball rose unsteadily into the sky. Standing amid the flames, Jialai Yinghuo glanced back at his guards, face absent of fear.

It came to Chen Qingxu that Jialai Yinghuo must have known all along the temple would combust the instant it caught fire... He had prepared for this outcome and was content at last. The Wolf King was merely looking for a more splendid death.

The temple's outer walls began to crumble—they would collapse any second. Chen Qingxu gritted her teeth and threw caution to the wind. Slipping through a tiny gap in the flames licking in all directions, she pursued Jialai into the temple as his royal guard looked on. With a massive rumble, the temple's outer walls caved in.

Cao Chunhua had lost track of Chen Qingxu halfway through their mission; he had no option but to stay behind and rendezvous with Gu Yun's party. Only when the Black Iron Battalion had slaughtered their way into the Grand Capital did he learn from a captured royal guard the approximate direction of Jialai Yinghuo's flight. Cao Chunhua was deeply familiar with the northern barbarians' capital; a rough explanation was enough for him to guess Jialai Yinghuo had run off to the Temple of the Goddess. With the feverishly anxious Shen Yi in tow, he raced over just in time to see the temple walls give away.

His pupils contracted, his cry of alarm trapped in his throat. Shen Yi shed his light pelt without the slightest hesitation and, ever resourceful, proceeded to roll across the snow-covered ground. After covering himself in the ice and snow of this frigid land, he charged fearlessly into the raging inferno.

The Wolf King's dazzling ending left his personal guards stupefied. The group of elite soldiers stood frozen in place like a cluster of wooden stakes thrust into the ground. They seemed incapable of summoning any resistance; the Black Hawk soldiers mopped them up with little effort. The contaminated violet gold didn't burn hot enough to melt through the icy field, but it generated a suffocating smoke. Chen Qingxu struggled to open her eyes amid the fumes. Her field scope was soon covered in a layer of ash; she pulled it off and threw it aside.

Jialai, she realized, had likely chosen death the moment he fell out of that suit of armor. For someone with such a fatalistic mindset, interrogation by torture would be useless—not that she was capable of such a thing in the first place. In that case, she could only hope the secrets she had sought for so many years were hidden somewhere within the temple itself.

Chen Qingxu wove through the collapsing temple in a single swift leap and spotted Jialai's figure as he crawled through the soot-blackened rubble. She cupped a hand over her nose and mouth and squinted in the direction he was headed, noting how he ignored the deafening conflagration, eyes fixed on the stone altar in the center of the temple.

What did that stone altar hold?

One of the temple's enormous roof beams crashed down directly over Chen Qingxu, forcing her to dodge to the side. Bracing a foot on the broken rubble, she took off for the stone altar. If the original architect had hoped to turn the temple into a giant kite, then given the altar's position, it would have served as the mast that stabilized the whole. Its stone slabs were etched with a circular loop of barbarian script distinct from the unintelligible incantations inscribed on the temple doors—this was the written form of the eighteen tribes' language.

On her previous trips beyond the border, Chen Qingxu had spent some time learning the barbarians' language. She could roughly make out this script as a written record of the history of separation and reunification of the eighteen tribes. Nowhere in the inscription did it make mention of the barbarians' shamanic techniques. Chen Qingxu, coughing from the thick smoke, finally began to despair—could it be that this really was just a crumbling temple with no clues about the barbarians' poisons?

Another explosion rocked the earth somewhere nearby, and a large slab of stone pitched toward her. Chen Qingxu instinctively stepped back, but the dense smoke obstructed her vision; she lost her footing and toppled toward the base of the altar. At this rate, she would be crushed. In desperation, Chen Qingxu flung out the rope hidden in her sleeve, catching on something atop the stone altar. Coughing furiously, she yanked on the rope to pull herself up. But whatever she had snared wasn't anchored down; it gave way with the lightest pull, leaving the rope slack in her hands.

Chen Qingxu's heart sank. *I'm done for.*

At that moment, a shadow bolted over and grabbed Chen Qingxu, rolling them both to the side. The huge slab of stone crashed into the ground where she'd lain, so close she could feel the rush of air on her face. Covered in filth from tumbling through the debris at the base of the altar, Chen Qingxu looked up in shock to see a battered General Shen.

Shen Yi yanked her to her feet by her collar, furious. "Are you trying to get yourself killed?!"

Chen Qingxu's eyes widened slightly.

The instant Shen Yi met those eyes, he quailed, his surging fury fizzling to smoke. He bent to grab the length of white silk rope hanging from her sleeve and muttered, "Let's get out of here first... What the hell is this?!"

Caught on the other end of Chen Qingxu's grappling hook was a strange object the size of a grown man. At first glance, it resembled a carved stone statue, but perhaps because it was hollow, it was incredibly light. Shen Yi tugged lightly on the rope to pull it over and reveal the figure's face.

It was a lifelike sculpture of a woman, eyes closed and expression serene.

Looking at this expertly crafted statue, Shen Yi inexplicably broke out in gooseflesh. Chen Qingxu was likewise taken aback. Crouching in the rubble, she brushed away the dust covering its surface, revealing the object's original light color under the grime. Astonishingly, it was soft to the touch.

"Human skin," Chen Qingxu said quietly.

Shen Yi thought for a moment he had contracted Gu Yun's deafness. "What?"

Chen Qingxu looked up and spotted a hidden recess behind the collapsed stone altar. This beautiful statue—or corpse—had originally been stored there.

Was it for this that Jialai had come?

Thoughts a tangle, Chen Qingxu acted on instinct. She bent to pick it up.

"I'll do it," Shen Yi hastily interjected. "Let's go!"

Lifting the figure in one arm and grabbing hold of Chen Qingxu with the other, Shen Yi dashed for the entrance at top speed.

Fire exploded in all directions, filling the air with thick smoke. From within the roaring flames, a hoarse voice slurred in stops and starts, "The purest spirit of the grasslands...even the heavenly winds seek to kiss...the hem of her skirt..."

The pillars and rafters of the temple collapsed like dominos. The two had nearly reached the exit when there was a deafening roar as a column of purple-tinged flame licked the sky. A huge pillar—so thick it would require seven or eight men holding hands to span its circumference—listed to the side as the temple's sprawling roof, finally unable to bear the strain, collapsed completely.

Shen Yi's face was gray with ash. He struggled to breathe, overcome by a sudden wave of despair at the thought that this temple might very well become his grave. Making a split-second decision, he shoved that unsettling human figure into Chen Qingxu's arms, slung his windslasher over his shoulders, and bent his back in an attempt to shield the person beside him with his own body.

Stunned by this gesture, Chen Qingxu couldn't describe the feeling welling up in her heart.

It was then that the scream of Black Hawks came from overhead, followed by the grinding of metal on stone. Shen Yi looked up in shock to see a team of Black Hawks with steel cables as thick as a man's arm gripped in their iron claws, hauling the temple's collapsed dome back aloft.

Gu Yun had arrived.

Shen Yi dared not linger. Wrapping his arm protectively around Chen Qingxu, he ignored the bits of rubble peppering his body and dashed toward the exit in a treacherous sprint. They had scarcely stepped beyond the bounds of the temple when one of the steel cables the Black Hawks were holding snapped. The Black Steeds waiting for them at the fore dragged the pair to safety in a chaotic tangle of limbs as the roof crashed down behind them.

Gu Yun had nearly spurred his horse straight into the sea of fire when that cable snapped; only when he saw the soot-covered Shen Yi and Chen Qingxu come barreling out of the conflagration did he yank back on his reins just in time. He ran a soothing hand over his terrified horse and breathed a sigh of relief, his face unreadable. With a long whistle, he signaled the Black Hawks in the sky and the Black Steeds on the ground. "Fall back!"

They could no longer hear Jialai Yinghuo's faint singing.

After standing tall for centuries, the eighteen tribes' temple was reduced to flying ash, rising in thick plumes of smoke into the boundless, eternal sky. A gust of wind tore away half the wolf banner, singed by the flames of war, and carried it roaring into the distance where it was swallowed by raging fire and choking dust.

The long river of time flowed ever onward as the bold and vibrant Celestial Wolf Tribe quietly took its final bow.

And the violet gold continued to burn.

THE STORY CONTINUES IN
Stars of Chaos
VOLUME 5

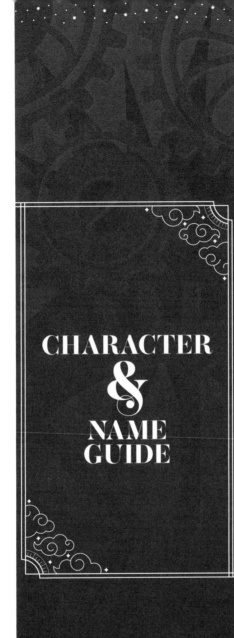

CHARACTER & NAME GUIDE

CHARACTERS

The identity of certain characters may be a spoiler; use this guide with caution on your first read of the novel.

Note on the given name translations: Chinese characters may have many different readings. Each reading here is just one out of several possible readings presented for your reference, and not a definitive translation.

MAIN CHARACTERS

Chang Geng

MILK NAME: Chang Geng (长庚 / "Evening star" or "Evening Venus")

GIVEN NAME: Li Min (李旻 / Surname Li, "Autumn sky")

TITLE: Prince Yan (雁 / "Goose")

Chang Geng spent nearly fourteen years living an uneventful life on the northern border, only for his world to be turned upside down when he learned he was actually the long-lost fourth prince of Great Liang.

Gu Yun

MILK NAME: Shiliu (十六 / "Sixteen")

GIVEN NAME: Gu Yun (顾昀 / Surname Gu, "Sunlight")

COURTESY NAME: Gu Zixi (顾子熹 / Surname Gu; "Daybreak," literary)

TITLE: Marquis of Anding (安定 / "Order")

RANK: Marshal

The fearsome leader of the Black Iron Battalion and Chang Geng's beloved young godfather.

SUPPORTING CHARACTERS

Shen Yi

GIVEN NAME: Shen Yi (沈易 / Surname Shen, "Change" or "Easy")

COURTESY NAME: Shen Jiping (沈季平 / Surname Shen, "Season," "Even" or "Peaceful")

RANK: Commander in Chief of the Southwest Army

Gu Yun's loyal friend and right-hand man.

Ge Pangxiao

MILK NAME: Ge Pangxiao (葛胖小 / Surname Ge, "Chubby youngster")

GIVEN NAME: Ge Chen (葛晨 / Surname Ge, "Dawn")

Chang Geng's childhood tagalong who leaves Yanhui Town with Chang Geng after becoming orphaned. Ge Pangxiao has a fondness for machines.

Cao Niangzi

MILK NAME: Cao Niangzi (曹娘子 / Surname Cao, "Lady")

GIVEN NAME: Cao Chunhua (曹春花 / Surname Cao, "Spring flower")

Chang Geng's childhood admirer, who leaves Yanhui Town with Chang Geng. Cao Niangzi has a fondness for dressing up as both women and men, and is an expert at taking on different roles.

Chen Qingxu

GIVEN NAME: Chen Qingxu (陈轻絮 / Surname Chen, "Gentle," "Silk floss")

A jianghu physician with a cool demeanor whose family specializes in medicine. A member of the Linyuan Pavilion.

Liao Ran

DHARMA NAME: Liao Ran (了然 / "To understand," "To be so")

TITLE: Great Master

A multi-talented monk from the National Temple and member of the Linyuan Pavilion.

THE EIGHTEEN TRIBES

Chikuyou

NAME: Chikuyou (哧库犹)

Wolf King Jialai Yinghuo's trusted aide and captain of his personal guard.

Xiu-niang

ALIAS: Xiu-niang (秀娘 / "Refined lady")

GIVEN NAME: Huge'er (胡格尔 / "The violet gold at the center of the earth")

Chang Geng's "mother," who turns out to be his aunt. She is a member of the Celestial Wolf Tribe and their agent inside Great Liang.

Jialai Yinghuo

GIVEN NAME: Jialai (加莱)

NAME TRANSLATED INTO CHINESE: Yinghuo (荧惑 / "Glimmering deceiver" or "Mars")

TITLE: Wolf King of the Celestial Wolf Tribe

The crown prince and later king of the Celestial Wolf Tribe. He orchestrates the infiltration and attack on Great Liang at the beginning of the story.

THE CAPITAL

Du Wanquan

NAME: Du Wanquan (杜万全 / Surname Du, "Perfectly safe")
A wealthy and powerful merchant known as the "God of Wealth,"
and a member of the Linyuan Pavilion.

Emperor Wu

The reigning Emperor of Great Liang prior to the Yuanhe Emperor
at the start of the story. Gu Yun's maternal grandfather.

Fang Qin

NAME: Fang Qin (方钦 / Surname Fang, "To revere")
TITLE: Minister of Revenue
The leader of a faction of rich and powerful noble families within
the imperial court.

Li Feng

GIVEN NAME: Li Feng (李丰 / Surname Li, "Plentiful")
ERA NAME: Longan (隆安 / "Grand Peace")
Chang Geng's elder half-brother, the crown prince, who ascends the
throne after the death of his father, the Yuanhe Emperor.

Liao Chi

DHARMA NAME: Liao Chi (了痴, "To understand," "Infatuation")
TITLE: Abbot of the Temple of National Protection
Abbot of the National Temple and Liao Ran's shixiong.

Jiang Chong

GIVEN NAME: Jiang Chong (江充 / Surname Jiang, "Abundance")

COURTESY NAME: Jiang Hanshi (江寒石 / Surname Jiang, "Cold stone")

TITLE: Chief Justice of the Imperial Court of Judicial Review

Shen Yi's senior via the imperial examination system, a friend and ally of Gu Yun, and member of Chang Geng's Grand Council.

Lü Chang

GIVEN NAME: Lü Chang (吕常 / Surname Lü, "Constant/ Unchanging")

COURTESY NAME: Lü Yannian (吕延年 / Surname Lü, "To prolong life")

TITLE: Assistant Minister of Revenue

The head of the well-connected Lü family, and a key player in Fang Qin's faction of nobles.

The Noble Consort

TITLE: Noble Consort

TITLE: Goddess of the Celestial Wolf Tribe

Chang Geng's birth mother. As the goddess of the Celestial Wolf Tribe, she was gifted to Great Liang after their surrender, and became the sole noble consort within the imperial harem.

Prince Wei

TITLE: Prince Wei (魏 / "Kingdom of Wei")

Chang Geng's elder half-brother, the Second Prince. Son of the Yuanhe Emperor. Colluded with Dongying nationals in an unsuccessful plan to overthrow the Longan Emperor by striking the capital from the East Sea.

The Yuanhe Emperor

ERA NAME: Yuanhe (元和 / "Primal," "Harmony")

The reigning emperor of Great Liang at the start of the story. Chang Geng's birth father.

Wang Guo

NAME: Wang Guo (王裹 / Surname Wang, "To enfold")

The Longan Emperor's maternal uncle and the most favored official in the imperial court.

Xu Ling

NAME: Xu Ling (徐令 / Surname Xu, "To command")

COURTESY NAME: Mingyu (明瑜, "Bright," "Virtue")

TITLE: Right Assistant Supervisory Commissioner of the Department of Supervision

An earnest court official sent to assist Chang Geng on his mission to Jiangbei.

Zhang Fenghan

COURTESY NAME: Zhang Fenghan (张奉函 / Surname Zhang, "To present a letter")

The director of the Lingshu Institute known for his stubbornness. A member of the Linyuan Pavilion.

OTHER

He Ronghui

NAME: He Ronghui (何荣辉 / Surname He, "Glory," "Splendor")

RANK: Commander

The commander of the Black Hawk Division of the Black Iron Battalion.

Cai Bin

NAME: Cai Bin (蔡玢 / Surname Cai, "A type of jade")

RANK: General

Originally the commander of the Central Plains Garrison. Interim commander of the northern front.

Lord Jakobson

ALIAS: Mister Ja

A mysterious operative from the Far West. He is the right hand of the Western pope, who, in the world of Stars of Chaos, is a military leader as well as a religious one.

Yang Ronggui

NAME: Yang Ronggui (杨荣桂 / Surname Yang, "Glory," "Osmanthus")

TITLE: Governor of Liangjiang

Governor overseeing the region of Jiangbei, which lies on the front line of the territory occupied by the Far Westerners, and a member of the well-connected Lü family by marriage.

Yao Zhen

GIVEN NAME: Yao Zhen (姚镇 / Surname Yao, "Town")

COURTESY NAME: Yao Chongze (姚重泽 / Surname Yao, "Great favor")

TITLE: Regional Judiciary Commissioner of Yingtian

Gu Yun's longtime acquaintance and a local official in Jiangnan.

Zhong Chan

GIVEN NAME: Zhong Chan (钟蝉 / Surname Zhong, "Cicada")

RANK: General

A general who was dismissed from his post after defying the emperor, and both Gu Yun and Chang Geng's shifu in martial arts.

INSTITUTIONS

The Government of Great Liang

The emperor is the highest authority in Great Liang, an autocratic monarchy. The top-level administrative bodies of the state include a number of departments and ministries, such as the Ministry of Revenue and Ministry of War.

Years ago, the militant Emperor Wu expanded the borders of Great Liang and built the nation to the height of its power. Due to his lack of male heirs, the more compassionate Yuanhe Emperor was selected as his successor from a different branch of the imperial royal family. The Longan Emperor, the son of Yuanhe Emperor, takes after his father in temperament.

The Military of Great Liang and the Black Iron Battalion

The armed forces of Great Liang consist of eight major military branches—the Kite, Carapace, Steed, Pelt, Hawk, Chariot, Cannon, and Dragon Divisions—each of which specializes in a particular type of warfare. Troops are divided between five major garrisons located in five different regions throughout the country.

Chief among these is the Black Iron Battalion, which is presently stationed in the Western Regions. An elite group of soldiers widely considered to be one of the most powerful military forces in the known world, the Black Iron Battalion is currently under the command of Marshal Gu Yun and comprises the Black Hawk, Black Carapace, and Black Steed Divisions.

The Temple of National Protection

The Temple of National Protection, also known as the National Temple, practices Buddhism, the religion of Great Liang's imperial family.

The Lingshu Institute (灵枢 / "Spiritual pivot")

An academy directly under the emperor's authority that develops the equipment of Great Liang's military, as well as other mechanical inventions.

The Linyuan Pavilion (临渊 / "Approaching the abyss")

A mysterious organization of people from all levels of society that emerges to aid parties they find worthy in times of chaos. The decision to intervene in worldly affairs is determined by the formation and bestowment of the Linyuan tablet. In addition to granting its bearer access to the full extent of the Linyuan Pavilion's resources, the tablet also allows for the mobilization of the extrajudicial body responsible for meting out punishments to organization members known as the Daofa Court.

LOCATIONS

GREAT LIANG

The Capital

The capital city of Great Liang.

Dagu Harbor

A naval base in the Beihai region, several days' ride south of Great Liang's capital.

Jiayu Pass

A fortress in the northwest and an important waypoint of the Silk Road.

Liangjiang

A fertile region in Great Liang's southeast that encompasses Jiangbei and Jiangnan.

The Southern Border

The mountainous southernmost region of Great Liang, where bandits run rampant.

Yangzhou City

A city in Jiangbei, north of the Yangtze River.

Yanhui Town (雁回 / "Wild goose's return")

A town on the Northern Border of Great Liang, where Chang Geng grew up.

Yingtian Prefecture

A prefecture in Jiangnan Province, south of the Yangtze River, near the East Sea.

FOREIGN POWERS

The Eighteen Tianlang (Celestial Wolf) Tribes

A people residing in the grasslands north of Great Liang, where violet gold is plentiful. They pay an annual tribute to Great Liang after being defeated in battle by the Black Iron Battalion.

Grand Capital

The principal settlement of the Eighteen Tianlang Tribes, where Wolf King Jialai Yinghuo resides.

Loulan

A small but prosperous nation in the Western Regions located at the entrance of the Silk Road. They have a friendly relationship with Great Liang.

Qiuci

A tiny nation in the Western Regions that acquired a suspicious number of sand tiger war chariots.

Qiemo

A tiny nation in the Western Regions that came into conflict with Qiuci.

Dongying

An island nation to the east of Great Liang.

The Far West

A region far to the west beyond the Silk Road that excels in seafaring trade and creating violet-gold-powered devices.

NAME GUIDE

NAMES, HONORIFICS, AND TITLES

Courtesy Names versus Given Names

A courtesy name is given to an individual when they come of age. Traditionally, this was at the age of twenty during one's crowning ceremony, but it can also be presented when an elder or teacher deems the recipient worthy. Though generally a male-only tradition, there is historical precedent for women adopting a courtesy name after marriage. Courtesy names were a tradition reserved for the upper class.

It was considered disrespectful for one's peers of the same generation to address someone by their given name, especially in formal or written communication. Use of one's given name was reserved only for elders, close friends, and spouses.

This practice is no longer used in modern China, but is commonly seen in historically-inspired media. As such, many characters have more than one name. Its implementation in novels is irregular and is often treated malleably for the sake of storytelling.

Milk Names

In China, babies are traditionally given their 大名 (literally "big name," or less literally, "given name") one hundred days after their birth. During those first hundred days, parents would refer to the child by their 小名 (lit. "little name") or 乳名 (lit. "milk name"). Milk names might be childish, employing a diminutive like xiao- or doubling a syllable, but they might also be selected to ward off harm to the child, for example Cao Niangzi's milk name meaning "lady." Many parents might continue referring to their children by their milk name long after they have received their given name.

At the beginning of *Stars of Chaos*, Chang Geng is already thirteen or fourteen years old, but has not been given a "big name." Since Yanhui Town is a backwater border town, this is not terribly strange—historically, many rural families have tended to give their children given names much later in life than the hundredth day. This may be because life in the countryside was harsher and it was more difficult to raise children to adulthood.

Diminutives, Nicknames, and Name Tags

A-: Friendly diminutive. Always a prefix. Usually for monosyllabic names, or one syllable out of a disyllabic name.

XIAO-: A diminutive meaning "little." Always a prefix.

-LAO: A suffix attached to the surname of venerated elders. Denotes a particularly high degree of respect.

Family

DAGE: A word meaning "eldest brother." It can also be used to address an unrelated male peer that one respects. When added as a suffix, it becomes an affectionate address for any older male. Can also be used by itself to refer to one's true oldest brother.

DAJIE: A word meaning "eldest sister." It can be used as a casual term of address for an older female.

ERGE: A word meaning "second brother."

JIEJIE: A word meaning "elder sister." It can be attached as a suffix or used independently to address an unrelated female peer.

NIANG: A word meaning "mother" or "lady."

XIONG: A word meaning "elder brother." It can be attached as a suffix to address an unrelated male peer.

YIFU: A word meaning "godfather" or "adoptive father." (*See Godparentage Relationships for more information*)

Martial Arts and Tutelage

SHIDI: Junior male member of one's own school or fellow disciple/ apprentice under the same master.

SHIFU: Teacher or master. For one's master in one's own school. Gender-neutral.

SHISHU: The junior fellow disciple of one's master. Gender-neutral.

SHIXIONG: Senior male member of one's own school or fellow disciple/apprentice under the same master.

XIANSHENG: A respectful suffix with several uses, including for someone with a great deal of expertise in their profession or a teacher. Can be used independently.

PRONUNCIATION GUIDE

Mandarin Chinese is the official state language of mainland China, and pinyin is the official system of romanization in which it is written. As Mandarin is a tonal language, pinyin uses diacritical marks (e.g., ā, á, ǎ, à) to indicate these tonal inflections. Most words use one of four tones, though some are a neutral tone. Furthermore, regional variance can change the way native Chinese speakers pronounce the same word. For those reasons and more, please consider the guide below a simplified introduction to pronunciation of select character names and sounds from the world of *Stars of Chaos*.

More resources are available at sevenseasdanmei.com

Shā pò láng
Shā as in **sho**p
Pò as in **pu**t
Láng as in **long**

Cháng Gēng
Ch as in **ch**ange, áng as in l**ong**
G as in **g**oose, ēng as in s**ung**

Gù Yún
Gù as in **goo**se
Y as in **y**ou, ún as in b**in**, but with lips rounded as for **boon**

GENERAL CONSONANTS

Some Mandarin Chinese consonants sound very similar, such as z/c/s and zh/ch/sh. Audio samples will provide the best opportunity to learn the difference between them.

X: somewhere between the **sh** in **sh**eep and **s** in **s**ilk

Q: a very aspirated **ch** as in **ch**arm

C: **ts** as in pan**ts**

Z: **z** as in **z**oom

S: **s** as in **s**ilk

CH: **ch** as in **ch**arm

ZH: **dg** as in do**dge**

SH: **sh** as in **sh**ave

G: hard **g** as in **g**allant

GENERAL VOWELS

The pronunciation of a vowel may depend on its preceding consonant. For example, the "i" in "shi" is distinct from the "i" in "di." Vowel pronunciation may also change depending on where the vowel appears in a word, for example the "i" in "shi" versus the "i" in "ting." Finally, compound vowels are often—though not always—pronounced as conjoined but separate vowels. You'll find a few of the trickier compounds below.

IU: **y** as in **y**ou plus **ow** as in sh**ow**

IE: **ye** as in **ye**s

UO: **wa** as in **wa**rm

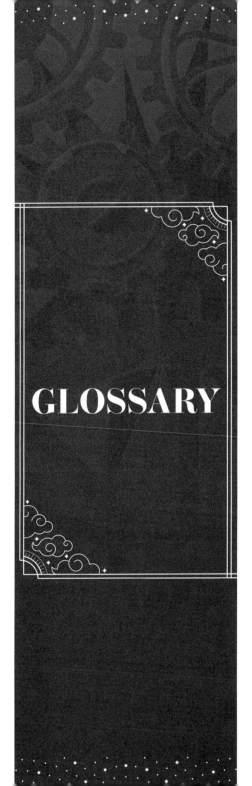

GLOSSARY

GLOSSARY

While not required reading, this glossary is intended to offer further context to the many concepts and terms utilized throughout this novel and provide a starting point for learning more about the rich Chinese culture from which these stories were written.

TERMINOLOGY

BALD DONKEY: A derogatory epithet used to describe Buddhist monks. It stems from the stereotypical image of a bald monk riding a donkey while begging for alms.

BOWING AND CURTSYING: As is seen in other Asian cultures, standing bows are a traditional greeting and are also used when giving an apology. A deeper bow shows greater respect.

BUDDHISM: The central belief of Buddhism is that life is a cycle of suffering and rebirth, only to be escaped by reaching enlightenment (nirvana). Buddhists believe in karma, that a person's actions will influence their fortune in this life and future lives. The teachings of the Buddha are known as The Middle Way and emphasize a practice that is neither extreme asceticism nor extreme indulgence.

CALLIGRAPHY: Chinese calligraphy is a form of visual art and a central part of Chinese culture. It is considered one of the traditional "four arts" of gentlemen scholars, along with guqin, weiqi, and painting. Calligraphy by notable masters is highly sought-after by collectors. A gift of calligraphy is a great honor for both the giver and the recipient.

CONCUBINES AND THE IMPERIAL HAREM: In ancient China, it was common practice for a wealthy man to possess women as concubines in addition to his wife. They were expected to live with him and bear him children. Generally speaking, a greater number of concubines correlated to higher social status, hence a wealthy merchant might have two or three concubines, while an emperor might have tens or even a hundred.

The imperial harem had its own ranking system. The exact details vary over the course of history, but can generally be divided into three overarching ranks: the empress, consorts, and concubines. The status of a prince or princess's mother is an important factor in their status in the imperial family, in addition to birth order and their own personal merits. Given the patrilineal rules of succession, the birth of a son can also elevate the mother's status, leading to fierce, oftentimes deadly, competition amongst ambitious members of the imperial harem.

CONFUCIANISM: Confucianism is a philosophy based on the teachings of Confucius. Its influence on all aspects of Chinese culture is incalculable. Confucius placed heavy importance on respect for one's elders and family, a concept broadly known as filial piety (孝). The family structure is used in other contexts to urge similar behaviors, such as respect of a student toward a teacher, or people of a country toward their ruler.

COUGHING OR SPITTING BLOOD: A way to show a character is ill, injured, or upset. Despite the very physical nature of the response, it does not necessarily mean that a character has been wounded; their body could simply be reacting to a very strong emotion.

CROWS: An inauspicious symbol in Chinese culture. A person "has the beak of a crow" if they are prone to saying inauspicious things.

CULTIVATION: A practice in Daoism-inspired Chinese myth through which humans can achieve immortality and non-human creatures can acquire higher forms, more humanoid forms, or both.

DHARMA NAME: A name given to new disciples of Buddhism during their initiation ritual.

DAOISM: Daoism is the philosophy of the dao (道 / "the way"). Following the dao involves coming into harmony with the natural order of the universe, which makes someone a "true human," safe from external harm and able to affect the world without intentional action. Cultivation is a concept based on Daoist beliefs.

DRAGONS: There are several kinds of dragons in Chinese mythology. Jiao (蛟) or jiaolong (蛟龙), "flood dragons," are hornless, aquatic dragons that can summon storms and floods. Zhenlong (真龙), "true dragons," also have water-related powers, but are capable of flying through the clouds. "True" dragons are a symbol of the divine and the emperor, hence the translation as "imperial dragons" in this story. According to myth, flood dragons can transform into true, or imperial, dragons by cultivating and passing heavenly tribulations.

ERA NAME: A designation for the years when a given emperor was on the throne (or some part of those years). This title is determined by the emperor when they ascend the throne, and can be used to refer to both the era and the emperor himself.

EYES: Descriptions like "phoenix eyes," "peach-blossom eyes," or "triangular eyes" refer to eye shape. Phoenix eyes have an upturned sweep at their far corners, while peach-blossom eyes have a rounded upper lid with gentle upward tilt at the outer corners and are often considered particularly alluring. Triangular eyes have eyelids which droop at the outer corner and are considered harsh and keen.

FACE: Mianzi (面子), generally translated as "face," is an important concept in Chinese society. It is a metaphor for a person's reputation and can be extended to further descriptive metaphors. For example, "having face" refers to having a good reputation, and "losing face" refers to having one's reputation hurt. Meanwhile, "giving face" means deferring to someone else to help improve their reputation, while "not wanting face" implies that a person is acting so poorly or shamelessly that they clearly don't care about their reputation at all. "Thin face" refers to someone easily embarrassed or prone to offense at perceived slights. Conversely, "thick face" refers to someone not easily embarrassed and immune to insults.

FIRESTARTER: An ancient "lighter" made of easily flammable material inside a bamboo tube. It can be ignited by shaking or blowing on it.

FOOT BINDING: A process used to create artificially small feet, which were seen as an attractive trait for women during certain periods of Chinese history. The process involved breaking and tightly binding the foot to mold its shape. The foot might also be bound with pieces of broken crockery in order to induce necrosis in the broken toes and cause them to fall off, leading to a smaller final result.

GODPARENTAGE RELATIONSHIPS: Similar to the idea of "sworn brothers," gan (干) relationships are nominal familial relationships entered into by non-blood-related parties for a variety of reasons.

In the setting of *Stars of Chaos*, the border towns have a tradition where a debt of gratitude that a person could not repay by other means would be recognized by either the recipient or their descendants naming their benefactor as their godparent. Entering this relationship means that the recipient (or their descendant) now acknowledges filial duties toward their new godparent, such as making sure they are taken care of in their old age.

INCENSE TIME: A common way to tell time in ancient China, referring to how long it takes for a single incense stick to burn. Standardized incense sticks were manufactured and calibrated for specific time measurements: a half hour, an hour, a day, etc. These were available to people of all social classes. "One incense time" is roughly thirty minutes.

IMPERIAL EXAMINATION SYSTEM: The official system of examinations in ancient China that qualified someone for official service. It was a supposedly meritocratic system that allowed students from all backgrounds to rise up in society, but the extent to which this was true varied across time.

An examination mentor presides over the highest level of the imperial examination, with the emperor occasionally proctoring the test himself. The first-, second-, and third-ranked candidates are bestowed the titles Zhuangyuan, Bangyan, and Tanhua, respectively.

JIANGHU: The jianghu (江湖 / "rivers and lakes") describes an underground society of martial artists, monks, rogues, artisans, and merchants who settle disputes between themselves per their own moral codes. For members of the jianghu, these moral codes supersede laws mandated by the government. Thus, the jianghu typically exists outside of or in opposition to mainstream society and its government, with its members customarily avoiding cooperation with government bureaucracy.

The jianghu is a staple of wuxia (武侠 / "martial heroes"), one of the oldest Chinese literary genres, which consists of tales of noble heroes fighting evil and injustice.

LOTUS FLOWER: This flower symbolizes purity of the heart and mind, as lotuses rise untainted from the muddy waters they grow in. It also signifies the holy seat of the Buddha. An extremely rare variety known as the bingdi lian (并蒂莲) or "twin lotus" is considered an auspicious sign and a symbol of marital harmony.

MANDARIN DUCKS: Famous for mating for life, mandarin ducks are a symbol of marital harmony, and are frequently featured in Chinese art.

MOURNING PERIOD: The death of a parent was a major event in historical Chinese culture. Children who survived them would be expected to observe a mourning period during which they wore only plain white clothes, stayed at home, and ceased to partake in entertainment and social events. The exact length of the mourning period varied, and there could be exceptions if, for example, the child had important duties they had to attend to.

SHA PO LANG: Sha Po Lang (杀破狼) is the name of a key star formation in Zi Wei Dou Shu (紫微斗数 / "purple star astrology"), a common system of astrology in Chinese culture. It refers to an element of a natal star chart in which the stars Qi Sha (七杀 / "seven killings"), Tan Lang (贪狼 / "greedy wolf"), and Po Jun (破军 / "vanquisher of armies") appear in four specific "palaces" of the sky.

Sha Po Lang in a natal horoscope foretells change and revolution, a turbulent fate. The fortunate among those with this in their star chart gain talent and fortune amidst chaos, while the less fortunate encounter disaster and destitution. Those with this formation in their natal horoscope will encounter great ups and downs, yet have the potential to make their name in dramatic fashion. Many great generals of ancient times were said to have been born under these stars.

SIX ARTS: The basis of education in ancient China, the six arts comprised the disciplines of rites, music, archery, chariotry, calligraphy, and mathematics.

THREE IMMORTAL SOULS AND SEVEN MORTAL FORMS: Hun (魂) and po (魄) are two types of souls in Chinese philosophy and religion. Hun are immortal souls which represent the spirit and intellect, and leave the body after death. Po are corporeal souls or mortal forms which remain with the body of the deceased. Different traditions claim there are different numbers of each, but three hun and seven po is common in Daoism.

TIGER TALLY: A token used as proof of imperial authorization to deploy and command troops. In *Stars of Chaos*, there are three Black Iron Tiger Tallies total, which can command the eight branches of the Great Liang military in times of emergency. They are held by Gu Yun, the imperial court, and the emperor, respectively.

TITLES OF NOBILITY: Titles of nobility are an important feature of the traditional social structure of Imperial China. While the conferral and organization of specific titles evolved over time, in *Stars of Chaos*, such titles can be either inherited or bestowed by the emperor.

In the world of *Stars of Chaos*, a notable feature of the ranking system with respect to the imperial princes is that monosyllabic titles are reserved for princes of the first rank while disyllabic titles designate princes of the second rank.

Princes of the second rank are also known as commandery princes, so named for the administrative divisions they head. The title of commandery prince is not solely reserved for members of the imperial family, but can also be given to meritorious officials and rulers of vassal states.

TRADITIONAL CHINESE MEDICINE: Traditional medical practices in China are commonly based around the idea that qi, or vital energy, circulates in the body through channels called meridians similarly to how blood flows through the circulatory system. Acupuncture points, or acupoints, are special nodes, most of which lie along the meridians. Stimulating them by massage, acupuncture, or other methods is believed to affect the flow of qi and can be used for healing.

Another central concept in traditional Chinese medicine is that disease arises from an imbalance of elements in the body caused by disharmony in internal functions or environmental factors. For example, an excess of internal heat can cause symptoms such as fever, thirst, insomnia, and redness of the face. Excess internal heat can be treated with the consumption of foods with cooling properties.

QI DEVIATION: A physiological and psychological disorder believed to result from improper spiritual or martial training. Symptoms of qi deviation in fiction include panic, paranoia, sensory hallucinations, and death. Common treatments for qi deviation in fiction include relaxation (voluntary or forced by an external party), massage, meditation, or qi transfer from another individual.

UNBOUND HAIR: Neatly bound hair was historically an important aspect of one's attire. Loose, unbound hair was seen as highly improper, and is used as synecdoche to describe someone who is disheveled in appearance.

WEIQI: Also known by its Japanese name, Go, weiqi is the oldest known board game in human history. The board consists of a nineteen-by-nineteen grid upon which opponents play unmarked black and white stones as game pieces to claim territory.

WILD GEESE: A classic motif in Chinese poetry, the wild goose, or yan (雁), has come to embody a host of different symbolic meanings. As a migratory bird, it can represent seasonal change as well as a loving message sent from afar. Famous for mating for life, a pair of geese can allude to marital bliss, while a lone goose can signify the loss of a loved one.

WUXING THEORY: Wuxing (五行 / "Five Phases") is a concept in Chinese philosophy used for describing interactions and relationships between phenomena. The expression 五行 (literally "five motions") originally refers to the movements of the planets Mars (火星 / "fire star"), Mercury (水星 / "water star"), Jupiter (木星 / "wood star"), Venus (金星 / "metal star"), and Saturn (土星 / "earth star"), which correspond to the phases of fire, water, wood, metal, and earth, respectively. In wuxing cosmology, people are categorized according to the five phases and relationships are described in cycles.

Xiangke (相克 / lit. "mutually overcoming") refers to a cycle in which one phase acts as a restricting (and oftentimes destructive) agent on the other. The phase interactions in the ke (克) cycle are: wood breaks through earth, earth dams up water, water douses fire, fire melts metal, and metal chops through wood. When applied to people, these interactions take the form of karmic consequences, which are oftentimes directed at the children and other family members of the original actor. An example of one such cycle might be: An emperor killed many people to expand the nation → the adverse effects of his great deeds are directed toward his children in the form of early death.

Chinese superstition also holds that, due to their phase categorization, certain people's fate can "suppress" (克) the fates of the people around them. For example, if someone is categorized as metal, they may suppress people who have been categorized as wood. Similarly, if someone's fate is determined to be more tenacious than others, they may bring harm to their familial relations. In the case of Gu Yun's unmarriageable status, people have observed the misfortune that befell his family and concluded that he inherited a similar fate. Thus, any woman who marries him will suffer misfortune as her fate is suppressed by his.

YIN AND YANG ENERGY: The concept of yin and yang in Chinese philosophy that describes the complementary interdependence of opposite or contrary forces. It can be applied to all forms of change and differences. Yang represents the sun, masculinity, and the living, while yin represents the shadows, femininity, and the dead, including spirits and ghosts. In fiction, imbalances between yin and yang energy can do serious harm to the body or act as the driving force for malevolent spirits seeking to replenish themselves of whichever they lack.

THE WORLD OF STARS OF CHAOS

COPPER SQUALL: A horn-shaped device made of copper that amplifies the voice of the speaker when spoken into.

GIANT KITE AND RED-HEADED KITE: A large, amphibious airship, the giant kite is powered by steam and equipped with thousands of wing-like structures called fire pinions, which burn violet gold.

A variation of the giant kite is the red-headed kite. Unlike the giant kite, the red-headed kite is a small pleasure vessel that does not see use in the military.

GREAT CONDOR: An experimental ship which combines the propulsion system of hawk armor with the body of a small kite. This allows it to transport multiple passengers and fly far faster than clumsy giant kites. However, the prototype still suffers from fuel efficiency problems and lacks stability in inclement weather.

HEAVY ARMOR: A class of armor used in the military, heavy armor is powered by violet gold, allowing its wearers to traverse thousands of kilometers in seconds and lift objects weighing hundreds of kilograms. A single suit of heavy armor has the power to annihilate a thousand soldiers.

IRON CUFF: The part of light armor that encircles the wrist. Highly convenient, iron cuffs can be removed from full suits of armor and used on their own. A single iron cuff can conceal three or four silk darts.

LIGHT ARMOR: A class of armor used in the military, light armor is typically worn by the cavalry and can only support a small amount of propulsion. It relies primarily on man- and animal-power, and its primary advantages lie in how light and convenient it is.

LIGHT PELT: The lightest class of armor used in the military, the light pelt is specially designed for riding and weighs less than fifteen kilograms.

PARHELION BOW AND ARROW: A giant mechanical bow that runs on violet gold. When fully powered up, arrows released from such a bow can pierce through a city wall a dozen meters thick.

SILK DART: An extraordinarily thin knife that can be concealed in and fired from wrist cuffs.

VIOLET GOLD: A substance mined from beneath the earth which can be burned as fuel in high-quality mechanical devices. It is of such strategic importance that it is called the "lifeline" of Great Liang.

WINDSLASHER: A weapon used by the Black Iron Battalion. It looks like a staff when at rest, but spinning blades release from hidden incisions in one end when the weapon is spun.

WU'ERGU: A slow-acting poison of northern barbarian origin. It is purported to have the ability to transform someone into a great warrior, but those afflicted with wu'ergu are plagued with nightmares and eventually driven insane with bloodlust.